What It Should Be

BOOK 2 IN THE OFF ICE SERIES

GRAYCE RIAN

Dedication

To those who want a simp in the streets
and a sinner in the sheets…
I introduce to you: Carson Wilder.
You're welcome.

Content Note

This book contains mature themes and potentially triggering content, including on-page explicit language and explicit sexual references, mentions of loss and grief of a friend (off-page), mentions of loss and grief of a parent (off-page), on-page mental health struggles and panic attacks, and on-page verbal, emotional, and physical domestic abuse. Despite being a romance novel with a happily ever after, readers should be aware of these themes.

If you or someone you know are a victim of domestic violence and do not feel safe, please call 1-800-799-7233 for help.

CONTENTS

Playlist

Wildest Dreams (Taylor's Version) – Taylor Swift
Golden – Harry Styles
Cowboy Take Me Away – The Chicks
22 (Taylor's Version) – Taylor Swift
You're Not Sorry (Taylor's Version) – Taylor Swift
Heartbreaker – Warren Zeiders
Mama I Lied – Megan Moroney
The First Noel – Gabby Barrett
Girl in the Mirror – Megan Moroney
1 step forward, 3 steps back – Olivia Rodrigo
The Way You Look Tonight – Frank Sinatra
I Found – Amber Run
Stuck with U (with Justin Bieber) – Ariana Grande, Justin Bieber
Fall Into Me - Acoustic – Forest Blakk
Little Bit Better – Caleb Hearn, ROSIE
Lovin On Me – Jack Harlow
Am I Okay? – Megan Moroney
Can't Take My Eyes off You – Michael Bublé
Sparks Fly (Taylor's Version) – Taylor Swift
Hold On – Wilson Phillips
To Love Someone Else – Avery Lynch
She Likes It (feat. Jake Scott) – Russell Dickerson
Little Bit More – Suriel Hess
I Knew I Loved You – Music Travel Love
Sleepy – Ashley Kutcher
Growing Old With You – Restless Road

Spin You Around (1/24) – Morgan Wallen
Until Now – Abe Parker
Turning Page – Sydney Rose
This Side of Paradise – Coyote Theory
I Can See You (Taylor's Version) – Taylor Swift
Lover – Taylor Swift
Enchanted (Taylor's Version) – Taylor Swift
Electric Love – BORNS
Begin Again (Taylor's Version) – Taylor Swift
State Of Grace (Acoustic Version) (Taylor's Version) – Taylor Swift
Your Love – The Outfield
Think I'm Gonna Love You – Michael Leah, Caleb Hearn
august – Taylor Swift
Atlas: Two – Sleeping At Last
this is how you fall in love – Jeremy Zucker, Chelsea Cutler
Off My Face – Justin Bieber
Heartbroken – Jessie Version – Diplo, Jessie Murph
The Good Ones – Gabby Barrett
Those Eyes – New West
Unwritten – Natasha Bedingfield
Bruises – Lewis Capaldi
Take My Name – Parmalee

Prologue

CARSON - JULY

"Two on you! Fuck, I'm getting pushed. I'm dead!"

My noise-canceling headphones are removed from my head, and I peek up from my spot on the couch to find my twin sister's stern look bearing down on me.

"Carse, can you help me pick up real quick before she arrives?" McKenna asks.

I answer her with a question of my own, "Before who arrives?"

"You haven't been listening to a word I've said, have you?" she huffs, crossing her arms. "The nanny I'm interviewing to help watch Cadence a few days a week."

"Wait, you're hiring a nanny? Is she hot?"

She uncrosses her arms and places her hands on her hips, scoffing at me. "Seriously? No. Nope. You're not messing this up for Cades and me. I need someone I can trust to take good care of my daughter and not bone my brother!"

"I mean, multitasking is a great skill to have on a resume—definitely comes in handy while nannying."

"You're incorrigible. I wonder why you're still single . . ."

"Coming from my very single twin sister." I flash her a sassy smirk.

Mack rolls her eyes. "Can you just help me? Quickly. She will be here any minute. Just pick up the wrappers from the coffee table and fold the blankets on the couch. I'll do a quick sweep of the kitchen."

1

I'm just taking the garbage out to the garage when the doorbell rings. Mack answers the door, and a woman's voice floats through.

"Sorry, we can just sit on the barstools. We just moved in, so not all of the furniture has been unpacked yet," my sister explains.

"Oh, that's okay. I don't mind," a woman responds in a melodic voice—she sounds kind.

I tune them out as I gather a few snacks from the butler's pantry. It's the off-season, but I'll report to my first training camp with the Wolverines in a few weeks. Even though I try to stick to my nutrition plan throughout the year, I feel like treating myself today.

Original Pringles, check. Beef jerky, check. And . . . puff corn, check. Alright, that's good.

I round the corner out of the pantry to grab a Gatorade when my eyes land on the new nanny, or at least who I hope will be the new nanny.

My heart sinks to my feet at the sight of the woman before me. Her dark brown hair is parted in the middle and flows down to her mid-back in soft waves. She has a timeless look—a distinct jawline and high cheekbones frame her plush lips and button nose.

"Right, I have to apologize in advance. I'm a bit rusty when it comes to interviewing," the beauty in front of me informs Mack. She even has the perfect voice, soft, but there's a hint of an accent—perhaps a Southern twang.

"That's okay. I've never conducted an interview before. Think of it as a chance to get to know one another," Mack reassures her.

"Well, I graduated from college a couple of years ago with a degree in English. I've always loved working with kids of all ages. I babysat my younger cousins from the time I was twelve until I moved away for college," she pauses.

So, she's not only drop-dead gorgeous, but also intelligent and loves kids. This is the moment I'll remember when I think of how I met the woman of my dreams.

"When it comes down to it, I'm looking for something to do while I decide what to do next with my degree."

Just then, the two women turn their heads and notice me staring. Dream Girl has the most captivating emerald eyes framed by dark, long eyelashes and full, shapely brows, and I'm momentarily entranced. I blink out of it, flashing them my signature easygoing smile.

"Oh, hello! I'm Dakota. I'm here to interview for the nannying position." My eyes widen and my heart pounds when she smiles my way. She has a one-of-a-kind smile; it reminds me of Julia Roberts, the way it lights up her entire face.

Setting my snacks on the island, I cross my arms and lean against the edge of the counter.

Dakota. My dream girl has a name, and it's as beautiful as she is.

"You must be Mr. Wilder," she continues, holding out her hand for me to shake.

Why does hearing her call me Mr. Wilder make my dick twitch? I like it far too much.

"Carson, McKenna's twin brother. But you can call me Mr. Wilder if you'd like." I untuck one of my arms to shake Dakota's outstretched hand, chuckling at the way her face scrunches up at my remark.

"Oh my goodness, my apologies. It's nice to meet you, Carson." Dakota's breath hitches as our hands meet—electricity pulses between us. But she quickly breaks the connection, pulling it away as if she's been burned.

Mack interrupts us when she asks Dakota, "What is your availability for weekends and evenings? I'm on Abbott University's volleyball team, so I may need the nanny to watch her during games if my parents decide not to bring her."

"Honestly? I have practically no life. Most of my friends and family live out of state, so I rarely have plans that will conflict with your game or practice schedules. I'm assuming you're also looking for someone to watch her while you're in class?"

"Yes! But that's just two days per week. The rest of the nannying position would come for practice times and games. There may also be the occasional nights where Carson plays that I might want to watch, but the games would be too late for Cadence."

"That all sounds great." Then Dakota turns to me and asks, "Do you also play a sport for Abbott?"

"I did last season. I just signed my rookie contract with the Minnesota Wolverines."

When she continues to stare blankly at me, I smirk and add, "I am a professional hockey player."

"Oh my gosh, how silly of me. Apologies, I don't follow any sports aside from football. I don't have much of a choice there," she admits bashfully.

Now, my interest is even more piqued. "Why is that?" I ask.

"Well, growing up in Texas, it's ingrained in our way of life."

"Ah, so that's where that slight drawl comes from. I like it."

Dakota's cheeks turn the most irresistible shade of crimson.

"Then there's the fact that my older brother plays football for the Denver Mustangs."

Wait . . . "Shit, really? What's his name?"

"Brody Meyer, he plays—"

I cut her off. "Are you kidding me? Brody Meyer, one of the league's all-time greatest quarterbacks, is your older brother?"

Her cheeks, to my surprise, get even darker with heat.

"My one and only."

"Hey, Carse, could you go check on Cadence? I think I heard her just now. She might have woken up from her nap," Mack interrupts.

Without another word, I run from the room to grab my niece from her crib. "I'm coming, Cadey Cat!"

I enter Cadence's darkened room, and the motion-sensor night-light turns on, illuminating the space just enough for me to see my favorite little girl standing in her crib, making grabby hands at me.

Her wavy blonde hair stands up on end, making her look like baby Einstein.

She can't quite say my name yet, but she's getting close. It sounds more like Ca-Ca, which is cool with me. I have the sweetest little niece in the world, and she's got me completely wrapped around her finger.

"Come here, Cadey Cat. Uncle Car Car is going to change your stinky butt, and then we're going to woo your new nanny downstairs."

After I change her diaper, I carry Cadence down the stairs on my hip, humming her favorite song as we go. When we enter the kitchen, her face lights up when she spots her mama.

"What'd we miss?" I raise my left brow. Cadence looks from Mack to Dakota and smiles so big her little dimple pops. Cadence claps her hands together, wiggling her body excitedly in my arms.

"I offered Dakota the position. And I'm hoping she's about to accept the offer," Mack announces, looking over at Dakota expectantly.

Just then, Dakota stands up and heads over to me and Cadence. She's a petite little thing, easily a foot shorter than my six-foot-three frame. She's wearing a beige crew neck that says "Pemberley est. 1813" with a graphic of an estate on it.

Ah, so she's a Darcy girl. Dream Girl just keeps checking the boxes.

"Of course, I accept! Look at this darlin'. How could I say no to this smile?"

My face lights up at that. "I do have a great smile, don't I? I had braces for two years in middle school and haven't lost any teeth on the ice yet."

"I wasn't talking about you, Golden Boy." Dakota's taunt is so quiet I nearly miss it.

Golden Boy? Oh, I like this.

"Hear that, Mack? She's already got a nickname for me." I ruefully wiggle my eyebrows but don't break eye contact with Dakota. "Careful, Austen, I might develop a crush," I declare.

"I'm actually from Dallas," Dakota replies, looking puzzled.

Oh, I know. Any football fan in the country is well aware of Brody Meyer's roots. Instead of sharing that tidbit, I just shake my head and smile at the English major in a Pride and Prejudice sweatshirt.

Dakota must be someone who appreciates the classics, much like myself. I just met her, but I want to know everything about this woman. What's her favorite book? Favorite author? Where does she like to read? Is she a Kindle girl? I'd bet she isn't; she seems like the type of girl to curl up with a good paperback by the fire.

The moment Mack shuts the door behind Dakota after she accepts the position, she turns on me and pokes her pointer finger into my chest. "Stop whatever is going on in that flirtatious head of yours—she's married."

Hold up. What?

Married? My dream girl is married? She couldn't be more than twenty-five. Since when did all of the good ones get snatched up so young?

From the moment I laid eyes on Dakota, I was absolutely enamored. My stomach sinks at the realization that my attraction for her can't go anywhere. She's married, so boundaries will be respected, of course. But I'd be lying if I said I wasn't excited to get to know her more while she's hanging out with my little Cadey Cat. Perhaps the two of us can be . . .

I run my fingers through my hair before settling on the realization that we can only be one thing, and that's friends.

1

Carson

August

It's McKenna and my twenty-first birthday today. We didn't go out last night at midnight because she had a volleyball match this afternoon, but I'm taking Mack out tonight and told her I wouldn't take no for an answer.

"I already arranged for Dakota to watch Cadence while we're out celebrating. She's planning to stay the night and watch her tomorrow morning too, for the guaranteed hangover we'll have," I tell Mack as we drive back to my place from her match.

As I pull up to the stoplight, I glance over at my twin sister and see she winces at my words. "I don't know, Carse. You know I'm not a big drinker, especially in season and since I've had Cadence."

"Fine, no hangover for you. Just a few drinks to ring in our milestone birthday together."

McKenna has had a challenging two years, and I just want to give her the opportunity to let loose and have a reason to celebrate. Her childhood best friend and our next-door neighbor, Katie Turner, passed away almost two years ago in a car accident. Mack was in the car with her and, as a result, was in a coma for two days. She's had to deal with a lot of survivor's guilt along with her grief over losing her best friend.

Not to mention the fact that Katie's older brother, Griffin, was McKenna's boyfriend at the time. Katie's death tore them apart, and

Griff left my sister heartbroken. As if that wasn't enough, Mack discovered she was pregnant with Griffin's child a few months later. The fallout from her telling him was something I never anticipated.

Loss changes people—it certainly changed me. I never thought Griff would abandon my pregnant sister and his child, but I've also never lost my sister, who is my best friend. *Though I almost did.* I'm not trying to validate his actions because they're inexcusable, but I know I'd be lost without my sister. We've done everything in life together from day one, which is another reason I'm not allowing her to back out of celebrating our twenty-first birthday together.

"I already told Brooke to invite a few of your teammates, and Mom and Dad are joining us, so you have to show up at least," I add.

"How did you even get Dakota's number?"

"You have it on the fridge on the 'Cadence contacts' list," I explain. She doesn't need to know that I added it to my phone contacts the second I saw it on the fridge. I was itching for a chance to use it, and our birthday was the perfect excuse.

Mack also doesn't need to know that the handful of times Dakota has come over to watch Cadence, I've made it my mission to squeeze in a few extra minutes at home to get to know her better.

My conversations with Dakota have been few, but I look forward to each little interaction like an addict waiting for my next fix.

Speaking of my little addiction, Dakota opens the front door of my house with Cadence on her hip, waving excitedly to us as we pull into the driveway. Coming home to the two of them feels right. It makes me want things with Dakota that I know I'll never get.

You're just barely friends, remember?

Right, I told myself I could be her friend. She had said she didn't have many of them here in Minnesota since she grew up in Texas. I just needed to remind myself that's all we can be.

But god, she looks so cute in her jean short overalls with a white tank top underneath. Her long hair is pulled up into one of those clips she loves so much when she's nannying so Cadence doesn't tug her hair—it's my little stinker-butt niece's favorite thing to do.

Mack gets out in the driveway and runs up to them before I pull my truck into the garage. She never likes leaving Cadence, and she always feels guilty. Typically, I would bring Cadence to Mack's game with me, but today's match was during nap time, and believe me, it is in everyone's best interest that Cadence gets her beauty sleep.

I turn off the ignition to my truck and take a deep breath. Each time I've come home in the last few weeks since Dakota has started nannying, I've had to give myself a pep talk before going inside. Seeing her knocks the air from my lungs, my attraction to her still hasn't waned—if anything, it's gotten stronger.

Shaking those thoughts, I get out of my truck and walk inside through the garage door. I hang up my keys and take off my shoes in the mudroom before heading down the hallway into the kitchen.

This house wasn't what I envisioned myself getting at only twenty years old. I didn't think that instead of a bachelor pad condo in the city, I'd have a five-bedroom home in the suburbs for my rookie season in the NHL.

McKenna and I gained access to our trust funds earlier this month, and with the signing bonus I got from the Wolverines, I had more than enough money to buy Cadence and Mack the home they deserved.

The strange thing is, I don't even miss the bachelor lifestyle. Just because I didn't envision it working out this way doesn't mean I don't absolutely love coming home to Cadence and Mack living with me. I've never been good at being alone. I like to be supportive—to feel needed. It's what fills my cup when I'm running on empty.

I swear, the moment my little Cadey Cat came into my life, my world shifted and began to revolve solely around her.

Some have referred to me as the "funcle," the fun uncle . . . okay, so maybe I'm the only one that refers to me as that, but it's true. I know how to have a good time and make others around me feel at ease.

It's just that, for me, being in my head isn't always the most fun place to be. Ever since Cadence was born—hell, before that, if I'm being honest with myself—I've had crippling anxiety. I'm fucking scared all the time that something is going to happen to her, or Mack, or anyone I love and care about. I likely need to purge my insecurities and anxious thoughts to a therapist. But when you are the number three all-around draft pick and highly anticipated NHL prospect, you don't want to be seen coming in and out of a therapist's office. It doesn't photograph well. Online therapy? Sure, I could attempt that, but I don't have much time before the season begins.

Dakota, Mack, and Cadence are all in the kitchen now getting started on dinner. Mack connects her phone to the sound system, and soon "Wildest Dreams (Taylor's Version)" floods the space.

I can't hide the chuckle when Dakota picks up a wooden spoon and starts singing the chorus into it like it's a microphone. Mack has Cadence on her hip and is singing so off-key it makes me cringe, but I love her enthusiasm nonetheless. When they spot me laughing at them, Mack points to me and says, "Get to work! These veggies aren't going to cut themselves."

After washing my hands, I set up my cutting station beside Dakota. I lean down so she can hear me over the music. "Thank you for watching Cadey Cat earlier and for being willing to stay over tonight to watch her. I really appreciate it, Austen." I don't mean to, but we're so close that my cheek grazes hers as I pull away. Heat floods my system from the innocent touch just as Dakota's breath hitches.

She clears her throat. "No need to thank me. I love watching Cadence. And occasional overnights were part of the job description."

"I know, but this is different," I remind her as I stare into her emerald eyes. "Mack isn't playing volleyball tonight. And you're staying because I asked you to, not her. I just wanted to thank you again for your flexibility. McKenna doesn't get many opportunities to celebrate herself these days. I wanted this for her, and you're a big part of why this was possible."

She swallows, wetting her lips before she replies. "I'm happy I was able to help, birthday boy. Now, like your sister said," she points down before continuing, "those veggies aren't going to cut themselves."

I smile to myself as I get to work cutting up the vegetables. This feels domesticated as fuck, but I can't think of a better way to spend my birthday.

After dinner with our parents, they join us as we meet up with a group of our college friends at The Wolf Den, a bar close to the arena where I'll be playing my home games this season for the Wolverines. A few of my new teammates frequent this bar and told me we had to come by for a celebratory round.

It might seem weird to have our parents join us at the bars on our twenty-first birthday, but we're a really close-knit family. Losing all that we've lost recently has only brought us closer together.

I make my way to the booths in the back of the bar, where I spot Bennett and Jackson Wilson. They are two buddies of mine from high school who are now my new teammates. Bennett was recently appointed captain, and Jackson was invited to training camp that starts next month, where I hope he will earn himself a spot on the final roster.

After giving them each a handshake and back pat, I ask, "Have you been here long? Who else from the team is here?"

Bennett and Jax look like the brothers they are with their tall, broad stature, but their similarities stop at their looks and hockey. As far as their personalities and interests go, they couldn't be more different.

If I were to describe Jax, I'd say he's carefree, laidback, and easygoing. Bennett, on the other hand, is an extremely hard worker who likes structure and keeps things close to his chest.

As usual, Jax answers for the two of them. "It's just us so far. Hughesy and Pacer texted me a bit ago to say they were on their way. Happy birthday, Carsey-baby. I can't believe the babies of the group are finally twenty-one."

"Fuck off with that, Jax. You only turned twenty-one last month," I remind him.

"Semantics." He grins. "Let me get you a shot. Pick your poison wisely. It's about to be a long night."

"Not too long of a night, Jax. We've got conditioning tomorrow afternoon," Bennett says.

"It's not even an official conditioning. It's just the two of us," Jax replies.

Bennett sets his shoulders. "You haven't signed a contract yet, J. Being invited to training camp isn't a guarantee of anything. It doesn't matter how good of a season you had last year. That was college, and this is the show. You're going to have to keep working your ass off, never letting up, if you want to make the final roster this season."

There's the serious big brother I've come to know Bennett as.

Jax's jaw works before he lets out a scoff. "I'm more than aware of what's at stake. As if our daddy dearest reminding me every day wasn't enough, now I have to look forward to you busting my balls too. Maybe I should go back to Harvard this season."

I cut in, not wanting them to argue anymore. "And miss out on being on a line together again? Fuck that. Come on, Jaxy, let's get that shot, and then we can talk strategy about how we're going to pad our stats this season."

Jax's shoulders relax, and his easy-going smile takes over his face. "Damn, Carse. I missed you. It's good to be back."

We head to the bar, where Mack orders a drink with a few of her volleyball teammates.

"There she is! McKenna Marie, get over here, my little M&M," Jax says as he opens his arms for Mack.

She turns, running into his arms before he lifts her up and spins her around. "Jax! I missed you so much. How was Harvard, you fricken scholar?"

"Glad to see someone doesn't think I'm some Ivy League snob now." Jax sets Mack back down.

"Never! God, I've missed you. I haven't seen you since—" Mack trails off, not wanting to say it out loud. The last time she saw Jackson was at Katie's funeral. A day that pains us all too much to speak of.

"It's been too long, for sure. But I hear my M&M has been killing it on the court." Jax comfortably changes the subject.

"I don't know if I'd say killing it. But this season is off to a great start," Mack replies. She's being modest. She is killing it. Even after having Cadence, she played on the team last season. She didn't get a starting spot for most of last year, but this season, the coach hasn't taken her off the court for a single minute.

"Well, if I can get my shit together and make the final roster, I plan to come watch you kick some ass on the court," Jax promises. "And I need to meet the girl that has taken up residence in Carsey's heart."

My pulse skyrockets. How in the hell does he know about Dakota? I haven't told a single soul.

"I'll hold you to that. Feel free to come by anytime—I'd love for you to meet Cades. Though I must warn you, she's a little heartbreaker," Mack gushes as she pulls out her phone to show Jax some pictures on her phone.

Shit. Of course he was just talking about Cadence. Looks like I really need that shot after all.

By one shot, Jax meant ten. I am officially tipsy as I stumble out of my parents' SUV and walk up the front steps to my house. Mack is barely buzzed—something killed her mood after she started to have a good time dancing with my former college roommate, Ian. Though she's keeping tightlipped about what it is that's bugging her. I hate when she does that. It's got to be the twin thing, or maybe the older brother in me, but I can't stand to see her down like this.

After struggling to get my keys in the lock a few times, Mack grabs them out of my hand and lets us into the house. She quickly darts up the steps—to check on Cadence, I'm guessing.

I take off my shoes as quietly as possible so I don't wake anyone. I make it a few steps into the house before the sight in front of me has me stopping in my tracks.

Dakota has made a bed of blankets on the floor of my living room. She's nestled in front of the fireplace, reading a book I can't quite make out from here.

I knew she was a paperback-by-the-fire kind of girl.

"A fire in late August, Austen?" I tease.

Dakota nearly jumps out of her skin when she hears me. She must have been so enveloped in her book that she didn't hear us come in.

"Oh my gosh! You startled me. I'm so sorry about the fire. I got a chill and, well, it's just such a beautiful fireplace that I started a fire. But you're right. It's wasteful to start a fire this time of year. I don't know what I was thinking." Dakota shoots to her feet and turns off the fireplace.

I frown, my eyebrows pulling together in confusion. "Dakota, there's no need to apologize. I don't care if you start a fire every night you're here. I was just heckling you."

Her shoulders ease slightly at my words, but her face is still filled with worry, and she's hidden the book she was reading behind her back.

Needing to lighten the mood, I ask, "What were you reading tonight? *Pride and Prejudice?*"

"Um, no. *Jane Eyre.*"

I love asking her what she's reading. Her cheeks always blush, and she looks at me in wonderment as if my being inquisitive about what she's interested in is a bewildering thing to her. I have mixed feelings about it—I both crave that look in her eyes and resent it because it likely means she's not used to someone being fascinated by her. And everything Dakota does fascinates me.

"Ah, a Brontë-by-the-fire kind of night. I can see why you didn't hear us come in."

"I had the baby monitor right beside me in case Cadence woke up," she reassures me, pointing to the coffee table where the monitor is.

I just nod my head in acknowledgment.

"It's late. I should probably head to bed," she suggests.

"Do you need anything for your room?" I ask. This morning, I finished setting up the guest room where she'll be staying the night. I want to make sure I didn't forget anything. One last minute Target run had me buying all sorts of shit I never thought I'd purchase. And who knew there was an entire aisle just for candles? I spent nearly twenty minutes picking out the perfect candle to set on her bedside table.

"No, it's great. Thank you so much for putting that together. You didn't need to go through the extra trouble. I could've slept on the couch."

"I would've had you sleep in my bed before making you sleep on the couch," I say, my voice coming out rough.

She doesn't say anything. Her cheeks just blush an adorable shade of pink that matches her pink and white cotton pajama set. Her hair is down, pulled back from her face with a headband, and her face is clear of makeup. It strikes me again—her effortless beauty. I have to physically brush the tightness from my chest with my hand.

"Can I walk you up?"

"To my room?" she asks.

I nod in reply.

She laughs. "Your house is big, but it's not that big, Golden Boy. I don't think I'll get lost on my way upstairs."

That. That right there is something I love—her quick wit and hearing her give me shit. And I love hearing her call me Golden Boy. She's reclaimed a name that was once given to me by the media and made me long to hear it leave her lips.

"I won't apologize for wanting to be a gentleman. If you'd like, I'll even check under the bed and in the closet for the Boogeyman and tuck you in tight."

"Quite the host. Do you do that for all of the women you have stay the night?"

"The only women who have stayed the night in this house are my sister and my niece. You're the first guest I've offered my turndown services to." I wink and feel slightly more buzzed by the twinkle in her eyes flickering back to life.

Come on, Austen. Play with me.

Dakota squares her shoulders to me. "Is that so? Well, I'm just tickled pink to hear that I'm your first guest. What does this turndown service entail?"

I close some of the distance between us, giving her a rakish smirk. "Oh, you know. It includes turning back the comforter and shutting off the lights."

She taps her finger to her chin. "Hmm, sounds like any other run-of-the-mill service to me."

"Well, if you're a good girl, I'll even tuck you in and tell you a bedtime story," I rasp.

Her breath hitches, and her cheeks burn brighter. "I'm quite sure that if you did that, I would be the very opposite of a good girl," she breathes before slipping past me toward the stairs. "Goodnight, Golden Boy," she calls over her shoulder.

My stomach somersaults as I stand there dumbfounded, my jaw damn near on the floor.

"Goodnight, Austen," I reply when I finally regain my composure. I watch as she retreats up the stairway. My willpower not to follow her should be applauded. Dakota's presence tests me more and more with each encounter.

You can only be friends, I remind myself, repeating my new mantra for the thousandth time.

2

Dakota

September

My car starts with a wheezing sound that I definitely need to get checked out. I rub the dash and chant, "Thank you, Carol. I can always count on you, sweet thing."

At this point, I say a little prayer of thanks each time Carol starts. My brother Brody hates that I still drive my beat-up 1998 Honda Civic, which I got in my junior year of high school. He can't understand why Aaron hasn't bought me a safer, more reliable vehicle.

What Brody doesn't understand is that I don't want to owe Aaron anything other than a manila folder of neatly tabbed and signed divorce papers.

I'm leaving him, though he doesn't know that yet. No one knows.

But that is why it was imperative that my sweet Carol started today so I could get to my new job that I absolutely adore. It should only be about three more months before I'll have earned enough money to leave Aaron and file for divorce.

If I asked Brody for the money, I know he would give it to me in a heartbeat. Lord knows they pay him plenty to throw the pigskin in Colorado. But I couldn't bear to be another person asking for handouts from Brody.

If you would just tell someone about what you're going through, it wouldn't be a handout; it could save you.

No. I shake those thoughts from my head. Sure, I want to leave Aaron because I know what we have isn't love anymore—it may have never been. I think we were just young, and I was mystified by the fact that someone wanted to call me theirs.

But save me? From what? His words? His callousness? I could have it so much worse.

Thankfully, Aaron is just type-A and has control freak tendencies—he's very particular about a lot of things, like how I dress, how I do my hair, what perfume I wear, what the house looks like, how his suits are pressed, what I'm allowed to read, and what he deems worthy of my time. I used to appreciate his decisiveness; I thought it was a redeeming quality.

If he knew I got this nannying job, he would demand I quit immediately. Of course I had to tell him something to cover my tracks. I told him a former classmate of mine had a baby and needed someone to help watch her daughter until she could find a more permanent solution. He doesn't know I have a separate bank account where McKenna direct-deposits my paychecks.

Aaron was ecstatic for me to start "practicing" for our future children. When he said that, it was near impossible to hold back the gut-wrenching nausea at the thought of having children with him. That's another thing I've had to hide from him—the IUD I got at the women's free clinic a couple of months back.

I've been slowly coming around to the idea of leaving him for a few months now. Things took a turn when he thought I was "eye-fucking" one of his colleagues at a work dinner this summer. When we got home that evening, he was more cruel than ever. He showed me a side of himself I can't unsee.

Needing to change my headspace to ease my anxiety, I roll down my windows and blast one of my favorite songs, "Cowboy Take Me Away" by The Chicks, as I finish my drive.

A few minutes later, I put my car in park in front of McKenna's brother's house and roll up my windows before turning off the ignition.

Walking in through the front door of the house, I turn to hang up my coat and come face-to-chest with the most divine-smelling specimen.

"Whoa, Austin. Where's the fire?" he asks in a teasing tone as he catches me by the shoulders. Looking up, I find the most bewitching blue eyes sparkling back at me.

Carson Wilder is trouble with a capital T. It should be sinful the way my new employer's twin brother fills out a three-piece suit. His beachy blonde tresses are a slightly darker honey, still wet from the shower. The forest green suit he's wearing is paired with a crisp white dress shirt with one too many buttons undone on top—likely intentional so the gold chain he seems to never take off can peek out. My eyes trail down his expansive chest and catch on his antique gold Rolex adorned on his wrist. He finishes off the look with cognac loafers that match his dress belt. And when did I become so turned on by seeing a man's bare ankles peek from his tailored suit pants?

He looks as good as sin. I shouldn't be gawking at another man while I'm still technically married—especially a man who is much younger than I am. I mean, for Pete's sake, I'm two years shy of thirty while he just earned the right to legally drink alcohol.

But I can't help my attraction toward him. Anyone who says they don't find this man attractive is a bald-faced liar.

"No fire. I just didn't see you there." I take a few steps back. "Good morning, Carson."

"Good morning. I think I like it better when you call me Mr. Wilder or Golden Boy."

"Is that so?" I chuckle nervously.

"Mhmm. It makes me feel special," he muses with a cocky smirk.

"Well, it's a good thing you've got your first game today. I'm sure the thousands of people who will be cheering for you will make you feel extra special."

"There may be thousands of people screaming my name, but the only spectator I'm interested in playing for today is you. Are you ready to take in your first hockey game?"

I nod my head in response, causing a piece of hair to slip from the claw clip that's holding my hair up off my face. Ever the gentleman, Carson steps forward and brushes the fallen strands behind my ear. His movements aren't hesitant; confidence pours out of him at all times. Instead of pulling away, his hand lingers momentarily, his thumb swiping across my cheek. When he pulls away, his fingertips gently trace my jaw, causing my skin to erupt with goosebumps.

His touch is dizzying and dangerous. I take a large step back and he flexes his hand at his side. "I should probably go get Cadence ready for your game. Did McKenna say when she would be back from practice?"

Carson puts his hands in the pockets of his suit pants and rocks back on his heels, making him look relaxed again and effortlessly sexy. "She should be back within half an hour. I think she just had morning conditioning, not a full practice. I appreciate you coming earlier to help out."

"No need to thank me. It's part of my job, Carson."

"Even though it may be part of the job, I'd still like to thank you. I can see some of the weight has lifted off of Mack's shoulders since you started. She always felt guilty asking my mom for help watching Cadence. I'm not sure why, because my mom adores her granddaughter."

"I get where your sister is coming from. She told me she felt bad because she wanted your parents to be able to enjoy being empty nesters.

If anything, I should thank your sister for giving me this opportunity. I don't think anyone understands how badly I needed a fresh start." The words barely leave my lips before I wince at what I've just let slip.

Before Carson can ask me anything, I take off toward the playpen in the living room, where I see Cadence playing. She squeals in excitement when she sees me, and a sense of calm washes over me.

"How was your morning, little darlin'?" I ask as I pick her up in a hug.

"What did you mean by needing a fresh start?" Carson asks from behind me.

My shoulders stiffen at the sound of his voice. I close my eyes and scold myself for being so careless with my words. "Oh my, did I say fresh start? I meant to say something to bide my time. You know, until I figure out what I'd like to do with my degree." I don't dare turn around, knowing if I do, he will see how bad of a liar I am.

"Austin—" he starts but is cut off by an alarm sounding from his phone.

I start for the stairs and call out, "You better get going. You don't want to be late for your first game. Good luck today."

"Thanks," he reluctantly replies.

The crowd roars to life with electrifying energy after Carson scores a goal. McKenna screams before hugging her mom, the two of them jumping up and down in excitement.

"Scoring his first NHL career goal for your Minnesota Wolverines, number twenty-two, Carsonnnn Wilderrrr!" the announcer's voice booms through the sound system.

McKenna turns to give me a high five, and I don't bother to hide my smile as the crowd cheers, and fans chant his name.

Just as I finish giving myself a mental pat on the back for being right about the fans making Carson feel plenty special, my phone rings with an incoming FaceTime request.

I dig it out of my purse and see Aaron's name light up my phone. Knowing I can't let him hear the crowd, I reject the FaceTime request. My phone vibrates with an alert for the missed FaceTime, and that's when I notice the four missed call notifications and seven unopened text messages from him.

Shoot. How on earth did I miss these? Knowing I need to get out of here as quickly as possible, I go up to McKenna.

"Hey, something came up. Are you okay if I head out a few minutes early?" I found out today that there are three twenty-minute periods in professional hockey. There are only five minutes left in the third period now, so hopefully, my leaving now doesn't upset her. I really need this job.

"Of course, don't worry about it. Is everything okay?" she asks.

"Yes, I'm sure everything is fine. My husband is likely just worried about me being home in time for our dinner plans tonight," I assure her.

With the excitement of the game, I completely forgot that my brother is flying into town today for his game tomorrow. I wanted to get dinner with just Brody, hoping Aaron would go into the firm and work late like he does most Saturdays since one of the partners announced his upcoming retirement plans.

Ever since then, he has been working around the clock, practically living out of his office at the firm. I have had no complaints about his new work schedule. It means fewer interactions between us and less tiptoeing around his mood swings.

"Alright, I will see you on Monday. Have fun at your brother's game tomorrow!" she calls as I grab my purse and head out the door of the suite where we watched the game.

Right as I start my vehicle, my phone rings again. I swipe to answer. "Hey, Aaron."

"Jesus, Dakota. Where are you? I've been calling you for twenty minutes straight."

"Sorry, I'm just heading home now. I was babysitting. Did you see my note?"

"Do you honestly think a fucking note left on the kitchen counter is the smartest way to communicate with your husband in the twenty-first century?" he shouts his question through the phone.

So, he did get my note.

"I didn't want to disturb you at work." Truthfully, I didn't want him to figure out that I would be gone while he was at work and demand I come home.

"Don't be stupid, it's Saturday. We've been over this already, you can text me at work on the weekend. I can't have you just leaving the house without telling me where you're going. What if something happened to you? You know I'd be a mess without you, Belle."

I cringe at the name of endearment he coined for me when we started dating. Back then, he claimed he nicknamed me that because of my Southern roots, and it was also fitting because of my love of reading like Belle from *Beauty and the Beast*.

Lately, our life together has become one of Grimm's fairy tales instead of the Disney retellings. And instead of thinking it's cute when my head is stuck in a book, he chastises me for reading fantasies and romance instead of "something more worthwhile like nonfiction."

What I don't tell him is that I need the fictitious escapes—another world I can get lost in that will drown out the sorrow I feel from my current reality.

"I'm sorry. It won't happen again. I'll be at the house in fifteen minutes," I tell him.

"You should have been home when your brother arrived twenty minutes ago. I was left looking like a fumbling fool, not knowing where my wife was," he scolds.

"You're right. I lost track of time. Tell Brody I will be there as soon as I can."

"Too late. I sent him back to his hotel. I didn't know where you were, so I said you must have forgotten."

I'm barely able to hold back my sigh of frustration. "I'm going to hang up and give him a call."

"Did I give you the impression our conversation was done? If so, you are mistaken."

"I'm sorry. I just need to call Brody quickly, and then I can call you right back."

"Call me back in two minutes. Oh, and Dakota. There must be something wrong with your phone. Your location wasn't showing up on my app. Did you turn it off?"

Dammit. Yes. I've turned it off nearly every day I go to work, not wanting Aaron to know where McKenna lives.

"No, of course not," I lie, thankful that he can't see my face. Aaron is like a human lie detector.

"Hmm. We will have to go get a new phone then."

Panicking, I try to reassure him. "No, that's not necessary. I'm sure I just need to do an update or something."

"Don't be so careless, Dakota. Having your phone up to date and your location services on could be a matter of life or death. What happens if you were to get in a car accident and I didn't know where to look for you? That car of yours is an impending death trap."

"You're right," I placate. "I'm sorry. I'll make sure to update my phone right after I get home from dinner."

"You be sure to do that. Call your brother. I would hate for him to be as worried as I was about you."

Unease slithers its way down my spine at the switch of his tone. There's a lilt to his voice I haven't heard since this summer. I just hope he cools down by the time dinner with my brother is over. If not, I'll likely be in for a long night.

3

Carson

October

Inhaling deeply, the smell of the fresh sheet of ice beneath my skates floods my system as I take the first few strides of my rookie lap. The cool air fills my lungs as an awestruck smile takes over my face. My childhood dream of playing in the NHL is coming to fruition today.

Circling the net, I crossover to pick up speed as I snag a puck from the top of the circles and shoot it in the back of the net.

Fuck, this feels good—like I'm right at home.

Two blondes are cheering me on, banging on the glass beside the home bench, so I make my way over to them. When I get to the glass, I wave at Cadence, who's wearing a mini version of my jersey and noise-canceling headphones that take up most of her tiny head.

"Uncle Car Car loves you so much, Cadey Cat!" I holler so she can hear me, blowing her a kiss.

The announcer's voice sounds through the arena. "Make some noise for your Minnesota Wolverrriiiinnneeesssss!" Black and lime green jerseys flood the ice as my teammates join me out on the ice.

Our opponents, the Colorado Summits, also take the ice for their warm-up, but I refuse to look across the ice, knowing that if I do, my eyes will likely land on *him*, and I refuse to spoil this memory. Instead, I turn my back to the other half of the ice and squat down to stretch my legs.

"Careful, Carsey," Jax taunts, waggling his eyebrows as he pops a squat beside me. "If you keep stretching your hip flexors like that, you'll wind up with even more ladies fawning over you on TikTok."

He says this just as he spreads his knees wide and begins pumping his hips back and forth like he's fucking the ice.

Chuckling, I reply, "Nah, I'm pretty sure you're giving them all the content they need."

When he gets even more into it, looking up and winking at a group of girls with their phones aimed at the two of us, I playfully slash his shinnies with my stick.

"You're really leaning into that playboy image right now," I tell him, shaking my head at his theatrics.

Jax leans closer, voice lowering as he asks, "Can you believe we're about to play in our first NHL game together? How the fuck is this real life?"

"Right? It doesn't feel real. Want me to pinch you, Jaxy?"

"Oh, fuck off," he says, swatting my gloved hand away. "I'm not trying to make it dusty in here, but how surreal is it that we played on the same mini mites team together and now we both just took our rookie laps on the same sheet of ice for our NHL debuts?"

Unwilling to get too choked up, I hold my fist out for him as he bumps his glove against mine. "Let's do this," we say in unison, chuckling to ourselves.

Hours later, I've barely started down the player's hallway when Mack runs and jumps into my arms. Spinning her around, I bask in this moment with my twin. We've always been each other's biggest cheerleaders through every high and with every low, we've had each other to lean on. I can't imagine Mack not being here on my biggest day.

"Great game, Carse. I'm so unbelievably proud of you. Scoring a goal in your rookie debut? Amazing!" she tells me as she brings me in for another big hug.

"Thanks, Mack. I think it's because I had my good luck charm here tonight," I say, letting go of Mack and seeking out Dakota. I don't see her, but I do see my Cadey Cat. I make grabby hands at my mom, who's holding her. "Come here, Cadey Cat. Let Uncle Car Car hold his little lucky charm."

Cadence practically throws herself out of my mom's arms and into my outstretched ones. She looks adorable in her little Wolverines jersey. "How did she do?" I ask Mack.

"She did surprisingly well. She even tracked the puck and said Ca-Ca a few times," Mack gushes. That's our girl!

Ian, my college roommate and former teammate, slaps my shoulder. "Hell of a game, man."

He then wraps his arm around Mack's shoulder, and I watch as she stiffens from his touch. I've told Ian countless times that he and Mack wouldn't be good together. Not to mention, I don't think she's ready for a relationship. She can tell me all she wants that she's making strides in therapy to forget Griffin, but I *know* her.

"Ca-Ca!" Cadence exclaims. She adjusts in my arms and slaps my cheeks.

"Ouch!" I fake being hurt, rubbing my cheek.

Cadence's responding giggles make us all ring out in laughter, the sound echoing off the walls.

Mack's laughter is cut off and I stare at her in concern as I watch her demeanor shift, her face paling completely. I turn to see what has her so upset, quickly realizing it's not what, but who.

While the rest of the Colorado Summits continue to file out of the visiting locker room, Griffin Turner is stopped dead in his tracks. It took everything in me to focus on the fact that I was playing my first NHL game instead of wanting to punch him in the face again for walking out of her life almost two years ago.

"Mama! Look! Mama!" Cadence squeals, pointing toward a mural on the wall.

Mack grabs Cadence from me and wraps her into her arms, nuzzling her neck—breathing her in.

"Hi, baby," Mack coos to Cadence.

Cadence grabs Mack's cheeks, placing a big, sloppy kiss on her face before giggling.

Mack turns to me, leans in, and whispers, "I can't do this, Carse. Please get me out of here."

Before I can do just that, Griffin growls, "Can someone please explain what's going on?"

I wince at the tone of his voice. My mom quickly jumps into action, grabbing Cadence from Mack's arms, which is probably a good thing because Mack looks murderous.

"We'll take her to the restaurant and meet you both there," Mom tells us.

"Ian, why don't you ride with us," Dad suggests.

"Works for me," Ian replies.

Walking up to my mom, I wrap her and Cadence into a hug. "Uncle Carse loves you so much, Cadey Cat," I say before my parents swiftly head down the hallway with Cadence and Ian.

"What's her name?" Griffin demands.

"Wh-what? Whose name?" Mack stutters.

"Cut the shit, McKenna," he says in a chilling tone, one I've never heard him use before. "What's my daughter's name? She's mine, right? Jesus—of course, she's mine. Look at her eyes. They're a carbon copy of mine."

The anger I thought I had buried starts to resurface. "Alright, let's take this conversation back here. There's no one in the film room right now. We can talk away from where the media may overhear," I suggest before leading us to a room down the hallway.

Once we're inside, I turn to find Mack staring back at Griff with a thunderous expression. "Is this some sort of fucked up game you're playing, Griff? What is wrong with you?" she shouts.

"What is wrong with me? Who has a secret child and doesn't tell the father? Is she mine? Tell me right now."

"Yes—dammit! Of course, she's yours. Why are you acting this way—as if you're shocked? As if you didn't look me right in my eyes and tell me that you didn't care that I was pregnant and to stay the fuck away from you?" Her eyes are glassy now, filled with unshed tears.

"You're lying. You've never said a word to me about a baby—a pregnancy."

"What are you talking about? That night in Boston, when you played against Carson, I came to the after-party to tell you."

He recoils. "And you clearly forgot to tell me—hence why I had no clue I've had a daughter for the past two years—"

I cut in to correct him, "She's eighteen months. And I was there with Mack."

Placing my hands on Griff's shoulders, I say, "I was there that night with Mack when she told you. After seeing you when we got there, I should've never let her tell you by herself. I'd never seen you like that, man. It was like you had taken everything under the kitchen sink—you were crazy. She said she told you everything, and you laughed in her face and told her to get the fuck out of there.

"You were in no place to bring a child into this world. Mack was so terrified after that night that she contemplated giving the baby up for adoption instead of keeping her." Flashbacks of that night still haunt me. I take a deep breath and continue, "I got her out of there and got her home as quickly as we could. The moment she saw Cadence, the light came back into her eyes. Shit, she changed all of our lives for the absolute best."

She's everything, and instead of being the man I thought you were, you didn't just push them away—you threw them away.

"Apparently, everyone but me—her father. Jesus Christ, I have a daughter," he chokes out the words. "After everything we'd been through, did you think I didn't deserve another chance to know?" he asks Mack.

Her dark expression tells me precisely how she feels about his remark. A twin look of confusion passes between the two of us. *What does he mean he didn't know?*

"Can I see her?" he pleads.

"That wasn't the only attempt I made to tell you about her. I called you on the night she was born," Mack states, her voice trembling.

"When? If you called on the day she was born, I would have remembered. I got my shit together after that night in Boston. My dad came the next day, took one look at me, and I started therapy that same day. I haven't touched drugs or drank in excess since that night." His admission eases some of the aches in my chest. I should hate him for what he did to Mack and Cadence. I should hate him for not only throwing them away but also our lifelong friendship. But, fuck, I've missed him.

"I did tell you again. I called you from Carson's phone on the night she was born, but like every other attempt, it went to voicemail. So I texted you and told you that I had a girl and to call me. I took one look at her beautiful face inside the incubator they had her in, and I knew I had to tell you at least she existed. That you had a daughter who was a perfect little fighter," Mack tells him.

"Fuck. Goddammit," he curses.

"What?" we both ask in unison.

"When was she born?"

"March 29th," Mack says.

"As in right before the Frozen Four?" he questions.

"Yes, Griffin," she growls out.

"McKenna, shit, I'm sorry. I can't say for certain if I was in the right headspace to pick up the phone or not at that time, but I honestly didn't have my phone anymore. I gave it up after that night in Boston when I started therapy. My agent, Jared, had it, and he hired a publicist to take over my social media accounts. I still haven't been on social media in almost two years, which explains how I didn't know until today that you even had a child."

He could follow her on her socials all he wants, but it's one of Mack's top priorities to keep Cadence out of the media. A school reporter approached her last year, wanting to do a piece featuring Mack's life as a mother and college athlete. She immediately refused, and I couldn't agree more with her decision to make Cadence's privacy a top priority. It's become one of mine too.

"I'm having a hard time wrapping my head around everything. Why did you choose to disconnect your phone?" she asks.

"My therapist suggested blocking out things that triggered my anxiety and panic attacks I was having at the time. One major trigger for me was my old phone because of the photos on it and the social media memories that would come up. Every time I felt like I was coming up for a breath of air, a memory popped up on my phone, letting the grief resurface and pull me back under. So, I handed it over to Jared. He would tell me if anything major came up, but my dad, my coach, and my teammates all had my new number, so I didn't really use it much. I disconnected my old number when I signed with Colorado after the

Frozen Four. I didn't think to check my messages with the chaos of moving."

Is literally everyone seeing a therapist besides me at this point? I watch as they continue to ping pong questioning jabs back and forth.

"I'm sorry, but it's hard for me to believe you when the timing came literally days after I called to tell you about her, Griffin."

"And you don't think I'm having a hard time wrapping my head around the fact that I just now found out I have a daughter?"

"If I have to try to be understanding of your situation, you need to try to put yourself in my shoes."

Feeling like I'm interrupting a pivotal conversation, I quietly back out of the room and into the hallway, shutting the door behind me. I try to take a deep breath to ease some of the anxiety flooding me, but my chest is tight with fear and anger.

I'm shocked that Griffin didn't remember his conversation with McKenna about her pregnancy. All this time, I was sure he pushed aside his responsibilities and chose to abandon them. I'm riddled with guilt, knowing I didn't push Mack to reach out to him again, that I didn't just force his hand. If I had, I know I wouldn't have had to force him into anything.

The Griff I knew growing up was fiercely loyal and one of the most accountable guys I played hockey with. In my heart, I should've known he would never willingly abandon his child.

Fuck.

I rub at the tightness in my chest, willing it to subside when my phone buzzes with a text message notification.

Brooke:

Good game, All-Star. If you're back in town, there's a Halloween party at Kappa Delta on Tuesday night. Either way, convince your sister she needs to come. The team is dressing up as each of Taylor Swift's eras.

Shaking my head at my sister's friend and teammate's antics, I reply.

Me:

Thanks, B. But there's probably not a chance in hell she'll go for that. We've got trick-or-treating to do with our Wonder Woman.

I smile at that. Halloween is one of my favorite holidays. I've always loved it. There's something about fall that gets my blood buzzing. No, not something—everything. The way the leaves on the maple trees burn the brightest shades of scarlet, copper, and amber. The way the crisp Minnesota mornings make you reach for your favorite hoodie. And the fact that I'm the most basic of bitches and love every damn pumpkin-flavored thing should be the biggest sign that fall is my favorite time of the year.

I've made it my personal mission to ensure we go all out for my favorite holiday—I take dressing up for Halloween very seriously. Last year, Mack dressed as a lifeguard, and Cadence was a shark while I made a costume of a shark attack victim with a bloody bitten abdomen. It was epic. This year, Mack is Catwoman, I'm the Joker, and Cadence is Wonder Woman. I practically begged Dakota to join us as Harley Quinn, but she's shot me down every time.

Speaking of Dakota, where in the hell did she go? I pull up her contact and shoot her a quick text.

Me:

You joining us for dinner?

My message quickly changes from delivered to read before the reply bubbles appear.

Austen:

I can't. My brother is in town for his game, and we're headed to dinner now. Good game, by the way! Nice goal . . . It is a goal, right?

Holy shit. I forgot the Mustangs were playing the Minnesota Voyagers tomorrow.

Me:

> Thank you, Super Nanny. Yes, a goal, lol. I'm glad you were here for it. Where are you eating dinner?

Austen:

> Nice try! I saw the heart eyes you have for my brother. I'm saving him from the awkward fangirl moment you'd have.

Ha! Of course, I'd fangirl over Brody Meyer. Who wouldn't? The guy is a legend. But if she only knew the truth—the only heart eyes I have are for her.

Me:

> I see how it is. It's a low blow to deprive a man of meeting his idol and then bash him for a potential, totally appropriate, fangirl moment.

I wait a few minutes, but the text doesn't change to read, and a reply from my dream girl doesn't come. *Because she's married and she's probably eating with not only her brother, but her husband.*

A few minutes later, McKenna and Griffin exit the media room. Mack looks exhausted and like she's about two minutes from withdrawing into herself. I already knew I wasn't going to stay long at dinner tonight because I've got an early morning flight with the team to Dallas for a Monday night game. Now that I see the look on her face, I know the goal is to eat as quickly as possible so we can get her home.

4

Dakota

October

I've only made it three steps into the house when McKenna's dog, Ranger, comes barreling toward me. He leaps up to stand on his hind legs and assaults my face with kisses. I am *so* not a dog person. Or at least I wasn't a dog person until I met this sixty-pound Golden Retriever whose personality is scarily similar to Carson's.

Only after Ranger has thoroughly drenched my face in slobber do I hear someone command, "Ranger, down." The voice isn't one I recognize, and neither is the man in front of me. "That's my goodest boy," he coos to the dog as he pats his head.

The man notices my puzzled expression and introduces himself. "Hi, I'm Griffin. Kenna's uh . . . I'm Cadence's dad." Griffin smiles sheepishly, rubbing the back of his neck.

He doesn't offer his hand to shake, so I wave awkwardly. "It's nice to meet you, Griffin. I'm Dakota, Cadence's nanny." In the months I've worked for McKenna, we've talked from time to time. A few weeks ago, she mentioned Cadence's dad for the first time, knowing he would be playing against Carson at his debut game this last weekend. She called last night to inform me that Griffin would be in town for a few days getting to know Cadence before he flies back to Colorado.

"Yes, I've heard a lot about you. Kenna says you're a miracle worker with Cadence."

"Aw, I don't know about that. But that little darlin' sure makes it easy when she's such a sweetheart."

A door upstairs opens, followed by loud footsteps in the hallway. I've barely made out what he's wearing as Carson struts down the stairs like it's his own personal catwalk in full costume. He's dressed in a deep purple suit, completing the look with light green hair and full Joker makeup.

Today is Halloween, and Carson clearly went all out with the themed costumes he picked out for Cadence, McKenna, and himself.

"There she is! Happy Halloween, Austin. I've got your costume upstairs in my room." He thumbs behind him, before continuing, "I really outdid myself this year, if I do say so. Griff, I put your costume in the guest room."

Griffin is now the one wearing a puzzled expression. "Austin?"

"Inside joke," Carson replies without elaborating.

Griffin shakes his head, his face lighting up with a bemused smile before he heads up the stairs.

Carson watches him retreat for a second before he returns his gaze to me, tucking his hands into the pocket of his purple suit pants. How does this man even make a villain costume look attractive?

"So, what was today's pick?" he asks.

I slowly blink at him, trying to solve the riddle he sometimes speaks in. "Pick?" I question.

He shrugs his shoulders, hands still in his pockets. The move would look downright adorably boyish if it weren't for the way the creepy makeup on his face distorts his typical golden glow. "Yeah. Which book did you pick to read today?"

My cheeks heat the way they always seem to do under his attentive stare. "Oh, um, well, ever since I moved to Minnesota, fall has quickly become my favorite season." I pause, clasping my hands together, before realizing what I'm doing and dropping them to my side. "The crisp air and falling leaves feel sort of whimsical, which puts me in the mood to read fantasy books."

A lazy smile takes over Carson's face as he stares at me. It's unnerving having this man's full attention and unyielding gaze on me.

"Fall just so happens to be my favorite season as well. In fact, Halloween is tied with Christmas for my favorite holiday."

I chuckle at that tidbit. "You don't say . . . I would've never guessed," I say sarcastically.

"I know, I hide it pretty well. I've been told I have a great poker face," he goes on.

"You have not," I tell him in a fit of laughter.

"Alright, so I'm not exactly the best at holding back my emotions. But isn't that a good thing? When I like something, there's no hiding it," he explains, his deep voice sending a shiver down my spine.

"I suppose it's not a bad thing," I admit, hugging my arms to my chest. "Hey, did you say you had my costume upstairs?" I ask, and he nods in response. Dipping my head, I give him a shy "thanks" in response before slipping past him to get changed.

Upstairs on the bed, *his* bed, is a shirt that says "Daddy's Lil Monster," pleather pants that are red and blue, hightop Converse sneakers, and a blonde wig that is already pulled up into two pigtails, one dyed red, the other blue.

Dear god, please help me. I can't do this. I can't go out in public looking like this. If a photo of me ever got back to Aaron somehow, he would probably kill me for looking so indecent.

A few minutes later, I crack the bedroom door open and peek my head out. I see two figures dressed in all black at the other end of the hallway. I recognize McKenna's voice as she talks to Griffin. They are dressed as Batman and Catwoman, and Carson wasn't lying, he really outdid himself. All of these costumes look as if he stole them from the production set himself.

McKenna turns toward me, and I see a smiling Cadence dressed up as Wonder Woman.

"Look at you, Cadence! I love your costume," I say to her. She claps and squeals, her whole body going rigid in her mom's arms with excitement.

"Are we going to your parents' neighborhood to trick-or-treat?" Griffin asks.

"Yeah, I think Carson was just loading the stroller into his truck. Figured we could all ride over there together," she replies.

The four of us head downstairs to the kitchen to pack up a few snacks for Cadence—because as sweet as she is, Cadence goes from fine to melting real quick when she's hungry.

"I'll get the snacks while y'all get her bundled up," I suggest. It's only October, but in Minnesota, it gets colder for Halloween. Or maybe this Texan just hasn't adapted to the cooler climate.

Carson joins me in the kitchen once he's loaded his truck. He walks up to me with a twinkle in his eye. "Harley-girl, you look amazing," he compliments me as he grabs my right hand in his. "I almost forgot—a few of the accessories were still in my truck."

Before I can pull my hand from his, Carson's entire body goes rigid when he spots the bruises on my wrist. He doesn't tighten his grip, but he gently tugs my wrist closer while thoroughly inspecting my purpling skin.

He drops the studded cuff from his hand and looks up, his gaze meeting mine. "How did you get these bruises?" he questions.

Shit. Shit. Shit.

This can't be happening. Why didn't I just refuse to dress up? The sweater I was wearing covered my wrists, effectively hiding the bruises Aaron left there.

Think, Dakota.

I pull my hand from his grasp and try to play it off. "Oh, no. These look suspiciously worse than what happened."

"Then what happened?"

"What happened?" I echo his question.

"Yes, what happened? And please start talking fast, Dakota, because my mind is drawing a lot of conclusions."

I break eye contact with him, his piercing blue eyes feeling like they'll probe the truth right out of me.

"My husband and I were, uh, well, you know . . . being intimate?" My face heats from the lie, but Carson must mistake it as me bashfully blushing.

"So, just to clarify, these dark bruises on your wrist were consensual?" he presses.

"Carson, this conversation is completely unnecessary. These are the results of a moment of passion," I lie, intentionally avoiding answering his question. Though it isn't too big of a stretch—they are the result of a passionate argument in which my husband laid hands on me for the first time.

Can I even classify it as "laying hands on me" when all Aaron really did was tightly squeeze my wrist for embarrassing him in front of my brother the other night?

Yes.

No. Everything is fine. Aaron apologized profusely the next day when he saw my wrist. He even brought me an ice pack and promised he'd never lose his temper like that again. Besides, I've already decided I'm filing for divorce the moment I can afford to cut ties. I just need to stand my ground and play the part of a doting wife for a few more months.

Instead of stewing on the way my heart sinks at that, I push past Carson to grab my jacket before heading outside to get in the truck. I need fresh air away from Carson's imploring gaze.

We're a few houses down the street from Carson and McKenna's parents' house when Carson gets recognized for the first time by a group of women in their early twenties. They ask Carson and Griffin if they can take photos with them, but Carson politely declines saying, "I'm sorry, ladies. We're actually having some family time tonight. I would hate for the photos of what we're dressed up as to circulate and ruin our disguises. I'm sure you can understand, right?"

The women all nod their head in understanding, and Carson gives them an appreciative grin, adding a wink for good measure that looks downright wicked with his Joker makeup.

At that, he turns and runs over to Cadence, crouching down to pick her up and lift her onto his shoulders. Cadence squeals in delight and grabs onto the longer, now green, hair on the top of Carson's head.

"Ouch, Cadey Cat. Be careful with Uncle Car-Car's hair."

"Yes, you wouldn't want anything to happen to those golden locks," I tease. "Then what would the ladies have to grip on to?"

My eyes widen with panic. I'm not sure what possessed me to go there, but I regret the words the moment they've left my mouth.

Carson turns around to walk backward, his eyebrows shooting up his forehead as he slows his pace until I'm nearly toe-to-toe with him. "Are you flirting with me, Harley-girl?"

This man and his nicknames.

Also, am I flirting with him? I'm not even sure I remember what flirting is. But if the lowering of his voice and slightly crooked smirk on his face are any indication, I'd say he appreciates my accidental attempt at flirting. He's stopped walking now and is looking down at me intently, almost as if he's imploring me to play along.

Feeling slightly unsure of myself, I decide a change of subject and deflection is the right move here. "So, did you know those women back there, or is your costume maybe not as good of a disguise as you thought it was?"

He sends me a knowing look and softly chuckles at my pivot. "We went to high school with a few of them. My guess is they likely knew we'd be bringing Wonder Woman trick-or-treating around our parents' block, and they wanted to shoot their shot." I frown at that, and he casually shrugs his shoulders as if that kind of behavior is totally normal.

"I've had a lot of unwanted attention on me since high school. Things only got more intense after my college team won a national championship and I got drafted only a couple months later. I don't enjoy being in the spotlight, especially when Cadence is with me, but it's a small sacrifice to pay in order for me to play the game I've loved since I put on my first pair of skates."

It must be the cold air or something because my eyes start to tear up of their own volition. I can't imagine it's easy not knowing people's true intentions when you've got the level of popularity it sounds like Carson has had for years now.

"That sounds like it'd be really hard—lonely, even."

"Ah, shucks. Are you worried about me, Super Nanny?" he playfully brushes off my comment. "It's not so bad. Especially when I get to play with some of my former teammates, Bennett and Jackson Wilson.

It's been really good for me because they're going through the same thing. Honestly, it's even worse for Bennett—he's been somewhat of a hockey prodigy from a young age. He was drafted first overall straight out of high school. The attention surrounding him would be far more suffocating. It's probably why he has such a tough exterior." Carson chuckles to himself. "I'm sure you'll meet him sometime. Benny is a great guy, but he can come off as a standoffish dick from time to time."

"Well, I'm glad you've got them."

"And Griff too now. We might not be on the same team, but I'm hoping with him discovering Mack had Cadence that he will be around again more often."

At the mention of her name, Cadence perks up and tugs on Carson's hair again as if they're the reins to steer him away from this conversation and back to trick-or-treating. I look over my shoulder to find Kenna and Griffin both staring at us with a few feet of distance between them. Kenna's body language is guarded, and Griffin looks unsure of himself, like he wants to close the distance between them but isn't sure if he should.

I turn back to Carson and point my thumb over my shoulder. "I'm going to walk with your sister for a bit. Why don't you and Griffin bring Cadence to the next house?"

"Sounds good. Oh, and Austin, thanks for being such a good friend to Mack." I'm about to respond when he cuts me off, lifting one of his hands from Cadence's feet. "I know, I know. It's part of your job. But that doesn't mean I can't thank you for being so good to my girls."

I close my mouth and bite the inside of my cheek. He doesn't have to thank me, because Kenna's friendship has quickly become something I cherish.

And when he said his girls . . . I couldn't help but wonder—what would it be like to be his?

5

Dakota

December

I promised my mama I'd be home for Christmas this year, and if there's one thing I've learned in my twenty-eight years thus far, it's to not break promises to your mama. I'm thankful that it's unseasonably cold this winter so no one questions why I'll be wearing sweaters for the duration of my stay.

I'm not sure why I was so shocked when Aaron got upset again and left more marks on my wrists and arms. But when I showed up fifteen minutes late to meet him at a dinner party after McKenna's practice ran long, he was irate when we got home. He pinned me against the wall, squeezing my arms with such force that even after a week, my skin is still riddled with deep purple marks. There was also the hole in the wall that he made when he punched the drywall beside my head. He said I had to patch it myself because he wouldn't allow someone else to come clean up the mess "I'd made."

Taking a deep breath, trying to clear the thoughts from my head, I send up a prayer of thanks that Aaron wasn't able to come with me to Texas. He said he was working on a case that wouldn't allow him to be out of the office for five days.

Snapping me out of my thought spiral with his deep baritone, Brody says, "Come on, Kota. Don't pitch a hissy fit over this. There's no use;

46

you'll never win this battle. I'm your older brother, and I have every right to be concerned about your happiness, safety, and well-being."

"Brody Meyer, I know you're not fixin' for a fight with your baby sister on Christmas Eve," Mama scolds.

Yep. It only took one look from my big brother to know something was off about me. And without a moment of hesitation, he knew Aaron must be the cause of whatever was going on.

"It's no secret I've never liked Aaron, Mama. The first time I met him, do you remember what I told you?"

She shakes her head at him and gives him a look of warning, but Brody completely disregards her. "I said that man looks like a sheep-killing dog. And the girl you raised was no sheep." Brody looks me in my teary eyes. "Don't let that sonofabitch turn you into a sheep, Kota Lynn."

"I won't."

"You swear it?"

"I swear it, Bubs." With that, I get up and excuse myself. After placing my dessert plate in the dishwasher, I head up to my childhood bedroom to grab my book off the nightstand. I need to bury my head in a reality that isn't mine.

Just as I grab my tattered copy of *Little Women*, my phone lights up with a text notification. I tense, thinking it might be Aaron, but relax when I see Carson's name. Well, the name I put him under in my contacts. It's both a nickname and a cover in case Aaron were to see my phone.

Mr. Wilder:

Merry Christmas Eve, Dakota!

Me:

Dakota? Who stole your phone? So formal . . . you must want something from me.

Lol, it's just me. But I wouldn't hate it if you said hi to my idol for me.

Knew it!

Can you blame me for shooting my shot, Super Nanny?

Ah, there he is. You couldn't even go two minutes without a nickname.

It's a form of endearment. Like a love language.

So are you saying you love me, Golden Boy?

Shit. Why in the hell did I ask that? The text bubbles appear and disappear before reappearing again. What feels like minutes but is really only moments later, his reply pops up on my phone.

Mr. Wilder:

I'm really good at golf.

What? Well, that's one way to avoid my awkward question.

Okay . . .

We should go together sometime. It's my favorite thing to do in the off-season.

I'm not going to lie, you probably wouldn't want me to golf with you. I've never been before.

I could teach you.

It's not right. I'm older than you. You shouldn't be the one teaching me anything.

You can teach me anything you want. I'm a very eager student.

Carson Wilder makes my cheeks heat even from thousands of miles away.

I'll trade you baking lessons for golf lessons.

Deal. I'm holding you to it.

You've got it. I'm about to get lost in a book. Merry Christmas Eve!

What book?

I'm not sure if his interest in what I'm reading is genuine, but each time he asks, my chest tightens.

Little Women. I've read it every Christmas Eve since I was nine.

That's commitment. Which character is your favorite?

I'd like to be more like Josephine with her fiery personality.

Personally, Aunt March is my favorite.

That makes me laugh so loud I have to cover my mouth to muffle the sound.

"What has you laughing like a schoolgirl, Kota Lynn?" Brody's voice startles me.

I grasp my chest. "You scared me, Brodes."

"Seems like you startle easier than ever these days."

Shaking my head, I start to disagree, but he puts his hand up to stop me.

"Look, Mama told me to come up here and apologize for speaking out of place. But I'm not gonna do that." I snort at his bluntness. "You see, ever since Pops passed away, I made it my mission to become your protector. I won't apologize for having your best interests at heart."

My chest aches the same way it does every time I think of my daddy. He passed away when I was in middle school. He was diagnosed with brain cancer, and six months later, we were laying him to rest.

"Something is going on. You're acting different—skittish even. You can't expect me to just stand back and watch my sister be unhappy. I hope like hell you know you can come to me with anything, sis."

Swallowing past the lump in my throat, I whisper, "I know, Bubs."

And I do know. So why can't I muster up the courage to admit what is happening? Why can't I go to the people I love the most in the world and tell them I don't feel safe?

I know if I admit to Brody what has been happening with Aaron, he will jump into protector mode. He'll help me get a swift divorce and set me up with a new place to live. But I also know he can be hot-headed, and finding out Aaron has laid hands on me multiple times now could possibly land Brody in jail.

I'm so close to leaving Aaron and making it on my own that I can almost see the light at the end of the tunnel. By this time next year, I'll celebrate Christmas with my family as a single woman.

6

Carson

December

My truck rolls to a stop at a slick intersection a few blocks from my house. I spent Christmas Eve with my parents to allow Mack and Griffin time alone with Cadence. Thick, cottony snowflakes are falling, and "The First Noel" is playing on the radio. The scene is set for a storybook holiday, but I can't muster up the same spirit.

Christmas morning used to be one of my favorite times of the year. Nothing beats the innocence of running down the stairs on Christmas morning and seeing that Santa had come. Growing up, my parents would invite our next-door neighbors, the Turners, over to let McKenna and I play with Griffin and Katie while the adults enjoyed spiked hot chocolates and made a big breakfast spread.

I was naive to think those traditions would follow us into our adulthood. But as I walk through the garage door into my house and spot Griffin at the stove flipping pancakes, my heart both swells and aches.

Fuck, Katie should be here with us right now.

She'd eat this up—Griffin making pancakes in my kitchen for her best friend and niece, who, she would point out, he so stupidly pushed away. She'd probably say something like, "Get on your fucking knees and grovel, Griff. You better beg for her forgiveness."

I rub the physical ache in my chest that comes whenever I think of the spitfire girl I grew up with. Katie never hesitated to bust my balls and put me in my place. Sure, she was Mack's best friend, but you don't spend nearly every day interacting with someone in some small way or another, and not form a deep bond with them. She was ingrained into every memory of our childhood. Days like today feel like a punch to the gut when I realize she won't be joining us.

The days and months that followed her passing were filled with sorrow so deep I didn't know how to go on. But I didn't have any choice but to keep moving, because I had to be there for my twin when her world was crumbling.

Watching Griffin make my sister and my niece breakfast, I know the pain I feel on this day every year, the grief that threatens to pull me under, is nothing compared to the bone-deep despair Griffin has had to overcome. Yet here he is—putting in the effort and slowly proving himself to everyone that he can be the man they deserve.

"Merry Christmas, G. What are you making?" I ask.

"Merry Christmas, Carse. I'm making pancakes, scrambled eggs, and ground sausage. Kenna said Cadence loves all of those, so I thought it was a good choice for the first Christmas I get to spend with her."

I nod at him, really taking him all in. He's changed so much in the two years since I've seen him. Sure, we played each other in the Frozen Four tournament in college, but I could barely look at him then.

Goddamnit, I've missed him.

"You're doing a good job with her—with them. You know, I feel partly responsible for how things went down. I was hurting too, seeing you like that, hearing what you said to Mack. I didn't handle it well. Obviously, punching you wasn't one of my finest moments." I wince at the memory. Hitting my childhood best friend while he was high and insinuating my sister intentionally got pregnant to trap him . . . yeah, not something I wish to rehash.

I rub the back of my neck and continue, "I've always taken on the role of a caretaker in our group. I guess I liked the idea of Mack, and eventually Cadence, needing me. I should've backed off and suggested Mack continue to reach out to you. To not give you the option of skirting your responsibilities. Looking back and knowing you, if you were in your right mind, you never would've abandoned them. I'm sorry, G. I feel like I got in the way."

Griff turns off the burner and plates the last of the pancakes.

He clears his throat and turns to me, looking me in the eyes. "Honestly, I should be thanking you, Carse. If it weren't for you, Kenna wouldn't have had anyone to lean on after Katie's death. I carelessly pushed her away, fooling myself into thinking I was doing what was best for her. Then, instead of trying to grieve in a healthy way, I coped by drowning myself in alcohol and prescription pills. You were there for her when I should've been along every step of the way. And while I'm jealous as hell that it wasn't me, I'm also thankful for each and every time you had her back."

He doesn't need to thank me. My need to take care of Mack and Cadence has become one of my sole reasons for existing. Without the two of them, I don't know what I'd do.

"Shit. It's pretty early for these deep conversations. What do you say we hug it out and let the past stay in the past?" I give him a watery-eyed grin.

Griff smiles back, shaking his head at my theatrics, then brings me in for a real hug. He pats my back a few times, and we part when a throat clears from behind us.

"Care to share what has the two of you so emotional this morning? It's Christmas!" Mack stands near the kitchen island, holding a grinning Cadence on her hip. My sister and niece are in matching Christmas pajamas and both sporting some crazy hair. But as I look over at Griff, his face is lit up brighter than the damn Christmas tree. He is so enamored with the two of them, and I can tell my stubborn sister's walls are slowly lowering.

At this very moment, surrounded by my people, I know Katie is here watching over us.

I miss you, Kitty.

After we finished breakfast, Mack said it was time for Cadence to open her presents from Santa. She tore into the wrapping paper, squeals of pure joy filling the room.

Once Cadence finishes opening her last present, Griff gets up and goes to the tree.

"There're a few more to open up," he says as he places a gift bag in front of Cadence.

Cadey Cat dives right into her present, throwing the tissue paper aside and pulling out a small blue and white jersey.

Mack helps Cadence lift the jersey up, turning it around to show the ninety-one and "DADDY" across the back of a Colorado Summit jersey. It's fucking cute as hell, but Cadence obviously looks better wearing my Wolverines jersey.

"Oh, this is so cute! It's actually perfect for what we got you," Mack says, becoming bashful and hiding her face behind Cadence.

"And what's that?" Griff asks.

Mack pulls out her phone. Once she's swiped a few times, she turns her phone over for him to see.

I already know what she got him—two flights from Minneapolis to Denver for New Year's Eve day, with the return flight returning a week later.

"Sunshine, are you messing with me right now?" he questions. Sunshine, the nickname he used to call her, and I ate that shit right up.

She shakes her head at him. "I thought since my season is over, and I'm on winter break from school, Cadence and I could come visit you for a week in Denver. I looked at your schedule, and your team has a stretch of home games, so I thought it'd be perfect timing for us to surprise you. Your dad even said he could make it out for a few days to meet Cadence."

Griff goes silent and Mack's eyes widen in fear. "Oh my gosh. This was so presumptuous of me. I was so caught up in surprising you, I didn't stop to think if you'd even want us to come. Griff, I can get a refund on the tickets."

"No," he says firmly, shaking his head. "No, that's not happening. I want you two to come. This means so much to me, Sunshine. I've never loved a surprise more than this one."

She still looks apprehensive. "Are you sure?"

Griff scoops Mack and Cadence into an awkward sitting hug, placing a kiss on each of their cheeks. And that's my cue to go fill up my spiked hot chocolate.

When I get back into the living room, Griff pulls out two envelopes from his sweatshirt pocket, handing one to Mack and the other to me.

"What's this? You didn't have to get us anything," Mack starts, smiling in resignation.

"Should we open them together?" Mack and I ask in synchrony.

"Yeah," he replies.

I've barely got mine open when I hear Mack squeal, "What? How? Are these for real?"

Looking down at my own gift, I freeze. "G, are you serious? How the hell did you score floor tickets to Taylor Swift's sold-out Era's Tour?"

He just smirks. "I know people who know people. So, do you like them?"

"Like them? What's not to absolutely love? Tell me you got one for yourself too!" Mack squeals as she throws herself into his arms.

He nods his head to let her know he did. "I, uh, actually got four tickets. Figured Katie could be there in spirit."

Mack pulls back, her eyes pooling with unshed tears. "She's always with us, but I love that you got her a ticket, Griffin."

"I'm going to have no voice for a month after this concert," I say.

"I'm glad you love them, Sunshine. Does that date work for the two of you?" he asks.

I look down at the tickets. Fuck, how do I even tell him? "Uh, G, I don't know how to tell you this, but your people messed up. These tickets say the concert is in July in Milan. As in Milan, Italy."

"They didn't mess up. We're going to Italy for the concert," he says so matter-of-factly my jaw nearly falls to the floor.

"Griff, we can't just go to Italy. We have Cadence—" Mack starts.

Griff cuts her off. "I already asked your mom and Dakota if they could watch her while we're there for the two weeks."

"Two weeks? Griffin! That's crazy. You're insane. I haven't been away from her for more than two nights at a time. There's no way I'll be comfortable leaving her for that long."

"We can figure out the logistics and length of the vacation as it gets closer, Sunshine," he placates her.

Surely I don't have to stay with them in Italy, as what I imagine will likely be a third-wheel situation, for two weeks. Plus, that's two whole weeks where I wouldn't get to see Dakota.

Woah. Where did that come from? Maybe some time away would do me some good.

Yeah . . . no. Not only am I highly suspicious of what's going on in her marriage ever since Halloween, but now that I've gotten used to having her around and I'm getting to know her, that much time without Austen just won't do.

7

Dakota

December

Aaron is waiting for me in the foyer of our house with my black dress coat and a black sequin clutch when I've finished getting ready. Right, I guess I won't wear my favorite beige, knee-length coat then.

Slowing my steps, I pause a moment to take him in. At thirty-four years old, Aaron's once-dark hair is somehow already peppered with grays, and his lean runner's frame is looking like he's skipped one too many meals in favor of working through lunch. He was a third-year law student at Abbott University when I met him during the spring semester of freshman year. I used to appreciate our six-year age gap. He was more mature than the other guys I had dated—more grounded—and he knew what he wanted. I just didn't realize that when he said he wanted me, it meant he wanted to add me to his collection of possessions.

It didn't take long for him to propose, he even said he wanted to lock me down before I could realize I was too good for him. I naively thought that meant he knew what he had and he would always treat me like the queen he put on a pedestal while we were dating.

I wasn't quite so off-base. He did treat me well at the beginning of our marriage. But looking back on it, we married so quickly that I didn't wait long enough for him to show his true colors.

When he spots me approaching him, a deep frown spreads over his face. "What are you wearing?"

Smoothing my hands down the silk fabric of my floor-length, emerald green dress, I tense from the tone in his question. "D–didn't you say it was a black tie dress code?"

"I did."

"This is a black tie gown I got from that boutique you love in the city. The owner said it was on the list of the dresses you had pre-approved." That's a stretch. She said it was on the list of approved colors Aaron had given her. This specific dress, however, was not on the rack of preselected dresses he had chosen.

He scoffs. "I think I would have remembered selecting such a scandalous gown for my wife. Come," he commands, holding his arm out for me.

I press my shaking hand in his as he guides me toward the door.

Everything is fine. See? He's even holding my hand and letting the dress slide.

Those optimistic thoughts are quickly put to rest as soon as he shoves me in front of the floor-length mirror, the statement piece of our foyer.

My body turns rigid as Aaron stands behind me, his gaze running over my reflection in the mirror. "Do you want to know what I see when I look at you in this dress?"

I don't. I really don't.

He doesn't give me a chance to respond either way. "I see a pathetic little housewife, who is so lonely and needy for attention that she's decided to act out. What do you think the partners at my firm will think when the man they're grooming to join them as a partner shows up with such a stupid slut on his arm?"

His words cut deep, but they are nothing he hasn't called me before.

But what cuts deeper than his words is the harsh reality that's reflected back at me. He may see me as those terrible things, but what I see is so much worse. I see a woman scared, tired, and desperate to escape. I see a woman battered and willing to wave the white flag. I see a woman who has become so dejected that she might just give up.

Aaron scowls. "Unfortunately, we don't have time for you to change your dress. Being late is an even bigger sin than dressing like an escort." He roughly shoves my coat at me before opening the door for himself, not bothering to lock up or walk with me on the slick cement that leads to the town car waiting for us in the driveway.

One more week. That's all. And then I'm free.

I'm not sure how in the hell I didn't notice it before. Of course, Carson's father, the man in an expensive black tuxedo smiling next to his mother, is one of the founding partners of Procter & Wilder LLP. The very law firm where my husband is a senior associate. The same firm where one of the partners is set to retire in the next year. And the same firm that is hosting this very swanky end-of-the-year celebration on New Year's Eve.

Shit, this is so bad.

I've met Carson and McKenna's mom a few times, and I met their father at Carson's first hockey game. But up until this moment, I hadn't pieced together that their father was also the very man whom my husband plans to take over for when he retires. Carson doesn't know Aaron works for his father's firm, and he can't find out. He saw the cracks in my facade on Halloween, and he's been paying far too close attention to me since then.

I need to get out of here.

Excusing myself to the lady's room, I turn and take a few steps before I run right into a very broad chest. His black, velvet tuxedo jacket smells like notes of a spicy cologne I've become far too familiar with lately.

Carson gently grasps my shoulders to steady me. "Austin," he whispers breathlessly before audibly swallowing, making his Adam's apple bob in the most shockingly erotic way. "What are you doing here?"

I stare up into his ocean eyes and get lost for a moment.

"Dakota? What happened?" Aaron asks, and I've got to give him credit, he even sounds genuinely concerned. Carson's hands drop to his sides instantly.

No. No, no, no. This can't be happening.

"Excuse me, I'm such a clutz." Taking a step back, I try to sound lighthearted despite the panic that's causing my pulse to beat at a thunderous rate. "I don't believe we've met," I say, holding my hand out to Carson. "I'm Dakota, and this is my husband, Aaron Ackerman."

Carson stares back at me with a puzzled expression that he quickly schools. He must sense my need for him to play along. The moment his hand connects with mine, the feeling of warmth I get any time he touches me floods my system. "Hello, Mr. and Mrs. Ackerman. I'm Carson Wilder." Hearing him greet me as Mrs. Ackerman sounds like nails on a chalkboard. It sounds all wrong coming from his lips.

"Ah, right. You're Theodore and Elizabeth's son." Who? Oh, right. I've come to know them as Liz and Teddy, or Gaga and Papa, as McKenna calls them around Cadence.

"The one and only," Carson replies, holding his hand out for Aaron to shake. I don't miss the clench of his clean-shaven jaw.

"Ladies and gentlemen, I ask that you please find your assigned seats. The dinner service will begin shortly," the emcee for the evening announces. With that, Aaron drags me toward our table, which is, thankfully, a few tables away from Carson's.

But that doesn't stop his gaze from being fixed on me anytime I look up during dinner. Each time my eyes connect with his, he looks a little more vexed. His posture is rigid, jaw clenched, and his eyes discerning the truth behind my shriveling front.

The bar and another associate kept Aaron occupied for a good portion of the evening, giving me a reprieve from his suffocating presence. He just came to tell me he'd been asked to have a cigar with some of the partners. I'm hoping that will keep him occupied until he's ready to leave.

I'm just about to make an escape to hide away in the restroom when an outstretched hand appears before me.

"May I have this dance, Austin?" Carson literally bows down before me with his hand still outstretched. The sincerity in the question shining in his ocean eyes when he lifts his head has me throwing all of my good sense out the window.

His gaze is so intense that I'm left speechless. He must take my silence as reluctance.

Still unable to form any words, I place my hand in his outstretched one and nod. Nerves fill my belly as he guides us out onto the dance floor.

The opening notes of Frank Sinatra's "The Way You Look Tonight" begin to play as Carson spins me toward him. He places one hand on the small of my back, his other holding mine, and we start to sway to the classic melody.

Even with my four-inch heels, Carson still towers over me. He brings his head down, and for one foolish, reckless moment, I wonder if he will kiss me. Instead, he brings his lips to my ear and softly says, "You look absolutely stunning, Dakota. The shade of your dress makes your emerald eyes even more captivating. I didn't think that was possible, yet here you are, looking like a true vision."

What a stark difference his compliment about my appearance is from what Aaron told me before we left. Carson's tone is full of wonderment. As they seem to always do in his presence, my cheeks burn under his attention.

"I promise I don't mean any disrespect when I ask this, but I have to know. Are you happy with him?" As the question leaves his lips, Carson pulls back and stares so deeply into my eyes I fear he knows the answer without me having to say a thing.

Clearing the tightness from my throat, I reply, "I assure you, Carson, my happiness isn't anything you need to worry about. Happiness is a fleeting emotion. It comes and goes. It changes meaning based on the circumstance."

He sees right through me. And his next words only prove that. "Why do I get the sense that you're avoiding answering my question because you know the truth will set you free?"

If only answering him truthfully could really set me free from the shackles my marriage has imprisoned me with.

The hope shining in Carson's eyes scares me. What is his motive? Why does he want to know?

I don't like the way he pulls reluctant smiles from me. I don't like the way my heart races when he's near. I don't like the way I've started looking forward to seeing him while I'm at work. And I don't like the look of yearning in his eyes I see right now. I need to put an end to this.

"Not all of us have lived such a privileged life as you, Golden Boy. Some of us can't be set free by merely answering a prying question."

Carson rears back as if he's been struck. Sadness etches his features, and I curse myself for causing this man an ounce of pain.

I need to get out of here. Knowing what's done is done, I don't bother with an apology. Instead, I run out of the ballroom. As far away from Carson Wilder as I can get.

8

Carson

January

It's after one in the morning on New Year's when my doorbell rings for the second time. I roll myself out of bed and throw on a pair of gym shorts and a T-shirt before heading down the stairs.

When I open the door, all the air escapes my lungs as I take in the sight before me. A woman with dark hair is bent over, clutching her side. I have to bend down and pull back her hair to reveal who this woman is, but when I do, my heart shatters, and I nearly fall to the ground in shock.

Dakota lifts her chin, and her one green eye that isn't swollen shut connects with mine. Tears stream down her cheeks, her face is battered, her lips bloodied, and her arm is still holding on to her side.

Shock and anger paralyze me.

"I'm so sorry, I–I didn't know where else to go," she whispers.

Her words snap me back to reality.

"Who did this to you?" I somehow manage to grind out through a clenched jaw.

The only response is a gut-wrenching sob that escapes from Dakota's lips. Whoever did this must be punished, but that will have to wait. Right now, I need to get her to a hospital.

Fuck, I've been drinking, and I absolutely refuse to risk it. Instead of calling for a ride service, which I've been apprehensive about using since McKenna and Katie's accident in the back of one, I call a guy I know I can count on at all hours of the night.

"Hello?" he rasps.

"Bennett, hey, it's Carson. Listen, can you make it to my house as quickly as possible and drive me and my friend to the hospital?"

"Jesus, Wilder. What'd you get yourself into?"

"I really can't explain right now. If you can't bring us, just tell me so I can call someone else."

"No, I'm on my way now. It's New Year's. Everyone else is likely still out drinking."

He's probably not wrong. Most of our teammates went to a New Year's Eve party at a club in the city. I cozied up to a bunch of lawyers I don't even know at my father's firm's annual end-of-the-year celebration.

"I'll be there in ten. And, Wilder, you better not be getting me caught in the middle of a media shitstorm," Bennett warns.

"I'm not. Thank you, B. I really appreciate it." I hang up the phone just as Dakota sways on her feet. She groans in pain as I catch her around her waist to keep her from face-planting.

"I'm so sorry, Austen. Don't worry, I've got you. You're safe. I'm going to keep you safe."

And I mean every word—keeping her safe has now become my top priority. Most of my anxiety and fear since losing Katie is triggered when I think of losing another person I love and care for. Seeing Dakota bruised and battered—well, it fucking breaks me.

Dakota

Machines beep a steady rhythm even as my lungs fight to expand and contract. I wince as pain ricochets down my spine, but when I do, my face throbs, sending a new wave of pain. I struggle to open my eyes, only able to open my right one. The overhead fluorescent lights are dimmed, but I can make out that I'm in a hospital.

There's movement on my right side, and I flinch in anticipation of Aaron touching me.

"Austin, you're okay. I'm right here. You're safe." Hearing Carson's voice immediately puts me at ease. "You're in the hospital. I'll call the nurse to get the doctor in here."

I'm safe, but I'm far from okay. Aaron did this to me—he beat me so badly that I had to be hospitalized.

After pushing the call button on my bed, Carson takes my hand in his, giving it a gentle squeeze. Such a small gesture shouldn't make me feel so much relief, but it does.

"I'm so sorry, Carson."

His brow furrows in confusion. "You have nothing to apologize for."

Tears flood the vision in my right eye. "I was terrible to you on the dance floor. I never should've said those things. I didn't mean any of them."

Carson rubs slow circles over my hand. "You were right. I was prying. If anyone should apologize, it's me."

I start to argue just as a woman with platinum blonde hair slicked back into a tight ponytail wearing navy scrubs comes into the room carrying a clipboard.

"Hello, my name is Dr. Frederick. I'm the doctor on call this evening. Can you tell me your name?"

"Dakota."

"What is your date of birth?"

"8/30/96."

"Dakota, can I ask you a few questions in private?" the doctor asks before suspiciously looking over at Carson, causing my panic to spike.

"It-it wasn't him. He can stay. Carson brought me here when I showed up at his doorstep like this." I try to take a deep, calming breath, but it gets caught in my throat as pain slices its way through my chest.

The doctor pauses, chewing the inside of her cheek as she assesses the two of us. She seems to believe me, but she also knows someone did this to me.

"Alright. Your injuries were quite extensive. Your left lung collapsed upon your arrival. That, along with the three broken ribs on your left side, may make breathing painful, so we'll get you some more morphine. Your left kidney has a renal hematoma, also known as a bruised kidney. We're monitoring it for internal bleeding. You also had several lacerations that required stitches," the doctor explains before asking, "Dakota, do you feel safe?"

"Right now, yes."

"Do you feel safe at home?"

I don't verbalize my answer; instead, I slightly shake my head at her.

"Did someone you live with do this to you?"

Lowering my head, I'm too ashamed to look her in the eyes when I answer. "Yes," I whisper.

Carson gives my hand another reassuring squeeze, giving me the courage to speak my truth.

"My husband, Aaron Ackerman, did this to me."

"Thank you for telling me. Dakota, do you feel comfortable answering a few more questions?"

I nod my head in response.

"Perhaps I could ask you these questions in private?" The doctor looks over at Carson again, this time less suspiciously.

In this moment, Carson feels like my lifeline. "He can stay, if that's alright."

"That's okay, I just wanted to make sure you were comfortable. Some of these questions will be quite personal."

"I understand." Carson and I exchange looks, and it's as if a conversation passes between the two of us.

Are you okay with staying here?

I'll be here as long as you need me.

"Okay. Do you recall passing out or being unconscious for any amount of time during the assault?"

Wincing at that word and the flashback of the look on Aaron's face it brings, I reply, "No. The only time I recall being unconscious was when I was brought here."

"Was any part of the assault sexual in nature? Would you like us to run a rape kit?"

At that question, Carson goes completely rigid beside me.

"No," I answer truthfully. "I don't need a rape kit. Aaron didn't sexually assault me."

Dr. Frederick's features soften with sympathy. "Thank you for answering my questions, Dakota. There is also a police officer here to ask you a few questions. Do you feel comfortable answering them now, or would you like me to ask him to let you rest and return later?" Fear and panic slither their way back up my spine like vipers ready to strike.

"I'd like to rest, if that's okay," I whisper, my voice laced with unease.

"Okay. We'll be keeping you overnight for monitoring. Do you have any questions for me at this time?" she asks.

"No. Thank you," I answer.

With that, she gives me a soft smile, nods, and heads out into the hallway, closing the door behind her.

I close my eyes and struggle to inhale through my nose, attempting to calm my nerves, when I hear Carson shift in his seat. If it weren't for his hand still on mine, I'd have forgotten he was here.

"Dakota, I know you need to rest. I do. But I don't think you have a choice regarding pressing charges against Aaron. You'll at least want an order of protection against him so he can't come near you. My dad can help you. Once he hears about this, there's no way he'll stand for a piece of shit with no integrity to stay at their practice."

My breaths start to shallow as the monitor's beeping picks up speed. Trepidation and dread consume me as his words sink in.

"Carson, you don't understand. Aaron w-will kill me if he loses his job. It's all he's worked for—all he's cared about the entire time I've known him."

Still holding my hand in his, Carson gently squeezes my hand three times as he says, "I've got you."

I'm not sure why such a small gesture from a man I've only recently become friends with somehow both eases my terror while also earning my trust.

"I won't let anything happen to you, Austin. I'm going to take care of you, and I'll have my father help me take care of Aaron. You have my word."

Maybe it's the pain medication, maybe it's the conviction in his words, either way, I find myself nodding in acknowledgment as what I vow will be the last tears shed over my future ex-husband stream down my cheeks.

9

Carson

January

The sterile smell of Dakota's hospital room transports me back to haunting memories of my sister's coma and Katie's death. I feel like I'm stuck in a reoccurring nightmare I can't wake up from.

Dakota has been in the hospital now for three days due to complications with her lung collapsing again and her kidney needing continued monitoring. I just got off the phone with a frantic McKenna. Griffin hurt his knee in his game last night, and they flew back to Minnesota on a private jet in the middle of the night.

Mack wanted to get an update on Dakota and let me know she would probably stay at Griffin's until his surgery later this week to help him. Thankfully, my mom can help with Cadence, and Mack is on winter break from classes. But Mack said once I fly out for my game tomorrow, if Dakota is discharged, she can stay with them at Griff's house while they both recover.

But that's just the thing. I haven't gotten a good read on what Dakota plans to do once she's discharged. She's been incredibly tight-lipped with me since she overheard me talking to my dad on the phone about what Aaron did. Hopefully she'll come around once she hears my dad out.

Dakota's phone vibrates beside her on the bed for what feels like the hundredth time.

"Are you going to pick it up?" I ask, not needing to see the screen to know it's her brother.

"No, it's best he doesn't hear about this. He'd probably do something irrational, like fly up here and refuse to play in his game this weekend. They need to win it to clinch the wildcard for the playoffs."

"If you leave him in the dark and only text him, he'll probably get suspicious enough to fly up here regardless. Look, I'm not saying you need to FaceTime with him, but take the advice of an older brother who's a major worrywart—just let the guy hear your voice so he knows you're alive," I suggest.

She shakes her head in disagreement. "Once Brody hears my voice, he will know something is wrong. I'm not a very good liar."

"Then put the phone on speakerphone, and I'll do some of the talking to distract him."

A ghost of a smile dances across Dakota's face, and the sight of it makes my chest squeeze with pride. "Nice try. I know you're just trying to talk to your favorite football player."

I don't even try to deny it. "Guilty," I say as I hold my hands up. "But for what it's worth, I do think he needs to hear your voice—you know, proof of life and all that—otherwise, if he's anything like me, he'll fixate on why he hasn't heard from you. Didn't you say you usually talk on the phone every day? It's been three, Austen."

"Alright, alright. I'll call him on speaker. Just promise me you won't say anything about where we are."

Even though it goes against everything I stand for as a brother, I look her in the eye and hold my pinky out for her.

"Are you serious?" she questions, staring at my pinky in confusion.

"Yeah, my pinky promises are special. I pinky kiss promise that I won't tell him where you are right now."

"What in the world is a pinky kiss promise?"

"Hold up your pinky and cross it with mine," I start before she cuts me off.

"I know what a pinky promise is, Carson. But why on god's green earth would I kiss you?"

"Ouch! I'll have you know I'm a great kisser." I rub at my chest to feign hurt. "But that's not what this is, *friend*. It's just like a pinky promise, except you kiss your own hand to make it an extra-important promise. Kind of like an unbreakable vow from *Harry Potter*. Look, if Cadence can already do it, so can you."

Dakota reluctantly holds out her hand for me to link our pinky fingers. Once I do, the same rush of electricity engulfs me like every other time we've touched. I lean across her bed and kiss my fist just as she leans in slightly to kiss hers. Our eyes lock as we seal our promise. Except I'm not just promising to keep her secret from her brother. No, this is me promising far more than that.

I'll take care of you.

You are safe with me.

I'm never going to let him touch you ever again.

Not long after Dakota and I hang up with her brother—that's right, I got to chat with Brody fucking Meyer—my dad walks into the hospital room.

"Knock, knock," he says as he enters.

Theodore Wilder, or Teddy as most of my friends call him, is a six-foot-four brute of a man. His once light brown hair is now filled with salt and pepper, giving him more of a silver fox vibe. No matter the time of year, he always seems to have tanned skin, and even in his early fifties, he's still in pretty good shape. To others, he probably looks intimidating in his three-piece suit, with polished shoes and his clean-shaven face. To me, he looks like the most supportive dad, who has become one of my best friends as I've gotten older.

I get up and give him a big hug, needing to absorb his strength in this moment.

As soon as Dakota sees my dad, she looks like she wants to turn in on herself.

"Good morning, Dakota. It's nice to see you again, though I wish the circumstances were different."

"Hello, Mr. Wilder," she says, her tone laced with nerves.

Okay, I don't like that. I'm supposed to be Mr. Wilder, just like Mr. Darcy.

"You can call him Teddy or Theo if you'd like," I offer. Dakota nods her head, but I don't miss the heat of her cheeks.

"I brought some brunch for the two of you from that cafe down the street your mother loves. I figured you'd probably had enough of the hospital food," he says as he holds up two takeout bags before handing them over to me.

"That was very kind of you, thank you, Mr. uh, I mean, Theo."

"May I?" my dad asks as he points to one of the chairs beside Dakota's bed.

"Yes, of course," Dakota replies with a quick nod.

My dad undoes the button of his suit jacket, and once he's seated, he doesn't hesitate to get to the matter at hand. "Dakota, as I'm sure you know, my son has filled me in on the events that led to your hospitalization. I want to assure you that my partners and I have taken swift action and terminated Aaron's employment at the firm. We have a morality clause that Mr. Ackerman has certainly not abided by. I do not take his actions lightly, and we will not stand to have an employee who assaults his wife representing our firm. With that said, I want you to know that, should you agree, I would like to represent you. My services would be pro bono, of course."

Dakota is quick to shake her head. "Oh, no. Theo, I couldn't. You and your family have already done so much for me. I couldn't ask you to do that. Besides, the only attorney I'm hiring is a divorce attorney."

I busy myself with setting out the food on her bedside tray before taking a seat beside her on the edge of her bed.

She's still shaking her head when my dad says, "Alright, it's settled. I'll be representing Mrs. Ackerman in the matter of her divorce from Mr. Ackerman."

Biting her lip, Dakota nods in acceptance before adding, "I'd like to get my name changed back to Dakota Meyer, if that isn't too much trouble."

I like the sound of that much more than Dakota Ackerman. Not a single piece of her should have to remain attached to that piece of shit.

"Dakota, I'd like to move forward today with filing an order of protection against Mr. Ackerman. If you're okay with it, I can also begin the divorce filing by stating the marriage has been irretrievably broken. I'll also file a request for your name change when I return to my office. As for the assault charges, the prosecutors have moved forward with filing charges against Mr. Ackerman for assault in the first and third degree. If he is found guilty for either of those charges, he will be sentenced to prison."

I pray to god that the motherfucker gets prison time.

"Yes, I would like the order of protection and divorce to be filed." Dakota tries to take a deep breath but winces in pain. Every second she feels pain is another year that should be tacked on to his sentence.

"What do you need from your house? We can have an officer escort you and be sure Mr. Ackerman is not on the premises," my dad suggests.

"Nothing. I kept pretty much everything that I needed or was sentimental in the trunk of my car. I had been planning to leave him for a while—I was just saving up enough money so I could file for divorce and afford other housing."

"What about your clothes?" I ask, turning to face her.

"Aaron had picked out practically my entire wardrobe anyway. I don't ever want to step foot back in that house again," she says with finality.

"Have you found other housing?" my dad questions.

"No, not yet. I was thinking I'd just get a hotel room until I find something."

"Absolutely not," I practically growl out. Not wanting to frighten her, I take a deep, steadying breath. "Stay with me. I've got an extra bedroom, hell, I've got several extra bedrooms if you need more than just the one."

"Carson, I couldn't ask that of you." She shakes her head, looking down at her folded hands.

Reaching out, I gently lift her chin so she can see how serious I am. "You don't have to, I just asked you to stay with me. I'll get on my knees and beg if I have to. We can work this out, Dakota. Just stay with me so I know you're safe."

"You Wilder men sure don't take no for an answer, do you?" She looks from me to my dad, who is staring at me with a quirked brow.

I ignore his weighted stare, instead smirking at Dakota. "We do not. Stubborn as bulls because we've got hearts the size of Texas."

The reference to her home state earns me my first genuine smile from her for the day. And fuck if the sight of it doesn't nearly bring me to my knees.

"Alright, on that note, I'm going to head to the office to get to work on those filings right away." My dad stands from his chair and Dakota holds out her hand for him. He shakes his head with a slight smile before shaking her hand.

"I can't thank you enough for all of your help, Theo."

"It'll be my pleasure to take out the trash. In the meantime, be sure to keep my son in line." He winks at me and heads out the door.

Leave it to my dad to spend fifteen minutes with the two of us and sniff out my infatuation for Dakota.

10

Dakota

February

One month shouldn't feel like both an eternity and the blink of an eye. On one hand, it feels like only yesterday that I woke up in the hospital. On the other, each day of trying to heal has felt like time has dragged on at a snail's pace.

I officially moved in with my boss's brother the same week she temporarily moved in with her ex, who is now possibly her current boyfriend. Kenna and Cadence are staying with Griffin until he's healed from his knee surgery and goes back to Colorado. He surprised her with a house he purchased here in Minnesota over Christmas, and they've decided to live there together while he's rehabbing his injury.

I could tell Carson had mixed feelings about it. He assured me he loves the idea of Griffin and McKenna working things out, and for Cadence to have her parents raise her together. But I still felt as though he was anxious about the change.

The first few days I lived with Carson were spent resting, and meeting with his dad when I felt up to it. My divorce has been filed, and my order of protection has been granted, but unfortunately Aaron was released on bail until his hearing for my assault. I can't help but feel like I'm more skittish than ever, constantly looking over my shoulder and jumping at each and every sound.

"Do you need anything before I head to bed?" Carson's unexpected question startles me, causing me to let out a yelp.

"I'm so sorry, I didn't mean to scare you," he says, holding up his hands.

"No, it's okay. I was just so lost in my book, I didn't hear you," I try to reassure him, shaking my head as I take a deep breath.

I'd curled up on the couch in the living room after I saw Carson had started a fire. He's been doing that almost every night he's been home since I moved in. It's almost weird how quickly we've fallen into a routine—it shouldn't be this easy to find comfortable companionship with someone I've only known for about six months.

It's only when I look up from my book that I notice he's staring at me with that same look of worry he's had since he answered his front door on New Year's Day.

"I'm okay, Carson. Thank you for asking though."

"I'm curious," he pauses before asking, "What would your perfect day look like?"

I pause to think about my answer. "That depends on the mood I'm in."

"Okay, I'll bite. If you're having a down day, what would be the perfect day to make you feel better?" he questions, and it catches me off guard.

"When I'm feeling down, or having an off day, I like to double down and have a lazy day. Sometimes my favorite days are ones where I don't leave my sweats, I can hear the sound of the rain hitting the windows, and I snuggle up with a good book."

"Tell me, Austin, what do you consider a good book?"

I'm not sure why he insists on calling me Austin. I've told him multiple times now I'm from Dallas.

"I'm admittedly a sucker for the classics. But I have a list of books I'd like to read that's a mile long."

He taps his pointer finger to the side of his temple and says, "Storing that tidbit away for a rainy day. Pun intended." We both chuckle at that. "Are you sure you don't need anything? A blanket? Or a glass of water?"

I set my book down and reach for my water bottle with one hand while holding up a piece of the blanket draped over my legs with the other.

"Right," he claps his hands together in front of him before nodding toward the steps. "I guess I'll just head to bed then. Goodnight, Austin."

My lips turn up into a smile at his caretaking antics. He's gone out of his way each day to ensure I'm comfortable. Even when he's on the road and I'm staying at Griffin's house with McKenna and Cadence, he's texting or calling me to see how I'm doing.

"I'll actually head up with you."

"Okay, I'll turn off the fireplace and double-check the alarm is set," he says.

I'm not sure if he tells me that he set the alarm each night for his reassurance or my own, but I appreciate it either way.

While he's doing that, I fill up my water bottle and get one for Carson.

"Here," I say as I hand him his.

He takes it and flashes that bedazzling smile of his at me. "Thanks, you didn't have to do that."

"It's a water bottle, Golden Boy. Don't look too much into it," I tease. When his smile becomes too much to look at, I cast my eyes to my feet and clear my throat. "Besides, it's the least I can do for letting me stay here rent-free. I'm going to figure out a way to repay you."

Carson gently lifts my chin with his fingers, and I reluctantly meet his gaze once again. His voice is calm and reassuring as he says, "Dakota, I respect the hell out of you, so I don't mean any disrespect when I say this, but your money is no good here. The only repayment I'll accept is the assurance that you're safe and healing." His sincerity bleeds through with each word he says. I nod my head in acceptance, unable to speak past the lump forming in my throat.

We don't say another word as I reluctantly step away from his grasp. I instantly miss the warmth of his touch as we head upstairs together to get ready for bed. At the top of the steps, we both turn right down the hallway that leads to our respective bedrooms. Mine happens to be across the hallway from his bedroom, with Cadence and Kenna's being on the opposite end of the upstairs.

I pause in front of my door and take a deep breath. Keeping my back to Carson, I say the words that Carson has said to me each night, "Sweet dreams, sleep tight, I hope you dream of me tonight."

He chuckles softly before murmuring, "As long as they're filled with thoughts of you, they will be as sweet as ever."

"You're such a stupid fucking bitch. Did you really think I wouldn't notice? It wasn't enough to get caught up in your trashy little fantasies? No, it wasn't enough for my wife. Instead, you needed to go whore yourself out to my boss's fucking son! Well, now you're going to pay for making me look like a goddamn fool," Aaron says as the back of his hand strikes the left side of my face.

The force of the blow causes me to fall to my knees. I've barely touched the ground before his dress shoe connects with my ribs once, twice, three times. Pain slices through me with such vigor I forget how to breathe.

"Get the fuck up and properly accept your punishment."

Grasping on to what little strength I have, I try to get my feet under me. My attempt is feeble, and that only seems to spur his anger further.

"I. Said. Get up. You fucking bitch," he spits out, wrapping his fist in my hair and lifting me from the floor. My scalp throbs when he releases my hair, but the throbbing is quickly replaced by a shooting pain down my spine as Aaron punches my back before catching me around the throat to prevent my fall back to the ground. His grip around my throat tightens, and it's at this moment that I know he's going to kill me.

Fight. I need to fight back.

Black dots begin to cloud my vision, but I push past it as I reach down and grab my stiletto pump off my right foot. Aaron doesn't see it coming as I drive the sharp heel behind me. As soon as it makes contact with his head, I don't hesitate. Without sparing a glance back, I grab my purse from the ground and use every bit of strength I have remaining to get myself the fuck out of this house. Once I make it inside my car without him following, I realize the contact must have done some damage or temporarily stunned him.

"Austin. Hey, hey, shhh, you're okay," Carson whispers as he wraps me in his arms. "You're safe. I'm right here."

I open my eyes and use Carson as my focal point to gain my bearings. I'm safe. I'm at Carson's—he's right here, and Aaron isn't.

Carson's bare chest. Carson's ocean eyes. Carson's clean-shaven jaw. The sound of my pulse thundering in my ears. The sound of Carson's quick breaths. The soft pattering of rain from my noise machine. The feel of the soft sheets beneath my legs. The warmth of Carson's arms wrapped around me. The hardness of his muscular body pressed against mine.

I take a deep, calming breath as the fear from the flashback slowly recedes.

The same week I moved into Carson's house, I began seeing a therapist twice a week. Tasha has already taught me so much, but the 3-3-3 rule—three things I can see, hear, and touch—has been an absolute life saver on nights where I relive it all over again.

"I'm right here," Carson reassures me again as he rubs his palm up and down my back.

I try to speak, but my throat feels raw from what I can only assume were screams in my sleep. Clearing my throat, I start to apologize, "I'm sor—" but Carson stops me.

"Please don't apologize for something you have no reason to apologize for. You were having a nightmare. I'm just glad I was here."

If only it were a nightmare—a mere figment of my imagination, fear conjured up by my subconscious—instead of a flashback from a very real moment I couldn't wake up from. Instead of saying that to Carson, I move to sit up against the headboard.

"When I've had nightmares, it's helped me to watch TV. Do you want to watch something together?"

I only hesitate a moment before nodding in agreement.

In an attempt to make me feel better, Carson smiles as he jokes, "We can Netflix and chill, but like, truly just chill. Though, I wouldn't blame you if you wanted to use my smooth chest as a pillow. It's pillowy soft. I get it waxed, and my mom got me this new lotion for Christmas that makes it feel like butter."

Shaking my head, a small laugh slips out. I know his humor is his attempt at making me feel better, and I appreciate it now more than ever.

The TV above my dresser lights up before I hear the trademark *ta-dum* as the Netflix logo appears on the screen.

"Let's see, we've both probably watched far too much *Cocomelon* this week, so that's out," he says, waving the remote in the air as he scrolls through our options. I chuckle again at his theatrics. "Oh, I feel like this is something you'd like. We could try to watch an episode, it looks like each one is about an hour long. That should help take your mind off your bad dream."

His attempts to ease my mind are endearing. But when I look at the screen and see *Bridgerton* queued up, I laugh so hard that a very unattractive snort slips out. My cheeks flush as I cover my nose in disbelief that I just snorted in front of one of the most attractive men I've ever laid eyes on. "You can't be serious," I tell Carson.

He furrows his brow in confusion. "What's wrong with this? I thought you'd love something set in nineteenth-century London."

"I would. I mean, I do—the Regency era is one of my favorites."

Carson cuts in, "It's the *Reputation* era. Not a personal fav of mine yet, just because she hasn't released the Taylor's version. I'm more of a *Speak Now* kind of guy, if I'm being honest."

Is he seriously talking about Taylor Swift right now? In the few weeks we've lived together, I've learned Carson is a diehard Swiftie.

"What? I wasn't talking about Taylor Swift's eras, I was talking about the Regency era, which is when *Bridgerton* takes place—in nineteenth-century London." I turn onto my side to look at him. "Do you know what this show is about?"

A cocky smirk spreads across his face. "Of course I do. It's just like *Pride and Prejudice*. A simple caress of a hand will make viewers melt." He proceeds to dramatically fan himself with his hand.

Oh, I can't wait to see his reaction.

"You know what? You're right, I think the first episode would take my mind off of my nightmare." My smile is devious and probably makes me look unhinged, but Carson just shrugs and presses play.

As the opening scene plays and the narrator begins to speak, I quickly realize watching this with Carson will be interesting, to say the least. I haven't watched the show yet, but I've heard enough about it and read the series it's based on.

"Oh, I love an English accent. I used to have my Siri settings be a British accent," he informs me.

I side-eye him on his next line of commentary. "I can already tell Eloise is going to be my favorite. She's feisty."

Not a minute later, Carson straight up gasps at the scene unfolding in front of us where Anthony Bridgerton is in the throes of passion.

"What is he doing? Are they fucking? Against a tree?" He pauses the show, and the screen freezes on Lord Bridgerton's bare ass as he fucks his mistress against a tree. Carson looks over at me, and I must be doing a terrible job of hiding my humor because he says, "Oh my god, Austin! You totally knew there would be full-on fucking in this, didn't you? Have you watched this before?"

My last thread of constraint breaks when I see the perplexed look on his face. I cackle hysterically, so much so that my healing ribs become sore, and I have to hold onto my left side for support.

"Ouch, it hurts," I say as I continue to laugh through the pinch of pain.

"You swindled me, didn't you?" he questions but chuckles right along with me.

Once I get a grasp on my dignity, I breathe in through my nose and answer him. "I haven't watched the show but I have read the books. It's also rated TV-MA for a reason."

"I thought you read the classics. I didn't realize you dabbled in smut like my sister."

His comment immediately puts me on edge as I wait for his ridicule to follow.

But it doesn't come. Instead, he asks, "What are your favorite romance tropes?"

"How do you know what a trope is?"

"My sister talks about the books she reads, and over the past few months we've lived together, she's talked to me about them *a lot*."

"I've been meaning to ask her what she's reading, but I didn't want to be awkward. Sometimes people think reading romance is taboo, which I experienced firsthand with Aaron."

Carson's jaw tenses at the mention of my soon-to-be ex-husband. In hopes of distracting him, I answer his question. "I'm a mood reader, so I like a little bit of everything."

"Wait, you can read moods? Do you read auras, or how do you do it?"

At first I'm puzzled by his question. Auras? What the heck? And then it clicks. "Oh my gosh, I can't read moods, Golden Boy. I'm a mood reader, meaning what I read depends on the mood I'm in." I start to laugh again, and he just stares at me.

"You have the most beautiful laugh," Carson blurts, his cheeks staining the slightest shade of red in the darkened room.

I become bashful at his compliment. "Thank you," I say as I stare down at the bedding covering me. Clearing my throat, I continue, "My favorite tropes are small-town romance, friends-to-lovers, forbidden love, and, if I'm feeling up for it, a mafia romance."

"What about hockey romances?" he asks and wiggles his brows.

"I have yet to read a hockey romance. Mostly because I don't know much about the sport. But I've read more football romances than I care to admit. Oh, and bonus points if it's a brother's best friend football romance. Have you ever seen a man wearing football pants?" I'm only teasing, but I'm curious to see how he reacts. When I was with Aaron, I would never dare to joke about the idea of another man.

Carson scoffs. "Very funny, Austin. I know your love for football runs deep. And the football pants are indeed appealing. But have you ever seen a hockey player's bubble butt and tree trunk thighs in a pair of five-inch inseam shorts?"

When I just stare back at him, he chuckles. "Stick with me, Super Nanny, and you'll be in for a real treat this summer."

With that, Carson presses play, and Anthony Bridgerton's bare ass has nothing on the mental images swimming through my head of Carson Wilder in said athletic shorts.

Lord, have mercy on me.

11

Carson

March

"*It's Sunday morning, but that won't stop us from reporting on the latest happenings in the NHL. The breaking news of last year's Rookie of the Year, Griffin Turner, being traded from the Colorado Summits to the Minnesota Wolverines has sent shockwaves across the league. Rumor has it that Turner's daughter, who lives in Minnesota, was part of the reason he demanded the trade. Now, I won't speculate further on these rumors other than I'd like to point out how highly unlikely it is that a player in his rookie contract would get any say in trade decisions between the organizations.*"

My niece's birthday weekend was a wild one—not only did Cadence turn two, but Griffin was traded from the Colorado Summits and is now my newest Minnesota Wolverines teammate. I hope that once he finishes rehabbing his knee he'll be on a line again with Jax and me next season.

The press conference is this morning. Mack and Griff just dropped Cadence off at my place on their way to the arena so Dakota didn't have to drive over to Griff's house.

But today is also a rainy day in Minnesota, which means it's the ideal day for Dakota to get lost in a book.

"Knock, knock," I call out as I enter my Cadey Cat's toy room that's still set up in my house, though I wonder with Griff being traded to Minnesota, if that means Mack and Cadence will move in with him

"

permanently. It makes the most sense now that they're officially back together. Fuck, why does that make my stomach twist? I'm happy as hell for my twin and my niece. I'm even happier for myself that I got my best friend back. But I'd be lying if I said I wouldn't miss the hell out of them living with me. I've missed days like today—being with Cadence, stealing glimpses of Dakota playing with her, and having a house full of love and laughter.

Dakota rolls over and perches herself up on her elbows. "Hey, what's up?" she asks.

"It's raining," I state.

That makes her chuckle. "It is," she agrees.

"Rain! Rain!" Cadence squeals before running over to the window and pressing her face against the windowpane. Their laughter blends like the most beautiful harmony, and the sound seems to be the ice-breaker I need to shake the nerves I get whenever I'm around my dream girl.

"Well," I start but nervously clear my throat before continuing, "I know how much you like to have a lazy reading day when it's raining. And you've been helping with Cadence so much lately that I thought I'd let you take the day off while I bring my Cadey Cat on a funcle date."

Her face lights up at that. "It is *my* job to watch our favorite girl. But now I'm curious, what exactly does a funcle date include?"

Our favorite girl. Damn, I love the sound of that.

Crossing my arms as I lean against the doorframe, I answer, "I'll dress her up in one of her princess costumes, take her to the indoor playground, and then grab some lunch before heading back for her naptime."

"That sounds like a whole bunch of fun. What if I want to tag along?"

I smirk at that. "Next time. Today, soak up this weather with a good book. Besides, I can't have the first date I take you on be to an indoor playground followed by a happy meal." And I'm not teasing. I'm one hundred percent determined to take Austen on a date—when she's ready, of course.

"Isn't that puttin' the horse before the cart, Golden Boy?" she jests.

God, I love it when she calls me that. And I love that when she's being sassy, her Southern drawl really comes out.

"I could see how you might think that. But I'm a very patient man, and I'm quite certain a first date is in our near future." With that, I wink at her before scooping Cadence in my arms and leaving Dakota sitting in the same spot, her mouth now agape.

Yeah, I'm quite certain, indeed.

Everything about the funcle date had been going swimmingly until some scum bag with a big camera started following Cadence and me around.

At first, I wasn't sure what his deal was. I thought maybe he was a photographer hired by the company that owns the indoor playground, and he was taking photos for marketing materials. But then I noticed he left the playground at the same time as us before ending up at the same diner. Cadence's favorite thing to eat is any breakfast item, so it was a no-brainer to bring her somewhere that serves all-day breakfast. It's only now, after paying the check and buckling Cadence into her car seat, that I regret not just going home and cooking for her myself.

The same photographer from the indoor playground is outside the diner, taking photos of me buckling her into my truck. Do these guys have no fucking decency? Kids should be one hundred percent off-limits when it comes to paparazzi.

"Hey!" I call out to the guy after I shut the rear passenger door and round the tailgate of my truck. "Leave me alone and go find a real job, would you? She's a kid, man."

He lowers the lens of his camera, but with his black sunglasses and backward hat, it's hard to make out details of his face. "What is a young rookie like you doing with a baby, Wilder?"

I nearly growl at his questioning, my composure hanging by a thread. "I really don't see how that is any of your business, or anyone else's for that matter. I will only say this once more before I call the police: leave us alone."

The fucker just chuckles as he walks backward a few steps before turning around the side of the building.

God, I really don't understand how anyone could think I'm important or interesting enough to justify following me around. And where are the boundaries—the fucking morals—with these people?

Rounding the rest of my truck, I get into the driver's seat and press the ignition button. It's a colder spring afternoon with the light drizzle that's still coming down, so I turn up the heat in the rear of the truck to keep Cadence comfortable. If anything, I need the AC; I'm still fired up from dealing with that asshat. "Sorry about that, Cadey Cat. Uncle Car Car didn't mean to keep my princess waiting. Should we get Kota some ice cream on our way home?" Cadence calls Dakota 'Kota,' and it's the cutest damn thing.

"Yay! Ice cream for Kota!"

And that's all the confirmation I need as I back out of the parking spot.

We're stopped at a red light, and I've only just turned on Gracie's Corner's "Wheels on the Bus" when a vehicle rear-ends us, causing my truck to lurch forward into the intersection. Another vehicle slams its brakes but crashes into the front passenger side of my truck. The airbags deploy, but all I can think about is getting to my Cadey Cat and ensuring she's okay.

A startled cry breaks through the ringing in my ears before I hear someone shout that they've called 9-1-1. I get out of my truck and am nearly struck by the car that rear-ended us as it peels away from the scene, but not before I notice the guy who was photographing us behind the wheel. And, of course, he doesn't have any license plates on his black SUV.

I don't waste another second before opening the rear door to check on Cadence. Not wanting to move her in case something is broken, I choke on a sob when I realize she doesn't have any scrapes or cuts. The front passenger window is cracked, but thankfully, it didn't shatter.

"Shhh. You're going to be okay, Cadey Cat. Uncle Carson is right here. We're going to take a ride in a big vehicle that makes the 'wee-woo' sounds you love so much." As the words leave my lips, I hear the faint siren sounds of an ambulance approaching. "You're going to be okay," I repeat. And she will be.

She's got to be okay.

I shoot out of my chair in the hospital's waiting room when McKenna and Griffin walk in. Dakota stands alongside me. She arrived about a half hour ago after I called and told her everything that had happened.

"Fuck, McKenna. I'm so fucking sorry. I swear I don't know where the photographer came from. One minute, we were stopped at the red light, and the next thing I know, he rear-ended us."

"Carson, why are you apologizing? You and Cadence are both thankfully okay. We know you would never do anything to put her in harm's way. This isn't your fault," Mack tries to put me at ease, but there's nothing that will take away this gut-wrenching feeling inside of me.

I could've lost her. I was the reason one of the best parts of my life was put in danger. Shaking my head, I collapse back down into my chair and hold my head in my hands.

"Please, please tell me she's okay," I plead.

I feel a large hand on my shoulder before Griff's deep voice says, "Cadence is okay, Carse. She's okay, and you're okay. Katie and my mom would never let anything happen to her, and nothing did. After a full work-up, the doctors have reassured us that everything is okay. I had the hospital send her chart, along with all of her imaging, to my dad. He just got off the phone with us and confirmed everything the staff here had already determined. Now, I'd really like you to get checked out to make sure you're in the clear."

That makes me shoot my head up to look at him. "What are you talking about? I'm fine."

I had a minor cut above my left temple because of the impact of the second vehicle, but the paramedic was able to stitch me up. When we got to the hospital, I refused any further medical attention for fear they'd help me instead of focusing all of their efforts on Cadence.

It's Mack who speaks next. "You might be fine, Carse, but after all we've been through with my coma and losing Katie, could you at least let them do a head CT to rule out any swelling or bleeding?"

Fuck. Fuck! How could I be so selfish? Of course Griff and Mack are worried about a possible head injury. It was only two and a half years ago that we lost Katie and almost lost McKenna in a car accident. An accident that left my sister in a coma for two days due to her head injury.

"Shit, I'm so sorry. You're right. I'll tell them I'd like to be examined and given the all-clear," I tell them as I stand back up and head to the nurse's station just outside the waiting room.

Only an hour later, I'm not surprised to learn I've got a mild concussion, though thankfully, it's only my second. My mom also insisted a plastic surgeon restitch the laceration on my head once she arrived with our dad, who immediately went into lawyer mode with McKenna and said he was hiring a private investigator to find the photographer who fled the scene.

That guy should pray to whatever god he believes in that we never find him. Because while I may be harmless, I'm also my father's son, and when you hurt those we love, the apple doesn't fall far from the tree.

12

Dakota

April

"**Y**our hair." Carse stops when he sees me in the kitchen. He just got dropped off after a home game, but he still couldn't play due to his concussion. He'll be out for another week or two, depending on his symptoms.

Feeling self-conscious, I wipe my hands on my apron, then smooth my hair down and tuck the shortened strands behind my ear. "Yeah, I cut it. Felt like I needed a change." I haven't cut my signature long locks short since middle school.

"You didn't. But I like it. A lot. The shorter hair suits you."

I can feel my cheeks flush. I've never been good at taking compliments, and Carson gives them so freely I never know how to respond. So I just reply with, "Thank you."

Sensing I need a pivot, he asks, "What are you making? It smells amazing in here."

"I was feeling a little homesick after speaking to my mama, so I'm making her famous pecan pie," I explain.

"How famous are we talking? Is her pecan pie as famous as your brother?"

"Nope. It's even more famous. More grown men have cried after eating the last bite of my mama's pie than they have after watching the great Brody Meyer win the Superbowl."

Carson grabs a candied pecan from the counter, throws it in the air, and catches it with his mouth. The combination of him doing something so simple all while watching his broad body move in his navy game-day suit has me nearly coming undone. "I'm not sure if you've noticed this about me or not, but I've got no self-control when it comes to sweets."

"Oh, Golden Boy, I've known for a while that you've got a sweet tooth bigger than Texas."

He chuckles and shakes his head. "Here I thought I was doing a good job keeping it under wraps around you. What gave me away?"

"Well, let's see . . . it could've been the fact that you order a caramel macchiato with three extra pumps of caramel syrup and extra whipped cream. Or the fact that you add honey to just about everything that isn't already sweet. Or maybe it was how I've seen you take down an entire bag of saltwater taffy while we watched an episode of *Bridgerton*."

"Guilty. I'm just ashamed you caught me. Speaking of shame—have you been keeping something from me?"

My heart rate spikes at his question, even though his tone is teasing. "What? What are you talking about?"

"Have you been show-cheating on me while I'm gone?" I can see his cheek twitching as he holds back a smile.

"No, I only watch *Bridgerton* with you."

He lets out an exaggerated big breath of relief as if he'd been holding it. "Good answer," he says as he rubs his hands together. "Alright, let me taste test this bad boy, and then we can watch the first episode of season two."

I cut and plate each of us a slice of pie and top it off with a spoonful of my homemade whipped cream.

"Fuuuuckkk, Austin," Carson moans, and I pause my spoon midway to my mouth. That may be one of the hottest sounds I've ever heard leave a man's lips, and I suddenly want to hear more. "This is definitely better than watching your brother throw touchdowns."

Just as Carson shovels the last bite of pie into his mouth, his phone vibrates with an incoming call, and the most adorable photo of McKenna and Cadence lights up his screen.

"Dearest sister, you must come over for tea and a bite of Dakota's famous pecan pie," he tells McKenna as he accepts her call.

"Carse, why are you speaking with a British accent?" McKenna asks.

Carson puts the phone on mute and asks, "Do you think we've watched too much *Bridgerton*? Blimey, I am speaking with an accent, aren't I?"

"You certainly are, my lord," I reply, biting my lip to fight the laughter attempting to slip out.

"Damn, Austin. Don't call me that unless you want me to get bricked up."

"What in the world does bricked up mean?"

"You know . . . worked up. *Excited*."

My eyes widen, and I pretend to clutch my pearls as if I were shocked. "Don't scandalize me with your rakish ways, my lord."

"Would you consider this role-playing, *my lady*?" Carson's aqua eyes shimmer with amusement, and his voice drips with flirtation.

Holy shit. Are we flirting? What would it be like to role-play with Carson?

"Carse? Hello? Are you there?" McKenna, thankfully, snaps me out of my delirium spiral.

Carson unmutes his phone and continues his conversation while I get up to clear our plates. When I go to reach for his, he places his hand on mine to stop me. "I may not be a Southern gentleman, but my mama raised me with manners. You baked. Let me clean up."

"Are you sure? You don't need to do that. You just got home after a long day," I point out.

"I'm very sure. Go take a bath while I start a fire and make some popcorn."

"Okay, if you're sure?" I question.

"Positive. Now go." He quirks his eyebrow at me and nods his head toward the stairs. "You can use my soaking tub if you'd like. There are bath oils and salts on the shelf beside it."

"Thank you, Carson."

"I think I liked it better when you referred to me as 'my lord,'" he says before biting down on his plush bottom lip.

With that, I spin on my heel and practically sprint up the steps, but not before I hear McKenna begin assaulting him with questions. Questions that include my name at least twice before I disappear down the hallway and into his room.

Placing one hand on my chest and the other on my stomach, I try to calm my racing heart and the butterflies erupting in my stomach.

Carson Wilder could set my world ablaze, and I think I'd happily dance through the flames if it meant I got to be with him on the other side.

After my bath, I head downstairs wearing oversized sweatpants and one of my favorite new shirts, which reads "I closed my book, this better be worth it."

The smell of popcorn hits me even before I enter the living room, where a fire is roaring and Carson is playing a video game on the large TV.

I sit beside him on his sectional—it's the largest, deepest, and comfiest couch I've ever sat on. It's the kind of couch you want to veg out on for days on end. Only as I reach across Carson to grab the bowl of popcorn, does he notice me.

He takes off his noise-canceling headset and gives me a sheepish smile. "Sorry about that."

"You've been cleared to watch TV and play video games now, right? I don't want to break any of the rules and set you back."

Setting aside the controller and headset, he sits back and pulls my legs over his lap. "Yeah, I was earlier this week. We've just been so busy I haven't had a chance to tell you."

"That's exciting. How much longer until you can play?"

"Still out for another week at least. But I did get cleared for light activity today, so that's progress." He squints as he takes me in. "I like your shirt. I'm glad I was worth putting your book down for."

I give him a soft smirk. "Well, that's only because I finished my book while I was in the bath, and I didn't want to start a new one, or I'd probably stay up all night to finish it."

"No self-control with you bookworms," he teases, eyes narrowing as he looks at my legs. "Hey, are those my sweatpants?"

My cheeks heat and I bite my lip. "Oh, these? Are they? Hmm, I must have mixed them up in the wash."

They are most definitely his. I did accidentally find them in the wash, but once I put them on, I realized I was not going to be returning them.

Carson sends me a knowing wink. Nodding my head toward the TV, I ask, "What game were you playing?"

"COD."

When I stare back at him blankly, he says, "*Call of Duty.*"

"Haven't heard of that one," I tell him.

"Are you telling me Brody Meyer never played COD growing up?"

"We weren't too big into video games as kids. Our mama raised us on her own after my daddy passed when I was twelve. The only video games I've ever played are *The Sims* and *Madden*, but that wasn't really until Brody went to college, and I visited him there."

"I'm sorry to hear about your dad. How far apart are you in age from Brody?"

"He's three years older than me."

"Oh, I bet he loved having his jailbait sister come visit him at college."

I smack Carson's chest at that. "You're one to talk. I could probably go to jail just from living with you. I'm old enough to have been your babysitter."

"Age is just a number, Austin. You're barely older than me. Though, if you would've been my babysitter growing up, I would've begged my parents to go on date nights. Think of all the late nights we could've shared staying up late making our pretend family on *The Sims*. Whenever I used to play, I'd max out the number of kids you could have per family. My fake wife and I were 'woo-hooing' like rabbits."

Shaking my head at him, I try and fail to hold back my laughter. "You're something else, Golden Boy. I think your concussion is making you talk crazy."

Carson just shrugs in response as he reaches for a blanket from the back of the couch and drapes it over my legs and his lap, leaving my bare feet exposed. Before I can ask him to cover them up, he begins massaging the arch of my left foot, and the moan I let out has us both freezing.

"Is this okay?" he asks.

I clear my throat before I respond. "It's perfect. I'm sorry, it's just I couldn't tell you the last time I got a foot rub. It feels really good."

That makes a smile spread across Carson's face. "How about this—I'll give you a foot rub each time we sit down to watch *Bridgerton* together."

"But there's only eight episodes in season two," I pout.

Carson throws his head back, laughing at me. "Doesn't season three come out next month?"

I roll my eyes at that. "Yes, but it's in two parts. So there's only a few episodes coming out in May, and then we have to wait like a whole month before part two comes out."

"Greedy girl," he rasps.

Holy. Hell. That sounded far too attractive coming from his lips.

"Why are they trying to do us dirty like that? Fine, I'll amend my proposal to be a foot rub for each time we sit down to watch a movie or a show together."

"Deal," I practically squeak out as I struggle to press play on the remote.

The first scene of season two plays, and I can't help the overwhelming sense of comfort and security that floods me. I'm sitting on the comfiest couch with a man who has quickly become a person I lean on, and he's rubbing my feet as he goes on about how badass Eloise Bridgerton is.

Carson catches me smiling to myself and returns it with one of his own dazzling smiles before squeezing my foot three times.

13

Carson

APRIL

Swiping right, I accept an incoming FaceTime call from Griff. Assuming he couldn't wait to propose and they're calling to tell me the good news, I start to say congratulations but stop when I see the stressed-out look on his face. "Oh, shit. Did she say no?" I cover my mouth with my fist to hold back my laughter.

"What? No. Why would you ask that? Do you think she's going to say no?" The panic laced in his voice would be hilarious if he didn't look like he was on the verge of a breakdown.

I lower my fist and take a deep breath to get my shit together. "No way, G. Mack has wanted to marry you since the day you moved in next door. If you haven't asked yet, then why the hell are you calling? You better not tell me you got cold feet."

"Never," he assures me. "I'm freaking out because Cadence just woke up from her nap, and I want to surprise Kenna by doing her hair. She looked so cute last week when Kenna did those pigtail bun things."

"Yeah, she calls them space buns. I love it when Cadence has those."

"Me too. Well, I did my best attempt, and they definitely don't look as cute as when Kenna does it . . . "

He turns the camera to show me a smiling Cadence with very loose and lopsided buns right above her ears.

"Those look like disheveled Princess Leia buns. How do you not know how to do pigtails at this point?"

"Carse, I'm being serious. Can you just please help a guy out?" Griffin pleads.

"Yeah, hold on. Let me see if Dakota is ready, and maybe she can help walk you through it." I head across the hallway and knock on her door. While I wait, I ask him, "Are you sure you're okay with me and Dakota driving up to get Cadence? Would you rather we stay at my parents' cabin while you guys stay at the place you rented next door?"

My stomach knots just thinking about driving Cadence again. I haven't gotten in a car with anyone since the accident. Luckily, I didn't really need to until today.

"I didn't tell you? I didn't rent it, Carse. I bought it."

At that news, my eyebrows shoot to my hairline. "Wait, what?"

"I know your parents' place is huge, but I thought it'd be nice for us to have our own space next door for when we spend time here in the off-season. Besides, that way, you can feel free to still throw rowdy parties without us holding you back."

Rowdy parties? Is G mistaking me with Jackson?

"I can't tell you the last time I hosted a rowdy party unless Cadence's first birthday party counts. It got pretty out of hand . . . " I deadpan.

"Yeah, you're right. But eventually, you'll have a family of your own to bring there, so I was planning for the future."

Before I can respond, Dakota opens the door, her cheeks flushed and her shorter hair tousled. She's wearing deep purple yoga pants that look like they were painted on, paired with a matching crop top.

"Hey, what's up?" she asks, a little breathless.

"Am I, uh, interrupting?"

Her cheeks flush deeper, eyes widening, and I can't hold back the smirk on my face. Oh, I was definitely interrupting something. Perhaps a little self-care? Fuck, I really wish Griff wasn't on the phone so I could press her on it.

"What?" she squeaks out. "No, not interrupting at all. What do you need?"

We're definitely circling back to this.

"I know we weren't planning to leave for another hour or so, but Griff is on the phone, and he needs our help doing Cadence's hair."

Dakota holds her hand out palm up and gestures for me to place the phone in her hand. I do so and move behind her to peek at the phone over her shoulder. Being this close to her, I'm engulfed by her jasmine perfume, which has hints of vanilla and sandalwood. I inhale deeply, now dying to know if she tastes as sweet as she smells.

Cadence fills the screen, and I watch Dakota hold back her laughter. "Well hello, little darlin'. How'd you sleep?"

"Kota! Hi!" Cadey Cat squeals as she waves at the phone. God, I love this little girl so much.

"It looks like you tried, at least, Griffin. But bless it, you cannot let her look like that on the night you propose to her mama. Alright, here's what you're going to do: I want you to just take out the one side and make sure your part is good and straight down the middle of her head."

Griff props the phone up against the mirror and stands behind Cadence. "I think I did that part right. I just don't get why they're so floppy."

Dakota bites her lip, but she can't hide a smile as beautiful and wide as hers. "That's alright, we can fix this. I want you to get the brush or the comb, whichever you used, a little wet under the faucet. Then, brush the one side of her hair back to the crown of her head. Getting it damp helps to keep the smaller pieces from falling out."

Griff does as she says, pulling her hair back. "Perfect. Now comes the hard part. Do you have those little elastic hair binders?"

"Crap, we're not past the hard part? Yes, I've got the elastic ones right here." He holds up a little pink container full of them.

"Good. Grab one of those and use your pointer finger and thumb to widen it around the pigtail. Wrap it around three or four times if you can."

The look of concentration on Griff's face as his tongue peeks out makes me chuckle. Dakota looks back, shaking her head and lightly elbowing me in the ribs when my chuckles get louder.

"Ouch!" I double over in laughter. "Sorry, I can't help it. His fingers are visibly shaking."

Griff scoffs at me. "You'd be visibly shaking too if you were about to propose to the love of your life and you wanted to ensure everything was perfect without ruining the surprise."

"Alright, you've got me there. Just take a deep breath, G. Like I said, she will say yes. And if I know my twin, she will love the surprise you've come up with. Doesn't she think the surprise is the fact that you purchased a cabin up at the lake?"

"I'm not sure. I'm a little shaken up because right before Little Ray woke up from her nap, I asked Kenna if she'd move in with me permanently. She didn't get a chance to answer me before I had to grab Cadence."

"She's going to say yes to all of the above, man. Don't worry so much," I tell him, even as my chest tightens just thinking about how alone I'll feel without them here with me. Sure, Dakota lives with me now. But what if she decides I'm too much? I mean, she said she wanted to get on her feet and then get her own place when she could. I wish I could make her see we could remain roommates, even though I'd be extending this sexual torture.

"The ponytails are done. Now, how do I get them into buns?" Griff asks.

"Those look great!" Dakota cheers.

"Yeah, they're surprisingly even too."

Dakota tries to elbow me again, but I dodge out of the way and grab her waist, tickling her so she bends over. And right as she does, her perfectly toned and round ass makes direct contact with my semi-hard dick. As if we're both in complete disbelief, we remain there frozen—her ass against my cock—the only movement is my hands tightening their hold on her waist.

Fuck. This feels too good to be true. Friends. We're friends. Move, fucker.

I take a large step back and turn around while Dakota finishes explaining how to make two buns to Griff. When she's done, I try to subtly adjust myself before turning back around.

Dakota sounds breathless, her chest rising and falling, causing me to look down at her pebbled nipples that peek through the fabric of her workout top. I want nothing more than to take them in my mouth.

Just a taste.

"Here," she holds the phone out to me. Her voice is both raspy and trembling—that alone could be my undoing.

"Thanks." I pocket my phone before taking her in again. "What were you doing when I knocked?"

"Yoga," she squeaks, then drags her tongue across her lips, wetting them.

I would give anything to bite down on her plump bottom one.

"Yoga?" I question.

"Yep. And meditation. It's so good for you. We should try it sometime during the off-season. Alright, I've got to get back to it. And pack. You said to pack a bag in case, right?"

"I did." I don't believe for one second that I didn't interrupt her self-love session. But I'll let her think I believe her excuse. "I've got to finish packing too," I say as I move toward the door.

When I reach the hallway, I turn to grab my door handle. "I'll lock it, just in case your yoga session gets a little heated and you can't resist temptation." I wink as the click of the lock sounds.

Once it's closed, I rest my forehead against her door and try to picture what Austen would look like with her legs spread, fingers dipping into her drenched pussy, and bare body on display.

That scene I've conjured up continues to play out in my mind as I start my shower. I should feel wrong for doing this, but I don't as I begin stroking myself to images of her. In no time, I'm greedily pumping my cock to thoughts of Dakota in the shower with me, only she's on her knees, and those plump lips are sucking the soul from my body. It doesn't take much before I'm groaning her name as I come against the tiled wall of my shower. Black spots dot my vision, and my chest heaves like I've just got off the ice from a two-minute shift.

Living across the hall from Dakota Meyer may very well be the death of me.

Dakota

I've never been more frustrated in my life—sexually, that is.

I'm broken. I know this, my therapist knows it too because she and I have discussed it at length.

I can't come. And I've tried. Oh, trust me, I've *tried*. My bedside drawer has two new additions that I thought would for sure do the trick, but nope. Not even a whisper of an orgasm.

After seeing Carson come into my room in a pair of those damn five-inch inseam athletic shorts he teased me about a few months back, and feeling his hard body pressed against my ass—I'm wetter and needier than I've ever been. And yet, I still can't come.

I shut off my clit stimulator and slam it onto the bed before covering my eyes with the back of my arm. Tears of frustration prickle in my eyes.

Aaron has stolen so much from me.

Each time I've been turned on in the past few months—which has been pretty much every time Carson is home lately—I think maybe this will be it, this will be the time I finally come. Only, each time I'm on the precipice of climaxing, my mind floods with images from the night Aaron assaulted me.

So, like I said . . . I'm frustrated. And even after months of therapy, I'm pretty sure I'm broken, and I'll never come again. Okay, that may sound a little dramatic . . . but *come on*. A woman can only take so much.

Living with Carson Wilder has made the tiny spark that ignited inside of me when we first met erupt into formidable flames. Each smirk, each teasing joke, each innocent touch of our hands, each accidental press of our bodies, each unextraordinary moment all of a sudden feels monumental because of this building tension between us that is rising to an all-time high.

There are days where I worry I'll spontaneously orgasm in the kitchen while we're cooking together. Well, I'm typically doing the cooking while Carson stands there looking like my own personal snack.

Oh. My. God. Get a hold of yourself, Kota Lynn.

I'm starting to sound like an unhinged cougar. But Carson would make the best prey.

Knowing I need to finish packing, I huff a breath and drag myself out of bed. After I clean and put away my useless toy, I finish packing my weekender bag. It's still April in Minnesota, so naturally, being the Texan I am, I packed for winter.

Once I've filled up my water bottle and put on my jacket, I grab my bag and head out to the garage to get into Carson's truck.

After the accident, Carson got a new decked-out white Ford F-150 with black rims, and it's as sexy as he is.

I notice it's already started as I round the truck to get in the passenger side. But I freeze as soon as I open the door and see the state Carson is in.

He's shaking uncontrollably, his face is coated in sweat, and he's holding his chest with both hands while gasping for breaths.

"Carson," I call out but I know he doesn't hear me. He's having a panic attack, and I need to talk him down.

"Carson, I'm here," I tell him as I drop my bag and set my water bottle in the cup holder. "Listen to my voice," I say before grabbing his hands in mine. "Feel the way your hands eclipse mine." I pause, listening to the sound of his breathing begin to slow. "Look at me."

He shakes his head. "Not like this," he whispers.

Taking one hand from his, I place my fingers beneath his quivering chin and lift it so his glassy eyes meet mine. "You don't have to fight this alone. I'm right here. Just like you were there for me."

"I don't understand why this is happening to me."

"How many times have you had a panic attack?"

"I don't know. Maybe half a dozen since the accident with Cadence? I used to get them infrequently after Katie's death. Typically whenever I had a flashback to Mack being in the hospital or someone I loved got hurt. But these feel different—more intense."

I take him in. Like really take him in. His shoulders are slumped, his hair is standing on end as if he's been running his hands through it, and his cheeks are stained from the few tears that slipped free.

"Have you thought about seeing a therapist?" I ask.

Carson shakes his head and grips the steering wheel. "I can't. The media would make a big spectacle of it. They'd make me out to be the weak rookie who can't handle the pressure now that I'm in the big league."

I rest my hand on his arm and give it a gentle squeeze. "Seeking help doesn't make you weak, Carson. When we're vulnerable enough to admit that we're in our darkest hours, there is nothing more powerful than that. You allowing me to see this side of yourself doesn't make me think any less of you. In fact, I see you now more than ever."

At that, he turns his head and looks at me. "And what do you see?"

I stare back into his ocean eyes just as intently. "Everything. I see every beautiful piece of you, Carson. My therapist has taught me daily affirmations that have truly helped the way I see myself. Will you repeat after me? Will you let me show you with my words how I see you?"

"Yes." He takes his hands off the wheel and turns his body toward me.

Taking his hands once again in mine, I say, "Repeat after me. I am kind. I am brave. I am strong. I am selfless."

I watch and listen in earnest as this enigmatic man repeats each affirmation back to me.

"That was perfect. You did such a good job."

I'm not sure if it's the exercise we just completed or if he enjoys the praise, but the most beguiling smile spreads across his handsome face. "Thank you. It means a lot to me," he says as he squeezes my hands in his three times.

My heart warms seeing his smile and feeling his hands in mine. This moment—his vulnerability—feels pivotal in our friendship. Needing to ease the tension, I ask, "Do you mind if I drive us up to the cabin?"

He chuckles at that. "I can't think of anything better than being your passenger princess while you drive my truck. I've got a playlist ready. Be prepared to be serenaded by yours truly."

"I can't wait to hear you sing T-Swift off-key the whole way," I joke. And it is a joke, because I'll take Carson singing off-key every day of the week over what I just witnessed.

Our overnight bags ended up being a good call. We met up with Kenna and Griffin after he proposed to grab Cadence so they could celebrate just the two of them.

Once we returned to Carson's parents' cabin for the night, we got Cadence ready for bed, and she has been out like a light for about half an hour.

"Knock, knock," Carson announces as he taps his knuckle on my open bedroom door from our adjoining Jack and Jill bathroom.

"Come in," I answer.

"What are you up to?"

Shutting my laptop, I set it on the bedside table and say, "Nothing much. What about you?"

"Same. I was wondering if you wanted to play a game with me."

"What kind of game?"

He shrugs. "Like Cribbage or Sequence. Or we could play Scrabble. Though I'll probably kick your ass."

"Oh, you're on, Golden Boy. I'm not sure if you know this, but I have an English degree."

"And I'm not sure if you know this, but your fancy degree doesn't dictate which letters you pull in Scrabble. You may very well get fucked over by a two-letter word like 'za' or 'qi.'"

"In our household, we always had a minimum of three-letter words to prevent my brother from winning like that."

"Sounds to me like you were coddled growing up. In this household, we're cutthroat. So buckle up, Super Nanny, you're about to get your ass handed to you."

"Such poetry you speak, my lord," I tease him because, after seeing his vulnerability earlier today, I just want to make him smile.

"Austin," he warns. "What did I tell you about you calling me that?"

"Something about it gets you excited. I'm hoping if I can accomplish that, you'll be too distracted to play ruthlessly against me."

"You play dirty."

"Oh, you have no idea." I shoot him a wink, and he narrows his eyes at me.

"You're a little minx, aren't you?"

I don't even try to bite back the laugh that slips out.

He chuckles right along with me. "Meet me downstairs in ten?"

Nodding in response, I bite the inside of my cheeks to hold back another laugh from slipping out.

The first thing I notice as I make my way down the steps is the eucalyptus and mint scent floating through the air that is similar to the bath oils in Carson's soaking tub. I pause at the bottom of the steps as I take in the large square coffee table in the living room that is now covered by a Scrabble board, two wine glasses, two bottles of wine, candles, and bowls of snacks.

"Carson, what is all of this?" I question in wonderment. His thoughtful gestures never fail to make butterflies take flight from low in my abdomen up through my chest.

Carson whirls around from where he was lighting a candle on one of the bookshelves next to the two-story stone fireplace—the statement piece of this room.

When he faces me, he looks apprehensive, and I hate when this otherwise confident man looks unsure of himself. He clasps his hands together, fidgeting with them, before deciding to slip them into the pockets of his worn, light gray sweatpants. "Well, this is me saying thank you for what you did for me today. I'm typically the guy that others can lean on. It's hard for me to be on the other side—to need someone else—but it was easier knowing I had you there for me."

Needing to close the distance between us, I make my way across the living room until we're standing toe-to-toe in our matching attire of socks, sweatpants, and oversized T-shirts. I grab his arms, pulling his hands from his pockets and clasping them in mine. "You never need to thank me for being there for you. We're friends, right?"

He gives me a smirk that doesn't nearly reach his eyes. "Friends, yeah."

"Your friendship means a lot to me. I know I told you this when we first met, but I don't have any friends here, really, outside of you, McKenna, and now Griffin. The few friends I had during college slowly pulled away after they met Aaron. They told me how they felt about him, and instead of listening, I closed myself off from them."

"You mean a lot to me too, Austin." He squeezes my hands three times, the way I've become accustomed to. "This is just me trying to show you how much I appreciate you."

Breaking apart from my grasp, he walks over to the coffee table and takes a seat on one of the cushions he's laid out for us to sit on. He pats the one around the corner from his, motioning for me to join him.

"I haven't really seen you drink much wine, so I wasn't sure if you're a white or red kind of gal. My guess was red."

"You guessed correctly. I love black coffee and red wine, but Aaron always worried it would stain my teeth so he tried to get me to drink tea and white wine." Thinking back on my relationship with Aaron, I see all of the red flags now for what they were. It's hard to trust myself knowing I didn't see them sooner. I can't help but wonder if I'm defective when it comes to choosing a healthy partner.

Carson's posture goes rigid. "It goes against everything in me to hate someone, but I genuinely hate that shit excuse of a human."

My pulse races just thinking of Aaron and where he could possibly be right now.

I go to sit next to him and decide a change of subject is necessary. "Can you believe your childhood best friend proposed to your sister today? That sounds like a great plotline for a book."

That makes Carson's shoulders relax and a genuine smile spreads across his face. "Yeah, I can. They were never able to hide their feelings from anyone but each other. Katie and I knew our best friends were into our siblings, we even used to make bets on who would crack first."

"Were you and Katie close?"

He breaks eye contact, looking down at his hands before nodding his head. "Yeah, we were. The four of us were pretty inseparable growing up. Katie and Mack were like sisters. Griff and I were the same, we bonded over hockey, and the girls both fell in love with volleyball. But even before that, we were always over at each other's houses, swimming together, riding our bikes, sneaking out to play capture the flag with the other neighbor kids."

"Sounds like y'all had a lot of fun together."

Carson looks up, brows furrowed as he works his jaw. "Does it make me a terrible person that I'm having a hard time knowing my sister is engaged? I mean, I'm so fucking happy for Griff, Mack, and Cadence, but I can't help wonder—where does that leave me now? Two of my best friends have each other for the rest of their lives. I feel like I'm losing my twin. And they're going to live together full-time, leaving me in a big house all alone."

I reach for his hand. "Hey, you've still got me. I'm not that bad of a roommate, am I?"

"For now, you mean. I've still got you for now. And you know you're the best roommate a man could ask for."

"I'd like to think you have me for more than just the short-term."

"Are you saying you want to go the distance with me, bestie? We can be lifelong live-in companions." His tone is teasing again, but that doesn't stop those pesky butterflies from reawakening.

Picking up one of the wine glasses, I go to pour myself some of the red when Carson grabs the bottle and glass from my hands. "Let me wait on you."

"Carson, I'm perfectly capable."

"I insist, my lady."

"Well, if you must." I chuckle, attempting to break the tension in the room.

"Besides, I've got to give you a heavy pour if I have any chance of winning this game."

"Trying to take advantage of me?" I ask in a teasing tone.

His response comes out surprisingly serious again. "I would never, ever take advantage of you."

"I know, Carson. I'm sorry I was only teasing that you would take advantage of me being tipsy to try to win the game."

"Oh, right. Well, I can't promise I won't try that. But when it comes to other things I could take advantage of, I would never. If the day ever comes where you decide you want to be more than friends with me, I don't want there to be an ounce of hesitation or influence."

"Carson," I start, but he holds his hand up to me.

"Don't, Dakota. I didn't say that to start this conversation." My face pulls into a frown, but I just nod my head in response.

Carson begins shaking up the tiles in the bag, before holding it out for me to grab my letter tiles.

I pull the letter "I" and hold it up for him. "Looks like I'm going to start off."

"Game on, Super Nanny."

I'm not sure what game we're playing at this point, or who the opponent truly is. I know that Carson wouldn't play games with me. But that doesn't mean my heart isn't playing tricks on me, making me consider what it would be like if I did decide to cross the line of friendship with him.

Carson

I'm barely able to keep my eyes open as I stumble my way into the bathroom the next morning. I've got no clue how early it is, so I try to be quiet as I take care of business.

When I go to wash my hands and brush my teeth, I notice a blue post-it note on the mirror that reads:

Repeat after me, Golden Boy: My emotions are valid and worthy.

I smile as I repeat it out loud. "My emotions are valid and worthy."

My smile fades as I think about last night. Would Dakota still think these things if she knew some of the emotions I feel toward her are anything but friendly? Would she find me worthy of her time and attention if we were more than friends?

I've been giving her time to work through and process her emotions from her breakup. I knew she needed time to heal before she would be ready to try for something between us. If my breakdown yesterday was any indication, she's not the only one who needs time to process and heal before we can be together.

I don't hesitate as I pull up the contact information Dakota sent me yesterday for her therapist's office. When I call to schedule my first appointment, it's closed, so I give them a pseudonym, telling the voicemail my name is Carson Meyer. I know there is such a thing as patient confidentiality, but that doesn't mean there aren't people who won't leak to the press that an NHL player is seeking therapy. I'll tell my therapist who I am, but I'd prefer to schedule my appointments under a different name.

Besides, Carson Meyer has a nice ring to it.

14

Carson

May

Never in my life have I been as sore as I am right now. We've just returned home from Colorado, where I played and lost my first two playoff hockey games. Playoffs just hit differently—they're more aggressive, the checks are harder, and the stakes are higher. My feet are quite literally dragging beneath me as I make my way inside my house and punch the code into the security system to disarm it, only to immediately set it again. Headlights fade from my driveway as Griffin heads home to Mack and Cadence.

Even though Griff is still rehabbing his knee, he was able to travel with the team for the away stretch of our playoff series. I love having my best friend and soon-to-be brother-in-law on the same team as me. But I also know how hard it is for him to sit out the playoff series against his former team.

It's just after midnight, so I try my best to stay quiet and not wake Dakota. But I can't help the groan that slips out when I step on one of Cadence's oversized Lego blocks in the living room as I go upstairs to my bedroom.

"Ah, fuck!" I shout just as I hear a woman shriek from the couch beside me.

"Dakota?" I call out.

"Carson?" she asks.

"

"Yes, it's me. Are you okay?"

"You just scared me. I'm fine. Are you okay? What happened?"

"It's nothing. I stepped on one of those Lego blocks. I'm just sore and in need of an Epsom salt bath."

"I'm so sorry. I thought I picked them all up after they left. They stayed here for two nights so Kenna could study and pack up their rooms to move to their place. I hope you don't mind, we kept quite a few things of Cadence's here in case she stays over or I watch her over here occasionally. We combined her toy room and her nursery into just one room, and Kenna thought her old playroom could be your new guest room. At least while I'm still staying here," Dakota explains somewhat frantically.

"That sounds great. Thanks," I say in a subdued voice, even though I want to reassure her that I'm being sincere. I'd never admit it out loud—because I am truly happy for my sister, Griff, and Cadence—but I can't help the cloak of melancholy that has fallen over me since Mack told me they're moving out. Maybe it's the fact that they don't need me anymore, along with the thoughts spiraling in my head telling me that's for the best.

It's probably a good thing I booked two follow-up sessions for this week with the therapist Dakota recommended. My third session is tomorrow, which could be a terrible idea, seeing as I need my head to be on right for these next two home games if we have any chance of winning the series in this first round of playoffs. But with how many panic attacks I've had since the accident, I know I shouldn't wait to get help. It's just that, after the first two sessions, I was left drained. The mental load I've been carrying is exhausting.

"What's sore? Did you get hurt?" Dakota asks as she walks up to me, her beautiful face now etched with worry.

"No. Thankfully, I didn't get hurt. Every inch of my body is just sore right now," I tell her.

"Oh," she replies, biting down on her bottom lip. The same lip I've been dying to sink my teeth into for what feels like forever.

"I think one of your hugs would make things better. Come here," I open my arms for her. She doesn't hesitate a moment as she crashes into me, knocking the air from my lungs and leaving a tightening in my chest.

Things have been different between us since the night of Griff and Mack's engagement. Our friendship has shifted from just friends to slightly . . . more. We haven't crossed any physical lines, but I'd be lying if I said she wasn't the first thing I think about when I wake up. The first person I text or call when I've got news. The last person I think about before I close my eyes at night. While on the road, I longed for the nights we spent together watching TV or playing games. When we'd go to eat together as a team, I craved Dakota's home-cooked meals and desserts.

"I missed you. It wasn't the same not having you here," she whispers into my chest.

Fuck. She doesn't know how badly I needed to hear that.

"I missed you too. More than you know," I rasp.

Dakota steps out of my arms and clears her throat. "Do you want to watch something together?"

"I'd love that. Do you care if I take that bath first? If you're still awake, I'd never say no to spending time with you. But if you're tired, don't try to stay up."

"I was fixin' to read a bit before bed anyway. I'll see you if I see you, Golden Boy. And nice goal tonight. Even though y'all lost, it was still a hard-fought battle."

Nodding my head, I thank her before heading upstairs with my suitcase and carry-on.

Once the water runs, I strip out of my light gray suit and set it aside for dry cleaning. My phone buzzes on my vanity with an incoming text.

Mack Attack:

Good game tonight, Carse. I know it's a tough loss, but you guys can come back.

Me:

Thanks, Mack. Did Griff make it home?

He did. Thanks for agreeing to ride with him. He feels like you've been distancing yourself from him over the last month. Please tell me it has nothing to do with the accident.

My stomach sinks as I re-read my sister's text. Of course I've been distancing myself due to the accident. I almost caused another person my best friend loves to be taken from him. If something had happened to Cadence that day, I don't think I could have lived with myself.

Me:

I didn't mean to. It's been busy with playoffs and trying to plan you two the best joint bachelor and bachelorette party there ever was.

Mack Attack:

Please let Dakota and Brooke help! They've both been champing at the bit to help in any way they can.

> I mean, you don't have to twist my arm to get me to spend more time with Super Nanny.

> Keep it in your pants, Carse. She has quickly become a good friend of mine.

> And yet, you're engaged to my childhood best friend. Pot, meet kettle.

> Apples to oranges, bro. You're comparing fiancés to flings.

> I mean, I heard wedding bells the second I met her.

> It's far too late for this discussion. Goodnight, Carse! Love you, mean it.

> Goodnight, Mack! I love you guys!

I shut out of my text thread with Mack and open mine with Dakota. I scroll through the few where I let her know I had landed and was heading home until I spot the one from Thursday afternoon when we landed in Denver.

Austen:

> Repeat after me: I am in control.

Me:

> Oh, that's a good one. The flight had more turbulence than I would've liked, so I kissed the tarmac when we stepped off the plane.

Wait, you actually kissed the ground?

I did. I'll see if the social media team got a picture of it.

Me clicking on the Wolverines' socials to see if said picture has been posted

Repeat after me: I am confident and capable.

You're right on again. I am confident that I should've packed a jar of your amaretto peach jam. The hotel jam tastes like preservative garbage.

Repeat after me: I am worthy of greatness.

Let's hope you're right on this one. I repeated it. But maybe if you say, "Carson is worthy of greatness" out loud, together we can manifest that shit.

Alright, Golden Boy. I said it. Now go out there and score me one.

That one was for you, Super Nanny.

Smiling to myself, I set my phone down on the counter and get into the tub. When I walked through this house, I knew it was the one when I saw this oversized soaking tub. It's the perfect size to fit my large frame and then some.

After my bath, I knock twice on Dakota's bedroom door. "Are you still awake, Austen?"

A few moments later, the door swings open, and the sight of Dakota wearing one of my college hockey T-shirts just about brings me to my knees.

"Yep," she replies, somewhat breathlessly.

"Nice shirt," I tell her as I pinch the hem of the short sleeve. When my finger brushes against the skin on her arm, I have to swallow the groan that wants to escape.

"It is. I'm not even going to try to lie, I stole it when I was putting away some of your laundry."

I chuckle at her honesty. "That would explain why a shirt I haven't worn since I've lived here wound up in your hands."

She hides her head in her hands. "I'm so sorry. This probably looks really weird, but I promise it's not like that. I saw it in your dresser, and it was a weak moment that had me missing you. If you want me to give it back, I'll go change."

"Keep it. I insist. Besides, I don't mind the way my last name looks splayed across your back." I also don't mind one bit that she's openly admitting that she missed me.

"You're unrelenting in your teasing, aren't you?"

"Of course. So, do you want to watch the show here or downstairs?" I ask, shifting the discussion back to the show to try to distract me from how turned on I am right now.

"Let's watch it here. I'm getting a little tired now, so I don't want to have to walk up the steps later."

Giving her shoulder a little nudge, I tell her, "You know, I could always carry you to bed if you're too tired to walk, Austen."

She stares back at me before blinking rapidly a few times as if she were lost in thought. I'd give anything to know what she's thinking right now as we get situated in her bed, while she's wearing what looks like possibly nothing but my shirt, and there's been a recent shift between us.

I'm not sure where she stands with everything, but hearing her admit she missed me brings a sense of ease that I didn't realize I needed until now. It gives me hope that someday she'll miss me as more than just her friend.

15

Dakota

May

I'd just like to point out that things have escalated quickly. Between McKenna and Griffin, that is. Well, amongst others as well, perhaps. But I'm not ready to go there yet.

Tonight is the night of Kenna and Griff's joint bachelor and bachelorette party. Yes, they've only been engaged for a month. Yes, their wedding is only a month away. And yes, they are the absolute cutest couple I've ever met.

"Tell me, what is your go-to karaoke song?" McKenna asks me as she curls her blonde, waist-length locks into the most stunning waves.

"Probably 'Wide Open Spaces' by The Chicks," I decide.

"The Chicks!" she exclaims. "Oh my gosh, I love them so much. We grew up listening to them every summer at our cabin with our mom."

"My mama used to play the best 90s country music in our house when I was growing up. The Chicks, Shania, Martina, Garth, Trisha, Faith and Tim. We'd clean the house, and she'd damn near blast the speakers on our stereo while we were doing chores." My chest squeezes with the same ache I get any time I think of home and my mama. Now that Aaron and I are officially divorced, I question why exactly I haven't moved back to Texas yet. Something keeps a hold of me here. Perhaps not something, but a few someones.

Kenna sets down her curling iron, walks over to me, and gives me a big hug. "I feel like we're celebrating so much more than just my engagement tonight," she says as she steps back. "We're celebrating your freedom as a newly single woman. And we're definitely celebrating the fact that you decided you're going to write a fricken book."

"McKenna!" I squeal, looking around the room to make sure no one else overheard. "I told you that in confidence. No one else on this earth knows I'm an aspiring author."

"I'm not sure why. It's completely badass. I can't wait to read it!"

"Look, I know how much you and I love to read. But the only reason I told you that was to make sure you were okay with me typing away on my computer while Cadence is napping or sleeping. I'm not ready for anyone else to know just yet."

"What about my brother?" she asks.

"What about your brother?" I mimic her question as I apply a coat of mascara to my lashes.

"Well, there's the fact that the two of you live together. He will most likely see you working your fingers to the bone as you write your book. And then there's also the fact that I thought the two of you were getting close." At that, I whip my head around to look at her. She has her arms crossed and a knowing smirk on her face.

Shit. Am I really that obvious?

"Define close," I say nonchalantly.

"Perhaps closer than you're ready to admit to me right now. Close enough that I noticed he has leaned on you more than me lately." She pauses before adding, "Look, Dakota, I don't know exactly what is happening between you and Carse, but I do know my brother. I've never seen him so enamored with a woman as he has been with you since meeting you at your interview. I also know my brother is a sweetheart with a heart the size of your home state. So, please, just make sure you're ready for whatever is happening between the two of you. I don't think I could take seeing Carson heartbroken."

It takes everything in me not to say *again*. This man has been heartbroken since the day of McKenna and Katie's accident, though he's never admitted that to me. And the accident with Cadence likely deepened the break.

Feeling slightly uncomfortable discussing my feelings for Carson with his sister when I don't even know how I truly feel, I tell her, "I care deeply for Carson. We became closer friends quickly after I moved in with him. He is someone I feel like I can open up to and be vulnerable with. I'll probably tell him about my book soon. But as far as a relationship goes, I just feel like he and I are too different, not to mention the age gap between us."

"I don't think you're that different from one another. You both sound ambitious in your pursuit of what makes you happy. His passion is hockey. Yours is writing. And you both are terrible singers, which we're about to see on full display tonight," she teases. "I'll leave it alone until you're ready to talk about it. But, please, don't let the stigma of an age gap keep you from happiness. I know I'm biased, but my twin is a pretty fucking great guy."

I smile at that because Carson Wilder is the best of the best. But as much as it pains me to say it, I just don't think he and I would work. The last thing any golden boy needs is a tarnished divorcée cougar.

Carson

We're at one of my favorite bars of all time, The Watering Hole. It's a hole-in-the-wall place on Lake Mille Lacs—the same lake my family's cabin is on, and also Griff and Mack's new cabin next door.

We decided to throw their joint bachelor and bachelorette parties up here between the two houses. It's Memorial Day weekend, so it's pretty packed on the lake, but it also means The Watering Hole is having its annual karaoke contest. This weekend came together a little last minute since we weren't sure if we'd still be in the playoffs or not. Unfortunately, we lost out in four games to Colorado.

Tonight is the first of the three-night celebration. Jackson, being the party planner he is, helped me plan the ultimate weekend for Mack and Griff. Each night has a theme. Tonight is reverse cowgirl—Jax's idea, not mine—where everyone dresses up as cowboys and cowgirls. Night two is golf pros and tennis hoes—again, Jax's idea—where the guys stay dressed in their golf attire, and the girls dress up in tennis skirts. Night three is the blackout, where everyone dresses in black except for the future Mr. and Mrs., who will be in white.

The ladies were finishing up a drinking game at the cabin, so they told us guys to go ahead and get a few tables for the group. Following the theme of the night, we're all dressed in cowboy hats, boots, and a variety of outfits. Griff went full-blown Garth on us with his black cowboy hat, black cowboy boots, black button-up, and dark jeans. Jax is feeling right at home with tonight's theme, as he typically dresses in a midwest country boy wardrobe. He's got on a camo button-up with his light brown cowboy hat. I opted for a tan cowboy hat with the tightest bootcut light-wash jeans I could find, an obnoxiously big belt buckle that says "Ladies, my eyes are up here," a plain white T-shirt, and cowboy boots that Dakota helped me pick out.

Then we've got Bennett, the serious and stoic captain of the team, who also happened to be the loser of our fantasy football league this year and who is long overdue for his punishment. Because of this, we decided that we'd each get to pick out his outfits for the weekend. Tonight's outfit is brought to you by Jax—Bennett has a straw cowboy hat, a cutoff flannel shirt that also looks like it may be a cropped top, and a pair of cutoff jean shorts that are practically glued to his thick hockey thighs and show off his crocodile cowboy boots. I just about spit my beer out when I saw him walk down the steps at the cabin. Needing the liquid courage to get through the night in the ridiculous outfit his little brother picked out for him, Bennett pre-gamed heavily back at the cabin and is now owning the outfit. I'm not sure I've ever seen him tipsy.

We've just ordered a round of whiskey for the guys when the bar's emcee for the night announces they'll be starting karaoke soon.

"Will you be singing 'Should've Been a Cowboy' tonight?" Griff asks me. When I send him a questioning look, he breaks out in a fit of laughter. "You know, because you've got heart eyes for the nanny from Texas."

Before I can attempt to deny it, a roar of catcalls and wolf whistles break out over the bar as a group of women enter the front door. I see Mack dressed in a white minidress with coordinating white cowgirl boots and a matching white cowgirl hat with a short veil spilling out the back. She's got a white sash that says bride-to-be on it and a blinding smile that lights up her face. She looks so fucking happy, and I love that for her.

Behind her are her teammates, Brooke and Alexa, but I don't immediately see Dakota. That is, until it feels like the world stands still, and the door opens in slow motion as my Texan dream girl walks in.

I hear a low whistle beside me as Jax says, "Well, well, well. It turns out the nanny-turned-roommate didn't fuck around with tonight's theme."

He's not lying. She's wearing a jean miniskirt that should be illegal with how sexy it makes her legs look, a cropped hot pink shirt that says "Kenna's last hoe down" showing off the most delicious peek of her tanned and toned stomach, a black cowgirl hat, and knee-high rhinestone cowgirl boots.

Holy fuck. She looks absolutely amazing. And she's making her way toward the bartop tables I'm sitting at.

Dakota freezes in place when she spots me, not even bothering to hide her blatant ogling as she takes me in. I ogle her right back because, honestly, how could I not?

I grab my glass of whiskey and slowly walk toward her like a predator stalking its prey.

"My god, Austen. Look at you. You're absolutely devastating in a cowgirl hat and boots."

A shy smile spreads across her lips. She looks up at me through dark lashes, and the second her emerald eyes meet mine, I'm a goner. "You don't look so bad yourself, purty boy. Shoulda known you'd be a cowboy who thinks it's a good idea to wear white. You wouldn't last a day on my family's ranch."

"Oh, and I take it you typically wear those rhinestone cowgirl boots on the ranch?" I taunt.

"My mama would pitch a hissy fit if she saw me wearing these boots while riding Buttercup."

"Ah, Buttercup is your horse back home, right? Isn't she an apple-something?"

That makes her chuckle. "Yep. She's the sweet girl that makes me homesick whenever I think of her. And she's an Appaloosa."

"Well, if I weren't deathly afraid of horses, I'd offer to be your riding partner when you eventually take me home to meet your family. But seeing as I'd like to make a good impression, I should probably steer clear of the horse barn."

That makes her eyebrows shoot up. "Don't count your chickens before they hatch. I never asked you to come home to meet my mama. Besides, I know this is just another ploy to get closer to my brother. You're unrelenting."

"I've let up quite a bit since he somehow got my number and FaceTime-interviewed me to make sure I wasn't, and I quote, 'a serial killer forcing his baby sister to live with him.' Jolene loves me already after only chatting with me on a few of your calls, and that just kills you, doesn't it?" The smirk that takes over my face is cocky as hell.

"Well, you'd make quite the first impression with them if you dressed like that." Dakota gestures toward my belt buckle. "Did you choose the most obnoxious belt buckle you could find?"

"Oh, you know it. It was either this or the assless chaps, but I thought I should save those to live out one of your personal fantasies together someday."

"Bless your heart, Golden Boy."

"You did not just 'bless your heart' me." I mock-gasp and grab my chest as if I'm appalled.

"I absolutely did. Now, will you be a good boy and buy me a drink?"

I'll do anything she asks if she's calling me a good boy. A new kink has officially been unlocked.

"Sure thing. What can I get for ya, darlin'?" I ask with a tip of my cowboy hat.

"I'll take a margarita on the rocks, please, and thank you," she singsongs, clearly already a bit tipsy from the girls' drinking games.

I've barely placed the drink in Dakota's hand when my sister hooks arms with her and says they need to go dance.

Meanwhile, I'm frozen in place at the bar, completely captivated by Dakota's hips as they twist side to side in her little jean skirt. She's teaching the girls a line dance. And when Mack pulls out the classic sprinkler dance move, I watch Dakota hold on to her hat with one arm and tip her head back in laughter.

Goddamn. She's so fucking pretty when she's comfortable and secure enough to be carefree. I love getting to see her this way.

"Oh, fuck. Is Bennett actually hitting on her?" Griff asks, nudging my shoulder with his and pointing his glass of whiskey toward the end of the bar where Bennett is standing next to a woman with long, auburn hair.

"No way. Not my big brother. I mean, he's not celibate, at least I don't think he is at the moment—though, I wouldn't put it past him as punishment for losing in the first round of playoffs—but he hasn't sought out a girl *ever*. They come to him, and on the rare occasion he deems them worthy of his time, he doesn't have to do or say much to seal the deal," Jax clarifies, shaking his head in disbelief.

"It looks like our Benny boy is not only hitting on this girl, but did I just see that stoic motherfucker laugh?" Griff questions, raising his eyebrows.

"Holy shit. He did. He didn't just chuckle. He fucking cackled at whatever she just said," I point out, nearly spitting out my drink.

"Carse, go see if he's hitting on her. Ten bucks says he gets shot down wearing that outfit. No way is anyone going to take him seriously." Jax beams manically.

"Deal," I say, wandering over to the other side of the bar, where Bennett is talking to and most definitely hitting on a girl who looks to be about my age.

"Come find me later, Benny," the girl waves as she walks toward the front of the stage, where a group of her friends are waiting.

"Wilder, get your ass over here," Bennett commands, and I immediately do as I'm told. When Bennett asks, no, tells me what he plans for us to do, I can't hold back my grin. We split ways as he goes up toward the stage to complete his mission.

I practically run back to the bar to give the guys an update. "Shut the fuck up. You'll never believe what Bennett just asked me to do."

"What?" Jax and Griff ask at the same time as they turn toward me.

"Bennett fucking Wilson just asked if I would join him up on stage to sing the girl he's been hitting on all night's favorite song."

"Fuck, I think our boy is smitten," Griff beams.

"What song?" Jax asks, wearing an expression I can't quite discern.

Before I can answer, I see Bennett nod toward the stage as the emcee calls our names, signaling that it's our turn. The starting notes of "Can't Take My Eyes Off You" sound through the speakers.

Making my way up on stage, I don't miss the cocky smile and wink Bennett shoots toward the redhead he was talking to only moments ago. She shakes her head at his antics before raising her glass to salute him.

He brings the mic up to his mouth, and my jaw hangs open when he starts singing the song's opening lines. Bennett Wilson can actually sing. I always thought Jax was the only musically inclined sibling in their family, but I'll be damned.

I look out into the crowd, and it looks like I'm not the only one impressed by his voice. The little redhead is staring up at him with fucking stars in her eyes.

Knowing I can't hold a tune, especially in comparison to the Wilson brothers, I mouth to Bennett that he's got this. I stay on stage, mostly for moral support and backup singing, but I leave the lead vocals to "Benny," as the redhead called him.

Once the song is over, I decide to take a page from Bennett's book and serenade the girl I've been pining over for far too long. I write my karaoke selection on the sign-up sheet and wait my turn to be called back to the stage.

Two songs later, the emcee calls for Golden Boy as the opening notes of "Sparks Fly (Taylor's Version)" float through the bar.

I don't even bother to take my eyes off Dakota as I serenade her with some of the queen's best lyrics. The chorus of this song makes me think of my green-eyed dream girl every time I hear it. When the second verse starts, I throw a wink at her once the third line leaves my lips. As the bridge hits, I point to Dakota, causing her hands to cover her reddening cheeks.

I love it when my dream girl is bashful. But I love it even more when after the song is done, she damn near jumps into my arms and whisper-shouts, "That was ah-mazing! But terrible at the same time. You can't sing for shit, Golden Boy."

My heart races in my chest each time I get to have her in my arms like this. With her body pressed against mine, I feel invincible.

Dakota Meyer doesn't know it yet, but she's the woman of my dreams. I can't wait to prove her wrong when it comes to the differences she thinks exist between us. There may be obstacles we have to overcome, but I'm confident that with her by my side, we can get through anything.

Last call and last song were just announced. It doesn't take more than two bars of "Hold On" by Wilson Phillips for Griff, Jax, Bennett, and me to go nuts. This was our pregame song in the varsity hockey locker room when we all played together.

"Fuck yeah!" I shout as I grab Jax around the neck and throw my arm around Griff.

"Honestly, when this song comes on, I could kick a steel door off its hinges," Jax yells.

"Let's go boys! It's our little G-Baby's last hoorah before he becomes a married man," Bennett slurs as he closes us into a circle, he is definitely feeling the shots he downed to get through this night.

Griff throwing his head back to scream-sing the lyrics gets me in my feels. When the chorus starts, the four of us jump in the air and join Griff in screaming the lyrics. I'm so fucking excited for G to join the three of us on the ice in the same jersey next season. But I'm even happier that he's going to officially become my brother in a few weeks.

We're all feeling good by this point in the night, the ladies included. I break from our bro circle in the middle of the dance floor in search of my dream girl.

Dakota is holding her phone in the air like it's a microphone with her other hand on the top of her cowgirl hat to keep it from falling off. She looks so effortlessly sexy and in her element like this—stomping her boots and swaying her hips to the music.

I've got to be the most luststruck fucker in this bar.

Walking over to her, I bend down and brush back her hair behind her ear before leaning in so she can hear me over the music. "After seeing you dressed like this, I think I want to quit hockey and become a cattle rancher in Texas. What do you say—will you take me home, Austen?"

She doesn't say anything as she turns around and wraps her arms around my neck. "You might look the part right now, but I'm afraid all the dirt and dust will dull your shine, Golden Boy." Dakota bites down on her tempting bottom lip and I damn near beg her to let me have a taste. "Besides, you were meant to be out on the ice, living your best biscuit life."

Throwing my head back laughing, I just shake my head when I'm finally able to rein it in. "You're one of a kind, Dream Girl."

"What did you just call me?" She stops dancing and her face sobers as she searches my eyes.

I duck my head back down to her ear so she can hear me better. "Don't pretend you don't know what you do to me. You've had me completely off-kilter for almost a year, and you're right, I balance on tiny blades for a living, so that's saying something."

"Oh," she breathes.

"Cat got your tongue, Kota Lynn?"

Good. Maybe she's finally coming around to what I've known all along. I'll continue to be patient with her, but progress is progress, and fuck does it feel good to see her affected by me even slightly.

"Please do not call me what my brother and Mama call me. It's weird." Her face scrunches up in the most adorable way.

I smirk in response, shaking my head. "My bad, Austen. Won't happen again."

"There, much better. I like when you call me that, even if I still don't understand why you call me the wrong city. Maybe you should take to callin' me Dallas." Her suggestion ends on a hiccup.

"I'd let you in on my little secret, but I'm afraid you're too tipsy to remember tomorrow. The time is coming for me to spill it all soon though." I bite my cheek when I realize what I've just said.

Keeping eye contact with me, she tips her hat at me before saying, "I sure hope so, cowboy." She chuckles, throwing a wink my way then pats my chest before walking backward toward the girls.

It's after two in the morning when Dakota and I stumble through the front door of the cabin.

"I've got a secret, but I can't tell you," Dakota taunts as she skips toward the steps.

"Am I going to be an uncle again?" I guess. I'd fucking love for Griff and Mack to have more kids when they're ready. But seeing as I don't think the drinks Mack was drinking tonight were virgin, I will take a guess and say that's not her secret.

She stops as she hits the first step to go upstairs and turns around. "Not that I'm aware of. It isn't a secret about nobody but little old me." Dakota points to herself, bopping her nose and hiccuping simultaneously. "I think I'm a wee bit tipsy, my lord."

Fuck. I don't know what it is about her calling me that, but it gets my dick going from zero to sixty in two point two seconds.

"Does my lady need help turning in for the night? If so, me thinks she may spill her deepest, darkest secrets to me."

"I may have big lips, but they are sealed on this matter."

Those lips. I've told myself countless times that I won't have her lips until she's fully ready for me without any hesitation. I thought we were making good progress on that, but then I overheard Dakota and Mack talking when they were getting ready earlier tonight. She thinks the age gap between us will cause bad publicity. But I don't give a fuck about my image.

"Will you come with me for a minute? I want to show you something. I promise I'll get you tucked in in a little bit."

She cocks a brow in suspicion. "Where are you taking me, cowboy?"

That earns her a smile. "Some place that's special to me. A place I think you'll like too."

With that, she takes the few steps back down the stairs and grasps my outstretched hand, lacing her fingers in mine. "Show me," she whispers.

I'd show her the entire fucking world if she'd let me. But I'll start with one of my favorite places for now.

The path to the boathouse is lit by solar-powered lanterns. Keeping Dakota's hand in mine, I lead her down the stone steps and pathway until we're standing outside the two story boathouse.

I key in the code to enter before nodding toward the steps to let Dakota know we're headed up there. On the second level is a small guest suite that has a full wall of windows overlooking the lake that butts up to the A-frame glass roof. This may just be the best place to stargaze in the entire world. And it also serves as one of the best spots to watch the sun set over the lake.

When we get to the top of the steps and I open the door to the suite, Dakota gasps as she takes in the glass paneling along the west-facing wall and ceiling. "Carson. This is so beautiful."

My mom renovated and decorated this space to be my personal oasis.

"When my parents inherited this cabin from my grandparents, they did a pretty big remodel of the whole house and this boathouse as well. My mom and dad decided Mack and I should each have a space of our own for when we come here. Sure we each have rooms upstairs in the main cabin, but Mack got to choose what to do with the space over the garage, and I got to choose what to do in here."

Dakota runs her fingers over the charcoal gray king-size bedding before falling onto her back to take in the view of the clear night sky.

"I love this space so much."

"Does it put you in the mood to share secrets?" I query.

"I don't know. The bed is feeling too cold and lonely for me to share my secrets. Maybe if I could use you as my own personal heater then I'd spill the beans."

That earns her a laugh from me as I make my way over to the bed. I crawl in beside her and slip my arm under the crook of her neck. Pulling her against my chest, I say, "I'll go first. I've been keeping a secret from you, Austen."

"Oh yeah? What's the secret?"

"I've had a slight crush on you since the day I met you. But after Mack broke the news to me that you were married, I told myself that we could only be friends."

"I'm not sure that was exactly a secret. Even if Mack didn't share that tidbit with me earlier, I think I've seen the writing on the wall. But you were right, we are friends. You've quickly become one of my best friends, Carson."

My stomach does a weird fluttering and sinking feeling at the same time. Pushing aside my apprehension from her admission I heard earlier with my sister, I say, "Is that so? Do best friends typically share secrets with each other?"

She nods her head against my chest. "They do." She pauses to inhale deeply, burying her head in the crook of my neck. It tickles when she exhales, and the scent of the tequila she drank floods my senses. "I'm thinking of doing something I've always dreamed of since I was a little kid."

"I'm on the edge of my seat, Austen. What is it? You can tell me anything, and I'd support the hell out of you." I give her shoulder three gentle squeezes, silently urging her to continue.

"Well, I'd like to put my degree to use. I'm writing a novel. Perhaps even a series if I can get through the first one." When the admission slips from her lips, she covers her mouth as if she can't believe she spilled her secret to me.

Rolling her onto her back, I push myself up on my elbow and stare into her ensnaring emerald eyes. "That's fucking amazing. When did you decide to do this?"

"Yeah? Don't you think it's weird I'm chasing a dream with no fallback plan? Without a safety net?" Her brow furrows, and she bites her bottom lip as she awaits my answer.

"Yeah, it's fucking amazing. And you won't need a backup plan. Do you want to know why? Because you're destined for greatness, Dakota. I can't wait to read it when it's ready."

"What? You can't read it! I think I'd die of embarrassment." She tries to hide her face in the crook of my elbow, but I pull her chin up so she has no choice but to see the sincerity on my face.

"The words you write to me each and every day without pause have slowly begun healing me and my anxious thoughts. You're damn right I'm going to read your whole-ass novel. And there's not a damn thing you can do about it." I punctuate my statement with a long kiss on her forehead. I breathe her in before rolling us over onto my back and resting her head against my chest again.

I'm the most fortunate man in the world because this woman chose me to divulge her deepest hopes and desires to. I only wish that I could convince her—prove to her—that I can be the man by her side, being her biggest cheerleader, as she achieves her aspirations.

16

Dakota

May

My head is pounding so badly that I can hear and feel each beat of my pulse. And why in the hell is my face so warm?

I try to crack open an eye but immediately decide against it when I see how bright it is. Groaning, I fling my hand over my eyes, only for my fingers to connect with something hard. Did I think it was a good idea to sleep on a brick? Testing out the pillow, I move my head side to side to see if it becomes any comfier.

"Mmm," I hear from just above me.

What the hell?

Peeking my eye open again, I make out a circular, gold pendant resting against a firm, tanned chest.

Holy shit. Why was I just asleep on Carson's bare chest? And why do the sounds Carson makes first thing in the morning have me squeezing my thighs together?

Heat pools low in my stomach as I take in this innocent accident, noticing certain *things* about Carson. Like the way his body is hard in all of the right places. His lean muscles and sharp jawline look as if they were carved by Michaelangelo. God sure took his time creating this man. I squint to get a better look at the medallion he never seems to take off his chest. It looks to be Saint Christopher. That explains . . . a lot about Carson. It feels like he carries the weight of the world on his shoulders, always trying to protect those he loves.

I shift to try to take him in more at the same time as his palm connects with the bare skin of my lower back.

That feels *amazing*. It feels so good that I give up trying to take him in because I'd rather melt back into him and pretend I'm still asleep—to extend this time together—before the reality of what I'm letting happen comes crashing to my conscious brain.

I'm not that lucky, though. Just as I nestle my head into the crook of his neck between his collarbone and jaw, Carson shifts again, moving his hand around my side. When his large hand grips a hold of my waist, I have to bite back the moan that nearly escapes my lips.

"Funny meeting you here, Austin," he murmurs, sleep making his voice gravelly. I perch myself up on my elbow to take a peek at him, but I'm met with his aqua eyes already taking me in. A lazy smile spreads across his face, and in the morning light flooding through the glass panel ceiling, he looks god-like.

Knowing I probably have mascara smudged beneath my eyes, I perch myself up on his chest and cover my eyes with my hands. "I'm a mess."

Carson gently tugs my hands down. "Don't talk about my favorite author like that."

My stomach pulls taut like the strings of a bow hearing that word leave his lips.

Biting my lip in apprehension, I ask, "I let that slip, huh?"

"You sure did." He slowly dances his fingers across the exposed skin of my lower back. "So tell me, what is this future bestseller of yours about?"

"That is highly unlikely." Pausing, I avert my gaze. "I'm writing a romance novel about two clandestine soulmates forbidden to fall in love. Sort of a modern spin on *Romeo and Juliet*."

"Why is it forbidden?"

"I'm still mapping out the plot, but I think the main male character is going to be a professional football player who falls for his assistant."

"And by football player, you mean hockey player. That doesn't seem very forbidden."

"You're right. Until you find out the assistant is his rival's daughter. And it's most definitely going to be a football player. It's the only sport I know."

"Okay, I'm hooked already. We'll circle back to the football detail at a later date. When can I read it?" I can't help the questioning look I send his way, but he looks so sincerely intrigued.

"I haven't written more than the first two chapters. So, not for a very long time. Or quite possibly ever."

"Wait, why can't I read it?"

"It's a romance novel. You don't think that'd be weird to read your friend's romance book?"

"Not really. I mean, I read the books you leave around the house all the time."

"What?" I squeal. "No, you don't."

"Oh, I do. Once we started watching *Bridgerton* and I realized you read more than just the classics, my curiosity was piqued." He sends a shameless wink my way.

I cover my face again, this time in utter humiliation.

"Ohmygodthat'ssoembarrassing," I mumble through my palms.

His chest shakes with laughter beneath me, and I peek a glimpse at him through my fingers. I can't help but drown in the current that is Carson Wilder. I'm amazed at how easily he breaks down my walls and pulls me in. His golden hair shines in the light of dawn, and even though it's only just started to get warmer, his skin already has a bronzed glow. He looks ethereal.

Pulling my hands from my face again, he says, "You're so fucking beautiful when you're bashful first thing in the morning."

My breath hitches as his words sink in. I lick my lips, and his gaze locks on the movement.

Carson's phone vibrates on the nightstand, thankfully breaking the tension that was building. I shift to grab his cell for him. "You're popular this morning, Golden Boy."

He takes his phone when I hold it out for him. "Thanks. It's probably the guys looking for me. I think we're all eating breakfast together before our tee time this morning."

I start to roll out of bed when he grips me by the waist, halting me in place. "Whoa there, where are you running off to, Austin?"

"I should get back up to the house and change so I don't look like I'm doing the walk of shame."

His lip quirks up at the corner. "There's no shame in two friends spending an innocent night together, right?"

"You'd be right if I didn't admit that this is starting to feel less . . . innocent," I murmur. "I really should go."

Moving out of his grasp, I slip from beneath the covers and start looking for my boots.

I'm just pulling on my second rhinestone boot when Carson stands from his side of the bed. He stretches his arms above his head, and my gaze slides down the sinew of his arms, across the expanse of his broad chest, to each rivet of his defined abs, until I reach the V that leads beneath the very low waist of his faded blue jeans.

Yeah, the way he's turning me on right now is far from innocent.

He relaxes his arms and lightly scratches his bare chest. "I hate to watch you leave, Austin."

Yeah, but I bet you'd love to watch me come.

Fudge. I need to get out of here.

"Then don't." I circle my hand in the air, motioning for him to turn around.

"Right." He claps his hands together in front of him in the way I've come to know he does when he's nervous or unsure. Pointing behind him, he says, "I'm going to take a quick shower down here before breakfast."

"Okay. I'll see you up there," I tell him as he closes the door to the small en suite.

Grabbing a pen and notepad out of my purse, I leave Carson with a little token to remind him of me. Today's Post-it affirmation reads:

Repeat after me, Cowboy Carse: My inner strength and confidence are attractive to others.

I'm still smiling to myself, thinking about how much shit he's going to give me for that one as I head up the path back to the cabin.

This place is so peaceful and serene. I can see why Carson's parents wanted to make sure they took time every summer to come up here as a family and make memories.

I'm pulled from my thoughts as a slender arm wraps around mine. "Good morning, bestie. Where did you run off to last night?" Kenna asks.

My stained cheeks don't stand a chance against her knowing eyes.

"The boathouse is a favorite spot of one of the twins, but I can't think of the last time I was up there since my mom and dad redecorated it for Carson." She pauses, putting her hands on her hips. "And considering the guys have been looking for him for the past ten minutes, I'm going to guess the two of you had a little boathouse slumber party."

Shit.

My stomach churns with guilt. "I'm so incredibly sorry, Kenna. We honestly didn't mean to fall asleep up there. He wanted to show me the space, and then I told him about my book, and then we were drunk and must have passed out."

Kenna claps her hands together and lets out a howl of laughter. "Oh my gosh! You should see your face right now. Dakota, you're fine! I was only giving you a hard time."

I let out a breath I didn't realize I was holding. "Oh, you're mean."

"Wait. Did you just say you told Carse about your book?"

Groaning, I mutter, "I did. Why do I have the loosest lips when I'm drinking?"

"Girl, I don't know. But I'm here for it. I was having the hardest time keeping it a secret from him. The second I told Griff about it, he made a bet with me, saying I'd crack and spill the beans to Carse within a week. Thankfully, your tipsy ass helped me win the bet!"

"I'm glad I could be of service," I deadpan.

Kenna shakes her head before throwing her arm around my shoulder. "If it weren't already obvious, you're stuck with me, Kota. It's a good thing we're getting facials today. Maybe they can wipe that scowl off your face."

I shoulder her lightly and make my way into her parents' cabin while she takes the path between the houses to her and Griff's new place.

McKenna doesn't realize how serendipitous it is that she came into my life. I found her post about needing a nanny in the college bulletin the same week my school email was about to expire—only a week after Aaron first showed me his true colors.

The Wilder twins have changed my life for the better. I know I wouldn't be here today without them, and that's the only sobering thought I need to realize I shouldn't risk my friendship with them just because a swarm of butterflies erupts in my stomach every time Carson smiles at me.

The theme for today is golf pros and tennis hoes. I'm honestly not sure where Cason and Jackson came up with these ideas, but I'm somewhat in love with them.

Last night, Carson stole the breath from my lungs when I saw him in his cowboy getup. Who knew a cowboy wearing a chain could be so hot?

Today's theme has Carson looking even more in his element. He's wearing a teal shirt that makes his eyes look like the turquoise waters of the Caribbean, a backwards white golf hat, and white golf shorts with that damn five-inch inseam that show off his powerful thighs. Since when did I become turned on by a man's legs? I officially feel like a creep for being attracted to the definition of his tanned calves.

I was surprised to find out the ladies weren't joining the guys for their round of golf, considering I'm the only non-collegiate or pro athlete in the group. Instead, we're going for a spa day and I couldn't be more excited to have a little girl time with McKenna, Brooke, and Alexa.

Carson spots me filling my plate from the smorgasbord worth of food Griffin cooked everyone this morning. He saunters over to me and says, "Who wakes up first and cooks breakfast for the entire group at their own bachelor party? That is a major red flag. I should warn Mack before it's too late."

I love an at-ease Carson.

"Someone woke up and chose violence this morning, Carse," Kenna says from behind us. Carson turns around, resting his hips against the kitchen island. "I know you're not talking about my soon-to-be husband having red flags. If Griff heard you, I think he'd revoke your best man privileges."

"Is that so? For some reason I don't think I have anything to worry about," Carson quips as he tosses a strawberry in the air and catches it in his mouth. I watch, no, ogle the way his jaw works as he chews. When he swallows, I'm entranced by the lift of his Adam's apple, which I have the strangest urge to bite right now.

What is happening to me?

He leans in when he catches me staring and whispers, "If you think watching me eat a strawberry is drool-worthy, you should see me eat a peach." His lips brush my ear, causing goosebumps to erupt across my skin.

"You don't play fair," I whisper.

He pulls back, sporting a rakish grin. "When we get home, will you teach me how to make your mama's peach cobbler?"

Home. Why does warmth flood my chest from that one word leaving his lips?

I set my plate on the island and face him, crossing my arms and leaning against the counter. "I'm not sure you've earned the privilege, Golden Boy. You're acting like a brat."

He tries to bite back his chuckle. "I like when you call me names, it turns me on."

"Down, boy."

"You're probably right. Can't afford to get *excited* in these shorts." The waggle of his brows has me snorting.

"Oh my goodness. Chivalry is indeed dead."

"Oh, I can be quite chivalrous, my lady. You just haven't allowed me the opportunity to show you."

"Is that so?" I muse. "And when would such an opportunity arise?"

"Let me take you out, Austin."

My eyes widen at his request. I'm just about to ask him what he means by that when Jackson steps between us to grab a strip of bacon.

"Are you excited for the spa day today, Super Nanny?" Jackson asks me before eating the entire piece in one bite.

I have to bite the inside of my cheek to stop the smile from spreading across my face at the look on Carson's face. His brow is furrowed and I fear he may crack a molar from how hard he's clenching his jaw. Note to self: he doesn't like when others call me by his nickname.

It's strange. I should find his possessiveness worrisome. Instead, I find it endearing. Clearly, I'm even more broken than I realized.

"Alright, alright, Jaxy. Super Nanny has a name. Dakota deserves your respect just like all of the other females here," Carson says.

Jackson throws his head back and smacks Carson on the back. "You're acting like a Neanderthal, Carsey-baby." He shakes his head, laughing to himself as he walks over to his brother.

"On that note, I'm going to eat in my room so I can finish getting ready." I reach to pick up the plate I set aside when his long, deft fingers eclipse mine. My skin prickles beneath his touch, and my heart rate skyrockets when he brings me in for a hug. There's nothing I want more than to stay in his warm embrace.

"I wish I could join y'all at the spa today," Carson breathes into my skin before pressing a soft kiss on my forehead.

God, this feels too good.

"Y'all, eh?" I question as I reluctantly step out of his embrace.

"Yeah, y'all. What can I say? You're rubbing off on me, Austin," he says with a devilish smirk. "Looks like I'm not the only one, *eh?*"

"You're incorrigible."

"You're right. I am incredibly cute."

Rolling my eyes, I feign annoyance. "Case in point."

"You love it."

"Hardly."

"Dakota Meyer . . . she's a real smitten kitten for the golden retriever of the group."

"Dream on, Golden Boy."

"I didn't even have to dream last night with you in my arms. Best night of sleep I've ever had."

It was for me too. But I'm not about to fan the sparks of hope in his eyes. Grabbing my plate, I head up the steps to add some much-needed space between the two of us.

No matter how attractive he is. No matter how easy it is to flirt and banter with him. No matter how nice it is to *feel* again. We wouldn't work. I'm far too broken, and I refuse to tarnish his shine.

17

Carson

MAY

"**Y**ou fucking sliced it, Carsey!" Jax hollers.

"Shut the hell up," Bennett whisper-shouts.

"What's gotten into you today? You're typically my scratch partner, but even G is showing you up today." Jax scowls at me while flipping his brother the bird.

My golf game has gone to shit today. I wasn't lying when I told Dakota I'd rather go to the spa with them than golf. It doesn't help that I tried to shoot my shot by asking her out just in time for Jax to interrupt us. I really thought we were getting somewhere, but I should've known she wasn't ready yet.

"Maybe I'm trying to let the man of the hour win, considering it's his last hoorah," I quip, shrugging my shoulders.

Jax shakes his head. "I call bullshit. The two of you are almost as competitive with each other as me and Benny. No, that's not it. . ." He trails off before snapping his fingers at me. "Ah, I know. It's the fucking nanny, isn't it?"

Turning my back to him to avoid eye contact, I try to focus on Griff teeing up his ball on the last hole. Unfortunately, Jax is like a dog with a bone now that he thinks he knows what's eating at me.

"Jax," I warn.

"Don't give me that shit. I can tell you're into her. So what's holding you back?"

"Well, for starters, when I asked her to go out with me this morning, you chose the perfect time to interrupt our moment by shoving an entire piece of bacon in your mouth," I bite out, my frustration for playing poorly and being interrupted earlier is bleeding through my tone.

"Ah, fuck. I'm sorry, Carse. I didn't realize." Jax lifts his hat and scratches his forehead before smoothing it back on his head. "So, I take it she didn't give you an answer?"

"You think? What gave you that impression?"

"Oh, I don't know. Probably the case of blue balls and the giant stick you've got up your ass."

"And tell me, Jaxy, how has the giant case of blue balls been working for you over the last two and a half years?"

"Great deflection," he scoffs. "But I'm not falling into that trap. So what's the deal with the two of you? You've been pretty tight-lipped, but from what I've gathered, Dakota moved in with you after New Year's Eve when Benny brought the two of you to the hospital. Is she divorced now?"

"Yeah, for about a month now. My dad was her attorney. I wanted to give her space to heal, and I've been working on myself too. But with the two of us living together, we've grown really close. Have you ever met someone and just knew the moment you laid eyes on them that they were meant to be in your life? I've been gone for her since the day I met her."

Jax looks at me incredulously. "I have—you know I had that with Tae—but I never thought I'd see the day where playboy Carse settled down."

"Who are you calling a playboy? You're the one with the party boy, womanizer reputation, not me."

And he is. Ever since Jax and his high school sweetheart, Tae, broke up the week he had to leave for Harvard, he has made it his mission for everyone to see him as this party-hard fuck boy. Those of us that are close to him know the truth. He throws these over-the-top parties just hoping they'll go viral and it'll get back to his ex, who is currently on tour for her debut album opening for one of the most recognizable male country artists. I also happen to know that even though Jax is photographed flirting, dancing, and kissing women nonstop, he has an even bigger case of blue balls than I do. From what he told me when we got drunk on my twenty-first birthday, he hasn't been able to move on even after almost three years. Not just emotionally, but physically too.

"Guess we're just a bunch of lovestruck fools lusting after women who don't return our feelings," he murmurs as he punches his foot down on the gas pedal of the golf cart.

Jax thankfully drops the subject of my current predicament for the rest of the afternoon. We're grabbing a drink in the clubhouse after our round when Bennett takes a seat next to me at the bar. Griff and Jax went to look at the golf apparel in the store downstairs, so it's just the two of us.

"How's it going, Cap?" I ask him, knowing he hates being called that.

"You're such a little shit sometimes, *Rookie*."

"Tou-fucking-ché."

Shaking his head, he takes a long pull from his beer before setting it back on the bar and turning toward me. "You good, Carse?"

Avoiding eye contact with him, I stay facing ahead as I study the label of my own drink. "Of course. I'm always good."

Bennett nudges my shoulder, causing me to look up at him. "That would've worked on me a few weeks ago. But after witnessing you having a panic attack in our shared hotel room in Denver, I'm having a hard time believing that's the case. What's going on?"

My shoulders tense at his questioning, and I look away again. "I told you, it was just a lot of pressure playing in my first playoff series, especially with all of the media attention surrounding me after my concussion."

"You mean after the car accident you were in with Cadence?"

I snap my eyes back to him and find him shaking his head at me. "Carson, any one of us would be fucked in the head if that happened to us. It's even more understandable that you'd be affected after what happened to Katie and McKenna. But don't shut us out, man. The three of us are your brothers, we'll always be here for you."

Biting the inside of my cheek, I swallow past the lump forming in my throat. "You're right. We are brothers, and I don't want to shut you guys out. It's just I'm used to being the guy others can lean on, not the fragile guy whose most vulnerable moments get broadcast to the world."

Placing his hand on my shoulder, he gives it a squeeze. "Being vulnerable with us doesn't mean you're not also the guy that we lean on."

Nodding my head, I reply, "I know. But I think I'm on the right path. Dakota set me up with a therapist that I've been working with for a few weeks now. I've gained some coping mechanisms and strategies to help me process my feelings and work through the anxiety I'm feeling. I feel good about it and am making my mental health a priority."

That makes a genuine smile spread across his face, which is rare for Bennett Wilson. "I'm glad to hear it, buddy. I think that even though Dakota has clearly knocked you on your ass, she's good for you. How's the pursuit going?"

I smile at the mention of Dakota being good for me. "The pursuit is slow-going, but I'm a patient man who knows what he wants. And what I want is her. She's it for me, man. So whether I have to wait a few more weeks, months, or hell, even years, I'll gladly do it."

"Our little Carsey-baby is all grown up," Bennett mocks.

"Don't act like I didn't see the pursuit you were on last night, Benny," I jest right back, pointing my beer bottle at him. "If I recall right, you serenaded a certain redhead."

"I was two sheets to the wind last night. I can't be sure who I was singing to," he counters.

"Right, right, right. Cool. You definitely weren't enamored with . . . who was it that you dedicated the song to?" I pause, tapping my chin. "Oh, I remember. Little Red."

"You know what, the guys in the locker room were right. You can be a pesky little shit."

"Oh, fuck right off. So what's her name?"

He chuckles and shrugs. "She wouldn't tell me. That's why I had to call her Little Red."

"Ah, playing hard to get. Did you get her number after your beautiful rendition of 'Can't Take My Eyes Off You,' or did she leave you hanging?"

"Nah, she said if fate put us in the same place at the same time again, she'd give me her number. I'm not sure how she figured that'd happen, considering the only detail I know about her is that she was there for her best friend's twenty-first birthday, and she loves *10 Things I Hate About You*."

"At least she's got good taste in 90s rom-coms. Now the song choice makes more sense," I point out.

"Yeah, well, it's probably for the best. She seems like someone who could easily become a distraction, and we're not going to win the cup if our team captain is preoccupied."

"Wow, for a superstitious motherfucker, you sure went there about winning the cup," Griff quips as he and Jax each take a seat at the bar.

We shoot the shit, sharing our excitement for next season when the four of us will be back on the ice wearing the same jerseys for the first time in seven years. It's getting late by the time we make our way in the golf carts back to our cabins.

When we walk in the front door of my parents' place, I realize I've died and gone to heaven. My mouth waters as I breathe in the spices of what can only be my favorite meal.

"Holy shit, please tell me this isn't a dream. Did someone make chili?" I ask, my question echoing down the hall.

Mack slides off the bar stool she was perched on at the kitchen island and runs up to Griff. "I missed you, Hotshot. How'd you play?"

"Surprisingly well, considering your brother choked on the back nine," he wisecracks.

"Hello? Did anyone hear my question? Do I smell chili? God, it's like the two of you are getting married or something," I whine.

"You're awfully needy this evening, Golden Boy," I hear Dakota say from the kitchen.

My feet move to her of their own volition. When I round the corner that opens up into the kitchen, I halt so I can take in the sight of Dakota in a white tennis skirt that barely skims her mid-thigh, an emerald green racerback crop top, and one of those neon green transparent visors that those dogs smoking cigars while playing poker wear in that famous painting. She looks so fucking good.

And holy hell, she looks even better when she pinches a dash of salt over the large stock pot that has to have chili in it. I can't stop myself from standing behind her, wrapping my arms around her shoulders to bring her in for an embrace. "Did you make my favorite meal to try to get me to like you even more? Because if you did, it worked."

She sets the ladle she was using to stir the simmering chili down and brings her hands up to grasp my arms. "Actually, I made this a few weeks ago for Kenna and Cadence when y'all were in Colorado, and the bride-to-be asked me today if I'd make it again."

"So this has nothing to do with the fact that the other night when we were watching *Bridgerton* and you asked me what my favorite food is I immediately said chili and cornbread?" I question.

"It was at the request of the bride, my lord," she jests as she moves out of my embrace and slips on an oven mitt to take out the most scrumptious-looking cornbread I've ever seen from the double oven.

"How soon is too soon to drop to one knee, Austen?" I ask in disbelief.

"I'd say you should probably taste it before you commit to a lifetime with someone who might not even be able to make your favorite meal."

"What is it I'm tasting?" I waggle my eyebrows. "You should specify. I can think of a few things that could be my favorite meal."

Dakota grabs the dishrag from the counter beside her and whips my shoulder with it.

"Easy, easy!" I try to exclaim through my chuckles.

"You're hopeless," she mutters as she drops the towel onto the counter.

"Hopelessly devoted to you," I singsong with my arms wide open in reply.

"You should be more devoted to soaking up some of the alcohol that's clearly got you talking crazy, Golden Boy." She cuts a small piece of the cornbread and brings it up to my lips. "Here, have a taste," she suggests, her green eyes twinkling with mirth.

Fuck. Me. She looks so sexy when she's teasing me.

"A taste?" I ask in a daze.

"A taste," she repeats, still holding the cornbread in front of me. I lean down and eat the small piece in one bite. She begins to lower her hand, but I grasp my fingers around her wrist and bring them to my mouth. "You've got crumbs on your fingers. May I?"

Her breath hitches at my question. "Yes," she whispers breathlessly, her chest rising and falling more rapidly now.

I bring her pointer finger to my mouth and flick my tongue against the tip of it, lapping up every crumb before moving to her middle finger. When I take the tip of her thumb into my mouth and quickly flick my tongue against it, she lets out a soft whimper.

That noise alone just about does me in before Griff interrupts us, asking if everyone should dish up. The question breaks the tension like a cold bucket of water. Pulling her hand from my grasp, she brings both hands behind her back as if she's hiding the evidence of what just happened.

"Shit. I'm sorry. I didn't realize I was interrupting," Griff says sheepishly.

"No! You weren't," Dakota squeaks.

Knowing she's about to turn in on herself and not wanting to have this affect the rest of the night, I wrap my arm around her shoulder and give her three gentle squeezes. "Bon appétit, everyone! Dakota made her famous chili and cornbread. If you don't dish up now, I don't want to hear shit for eating the whole pot myself."

Dakota looks up at me, clasps my hand around her shoulder, and returns my three squeezes with three of her own. If only she knew what I was trying to convey to her each time I did that. One day I'll clue her in. For now, I'll keep trying to show her through each moment we spend together.

18

Carson

June

It's the twenty-first of June, and today is officially Mack and Griff's big day.

Clasping the cuff links they got me as a groomsman present, I look out over the lake from where I'm getting ready in the boathouse.

It's the perfect backdrop for the two of them to become husband and wife. This place holds so many special memories for them. Every summer when we were growing up, Griffin's family would join ours on our annual Fourth of July trip, where we'd head up here for two weeks of uninterrupted time together. No matter how old we got or how busy our schedules became with sports, our parents made it a priority to take those two weeks off.

Even after Griff's mom, Catherine, passed away from cancer when they were younger, his dad and my parents kept the tradition alive. The summer after our high school graduation was the first time we broke tradition and our parents didn't join us for the full two weeks. Then, after Katie passed away, the tradition was officially broken when Griff and his dad moved to Boston.

This year will be the first time since Katie passed that we're all back here together. Although, this year, we came up a few days early so we could get everything ready and have the groom's dinner.

"Hey, Carse, you just about ready? The photographer said it's almost time for your first look with Kenna," Griffin interrupts my moment of reflection.

Clearing the emotion in my throat, I turn to find him watching me. "Yeah, I've just got to get my jacket on." I move to the wall of windows where my jacket is draped across the writing desk I recently added to the space, hoping my little oasis could become a place of inspiration for Dakota's writing.

"Here, let me help," Griff says as he grabs the jacket from my hands. I slip my arms in the jacket and Griff smoothes the shoulders once I get it on. Turning to face him while I fasten the stop button of my black tux, I take a moment to soak in this moment with my best friend. Tears well in my eyes and I have to bite the inside of my cheek to stop my lip from quivering.

Griff hangs his head back and brings his hand to pinch the bridge of his nose. "Ah, fuck. Don't do this to me, Carse. You already know I'm going to be a goddamn puddle when I see Kenna."

"I can't fucking help it, G. You were like the brother I never had growing up. And today you officially become my brother for life," I choke on the sob that threatens to escape.

Shit, I'm way too emotional for this. How in the hell am I going to get through Mack walking down the aisle?

"You've always been my best friend, Carse. Even when I was figuring out how to handle my grief, you and Kenna were never not on my mind."

Griff pulls me in for a tight hug and we pat each other on the back, both trying not to lose it. When he pulls away, he gives my shoulder a squeeze. "McKenna and I wouldn't be here today if it weren't for you and Katie accepting our relationship in the first place. I'll never be able to repay you for being there for our girls when I couldn't be."

My chin quivers and I swipe the knuckle of my pointer finger beneath my eye as a traitorous tear slips free. "You'll never have to repay me for being there for the three of you. I've never been happier for my sister than I am today."

"Knock, knock. Carson, are you ready?" the photographer's assistant asks.

Blowing out a steadying breath, I nod my head and make my way down the steps and out to the gardens that Mack, Katie, Catherine, and my mom planted one of our first summers up here.

Once I'm standing beneath the archway in the corner of the garden, my chest fills with joy as I hear one of my favorite sounds. Cadence's giggles reach me before she comes running into view. I scoop her into my arms and spin her around, taking in the way her face lights up and her brown eyes twinkle in delight. Her blonde hair is just past her shoulders now and is pulled back with a pearly headband. She looks like a little princess in her white dress with pearls on it. "Look at you, Cadey Cat! You are so very beautiful!" I exclaim.

"Alright, I'm going to have the two of you turn around and then when McKenna is ready, we'll have her tap you on the shoulder and you can turn around," the photographer explains.

Turning around, I bounce Cadence in my arms, earning me more giggles. I rest her on my hip again as I hear the photographer giving Mack directions. I hear the fabric of her dress move against the grass as she makes her way closer to us. When she taps on my shoulder, I turn around, tears already filling my eyes again, and take in my twin sister looking stunning in her wedding dress.

"Holy shit, Mack. Griff is going to die on the spot when he sees you walking down the aisle. And Dad is going to weep like a baby." I turn to Cadence and tell her, "Look at your mama, Cadey Cat!"

"Mama so pwetty!" Cadence exclaims.

"Thank you, baby! Look at you—you're so beautiful, baby girl!" Mack tells her as her own eyes glisten with unshed tears.

The three of us pose for a few portraits together before I turn to Mack. "It's time to meet up with dad and walk down the aisle. Are you ready for this?"

She nods and dabs her eyes with a tissue she had wrapped around her bouquet. "How is he?" she asks. I don't need to ask her to clarify who the "he" is that she's referring to.

"Griff is fucking ecstatic to marry you so he can officially become my brother."

Mack rolls her eyes but lets out a soft chuckle. "I'm being serious. I know each new milestone he experiences without his mom and Katie here is hard for him. Hell, it's so hard for me too. But I know they're here today."

Shit. Just when I thought I had a handle on the tears.

Emotion clogs my throat, so I clear it before assuring her that he was good all morning when we were having breakfast and getting ready together.

Handing Mack off to my dad, I bring Cadence with me outside to where the rest of the wedding party is getting lined up. Griff is standing with his back to us with my mom's arm intertwined with his.

I place Cadence on her feet, and she immediately runs over and crashes her body against Griff's leg. "Daddy! Mama so pwetty," she tells him.

Griff lets go of my mom's arm and scoops Cadence into a big hug. "Oh my goodness, Little Ray. You look so pretty! I bet Mama looks like a princess if she looks as beautiful as you!"

Cadence nods her head and squeals in delight. "Mama a pwincess!"

I'm watching my mom begin to fawn over Cadence as someone hip checks me playfully. Out of my periphery, I can make out that it's

Dakota. If her short stature didn't make it obvious, her signature jasmine scent would be a dead giveaway.

"You sure clean up nice, Golden Boy," she remarks.

Turning to face her, my breath seizes and my heart stops in my chest as I take her in.

My dream girl looks bewitching in a lacy, black mid-length dress. The top looks like a corset and the skirt flows from her hips, making her look like a fucking goddess. Her hair is curled, falling just above her shoulder, and her caramel highlights shine beneath the sun's beams. Dakota's lips are painted a deep red, and the smoky eye shadow she did somehow makes her eyes even more mesmerizing.

She bites her lip to try to hide her amusement at what must be the awestruck look on my face. Standing on her tiptoes, Dakota reaches up to straighten my bowtie. When she's satisfied with her adjustments, she slides her hands down the lapels of my tux jacket. I don't hesitate to bring her into my arms for a hug.

"Austen," I breathe her in, letting out a low sigh of contentment. "You look divine—fucking ravishing."

"Thank you. You look quite debonair in your tux," she declares.

Swiping my thumb across the bare skin of her upper back, I thank her.

She steps back, grabs the side of her dress and gives me a deep curtsy. "I must take my seat, my lord. I'll see you after the ceremony."

She looks so fucking serene standing before me like this. But this just won't do. If either of us is to bow to the other, it will be me getting on my knees and bowing before her every fucking day.

When she rises to her feet, I tilt her chin up, and when her eyes find mine, my heart skips two beats one after the other. "Will you save a dance for me, my lady?"

Dakota licks her deep red lips and my eyes track the movement. "You may have them all." Tucking her hair behind her ear, I brush my thumb across her cheek.

With our gazes locked, I pull her in and place a lingering kiss on her forehead. When we pull away, she walks down the aisle to her seat, but not before pausing to look back at me over her shoulder. A shy smile spreads across her face, and it's like a slapshot straight to my heart.

I may have said that I hate to watch her go, but when it comes to watching her walk down an aisle, nothing has ever made me feel more euphoric.

Silverware clinking against glass rings out over the space in the backyard which has been transformed into a fairytale wedding venue. The A-frame paneling of the clear-top tent is strung with bulbed lights and chandeliers that, combined with the golden hour of the setting sun, gives Dakota an ethereal look to her as she sits beside Cadence at their table for dinner.

I don't take my eyes off her as I clap mindlessly at what I'm sure is Griff and Mack's tenth kiss since they sat down for dinner. I'm still staring in awe as Dakota throws her head back in laughter at something Cadey Cat said to my mom when the DJ walks over and hands me a microphone for my speech.

Shaking myself out of my haze, I clear my throat and chuckle. "That time already?" I ask.

Mack walks behind me and wraps me in a hug just as Griff gives my arm an assuring squeeze.

"You've got this, Carse," Mack whispers to me.

"Of course I do. I'm about to captivate the hell out of this room all while embarrassing the hell out of Griff," I tell her as I stand up and button my jacket before grabbing the mic.

"Good evening, everyone, and thank you for being here to celebrate Griffin and McKenna on their big day. For those of you who don't know me, I'm Mack's twin brother, Carson. I arrived two minutes earlier, which does, in fact, make me her older brother." I pause as guests chuckle and Mack rolls her eyes at my antics. Shooting her a quick wink, I continue, "But I'm not just the brother of the bride, I also happen to have the great honor of being the best man, because this guy right here decided to marry his best friend's sister." I place my hand on Griff's shoulder and give him a playful shove.

"Some of you might be wondering if that was weird for me, or if I ever got upset with him. The short answer to that would be: no. The longer answer is that I have a lot of feelings about the two of them being together. I have feelings of vindication that lead me to feel bittersweet all at the same time. You see, I, along with I'm sure many of you, knew that Mack was obsessed with Griff for a very long time before Griff eventually got a clue." That earns me a chuckle from Griff.

"I also had a years-long bet going with Griff's little sister, Katie, or Kitty as I liked to call her. Kitty and I both knew for years that our siblings had crushes on our best friends, and we made a bet as to which would crack first, and another side-bet to see when it would happen. I thought they'd cave earlier and become high school sweethearts. Katie bet otherwise, and of course won. When did we make this bet, you ask? Let me set the scene for you in a way that Kitty would be proud of," I say as I move to pick up a remote control clicker from beside my place setting and aim it at the projector screen in the front corner of the tent where a picture of me, Katie, Mack, and Griff in our pre-teen phase lights up the screen.

"It was the summer of 2012 when nine-year-old Katie and Mack were in our basement watching their favorite movie for the hundredth time. Meanwhile, an eleven-year-old Griff was playing an intense game of knee hockey with me. Just a typical day in the Wilder household, until Katie and Mack begged us to act out a scene from their favorite movie with them. Now, Griff and I were pretty great brothers growing up, we didn't get annoyed by our sisters very often, but this time crossed a line for me."

I click to the next slide where a movie poster for *Hannah Montana: The Movie* takes up the screen. "*This* was their favorite movie, and the particular scene they wanted to act out was the 'Hoedown Throwdown' dance. I didn't want to be embarrassed in front of my teammate and best friend, so I refused to do the dance. At least, I did until Griff walked over and picked up a sequined scarf and wrapped it around his neck and told the girls he was only doing it once and they better make it quick. I was stunned. The cool-as-hell guy I idolized was willing to do a dance just because his little sister asked nicely. And he didn't just go through the motions—nothing Griff does is half-ass, especially when it came to making Katie smile."

My voice cracks and I take a deep, quivering breath just as Mack uses her dinner napkin to dab at her eyes. She gives Griff a watery smile, and he wraps his arm around her, rubbing his hand up and down her own.

"Naturally, Griff gave it his all and got into the dance. I mean *really* into it. But I don't feel like my words can really do it justice, so I thought I'd show you instead," I say as I press play on the next slide where a grainy video of the four of us is displayed.

"Oh my god. I'm going to kill your brother," Griff murmurs as he hides his face in Mack's neck. Mack's face lights up as she takes in the video. While it isn't the greatest quality, you can clearly see me and

Griff wearing sequined scarves and cowgirl hats that barely fit on our heads as we stand beside our sisters and reenact the ridiculous dance.

The guests laugh as they take in the video clip that ends with Griff spinning Mack into his arms and dipping her low. I pause the video and turn to them. "Let's hope your first dance tonight goes a lot better than this one did," I explain, pressing play on the video where Griff drops Mack onto her back mid-dip.

The guests erupt with laughter, and when I can finally catch my breath between the laughs, I go to stand behind the two of them.

"In all seriousness, I learned a lot about Griff that day. I learned that suddenly his cheeks turned pink any time Mack talked to him. I learned that he couldn't dance for shit. And I learned that he would do just about anything for not only his little sister, but mine too. Suddenly, the list of reasons why I idolized him grew from beyond just hockey."

I sniff and quickly swipe my thumb under my eyes. "Griff is a protective, loving, and caring guy, and I promised myself that if one day he and my sister finally realized their feelings were mutual, I'd never be someone to stand in the way of their relationship. Today was predestined."

My voice cracks again, and I swallow past the lump in my throat. "The kind of love Griff and Mack share is once-in-a-lifetime—it's a love written in the stars. But I think even if you two didn't find your way back to each other, Katie and Catherine would've intervened—I mean, who's to say they didn't?"

I take a deep, steadying breath as I stare down at the two of them as they stare at each other with stars in their eyes.

"And while their love is unlike any other, so is the bond the four of us shared growing up. I'm fucking ecstatic to officially be able to call Griffin my big bro. And I know with everything in my heart that Kitty is here with us today."

Reaching around Griff, I grab my glass of champagne.

"I ask on behalf of the maid of honor, who is joining us from above, that you raise your glasses to the happy couple. Let's have a great night of dancing and celebrating love. Cheers to the beginning of your forever, I love you both," I tell them as I raise my glass in the air.

I've barely set my glass down on the table with the mic when Mack throws her arms around me in a tight hug. "I love you so much, Carse. Thank you for being the best brother and uncle in the world."

Backing out of her arms, I look at Griff and say, "I learned from the best." Griff pulls me into a hug that has both of our shoulders shaking with emotion.

"I love you, brother," he tells me, and fuck if that doesn't put the biggest smile on my face.

"I love you too, you two-left-footed fool. Let's hope you took some dance lessons in the last two months," I tease.

Dakota

There wasn't a dry eye during Griffin and McKenna's touching ceremony. It was perfect from the thoughtful ways they memorialized Katie and Griff's mom, Catherine, to the adorable way Griff couldn't help but steal a kiss before Bennett, who officiated the ceremony, told them to kiss, to the meaningful vows they wrote and exchanged.

I couldn't keep count of how many times my gaze strayed to Carson. He was holding on to Cadence for the majority of the ceremony until she wanted to be put down and raced over to sit between me and her gaga Liz. The next time my eyes wandered toward him, he was already staring at me. The wink he shot my way made my stomach swirl in anticipation.

I'm snapped out of the haze I was in when the guests cheer and whistle as Griff successfully dips Kenna and kisses her during their first dance.

Jackson is up on the stage singing Restless Road's "Growing Old With You" while Bennett plays guitar and harmonizes with him.

The whole scene playing out in front of me is straight out of a fairytale love story. And that includes watching Carson dance with Cadence in his arms off to the side of the dancefloor where I can tell he's choking back his emotions.

Kenna's blinding smile makes my chest tighten, but it's the single tear that drops down Griff's face that cracks my chest wide open. Maybe being a recent divorcée should make me cynical when it comes to love and marriage, but the two of them prove that true love can persevere even in the darkest storms. The love reflecting in their eyes is so different from the feelings I felt on my own wedding day with Aaron.

Griffin loves and cherishes McKenna in a way that every girl dreams to experience one day. And he better, or I'm sure Carson would never stand for it. My chest aches at that thought—knowing Brody would never have stood for what Aaron did to me either. I want to come clean to him and tell him what happened, but I don't know where to start. Of course Brodes and my mom know I'm divorced, but they have no idea about the abuse or my hospitalization. I'm worried that when he finds out I hid it from him for so long that he'll be hurt I didn't tell him right away.

Jackson and Bennett sing the last line of the song, and as the music begins to fade, Griff picks Kenna up and twirls her around in his arms as she tosses her head back in joyful laughter.

Walking over to the bar, I spot Bennett getting a refill.

"Whiskey, neat, please," he tells the bartender who then looks at me, waiting for my order.

"Oh, um, I'll have a tequila sour, please."

Unsure of what to do, I ask, "Who knew the karaoke night wasn't a one-off?"

Bennett turns toward me, quirking a skeptical brow.

"Good job up there. I didn't know you could play the guitar." I'm trying to make polite conversation, but something tells me he isn't the kind of guy to make light conversation with an essential stranger.

"Thanks," he murmurs.

Right. So not a fan of small talk.

"Hey, Benny. Isn't that the girl you were drooling over at Griff's bachelor party?" Carson asks, thankfully saving me from this awkward moment.

I look to where Carson is nodding across the other side of the bar and notice a woman standing with her back to me. Her long, auburn hair flows to the middle of her back, just above the hem of her backless navy dress.

Bennett's head whips around surprisingly fast to where Carson is pointing. I watch with rapt attention as the girl turns around, and Bennett's mouth hangs open when he recognizes her.

"How is she here right now? I mean, only family, close friends, and teammates were invited. Does McKenna know her? She has to, right? I mean, why else would she be here?" Bennett rattles off.

Carson shrugs. "I don't know. Maybe she lives on this lake, and that's why she was at the bar that night, and now she's . . . I don't know, wedding crashing or something? I have a good idea—why don't you go ask her?"

Bennett shoots an unamused glare at Carson. "Funny."

"Well, if you're not going to shoot your shot, I'm going to at least shoot mine," Carson says, and my stomach sinks at the thought of him approaching her.

Instead, to my surprise, Carson turns toward me with an outstretched hand and asks, "May I have the honor of this dance, my lady?"

My chest warms and heat floods my cheeks in both relief and embarrassment for being jealous when I have nothing to be jealous of. The way Carson is looking at me—with a twinkle in his eyes as if I were the beginning and end of his whole world—should give me all the reassurance I need. He likes *me*. He wants to pursue *me*. And I'm getting so tired of coming up with reasons why we wouldn't work, why this shouldn't happen.

So, I decide to take a step toward him, willing myself to explore what it might be like to be the woman Carson Wilder spins around the dance floor. When I place my hand in his, the smile that eclipses his face is otherworldly.

We've just gotten out on the dance floor as a song the DJ was playing comes to an end. Instead of playing another, he announces that there was a special request. Jackson takes the stage again, this time picking up the guitar Bennett was playing earlier. He sits on a barstool and lowers the mic before strumming a few chords on the guitar. A moment later, I recognize the opening chords of Morgan Wallen's new version of "Spin You Around."

"I love this song," I tell Carson as he pulls me into his embrace. Resting my head against his chest, I listen to his racing heart for a moment before admitting, "Everytime I hear it, it makes me want to dance in the kitchen with you."

This little bit of vulnerability is more than I've shown him when it comes to returning any sort of feelings for him. Too nervous to peek at his face, I keep my head where it is. That is, until I feel the deep rumble of his laughter. Looking up, I find Carson peering down at me with a bewildered expression.

"What are you laughing at?" I demand.

He shakes his head. "Nothing. Well, no, that's not true. It's you. I'm laughing at the fact that we've lived together for over five months, almost the exact timeline of when this song came out. And we've cooked together in the kitchen—"

I cut him off, "Correction, I cook in the kitchen, and you stand there and look pretty."

His eyes glimmer in amusement before he continues, "I've been in the kitchen with you while you've cooked more times than I can count, and not once have you ever mentioned wanting to dance with me."

Feeling bashful, I try to look away but Carson guides my face to look back at his with his hand beneath my jaw.

"Don't shy away from me, Austin. Not when I feel like you're finally letting me in."

My pulse hammers against his hand as he holds my stare. I could lose my head in the enchantment that is Carson's turquoise eyes.

The way he stares at me as if I'm the only person he sees sends a thrill down my spine, it's intoxicating.

Wetting my lips, I watch him shake his head again at me.

"Don't do that," he softly pleads.

"Do what?" I ask because I genuinely don't know what I did.

"Don't make me want to go against every rule I set for myself," he replies.

Carson must see the question on my face because he clarifies, "I'm not kissing you tonight. Not like this, not until you're ready. Because once I kiss you, Austin, I know I'll never be able to let you go. There's not a chance in hell once I've tasted your sweet lips that I'll ever be able to go back to pretending I'm okay with being just your friend. It won't be enough at that point."

Why do I have the inclination that it isn't enough now? For either of us.

"So I'm going to be a good boy and pivot this conversation to something I've been dying to know."

I let out a long sigh. "And what would that be?" I ask.

"What inspired you to write your book?"

His question catches me off guard, so much so I find myself blurting out, "You." I purse my lips together, cursing myself for admitting that out loud.

"How so?" he counters, his brows lifting in surprise.

"I should actually thank you for inspiring me."

"Me?" he asks incredulously.

Nodding my head, I reply, "Yeah. It'll probably sound silly to you, but watching you live out your dream and coming alive out on the ice made me really question what I'm passionate about enough to bring me that much joy day in and day out." I pause, wondering how much I want to divulge. Deciding to go for it, I explain, "The more I thought about it, the answer always stayed the same. Writing. Storytelling. Crafting something that is completely my own."

Carson pulls me into a tight hug, resting his chin on top of my head.

"Tell me more about your book. I want to know everything you've got planned so far," he implores.

So I do. I tell him how the male main character gets assigned a new assistant, who happens to be the female main character. The unexpected change upsets the MMC because he was close to his former assistant until she decided to retire so she could spend more time with her grandbabies. I tell him he doesn't realize the new assistant is his life-long rival's daughter, who was born when he was only in high school due to an accidental pregnancy.

When Carson asks more about the setting, I tell him it takes place in the MMC's off-season and he finds out he has to fly to Italy for some endorsement deals and photoshoots. The kicker is, his former assistant was supposed to go with him. But now this new, younger assistant, who he finds himself far too attracted to, has to go with him instead.

"This sounds awesome. What part of Italy are they going to?"

"Well, you see. That's the thing. I'm still debating if they just stay in Milan the entire time, or if they decide to extend their trip and go to all of the places I've only dreamed of going."

"Only dreamed of going?" he questions.

"Well, yeah. I mean, I haven't been there, but I've always dreamed of going. Who knows, maybe if this book is a success, I'll be able to go there one day."

"Wait, hold on. Are you telling me you've never been to Italy?" He pulls his head back to look at me.

Pursing my lips, I roll my eyes at him. "Look, just because I haven't been to Italy doesn't mean I can't write a book that takes place there."

He snorts. "Duh, I know that. J.K. Rowling wrote a whole series that takes place at Hogwarts without ever having been there."

I can't help but throw my head back laughing at how adorable he is with his random references to Taylor Swift and *Harry Potter*. "You're right. But J.K. Rowling wrote a fictitious fantasy series. Not a contemporary romance novel."

That earns me a scoff. "Rude. *Harry Potter* is magical realism, not fantasy."

"That's beside the point," I gripe. "I'm perfectly capable of doing enough research to do my novel justice without having been there."

Carson nods his head eagerly. "And I don't doubt your capabilities at all. But why would you do that when you literally know and live with someone who is going to Italy in two and a half weeks?"

Now it's my turn to scoff. "I am not inviting myself to join the three of you in Italy."

Completely ignoring me, he adds, "As long as I keep up my workout regimen, I can be gone for probably four to six weeks."

"Weeks?" I squeak. "Don't you mean days?"

"I said what I said, Austin. Weeks. You're going to need a few weeks immersed in the culture to get a better understanding of the culture for your book, right?"

"Carson, that's too much. I can't—we can't. What about Cadence and McKenna? I'm supposed to watch Cadence while the three of you are gone."

"They have Griff now, and it's his off-season too. They're fully moved into their new house. If they need someone to fill in for you, my mom would be ecstatic to watch Cadence. She'll love the extended snuggle session with her granddaughter."

Shaking my head, I say, "I don't want to impose. It'll practically be their honeymoon."

That makes him rear his head back. "And you think I want to be a third-wheel on my sister's honeymoon? Come on, you'll be doing me a favor. They're going to be in the literal honeymoon phase, and if you don't go I'll be the pathetic single brother tagging along."

"I couldn't afford it."

"You wouldn't have to. Griff already purchased a fourth ticket to the concert. And I'll cover everything else."

"He purchased that ticket for Katie. Not for his daughter's nanny to tag along, *uninvited*, might I add."

"I'm not sure how you can say you're tagging along. I invited you. Hell, I'm begging you to come with us at this point. Do you have a current passport?"

"Yes."

"Good. Then it's settled."

I practically growl at the man as I ask, "What is settled?"

"You and I are going to Italy together for the next month. I'll have everything covered. I will ensure you're immersed into the culture for your book, along with providing you the eye candy and male main character inspiration you need." He winks at me, but I glare back, unamused as he continues, "And you will eat, pray, love the shit out of Italy every day before typing your fingers to the bone each night. This is going to be great, Austin. I can feel it."

What he needs to feel is my knee to his groin. Maybe that will snap him out of his delusional spiral. "Listen to me very closely, okay? I'm. Not. Going."

19

Dakota

This country girl has never flown halfway across the world. I'd been to Mexico a few times growing up. We even took a family vacation to Canada a few years ago. But the farthest I've ever gone over an ocean was when I went to the Bahamas for my honeymoon with Aaron. We both got food poisoning, and it honestly was probably one of many ominous signs of how our marriage would be.

I did fine with our flight from Minneapolis to New York City, where we had a long enough layover that Griffin was able to arrange for a few of his friends and former Boston teammates to fly into the city to meet us. His friends Maksim, Nicolai, and Emmett flew down on a private jet, as if it were no big deal to fly into a city to catch up over lunch with their former roommate for four hours.

But as soon as our flight from New York City to Milan took off over the Atlantic, I became riddled with anxiety.

Carson somehow was able to get us seats next to each other, even with adding me to the trip last minute. I tried to protest the first class ticket he insisted on purchasing, but my efforts fell on deaf ears.

When he notices my hands white-knuckling the arm rests, he places a hand on top of mine and rubs his thumb slowly over each of my knuckles. Squeezing my eyes shut, I try not to look out the window to where the vast ocean threatens to swallow us whole.

The moment the seatbelt light turns off, Carson unbuckles his before doing the same to mine.

"Here, why don't we switch," he suggests.

Peeking my one eye open, I see his face is etched with concern. "What? No. You've got long legs—you're a giant compared to me—you need the aisle seat," I tell him.

"Austin, I don't need the aisle seat. I actually wouldn't mind taking the window seat so I have something to lean against. Come on, let's switch." He stands up and gestures for me to follow him into the aisle so he can switch seats with me.

I do, and as soon as I sit back down, Carson scoops up my legs and places my feet in his lap. The feel of his warm palm resting against my bare ankle fills my stomach with warmth, and when the rough pads of his fingers begin tracing circles on my calf, goosebumps erupt on the spot, sending a chill up my spine.

I've never experienced such immediate relief from another's touch. Sure, a long hug from my mama growing up would calm me. But it's as if Carson's touch is my own personal elixir.

"Hey, I downloaded some of the classics onto my iPad. Do you want to watch a few movies together to take your mind off things?" he asks.

I simply nod in response.

When he queues up *Twilight*, my eyes shoot to him. With my brows still furrowed in confusion, I ask, "I thought you said you downloaded the classics?"

Scoffing, he clarifies, "I did. Edward and Bella's love story is a classic."

"You're absurd," I inform him.

We watch the first three movies in the saga, and after the third we decide to take a nap for the remainder of the flight. That way we can watch the last two on the flight home.

I'm woken up by the flight attendant tapping me on the shoulder asking me to return my seat upright and fasten my seatbelt as we prepare for landing. Unsure of when it happened, I find I'm currently burrowed under Carson's arm, my head against the hard plane of his chest while he rests his head on his sweatshirt he's using as a makeshift pillow against the plane's window.

I begin to shift in his arms, which wakes him from what looked to be a peaceful slumber.

"Morning, Austin," he rasps, his voice still gravelly with sleep.

"Good morning?" I question, reaching over him to open the window's shade. Once it's open, I gasp as the first lights of dawn shine behind Carson's head, giving his golden hair an angelic glow.

Assuming I'm gasping at the scenery below, Carson shifts to take a look. I shoot out of his hold and begin to do as the flight attendant instructed, needing a moment to find my bearings.

I've heard you learn a lot about someone when you travel with them, and after two flights together, I would say that is accurate. For instance, I learned that even though we will be here for just shy of a month, Carson only brought a brown leather duffel carry-on, a backpack, and a special checked bag that holds two hockey sticks and his hockey gloves.

When I questioned him on the latter, he just shrugged and said it was part of his workout regimen he couldn't stray from.

Griff and Kenna, on the other hand, shared a checked bag that they packed in together, and then they each packed their own carry-on bags.

I feel . . . slightly self conscious at the amount of baggage that I brought on the trip. With two large checked bags, a carry-on that I could barely get to zip, and my oversized purse, I take the cake on overpacking. But in my defense, my carry on includes my laptop, two cameras I brought to capture aesthetic photos and video content, as well as a few lenses.

When Carson saw me packing up my equipment, he said he hadn't realized I liked photography. Growing up it was a hobby I was passionate about. I worked for our school newspaper as both a photographer and a journalist, as well as led the yearbook committee.

We've just grabbed our luggage and are at the rental car pickup. Both Griff and Carson chose to get luxury vehicles, so we're waiting on the sidewalk for the valet to bring the cars around. When a sleek black Range Rover pulls up to the curb, I roll my eyes at Carson and begin to wheel my luggage toward the back of the vehicle just as Griff says, "That's us." He guides his and Kenna's luggage to the rear of the vehicle.

"G, do you think we could fit some of our luggage in yours?" Carson asks.

Confusion knits my brow. I know I overpacked, but even if we got a standard size sedan, we can put some of the luggage in the back seat. My confusion wanes as another valet pulls up a gunmetal gray two-passenger convertible Ferrari.

"Carson—" I start but am cut off.

"Come on, Austin. Let me live out my fantasy of driving down the coast of Italy in the world's sexiest sports car with the world's most beautiful woman in the passenger seat."

"How in the heck are we supposed to fit all of our luggage in there once Griff and Kenna go back to the states?"

He doesn't even hesitate to answer. "I've arranged for a concierge service to transfer our luggage to each of the places we're staying for us. We'll each keep a carry on with us in the trunk while we're driving to each location, but they'll handle the rest."

With my hand on my hip, I say, "That sounds very expensive."

He shakes his head in disagreement. "I think you meant to say it sounds like I planned accordingly, and you can't wait to explore Italy with such a well-traveled man."

Taking a deep breath, I close my eyes and try not to let my own insecurities ruin this outrageously kind gesture of his. For almost the entire two weeks we were at his family's cabin over the Fourth of July, Carson was meticulously planning this trip. He would ask for my input for things I wanted to do or places I wanted to see, but he wouldn't let me lift a finger when it came to coordinating the logistics of our vacation. It's the caretaker in him, and I know it's the way he shows he cares, but I never want him to feel like I'm taking advantage of his generosity.

"I'm putting my foot down when it comes to the car. I've dreamed of driving a Ferrari Portofino M, but have never had the opportunity. This is my chance," Carson explains.

"Alright, alright. Who am I to stand in the way of your fantasy?" I playfully tease.

Carson's eyes seem to darken as he brushes his hand against the light scruff of his jaw. "Don't tease me, Austin. You have no idea how many fantasies of mine you star in," he rasps.

Leaving me there with my jaw hanging open, and a dumbstruck look on my face, Carson saunters over to the valet and hands him a tip as he grabs the keys.

Sitting against the hood of the Ferrari, he twirls the keys on his finger. "Your chariot awaits, my lady." He punctates that statement with a flirtatious wink.

I'm so incredibly screwed when it comes to trying to resist his charms.

Especially so, because when we check into the hotel, we're informed that the booking was only for two rooms. Not a big deal, considering Carson and I have lived together, so sharing a room shouldn't be too much different, right? Wrong. Each of the two rooms only has one bed. One. Singular. Bed. Oh, but we can just get a cot, right? Wrong again. No cots are available at this lovely five-star establishment.

Kenna turns to me, worry etched across her face. "Oh my gosh, I'm so sorry Dakota. I didn't realize I booked both rooms for only one bed. Do you want to have Griff and Carson room together and you and I can share a room?"

"Absolutely not," Griff blurts at the same time as I say, "That is not happening."

Kenna raises a brow at Griff, and he shrugs in response. "We're on our honeymoon, Sunshine. Can you blame me for wanting to share a bed with *my wife?*"

The possessive way he emphasizes her new title has Kenna melting in the palm of his hand.

Carson cuts in before Kenna can try to suggest any other arrangements, "Dakota and I shared a bed when we were at your bachelorette weekend." He slings an arm over my shoulder, and peers down at me. "This won't be any different, right?" he asks.

I clear my throat and will my jittery nerves to settle. "No, not at all," I lie, because this will be completely different. We're not at his parents' lake cabin, we're in one of the most romantic countries in the world on a once-in-a-lifetime vacation. And we were both drunk the night we accidentally fell asleep together. Now I'm going to be in my own head about whether I packed appropriate pajamas, if the smell of my shampoo is too strong, or if I hog too much of the bed. Clearly he likes to cuddle based on the position we woke up in that next morning. "Besides, they already took our luggage up to our rooms."

Carson grabs the key from Kenna's hand and, without another word, guides me toward the stairs, placing his hand on the small of my back.

His touch makes my nerves feel like they're frayed at the ends and about to ignite, sending small shockwaves down my body—I feel my will slipping with each step we take toward our room.

Kenna and Griff are in their own little world, completely wrapped up in each other as we explore and walk across the stone-paved square in front of Duomo di Milano. I learned a new term today: piazza, the Italian word for an open square in a city. So technically, we're exploring Piazza Duomo today.

The Duomo di Milano is a grandiose gothic cathedral in the heart of Milan. Stopping in the middle of the *piazza*, I stare up at a statue of a man riding a horse.

"Oh, I looked this one up. This is the Statua di Vittorio Emanuele II; he was the first king of a united Italy," Carson explains.

Turning my gaze from the statue to Carson, I'm struck with a sight even more picturesque than the historic structures surrounding us. He has my film camera strapped around his neck and he's wearing black Ray-Ban clubmaster sunglasses. I'm mesmerized watching the sinew of his forearms work as he rolls the sleeves of his long-sleeve white linen shirt. The top few buttons remain undone, and the peek of his gold chain against his tanned chest is enough to make me spontaneously combust. He completes the look with a pair of tan linen shorts and crisp white fashion sneakers.

He looks like he walked straight off the pages of a menswear magazine.

Lowering his shades so his blue eyes can stare into mine, he softly chuckles. "You should probably quit being so obvious about your ogling if you don't want to give me a big head, Austin."

Shaking my head, I start to walk toward the cathedral.

I halt my steps when Carson calls out, "Stop!" Turning around, I see he has lifted his sunglasses on top of his head and has my camera poised in his hands, pointing straight at me.

"Can I take a photo of you in front of the cathedral?" he asks.

"Oh, I don't really know how to be in front of the camera. I'm used to being behind it," I stammer, feeling awkward.

"Just look at me and smile, Dream Girl," he instructs.

And as soon as the term of endearment leaves his lips, a smile spreads across my face and warmth floods my chest. I hear the click and shutter of the camera, knowing he probably captured me looking like a lustful fool.

"*Perfezione*," he says, his accent scarily good.

Narrowing my eyes in suspicion, I ask, "Did you take some sort of crash course on how to speak Italian?"

"Nah, I've got a Rosetta Stone membership. I've been doing Italian lessons since Christmas when Griff got the tickets. I try to do a lesson on the way to each away game on the plane rides," he explains, placing his sunglasses back over his eyes.

"Tell me something else," I urge.

"*Mi sto innamorando di una bellissima donna*," he recites.

Before I can ask what that means, a couple standing next to us claps and cheers at us.

"*Bacio, bacio!*" they exclaim.

Carson's face lights up with an electrifying smile. "Should we give the people what they want?" he asks me as he hands the camera to the couple and asks them something I can't understand.

Confused, and clearly unsure of what I'm getting myself into, I shrug my shoulders in response.

"Come here," he requests, holding his hand out for me.

The moment I place my hand in his, he tightens his grasp on mine and spins me into his arms before dipping me so low I'd think he was going to drop me if it wasn't for his firm hold on my back and across my waist.

"Woah," I mutter breathlessly.

Carson leans in, his lips an inch from mine, and it's as if time stands still in this moment. He gazes longingly into my eyes as my ragged exhales hang between us. My heart lurches in my chest as he closes his eyes, angling his head to press the lightest whisper of a kiss against my cheek.

When he pulls me up, he has to steady my hips to keep me from swaying.

"Are you good, Austin?" he questions.

I nod in confirmation, because what the hell are words right now?

Clasping my hand in his, he thanks the couple as they hand my camera back to him. "Come on," he nods toward the cathedral. "I hear the view from the rooftop is to die for."

As we make our way up to the rooftop of the Duomo di Milano, Carson shares more facts about the breathtaking cathedral. He stops us along the way to capture photos of some of the sculptures and architecture.

"Hopefully at least some of these turn out okay so you can use them for inspiration while you're writing."

"That's a good idea, I didn't think of that. Thanks," I mutter, still feeling off-kilter from earlier. For a moment, I thought he was going to kiss me. And I can't help but wish he would've.

When we get to the rooftop, I gasp at the panoramic view before us.

"Aren't the architectural details stunning?" Carson gapes.

"This is unlike anything I've ever seen," I admit, taking in the beautiful city of Milan before us.

"Have I ever told you I was a history major in college?" he asks.

"No, I didn't know that. It makes sense why you're so good with dates and rattling off fun facts though."

"I don't think I would've done anything with my degree had I finished college; I was more so picking a subject that interested me."

"What would you do if you weren't a professional hockey player?"

"I'd be a pro golfer."

I snort. "Well, I've yet to receive my golf lessons, so you still owe me."

"I remember." He chews the inside of his cheek, before continuing, "Is it ridiculous of me to say that if I weren't a professional hockey player, I think I'd want to be a youth coach, or maybe run a camp some day?"

Vulnerability bleeds through his question.

"Not at all," I assure him.

"I wouldn't have a fancy degree or a profound profession, but I know it would fill me with joy to watch kids have the opportunity to play and advance in the sport they love."

"That sounds amazing, Carson."

"I've been playing around with the idea of approaching Griff and Mack to open a youth camp by where our parents' cabin is. My thought is that we could open a summer camp for hockey, volleyball, and maybe even golf. The kids would not only get to further develop their skills on the ice, court, or course, but they'd also get to do fun summer activities out on the water while meeting new friends."

I'm stunned speechless at the thought he has put into this.

Carson does the thing where he claps his hands in front of him and hangs his head. "You know what, I've barely thought it through, I'd probably be in way over my head. And Mack is already so busy with volleyball and finishing school, she probably would think I'm crazy for even suggesting it."

Placing my hands on his, I stop his nervous fidgeting. "Carson, stop doubting yourself. I think it's an incredible idea. It honestly sounds like a place I wish I could've gone growing up."

He lifts his head, hope shining in his eyes. "Yeah? You don't think I'm crazy?"

I let out a soft chuckle. "I wouldn't go that far. But your idea is definitely not crazy," I jest.

Carson scoops me into a hug before tickling my ribs and making me squeal like an idiot. I'm sure people are looking at us as if we're insane, but I honestly couldn't care less. Because on a rooftop in one of the most romantic countries in the world, I just realized that I'm irrefutably falling for my golden boy.

Once we finished touring the cathedral, we went shopping at Galleria Vittorio Emanuele II, one of the world's oldest and most iconic shopping centers. The roof is stunning, made of glass and iron, and the mosaic floors lead us to some of the most esteemed fashion and jewelry brands. We walk in and out of the shops for Cartier, Gucci, Prada, and Louis Vuitton.

I was just forced to try on a dress in the Versace store that I could never afford. I'll never admit it out loud, but the corseted black midi dress fits me better than any dress ever has, especially considering my petite frame. But the fact that Kenna and Carson are currently fighting over who is going to buy the dress for me has me putting my foot down. "Please do not buy that dress for me. I don't need it. And if you didn't remember, I have plenty of dresses in the two suitcases I packed."

Kenna's shoulders sink in defeat. "Ugh, fine. But for what it's worth, you looked gorgeous in that dress."

"She always looks gorgeous, no matter what she's wearing," Carson clarifies and then turns to me. "I'm sorry, Austin. It wasn't my intention to upset you, I just wanted to spoil you a little."

"Why don't you spoil me with some gelato instead? We passed a shop down the street," I suggest.

"It's your funeral," Carson replies with a devilish glint in his eyes. I narrow my eyes, confused at his remark.

The confusion is quickly cleared up the moment I watch him glide his tongue, far slower than is necessary by the way, along the edge of his cone of gelato. When he changes up the pace of his tongue strokes to lap up the melting gelato, I can't stop myself from groaning. "Oh, come on. That's completely unnecessary," I remark.

"First cornbread, now gelato?" He tsks, shaking his head at me. "I'm beginning to think you have a food fetish, Austin."

I'm beginning to realize I just have a fetish for anything and everything to do with Carson Wilder.

20

Carson

JULY

G riff and I just finished an intense evening workout in the hotel's gym, and nothing sounds better right now than a scalding hot shower.

I'm just about to tap my keycard to open the door when I hear a noise from inside the room that makes my step falter.

"Yes!" I hear Dakota moan.

"Carson, please!"

Did she just—did she just say my name? While she's . . .

"Fuck! Carson, yes! Don't stop!"

Holy fucking shit. She did. My hands tremble with need. I tell myself the right thing to do is walk away, yet my feet remain frozen to the spot.

"Oh, gimme a break!" Dakota growls.

That is one of the oddest things I've heard a woman say while climaxing. However, she sounds more frustrated than anything.

I swipe my keycard over the lock on the door. "Are you still awake, Austen?" I whisper as I cautiously enter the room.

There is a rustling of her sheets, followed by a drawer slamming shut. "Yep, wide awake," she huffs.

"And about as happy as a hornet. What's wrong?" I ask, but once I take her in under the glow of the lamplight, I can see it written all over her face—hell, I can feel the frustration coming off of her in waves.

"Nothing." She crosses her arms, making her sleep tank slide down to expose her supple breasts.

I can't help but take my fill of her as she stands from the bed. She's in a matching white cotton sleep set, and I can tell she's braless from the way the hard buds of her nipples are beckoning me. I'm a boob guy. Sue me. I have zero shame as my gaze remains fixated on her chest. "Yeah, I'm not buying it. I have a sister, remember? I know better than to fall for the 'nothing' response," I say, using air quotes for emphasis.

"Eyes up here, Mr. Wilder," she teases.

Snapping my eyes up to meet hers, I don't miss the seductive smirk on her lips or the playful glint in her eyes.

"What. Is. Wrong?" I grind out the question.

"Now you sound like the one who can't get off," she says, clearly regretting letting me in on that tidbit because her hands fly up to cover her mouth.

"Can't get off?"

She throws her head back, groaning, and not in the way I'd like her to. "Ugh, couldn't you just be a gentleman and act like you didn't hear me say that?"

"I told you, I'm no Southern gentleman. Why can't you get off? Did I interrupt?"

"No, it wasn't that. I don't even know why I'm standing here having this conversation with you," she bites out.

Holding my hands up in surrender, I say, "Alright, my bad. I'm pretty sore from my workout and all the travel, so I'm going to take a quick shower. Do you need anything from the bathroom before I head in there?"

She shakes her head. "No, I already got ready for bed. Thanks though."

I nod in response and grab a pair of clean shorts from the dresser to change into after my shower. I'm just about to shut the bathroom door behind me when Dakota calls out, "Shoot, wait."

Figuring she forgot something, I step out of the bathroom.

"I'm sorry for making things weird by . . . you know. Anyway, I'm also sorry for snapping at you. It's not your fault I'm broken."

"Broken?" I question in disbelief.

"Yes, but that's beside the point. Can I make it up to you?" She bites her bottom lip as she awaits my response.

"What did you have in mind?" The question comes out deeper, raspier.

"What about a massage?" she asks, looking happy with herself for suggesting it.

Hmm, I'm not sure. Let me think about that. *Would I like her to give me a massage? Would I like her hands on me? Yes, a thousand times, yes.* But I can't show her how excited that makes me. In fact, I should probably get in the shower as quickly as possible.

"Sure. That would be fine." I aim for nonchalance, but I know I have a terrible poker face.

After quickly showering and taking care of business so I don't embarrass myself, I walk back into the room in a pair of athletic shorts.

I've worked my ass off for the better part of my life in the gym and on the ice to get my body in prime shape. So, I'm not surprised to find Dakota openly checking me out.

"See something you like?" I smirk like the cat that ate the canary.

"How are you even real? I mean, I grew up around my brother's friends who were professional athletes, and this," she waves her hands up and down, gesturing toward my abdomen, "this is not realistic. I've seen the way you eat. There's no way you can have the V that women drool over when you can take down an entire bag of kettle corn in one sitting. Does it hurt being so hot?"

That makes me chuckle.

"I'm being serious. Does it hurt having women throw themselves at you every day?" She shakes her head before muttering something under her breath.

"What was that? I didn't quite catch that."

"You weren't supposed to, Golden Boy. Now get on the bed," she commands.

I wiggle my eyebrows. "Mmm. I love it when you're bossy." That gets me a scoff in return.

Climbing onto the bed and being surrounded by her jasmine scent has my cock hardening within seconds, making it incredibly uncomfortable to lay on my stomach. What Dakota does next doesn't help my situation at all. The moment the soft skin of her thighs makes contact with my bare skin as she straddles my waist, lust pulls at my spine, and I'm suddenly harder than I've ever been in my life.

She wiggles her ass on top of mine to get comfortable and asks, "Is this okay?"

Is this okay? Is she serious? This is fucking perfect.

"Yeah," I ground out before clearing my throat. "It's great."

The sound of a bottle being squeezed in her hand fills the room. When her warm hands start working the knots in my shoulders, I can't help the groan that slips out.

"Austen. That feels so fucking good."

"Yeah?" she questions.

"Fuck. Yes," I damn near moan the words in response when her knuckles knead into a stubborn spot on my shoulder.

After a minute she sits up, putting more weight behind her hands. And when she sits back down on my lower back, I am hit with the feel of her slick, cotton shorts rubbing against my bare skin as she continues to work my sore muscles.

A moan slips out, but it wasn't from my lips. Dakota, my fucking dream girl, is moaning as she rubs herself up and down my back right now. If anybody tries to wake me from this dream, I'll kill them.

"This, this isn't right," she practically whimpers.

Fuck that. It feels perfect. I'm mesmerized by the feel of her hips moving against my skin—it's like I'm caught in the most amazing dream.

In a move I'm not sure how I pull off in this dream-like state, I roll over onto my back and grip Dakota's hips before she can fall to the side.

"I can see you're worked up right now, Austen. Let me take care of you."

"We shouldn't be doing this." She bites down on her tempting bottom lip again, the same one I've craved since the moment I met her.

"Doing what?" I ask as I fold my arms beneath my head. "We're not doing anything wrong."

"This is so very wrong," she pants out.

"Use me." I grind my hips up into hers.

She moans louder in response. "What?"

"Use me to fall apart, Austen. I want to watch you come undone."

"I can't. I'm broken."

"There's not a damn thing about you that's broken," I reassure her.

She stills on top of me, swinging her leg off of me and falling onto her back. Turning to face me, she props herself up on her elbow. "I think you might be the only person who can fix me. This might be wrong of me to ask, but I'm desperate at this point. If you want me to use you, I'll only use your mouth."

"You don't get my mouth tonight, Dakota," I tell her, covering my eyes. I'm frustrated with myself for nearly going there with her. I didn't want it to be like this.

"That's not what I meant. Your words. I think I only need your words." Just then, she rolls over to grab something out of the bedside drawer. When she shows me a rose clit stimulator, I begin to understand what she was saying.

My dick becomes painfully excited at the idea of being able to make Dakota fall apart with only my words. I mentally tell myself to calm down and play it cool.

"It's my words you need?" I ask for clarification.

I watch as she bites her lip in hesitation before slowly nodding her head.

"If you want my words, I need to hear yours first, Dakota."

"Yes. I need you to tell me what to do. Should I get undressed?" she asks.

I shake my head. "No. You're going to keep those sexy pajamas on."

She looks puzzled but doesn't make a move to remove them.

"Turn the device on and slide it over your slit, but don't move your shorts."

Doing exactly as I say, she lets out a whimper when the device moves over her clit.

"That's it, just like that," I encourage her as I fight every instinct I have to grip her hips and take control. Keeping my hands to myself, I watch as she follows my directions.

"Ah, fuck. This feels so good," she mewls as her hand slips under her tank and she begins tweaking her nipple.

"Pinch those perfect tits. I'd give anything to have them in my mouth right now. Tease me with them," I command.

She continues to rock her hips over the clit stimulator while she works her tits, her movements becoming jerky.

"Fuck, Austen. You're soaked, aren't you?"

"Yes!"

"Show me how wet my words make you."

"More. I need more."

"Not until you show me, little tease."

She moves the stimulator aside and glides her fingers beneath her shorts, over her slit, and lifts them to show me.

"Goddamn. You're drenched. Push aside your shorts and imagine it's my tongue licking your sweet clit and my fingers deep inside your cunt. Come undone for me, baby."

Dakota begins to do just that, working herself into a desperate frenzy. "Oh, god! Carson!"

"Look at you taking what you need from me just like I told you to. You're such a good fucking girl," I praise. And that must do it for her because no sooner than the words have left my mouth, Dakota shatters. Her body shutters and quakes beside me, and I would give anything to be able to feel her pussy pulsing around my cock right now.

When she turns off her toy, she rolls over and locks eyes with mine. I'm completely bewitched.

"I told you, you're not broken. You're the most captivating woman I've ever met." I reach across to brush her short locks behind her ear, holding my hand against her cheek and refusing to break this spell she's put me under.

I watch as she rises to her knees. "I don't feel right if this isn't mutually beneficial."

Shaking my head, I tell her, "This was about you."

"Please?" she begs, and the last thread of restraint I had snaps.

My entire body feels deliciously warm as I thrust my hips forward, inciting a moan. Was that my moan? Fuck, it sounded too heavenly to have come from me. My hands glide up the cottony warmth before me, where I find the most perfect handful of skin that spills out of the cotton constraints.

I move my hips once again and am met with the most divine ass grinding straight against my dick. Another beautiful moan slips into a needy whimper as I brush my fingers against the bud of a pebbled nipple.

The whimper turns into a gasp, and the warm, pliant body I was just grinding against turns rigid.

My eyes shoot open. As the sleep clears, it only takes a moment for me to realize where I am—where *we* are.

Fuck. I shoot up from the bed.

"I'm so sorry," I rasp, my voice still laced with sleep.

She pulls the sheets up to cover her breasts that were spilling out of her sleep tank. "No, I'm sorry. It's my fault. You fell asleep last night while I was rubbing your back, and I didn't want to wake you. You looked so exhausted when you got back last night. Don't apologize," she motions to my erection before continuing, "I know it's a natural reaction in the morning."

Holy shit. That was a dream? It felt so fucking real.

I quickly grab a shirt from the dresser and use it to cover my dick which is standing at full attention. Using both hands to cover myself, I nod toward the bathroom door. "I'm going to uh—go take a shower."

"Yeah, I could use a shower right about now as well," she agrees.

That halts me in place.

"After you're done," she clarifies.

"Right. Of course." I fucking bow my head forward before dipping the hell out of the room. What the fuck is wrong with me?

Dakota has ruined me with only one dream, and fuck if I wouldn't give anything to turn that dream into reality.

21

Carson

"**A**lright, thank you, Brad. I appreciate your help on this," I tell the man on the phone before hanging up and looking over my shoulder to be sure no one overheard my conversation.

When I see a flash of movement behind me, I realize I should've known someone was eavesdropping. However, I'm not upset when I see Mack peek out from behind the corner of the stairwell.

"So, how much of that conversation did you snoop in on?" I query.

"I'm sorry, I didn't set out to listen in on your conversation. I was coming to see if you were almost ready to head out for breakfast," she clarifies.

"It's fine, sis. I was just talking to Brad Orwell about redoing a room in my house," I inform her.

"Yeah, I overheard. I also heard that you're redoing Cadence's old playroom and converting it into a library. Where did your sudden interest in reading come from?"

I do the thing with my hands that I can't help doing whenever I'm nervous, clapping them together in front of me. "It's not so much for my books as it is for Dakota's," I say sheepishly.

Mack smiles softly. "I kind of gathered."

"Do you think it's stupid? I probably shouldn't be renovating entire rooms in my house for a temporary roommate."

199

"It's sweet, not stupid, and I also don't think it's temporary. I've seen the shift between the two of you lately—for a while now, actually. Have you told her how you feel?"

"It's more than obvious to everyone how I feel about her. I haven't necessarily been inconspicuous in my pursuit."

That earns me a soft chuckle. "No, no, you have not. But if you recall, Griff and I had feelings for each other for years before we realized how the other felt. Even though it was evident to everyone around us, we remained clueless."

"Yeah, I remember. Katie and I had a front-row seat to the shitshow." My chest pulls tight, the way it always does wherever I think back on the memories from that summer. "That's not the case with Dakota, though. I've told her how I feel. I'm being patient and waiting for her to catch up."

Mack's face softens. "For what it's worth, I think you're going about it the right way. Building the foundation of your relationship on friendship will make a huge difference in her security within the relationship. Dakota told me once that her relationship with Aaron was very rushed, and she felt like they got married before she even realized who he truly was."

Biting the inside of my cheek, I mull that over. When will we ever get a better opportunity to truly get to know one another than while we're here spending uninterrupted time together for the next month? Probably never.

"So how do I show her that what she had with Aaron wasn't love?"

A wide smile spreads across my sister's face. "By showing her what it should be."

My own grin mirrors hers before we discuss the logistics of our most important mission yet: showing Dakota Meyer what falling deeply and indisputably in love is like.

Griffin and I are standing near the clear half-wall railing at the hotel bar's rooftop terrace that overlooks the city as we wait for Mack and Dakota. They opted to get ready together in our room, so I went over to change and shower in theirs. It didn't take long for Griff and me to get ready, thus the two of us sipping on negronis, a popular drink in Milan.

Tan arms wrap around Griff from behind, and once he sees her ring, he turns to pull Mack into his arms but stops midway to take in her outfit. "Fuck, Sunshine. You know I can't control myself when you wear red."

"Not something I needed to know," I mutter.

McKenna's got her long blonde hair pulled back into a wavy ponytail. The short red dress she's wearing, that has Griff looking like a lovestruck idiot, has red rhinestones all over it with straps that fall off her shoulders.

Mack's returning wink tells him she knew exactly what she was doing. "I was just choosing an era. And *Red* happens to be one of my favorites. I love how your shirt turned out, baby," she says innocently as she pulls him in for a kiss. Her makeup must be magic, because when she pulls away, there's not a trace of her red lipstick on Griff's face.

Griffin's shirt says "Fearlessly in love with my wife" with an arrow pointing to the side, where Mack is now tucked beneath his arm.

I look around in search of Dakota, but when I don't immediately see her I turn back to Mack. "Where's Dakota?" I ask. Maybe I'm just in my head, but I'm worried that after what happened this morning, she's going to pull away from me before I've even had a chance to convince her to stay.

"She was going to grab us a drink at the bar and then join us out here."

The nod I give in response hopefully comes off indifferent when I'm really feeling anything but. I'm nervous as shit to implement phase one of my mission: leave nothing unsaid.

When I notice I'm repeatedly fisting the hand not holding my drink, I slip it into the pocket of my light blue shorts and fidget with the contents of my pocket.

"Carse, you need to chill the fuck out. You look like you're playing pocket pool right now," Griff grumbles.

Pulling my hand from my pocket, I tip my head back and finish my drink.

Feeling a sudden, inexplicable need to turn around, I do, and when my eyes find my dream girl, my heart begins to hammer in my chest. Dakota makes her way toward us in a lavender sequin dress with a plunging neckline that has me biting my knuckles to hold in the groan that wants to slip out. Her short hair is curled and pinned back on one side. As she gets closer, I can see she has a lavender eye shadow with little rhinestones around the corners of her eyes. She completes the look with those sexy rhinestone cowgirl boots of hers.

Dakota hands one of the wine glasses she's holding to Mack. When she turns back to me and gives me a shy smile, I try to regain my composure. Clearing my throat, I tell her, "You can take the girl outta Texas, but you can't take the Texas outta the girl."

That makes a genuine smile spread across her face. "You like?" she asks, biting her lip and doing a playful spin so I can see her outfit.

The sun hitting off the sequins gives her an iridescent glow, and when she spins, the short flowy skirt of her dress moves to an almost indecent length. As she turns, I see the top of her dress is actually a halter top, leaving the tanned skin of her back exposed in the backless number.

Like? Is she serious?

Is death by attraction a thing? Because if it is, I think I'm on my way to my grave. My heart thrashes wildly in my chest, causing me to sweat and undo another button of my button-up shirt.

"I love it, Austen. You're like a living, breathing lavender haze."

That earns me a chuckle with a cute little wrinkle of her nose. "Thank you. Oh, and look. It even has pockets!" she exclaims, showing me the side of her dress where a concealed pocket is built into the fabric of the skirt. "And let me guess," she pauses. "You're in your *Lover* era?" She gestures toward my pink and light blue tie dye button up shirt. I do my own spin so she can see the back of my shirt where it has the album's logo across my shoulders.

"I'm never not in my *Lover* era," I declare.

I love the way we banter back and forth. This exchange is feeling very . . . us. And I guess after this morning, I really didn't think she'd be able to pivot so easily. But everything she does amazes me, so this should come as no surprise.

We didn't really get a chance to talk about the incident this morning. With all of us being a bit jet-lagged, we slept in and had a late breakfast with Griff and Mack. Then, Dakota and Mack went off to do a little last-minute shopping for tonight and got ready in our room.

Unsure if I should bring it up or not, I play with the medallion on my chain while I consider my options. Dakota must be a mind reader, or maybe I'm just that easy to read because she gives me the slightest shake of her head and mouths, "Don't," to me from her spot next to Mack.

Closing the distance between us, I offer her my hand. "Can we talk for a minute?" I ask her.

Her shoulders slump as if having this conversation with me is the last thing she wants to do. She puts her hand in mine and follows me to a quieter section of the terrace.

I reach into my pocket and am about to open my mouth to speak when she cuts me off. "Look, Carson. We don't have to have this conversation again. I know this morning was an accident, and honestly, if anyone should be apologizing here, it's me for my behavior last night. I'm not sure what I was thinking. In fact, I think my pent-up sexual frustration stole all my good sense. Then this morning happened, and well, as I'm sure you could tell, I wasn't immune to your touch. You see, it's just been so long since someone has touched me like that."

"I didn't bring you over here to talk about this morning," I clarify, my voice gravelly from her confession.

Her head tilts to the side in confusion and her cheeks stain my favorite shade of pink. "*Oh*. Oh my gosh." She tries to cover her face, but I gently pull her hands into mine. "Can you please spare me and pretend I didn't just confess all of that to you?"

A deep chuckle rumbles from my chest. "No way. I don't think I'll ever be able to forget you confessing that you're not immune to my touch, Dream Girl."

She turns her hands over in mine to lace our fingers together, but pauses and looks up at me skeptically when she feels something in my left hand. "What's this?" she asks.

"I made you a friendship bracelet for tonight," I stammer. My stomach churns with trepidation as I turn my palm over and show her the green and aqua beaded bracelet.

"Thank you, that is so sweet of you." Dakota whispers in reverence as she picks it up from my hand to examine it closer. I can tell once she's read the letters on the bracelet because her brow knits in confusion.

Taking her hand in mine again, I clarify, "I was never calling you by the name of a city I knew you didn't live near. I mean, of course I knew you grew up in the Dallas area as soon as you told me who your brother is." I silently will my nerves to ease so I can get through this.

"Do you remember what you were wearing the first day I met you?" I ask her.

Her face scrunches up in the cutest way as she tries to recall. "No, I don't."

"Well, I do. You were wearing this beige crewneck that said 'Pemberley est. 1813' on it. I also overheard you telling Mack that you were an English major in college. Being a guy who loves giving nicknames, I just couldn't help myself."

I can see the moment it registers for her. "Austen, as in my favorite author," she states.

"Yeah," I reply sheepishly. "I didn't correct your assumption that day, because I thought it was a cute inside joke between us, only you weren't completely in on the punch line."

She shakes her head and gazes up at me in wonderment. The one side of her bracelet says "Austen" and the other says "Dream Girl."

"Giving nicknames to those I'm close to is kind of my way of showing them I care. It's a term of endearment." Brushing my thumb over her knuckles, I continue, "From the moment I met you, I had this insane feeling that you were meant to be in my life. I looked into your big emerald eyes, and it was like this moment of clarification." I pause, clearing my throat. "Just know I would never want to push you into anything, Dakota. I'll gladly accept you in my life in any way you're willing to have me. Even if that means we remain just friends."

Dakota's green eyes bounce between mine, but the hesitation I expected to see isn't there. Instead, I'm met with emerald eyes that burn with yearning.

"Would you say we're *just* friends, Mr. Wilder?" She quirks a brow at me, her lips twitching with mirth.

I stare back at her intently as I squeeze her hands in mine three times. "The feelings I have toward you have never been friendly, Austen. Not even when I told myself you were someone else's—I held onto this false sense of hope that maybe one day you could be mine."

"And is that still what you want?" she whispers, before clarifying, "For me to be yours?"

My heart stops in my chest and the air seizes in my lungs at her question.

"Hey, Golden Boy?" she asks as she pulls her hand from mine and dips into one of the pockets of her dress.

"Yeah, Austen?" I reply.

She places something in my palm, and when I bring the lime green and black bracelet up to my face, I read "Golden Boy" just as she asks, "Remember when you said you wouldn't kiss me until I'm ready to be all in?"

My eyes shoot up to meet hers, hopeful glances being shared between us.

"I'm ready now," she whispers for only me to hear.

Stepping even closer to her, I wrap my arm around her waist, pulling her even closer. Cupping her cheek, I lower my gaze just as she licks her lips. Her lips that I've been dying to taste—to claim.

Lowering my lips to her ear, I ask, "You're sure?"

She wraps her arms around my neck, playing with the hair at my nape as she pulls back and stares back at me. "I'm yours if you'll have me."

My knees feel weak hearing those words leave her lips.

"Mine," I murmur, leaning in to finally claim her mouth.

"Carse, Kota? Are you guys ready to go to the stadium?" Mack asks from behind us.

Closing my eyes, I try but fail to hide my disappointment at the interruption. Dakota's forehead crashes against my chest as she sighs in frustration.

Slipping her hand into mine, I lift her chin and place a chaste kiss on her forehead.

"Something to look forward to later," I declare, shooting her a playful wink.

Because now that I know she's ready, I refuse to go another day without claiming her as mine.

22

Dakota

July

With Carson standing at my back, his strong arms wrapped around my waist, we stand in amazement as the renowned intro for The Eras Tour sounds throughout the stadium.

He grips onto my hips as the dancers lift the fabric from center stage to reveal the queen herself, Taylor Alison Swift.

The literal scream that comes from Carson shouldn't surprise me, but it does nonetheless. When Carson notices my shoulders tense, he pulls me closer to his chest and brings his arms up to wrap around my shoulders. He rocks us side to side as Taylor performs "Miss Americana & the Heartbreak Prince."

Out of the corner of my eye I see Kenna looking over at us. A wide smile spreads across her lips as she reaches her hand out and grabs mine.

Carson holds me in his arms like that until the opening beats of "Lover" begin to play. Spinning me around, he envelops me in his arms, leaving me to deeply breathe in his sandalwood and bergamot cologne. Resting his chin on the top of my head, he serenades me as we gently sway to the beat of the drum.

Pulling my head back, I look up at him and am captivated by his detonating grin before he brings me in for a crushing hug.

When the lights change and golden sparks start falling from the top of the stage, it's Griff who lets out a piercing squeal just as Taylor comes skipping out onto the stage with her rhinestone guitar to sing the opening lines of "Fearless."

The moment Carson hears "22" he lifts me into his arms and spins me around, shouting that that's his hockey number and asking if I remembered.

"Of course I know that, I watched nearly every game of yours this season!" I shout.

"Mack! We're going to be twenty-two next month. We've got to dance to this on our birthday," he pleads.

"As if not dancing to this song on our twenty-second birthday was ever an option!" she yells as she rolls her eyes at him.

It's only a few songs later when goosebumps erupt all over my body as Carson's fingers dance across the base of my spine, just above the dimples on my back.

Even when I notice the opening chords of my favorite song starting to play, I can't help but continue to stare up at Carson instead of turning toward the stage. The way the lights reflect in his eyes, giving them an almost violet hue, has me completely enthralled. As Taylor begins to sing the lyrics of "Enchanted," it's like he and I are in our own little world in this moment. The crowd's deafening chants, the thousands of people surrounding us, the lights and sounds from the amazing performance before us—it all melts away as his hands skim lower, over the curve of my spine. When he gives my butt a playful squeeze, there's a mischievous glint in his eyes, leaving my chest heaving as I struggle to catch my breath.

I want nothing more than for him to lean down and finally press his lips to mine.

When we were interrupted earlier, I could've cried from the depravity I felt in that moment. Since Griff and Kenna's wedding, things have shifted between us. Honestly, probably even before then. Carson went from being a complete stranger to someone I can't imagine going a day without talking to. I thought I'd be more guarded with my heart, but for him I think I'm willing to lay it all on the line.

We've lived together for over six months, but even before then, he was intentional with every interaction we had even though he knew it couldn't go anywhere.

If I had to pick my favorite thing about Carson I don't think I could pick just one. This man cares deeply, loves fiercely, lives freely, and I just know he'd kiss me fervently. He's compassionate, selfless, quirky, funny, loyal, and all of those things only make him sexier, if that's even possible, since he's drop-dead gorgeous.

The rest of the concert passes in the blink of an eye, and before I know it, Kenna and I are in line for the restrooms.

"I can barely speak, but hearing her sing 'Red' as her secret acoustic song had me deceased," Kenna croaks.

I giggle at her. "Girl, same. And watching Griff twirl you around in your sparkly red dress was unforgettable."

She does a little shimmy-twirl combination that is something I never would've pictured her doing when I met her a year ago. It's not that she wasn't the fun and sassy woman I've come to adore, it's just she wasn't as dauntlessly in love then.

"What about when I thought for sure Carson was going to finally kiss you?" she asks.

"Which time are you talking about? When you interrupted us back at the hotel, or when you pulled me from his arms so I could dance with you during 'Shake It Off'?"

"Wait, he almost kissed you at the hotel? When? Last night?"

My cheeks heat thinking about what I wish would've happened last night. "N-no. Right before we came here," I stammer.

Kenna's eyes flare in delight. "Oh. My. God. You blushed and stuttered when I mentioned last night. Did something happen?"

"What? No I didn't. Absolutely nothing happened last night," I say in a steadier voice than I feel. "We did, however, admit our feelings for each other. I hope that this isn't weird for you, what with me being Cadence's nanny and, I don't know . . . seeing Carson?" It comes out as more of a question because I don't know what we're doing, I just know I want to pursue him.

"Well, no offense, I don't want to know if anything did happen between you and my brother. Regardless, I'm happy for you both. I'm sure Cades will love having you become Auntie Kota." My eyes widen at her words, but the look on my face does nothing to stop her from continuing, "Oh, or maybe she should call you Auntie KoKo since she calls Carse Uncle Car Car."

Placing my hands on her shoulders, I tell her, "Slow your roll, Kenna. I think you've jumped ahead about forty chapters in the book to get to the spicy stuff."

"Forty chapters? What kind of slow burns are you reading? I'm more of a wham, bam, thank you ma'am in the first ten chapters kind of gal."

I'd never admit this to her, but I'm living in the quintessential slow burn at the moment, and I wouldn't mind one bit for more of that whamming and bamming she was just talking about.

"Wait, are you writing a slow burn? What are the tropes of your novel?" Kenna presses.

I smile at her excitement, because I'm genuinely so happy to have someone who loves books as much as I do to chat about my work in progress with. "For sure there will be an age gap, rival's daughter, pro football player, workplace romance, and I'm not sure if this is considered a trope, but vacation love."

"If it's not a trope, you're about to make it one. Ah! Dakota, that sounds so good. I can't wait to get my hands on it."

"They fall in love in Italy, that's why Carson insisted I come with. I hope you don't mind that I'm interrupting the first part of y'all's honeymoon. And I know my ticket for tonight was supposed to be for Katie, I told Carson I'd buy my own but he said he talked to Griff."

"Oh my gosh, you're absolutely not interrupting our honeymoon. If anything, having you and Carson join us has been an added bonus that we get to explore a new country with our friends. As for tonight's ticket, you actually didn't use Katie's—Carson purchased a fifth one when he was planning out the trip."

Learning that tidbit has me feeling relieved to hear that Griff's sweet gesture to include and memorialize his sister wasn't wasted on me.

Kenna pivots the conversation. "Have you started writing any scenes yet?"

"Yeah, I've been trying to write a few hundred words per night. It's kind of fun chapter mapping places my characters go and things they'll do as I get to experience them myself."

She tries and fails miserably to fight back a laugh. "I wonder if any other parts of your story will be inspired by what you experience on this trip."

Rolling my eyes, I give her a gentle shove, my petite frame doing nothing to her six-foot stature.

As her laughter fades, she grows more serious, biting her lip in hesitation. "How are you doing? Like, really doing? I feel like with all of the wedding planning that came together at the last minute, we haven't had as much time to talk. I can't believe I'm saying this, but I'm actually excited for hockey season to start back up again so we can have more sleepovers when the boys are traveling."

"I'm doing really well. I feel inspired to start this next chapter of my life by discovering what brings me joy—what I'm passionate about."

"And everything with your ex and the divorce? It's all settled and you haven't heard from him? Has he been convicted and sentenced yet?"

"Your dad is one badass lawyer. And as you know, I was able to get an order of protection. Once that was in place, the only communication I've received from Aaron has been through our lawyers as everything was finalized. I didn't want anything from him, I just wanted to be sure I never saw him again. The last update I got was that his court date for the assault continues to get pushed back."

"I'm really proud of you, and in awe of your strength, Dakota. You got out, and you're making yourself and your happiness a priority."

I grab Kenna's hand, squeeze it three times, and thank her. When I do, her eyes widen in disbelief. "Does your family do that too?" she asks.

"Do what?" I reply, confused by her question.

"Squeeze someone's hand three times to tell them you love them. Carse and I always used to do that growing up, and of course I'd annoy the shit out of him when I'd squeeze his a fourth time to say 'I love you more.'"

Hold the phone. Did she just say love?

Kenna must see my perplexed expression and realize that, no, my family does not do that. "By the look on your face right now, I'm going to guess that's a no and that you only recently had someone give you the three squeezes?"

Clearing my throat, I respond, "Yeah. But I think it means something different for me and Carson. He's been doing it here and there since I was in the hospital."

Looking uncomfortable, Kenna just shrugs in reply.

My mind starts racing at the possibility of what this means, it only quiets once we're out of the restroom, and Carson takes my hand in his once again. And he doesn't let it go for the entire car ride back to the hotel. Only when we arrive at the hotel does he let mine go as he rounds the car to open my door for me.

My feet have barely hit the pavement when he tosses the keys to the hotel's valet, and clasps my hand in his once again.

Carson leans in, combing my hair back with his fingers. "Will you come with me? I want to show you something," he murmurs into my ear, brushing his lips along my ear, sending chills down my spine.

"Yes," I whisper in reply.

We walk hand in hand down the cobblestone street of the Via Dante. Even though it is late, the city is still so alive with people dining together, conversation and laughter fill the air.

"Where are we going?" I question.

"There's a place at the end of the street a local told me about yesterday. He said seeing it lit up at night is a must-see while we're in Milan. He also gave me a few tips for the rest of our trip."

As we approach the end of the street, the most spectacular fountain sits in front of a colossal clock tower. The circular fountain is lit from within, with spotlights surrounding it.

"This is sensational," I gasp.

"Breathtaking," he agrees, but when I turn to look at him, he isn't taking in the fountain. Instead, his gaze is fixed on me.

The lights from the fountain cast a golden glow on his tanned skin and honey blonde hair, and the sight nearly brings me to my knees.

"Come here, Austen." When he pulls me toward him, I go willingly into his arms.

Carson cups my face in his hands, rolling his thumb over my bottom lip.

Wrapping my arms around his waist, I pull him closer to me, his warmth enveloping me.

"Do you have any idea how long I've been dying to claim these lips?" His stare is fixed on my lips, and when I wet them, he closes his eyes and lets out a low groan. The sound has my stomach turning molten.

"Show me," I practically whimper, lifting myself onto my toes to close the distance between us.

Tangling his fingers in my hair, Carson leans down and the moment his lips finally meet mine, my heart stops beating in my chest and time stands still. Everything around us ceases to exist. There is nothing in this life that feels more euphoric than the way his soft lips feel pressed against mine.

When he pulls my bottom lip into his mouth and rolls it between his, my mouth eagerly parts for him. He lets out a groan at the first swipe of our tongues, the sound causing a wave of heat crashing to my core.

Carson kisses me like time won't go on unless his lips are pressed against mine, and I don't think it would. Because this is the kiss that will change everything as we know it.

Nothing in my life made sense before Carson worked his way into it. Now that he's captured my heart, I can only pray he plans to keep it safe.

23

Carson

We've just loaded our day bags into the trunk of the sexiest fucking convertible on the planet. And nothing, I mean absolutely nothing, gets my blood pumping faster than when I look over and see Dakota's eyes hazy with lust when I rev the engine, and it purrs to life.

"Carson," she haphazardly warns.

"Do you trust me, Austen?"

Austen. Fuck do I like calling her that now that she knows what it means.

Her face softens at the term of endearment. "Without a doubt."

"That's my girl," I say as I take off down the crowded city streets. Peeking over at her out of the corner of my eye, I'm mesmerized by the way her dark hair whips in the open air. The dark red leather interior of the Ferrari against her tanned complexion makes my blood boil.

When we roll to a stop at the first stop sign, I turn to Dakota and pull her toward me for a lingering kiss. "I'd like to propose a new road trip rule," I suggest.

"And what would that be?"

"We kiss at every stop sign and red light."

She snorts as if what I've suggested is the most absurd thing she's ever heard. "We'll never make it to Venice."

"We'll make it there, but we've got a lot of catching up to do. I've wanted to kiss you for over 365 days now, and I only got my first taste of you last night. Besides, I'm the driver, and I made it a car rule, so as my passenger princess, you must abide by all car rules."

That earns me an eye roll, so I reach over and place my palm on her leg, giving the inside of her thigh a few squeezes that make her squeal out in laughter.

By the third stop sign, Dakota is the one leaning over the center console to kiss me. The moment her mouth opens for me, I groan in delight at the sweet taste of her. Without another car in sight, we get lost in this moment—in each other.

How I survived as long as I did without kissing her is beyond me. The feel of her lips on mine has turned me into the most ravenous man—now that I've had a taste, I'll never be able to get my fill. I want to kiss her every hour of every day.

A shrill honk comes from the car now behind us, followed by expletives shouted in Italian.

Dakota slides back into her seat, covering her mouth to muffle her laughter. I don't bother holding mine in as I bark out a deep chuckle. Taking a moment longer, I press play on my road trip playlist I made last night.

"Your Love" by The Outfield sounds through the speakers just as I hit the gas pedal. With one arm on the wheel, I use my fist as an imaginary microphone and waggle my brows at her as I serenade the first lines to Dakota.

The drive from Milan to Venice as we wind down the streets of northern Italy is breathtaking. We decided to stop about midway in Bergamo, which is a city full of Renaissance architecture and narrow stone streets. Only about an hour longer into the drive, we stopped along the shoreline of Lake Garda and explored the thirteenth-century castle there. We made one final stop in Verona, which brought out the history nerd in me. Dakota was fascinated that it was the setting for Shakespeare's *Romeo and Juliet*.

The sun is just starting to set as we enter Venice, one of the places I'm most excited about. As I park the Ferrari and put the top up, I open Dakota's door before grabbing our day bags out of the trunk.

When Dakota presses me up against the side of the car, I drop the bags to the ground and grab her around the waist, pulling her in between my legs to eliminate all space between us.

She runs her hands up my chest before raking her fingers through the hair at my nape. Her emerald eyes are alight with mischief as she asks, "We're stopped, aren't we, Golden Boy?"

Our lips crash together in a kiss that is every bit as needy as it is greedy. She takes charge, and when I open for her, I groan at the taste of her. Sliding my hands down, I cup her ass in my palms and give it a firm squeeze. Dakota lets out a soft whimper, and the sound goes straight to my hardening cock. With her pressed against me, I know she can feel what she's doing to me.

Nothing has ever felt better than kissing Dakota. When we got back to the hotel last night, we spent hours with our lips exploring and our limbs a tangled mess until we fell asleep wrapped up in one another.

I break away from her lips, and when I see hers red and swollen, I just about say "fuck it" and go back for more. "Austen, if we keep this up, we're going to be detained in a foreign country for indecent exposure," I warn.

Her cheeks break out in the most adorable blush before she hides her head against my chest. "Oh my gosh, I can't believe I just did that—in public of all places. I'm so sorry; I don't know what came over me."

Pulling her shoulders back, I lift her chin so she can see the sincerity on my face. "Hey, look at me, Dakota." Once her green eyes meet mine,

I continue, "You don't ever have to apologize for kissing me. I don't mind PDA if you're okay with it. But I knew if we continued to kiss like that for much longer, I'd be dealing with a different situation."

Biting her lip, she nods her head. "I've never been one for PDA. Heck, if I'm being honest, I've never been that into kissing. It always felt like something you do just to get to the next step—like going through the motions. But with you, kissing feels like we're creating a piece of art—I want to get lost in the craft of your lips, the strokes of our tongues, the way you bite my lip before sucking on it. And it seems I also don't give a damn who sees or where we do it. You're completely unraveling me, Mr. Wilder."

Her eyes widen as she finishes her admission, as if she didn't intend to divulge all of that to me aloud. I fucking love it when she turns bashful like this.

"Damn, Dream Girl. That was poetic, and I think I liked that admission far too much. I'm unraveling you, am I?" I tease, chuckling as I pull her in to give her another chaste kiss before wrapping my arm around her shoulder and grabbing our bags from the ground. "Come on, a boat is waiting for us on the Grand Canal to take us to our hotel. I'm really excited what I have planned, so I hope you're ready for what's in store for us here."

When we get to the boat, Dakota gasps as she takes in the serene scene before us. "This is stunning, Carson."

It absolutely is. The sun is setting over the buildings, painting the sky in pale pink and an array of oranges that reflect on the water. We get into the polished wooden boat, and the driver takes off toward the hotel. If she thinks this is stunning, I can't wait for her to take in the hotel I've chosen for our stay here.

"Did you know Venice is built on over 118 small islands, and there are 400 bridges for people to get around?" I ask her.

"I didn't, but the bridges are all so unique and beautiful," she says in awe. "Oh, like that one!" She points to the stone bridge ahead.

"That is Ponte di Rialto. It was constructed in the late sixteenth century, about the same time as the hotel we're going to stay at," I explain.

When we pull up to the Aman, a historic hotel that is situated on the Grand Canal, Dakota turns to me wide-eyed. "This isn't our hotel, is it?"

"Of course it is. Come on," I tell her as I step up onto the dock and offer her my hand. She grabs ahold and climbs out of the boat.

Placing my hand on the small of her back, I guide us to the reception desk to check in.

"*Buonasera*," I say to the receptionist.

While I'm checking in, I notice Dakota taking in the impressive lobby. I can't wait to show her some of the hidden gems this place has to offer. This is undoubtedly the nicest hotel I've ever stayed in, and I'm willing to bet she would say the same.

Once I've got our key, I guide her up the grand marble staircase to our room overlooking the Grand Canal. Entering through intricate wood-carved doors, we walk through the large entryway where the concierge has placed our luggage. There is a sitting room off to the left, with the bedroom to the right.

"I, uh, got a one bedroom. But they can set up the sitting room to be a second bedroom if you'd prefer not to share. I had originally booked it with that in mind, but after our stay in Milan . . . well, I'll just come out and say it. I loved sleeping with you in my arms, Austen."

A shy smile spreads across Dakota's face. "I don't want separate bedrooms either," she says as she walks into the room and takes it in. With my hands in my pockets, I lean against the doorframe and watch as she checks out the marble fireplace before turning and dragging her fingers across the plush comforter on the bed. "This place is majestic."

"When I saw the photos online, I thought maybe this place would inspire you. I requested they put a writing desk in the sitting room in case you had the urge to write," I admit.

She doesn't reply at first, instead she just stares at me with an unreadable expression. The moment I see her eyes begin to swell with tears, I push off the doorframe and take her in my arms. My heart pounds in my chest when I don't immediately feel her wrap her arms around me.

"Hey, what's the matter? I'm sorry if I overstepped."

Dakota shakes her head, wrapping her arms around my waist as she pulls back to look up into my eyes. "No, nothing is wrong. I-I'm just so thankful. You didn't have to do any of this—suggest I come, take extra time away from training to be here with me, plan the entire trip down to the smallest detail like requesting there be a writing desk in our room," she pauses to sniffle through the tears threatening to spill. "I can't believe you're real. And you're choosing to be here with me."

Rubbing my hands up and down her back, I reply, "Well, believe it, Dream Girl. Because there's nowhere else I'd rather be and no one else I'd rather have by my side."

Lifting up on her tiptoes, she places a soft kiss along the edge of my jaw, dragging her lips before placing another on my chin. With her lips still on my skin, she whispers, "I should freshen up, and then do you want to grab a bite to eat?"

"Yeah, I was thinking we could order room service for tonight, if that's okay with you?"

"That sounds perfect," she replies.

"Okay, I'll start unpacking while you're in there, and then I'll hop in the shower when you're finished," I tell her. Knowing she'll be in there naked and wet with soap running down her body is giving my cock unwarranted hope.

"I'll be quick," she says as she grabs a few items from her suitcase and heads into the ensuite.

I've just finished hanging up my suit when Dakota calls out, "Hey, Carson, could you help me for a second?"

"Yeah, what's u—" I cut off as I take in the sight before me.

Dakota is sitting in the large soaking tub in the middle of the bathroom. Sure, bubbles cover her body, but I know she's naked beneath them.

Clearing my throat, I try to play it cool. "What can I do for you?"

I take in her flushed cheeks, her hazy eyes, and the rapid rise and fall of her chest as it bobs up from the water before sinking back under.

"I can't reach my back," she states. "Could you wash it for me?"

Wash it for her? Fuck me.

I take a calming breath and reply, "Yeah, I can do that."

She grabs a sponge from the tray beside the tub and hands it to me. "Here you go."

"Thanks," I croak.

Get your shit together, man.

"No, thank you," she hums.

That sound, in combination with the way the bubbles disappear as she moves forward, exposing her full back to me, has my dick hard again within seconds.

Feeling weak in the knees as she gleams wickedly over her shoulder at me, I kneel down beside the tub and wet the sponge, squeezing it down her spine. I'm hypnotized, completely bewitched, as I follow the trickles of the sudsy water trail down her skin.

Heavy breaths fill the space between us, and I'm not entirely sure if they're hers or my own.

After two passes over her skin with the sponge, I drop it into the water and use my hands to massage her shoulders.

"Mmm, Carson. That feels so good," she moans, and it echoes against the walls.

"Here, let me wash your hair," I offer as I remove the clip holding it up.

Reaching into the water to find the sponge, I touch the soft curve of her ass, and when she presses herself further into my palm, I freeze.

"Dakota," I growl in warning.

"Touch me, please," she begs, arching her back, causing her dusty pink nipples to rise from the bubbles. They're pebbled and beckoning me to put them in my mouth for a taste.

"You know I can't say no to you," I rasp.

"So don't. I need you to touch me, Carse," she pleads, and I can't deny her.

I lace my fingers through her hair, bringing my mouth to hers, and when she bites my bottom lip before sucking it, I let out a low groan.

"Tell me what you like, Dakota. I want to make you feel everything."

"I don't know what I like. I just know that when you touch me, I feel more than I've ever felt before," she confesses.

Trailing my fingers from her lips, down the nape of her neck, to the slope of her breasts, I grab one into my hand and squeeze it.

"The perfect handful. Do you think you were made just for me?"

She whimpers in response.

"I think so too," I say, pressing my lips against her jaw.

Rolling one nipple between my fingers, I take her other nipple into my mouth, grazing my teeth over it before sucking it.

"Oh, Jesus," she keens as I remove my mouth with a pop and give the same attention to the other side.

Dakota arches her back further and squeezes her thighs together as she squirms in the water. I draw my fingers over her stomach, circling her hip bones and stopping my trail just above her pelvis. Her legs fall open, causing the bubbles to disperse, giving me the perfect view of her bare pussy.

"Fuck, Austen. Look at your pretty pussy, just begging to be played with. Is that what you want?"

She nods her head in reply as her chest heaves in my other hand.

"Give me your words, and I'll give you my fingers," I command.

She eagerly complies. "Play with me. Touch me. Please, Carson," she breathes.

Giving her what she wants, I drag my fingers through her slit before circling her entrance and teasing one inside her. She's so fucking tight that when I add a second finger, I'm met with resistance even though she's absolutely soaked.

"You're so fucking tight," I grind out.

I slowly pump my fingers in and out of her a few times before circling her clit with my thumb.

Sensing she needs more, I add a third finger at the same time as I take her nipple back into my mouth.

"Ah, fuck! Don't stop. I-I'm right there," she stammers.

Pumping my fingers harder, I hook them up, wiggling them back and forth against her g-spot when I feel her begin to clench around me.

"Carson!" she cries a moment later as her body finds its release, and she pulses around my fingers.

I release her nipple and crash my lips to hers as she rides out the aftershocks of her orgasm.

She whimpers against my lips when I pull my fingers out. Her eyes widen when I bring my fingers to my mouth and suck them clean. I can't help the low groan that slips out when I get my first taste of her.

"I-I think this place has to go in the book," she half stutters, half sighs as she sinks back into the water.

I chuckle at that. "Let me wash your hair while you brainstorm some scenes. Didn't you tell me the other night that you get your best ideas while you're washing your hair or driving?"

Dakota stares up at me as I reach for her shampoo. "How are you even real?" she asks.

Taking her hand in mine, I kiss the inside of her wrist. "These fingers will type a best-seller someday; I just know it. In the meantime, I've got to give you all the inspiration for what your male main character should be doing. Why do you think I read as many of the books you leave around the house as I can? If I want to be the best real-life boyfriend, I have to stack up to your book boyfriends."

She giggles at me, shaking her head as she moves her hand to cup my face and brushes my cheek with her thumb. "I don't want you to be like any of the men I read about in books. I like you just the way you are, Golden Boy. You're already far better than any fictitious man I could ever imagine."

I waggle my eyebrows at that. "And we haven't even gotten to the good stuff yet."

After I finish washing her hair, I dip my arms beneath the water, scoop her up in my arms, and carry her to our bed.

"Carson!" she squeals in disbelief when I toss her onto the bed. "I'm going to get it all wet."

"I don't care. I'll have housekeeping change the sheets after we order room service. For now, I just want to snuggle with you, Dream Girl."

And so we do. I tuck us in beneath the blankets and we order far too much room service for just the two of us. We stay up talking for so long that my voice becomes hoarse, and our eyes struggle to stay open.

When she trails off mid-sentence and her breathing turns shallow, I softly chuckle to myself.

Dakota came crashing into my life a year ago, and even though I knew she was my dream girl, I never anticipated we'd be where we are right now. I pull her tighter against my chest and gently squeeze her hand resting atop my chest three times before drifting off to sleep with a full heart.

24

Dakota

August

The next morning, Carson wakes charged with energy, buzzing about the secret plans he made for us today. I don't even ask what they are because I don't want to ruin the surprise he clearly put a lot of thought into.

Walking out of the bathroom in a white tank bodysuit tucked into a cream linen skort and white fashion sneakers, I grab my brown leather crossbody bag on my way out of the bedroom when a pair of strong arms wrap around me from behind.

I let out a shriek even though I know it's Carson.

"Sorry, I didn't mean to scare you," he murmurs into my ear before placing a trail of lingering kisses down my neck.

"You're fine, I knew it was you," I sigh, loving how his lips feel pressed against my skin.

"You look gorgeous," he tells me as I turn in his arms and wrap my arms around his neck. "Look at us coordinating without trying. We're already couple goals."

Trailing my eyes down his body, I take in his outfit. He's wearing a muted bluish-gray shirt, white shorts, and white sneakers.

"Did I miss the part where we became a couple?" I playfully tease.

His eyebrows crease in confusion. "You said you were mine, and you already know I've been yours since long before the night of the concert. I'm new to this relationship business. Did I miss a step?" he questions.

Wait, did he just say what I think he said?

"What do you mean you're new to relationships?" I ask.

He smiles sheepishly as he runs his hands up and down my back. "I-uh haven't really done this officially before."

"You've never had a girlfriend? Not even in high school?"

"No, I never really saw the point. I was so busy with hockey all the time, and I didn't want the distraction," he explains.

"So you had hookups and one-night stands? Did you have any situationships?" I press.

Carson's cheeks heat and I'm not sure what to make of the look on his face right now.

He takes a deep breath, and I love the way his hard chest expands against me. "I haven't had any one-night stands. I've messed around a few times at parties, but I never felt comfortable going there with complete strangers. I don't know if it was that I didn't trust them or if I was missing out on the genuine connection."

"Carson," I stammer, pausing to compose myself. "Are you a virgin?"

He must think the baffled look on my face is funny because he lets out a loud chuckle. "No, I'm not a virgin. I had a situationship, I guess you could call it, at the end of my freshman year of college into the beginning part of my sophomore year. It stopped when she met someone, which was cool with me because he was a nice guy, and she and I weren't serious. But by that time, I'd been drafted and had just won a college national championship so there was a lot of attention on me. With everything that was going on with Cadence and Mack, it felt weird bringing someone home when they moved in with me. And then, not long after they moved in, I met you, Dream Girl." He winks at me as a coy smile spreads across his face.

Taking the medallion of his gold chain between my fingers, I turn it over to examine both sides to avoid looking at his devastatingly handsome face while I ask, "Aren't you worried you'll grow tired of me? I mean, I'm older than you, and it's not that I care about experience at all, but don't you think you'll want to try being with other women so you know for sure what you want?"

I hate that I'm self-sabotaging right now, but I can't help the sinking feeling in my gut that someday he'll want to trade me in for the newer, younger model.

Carson pulls his hands from around my waist, grabs my shoulders, and bends so he's eye to eye with me. "Look at me when I tell you this." I comply, looking into his aqua eyes that are shimmering with sincerity. "Age is just a number, Austen. You're barely older than me. Stop trying to find excuses to stop this before we've barely begun. There is no stopping this. You and me? We're inevitable."

He pulls me against his chest, lacing his fingers through my hair as he rocks us side to side. Kissing the top of my head, he murmurs, "Besides, why would I ever want someone else when I hit the jackpot the first time around? I'm batting a thousand when it comes to girlfriends."

When I look back up at him, he has the cockiest smirk on his lips. "Just so you know . . . typically you *ask* someone to be your girlfriend before declaring she is," I tease.

Carson cradles my face in his hands as he stares down at me. His gaze is intense, but not in a way that frightens me. No, his gaze excites me—it ignites a passion I've never felt before but have longed for my entire life.

"Will you be mine, Dakota?"

"Only if you're mine too," I murmur in reply.

He places a chaste kiss on my lips before stepping back and grabbing my hand. "Then it's settled. Now, let me take my girlfriend on our first proper date," he says as we head out the door of our suite.

We walked about a mile from the hotel to a cafe, where we drank cappuccinos and ate brunch before we took in St. Mark's Square. Doge's Palace was unbelievable; touring it felt like we'd been transported back in time to a more regal period.

We're now walking hand in hand down the stone streets to our final destination for the afternoon before Carson has to get back to the hotel to do his virtual therapy appointment. I'm so proud of him for prioritizing his mental health, even while we're on vacation.

"Alright, we're almost there," Carson informs me as he looks up from his maps app.

"And where would 'there' be?" I press.

"It's a place I think you'll like," he vaguely replies.

And when we stand outside of the Libreria Acqua Alta, I leap into Carson's arms.

"Stop it! This is the only place I researched and wanted to go while we were here. I was going to suggest we come tomorrow," I squeal in delight as I take in the exterior of the iconic bookstore. There is actually a wooden sign in front that says "Welcome to the most beautiful bookshop in the world."

Carson chuckles at my excitement. "I'm happy that you're happy, Dream Girl. Now, let's get in there and shop 'til we drop."

When we get inside the bookstore, Carson's eyes widen at the cluttered chaos surrounding us.

"What happened here?" he whispers out of the side of his mouth as he takes in the stacks and stacks of books in bathtubs, gondolas, and disorganized shelves.

"This is why this place is so iconic. Sometimes the city floods, so they put the books in these bathtubs and boats so they won't get ruined," I explain.

"Yeah, but how are you supposed to find the book you're looking for?" he questions.

"I don't think you're supposed to come to this bookstore with a particular book in mind. It's more about uncovering a hidden treasure."

"Oh my gosh, is that an actual fricken cat?"

Before I can answer his question, Carson goes up and pets the black cat perched on top of a book stack. It immediately purrs in content from his attention.

"You're a cute guy, aren't you? With your big green eyes and your little purrs of perfection," Carson coos to the cat. "You know, I have a thing for green eyes." He nods his head toward me. "My girl over there has the most bewitching emerald eyes. I think you'll like her too. But lay off the charm, I don't share."

"I didn't realize you were a cat person. You and Kenna's dog seem so close," I interrupt his conversation with the cat.

"Ranger is the greatest dog of all time, hands down. But I don't discriminate. I like a good pussy as much as the next guy." He tries to play off his comment with a shrug.

I playfully hit his arm. "We're in public. What is wrong with you?"

He bends over in laughter. "Easy, Austen. You'll upset the little guy. How about I chill over here with my new friend while you go treasure hunting," he suggests.

"Alright, be back soon," I tell him as I reach up on my tiptoes to smack a chaste kiss on his cheek and give the cat a quick scratch behind the ears.

I'm still on cloud nine almost two hours later as I finish doing my hair and makeup while Carson is on the video call with his therapist.

When I walk back into our bedroom to get dressed, I halt when I spot something on the bed.

There is a familiar black dress on the bed, a pair of black stiletto pumps that have red bottoms, a black clutch, and a pair of what look to be diamond stud earrings. There is a note on top of the dress:

Dream Girl,

I know you said you didn't need this dress, but it was made to be worn by you. Do me a favor? Put this on and meet me in the lobby at six. I can't wait to continue our first date.

Xoxo,

Golden Boy

Damn him for being the sweetest man in the world. I can't find it in me to be upset with him for purchasing the dress when he was doing it out of the kindness of his heart.

After pacing in front of the bed a few times, I let out a defeated sigh and slip on the Versace dress and Louboutin heels. Grabbing the earrings, I stand in front of the full length mirror in our room and with shaky hands, fasten them in each ear.

Taking a deep, steadying breath, I grab my phone and the clutch from the bed and check the time. I take the steps down to the lobby, where Carson stands at the base of the steps with his back to me.

I feel like Rose in *Titanic* when Jack is waiting at the base of the steps for her. This moment turns even more surreal as Carson turns toward me in his sky blue suit that makes his eyes look like an even lighter shade of aqua, and the most enigmatic smile spreads across his face.

"Austen," he breathes when I get to the bottom of the stairs. "You look fucking exquisite."

No matter how many times he compliments me, I still blush each time.

"Thank you. For the compliment and the outfit. You shouldn't have, but I love the gesture nonetheless." I pause to take him in, grabbing the lapel of his jacket. "You look very suave in this suit."

With me still standing on the last step in heels, I come as close as I'll probably get to being eye-level with Carson. He wraps me in his arms and kisses me like he's been deprived for months instead of hours.

When he pulls away, his eyes are hazy with lust. "If I wasn't starving right now, I'd take you back up those steps and have my way with you," he admits as his stomach grumbles.

I mock gasp. "My lord, you use such dishonorable language."

Leaning in, he brushes my hair back. "I have no intention of doing honorable things with you tonight, my lady," he rasps before nipping at my ear.

The move has my nipples pebbling and desire pooling in my core.

We walk hand in hand to a restaurant in the hotel that looks like we're sitting at a bar top of a private kitchen.

"What is this?" I ask Carson as I take in the space.

"We're actually doing a private cooking class with the executive chef this evening," he informs me as he shrugs out of his suit jacket and sets it on the back of a bar stool.

"Wait, for real?"

"Yeah, I figured there's no better place to learn how to cook for my girlfriend than Italy."

Before I can say anything else, the chef enters to begin our cooking lesson. He hands us each an apron, and when I go to tie mine around my waist, Carson places his hands on mine. "May I?" he asks. The combination of his touch and his deep baritone sends a shiver down my spine.

I nod in response, my words getting caught in my throat. When he's done tying my apron, he rubs his hands up and down my arms, which are now covered in goosebumps.

"Are you cold?"

Shaking my head, I clear my throat. "No. I just caught a chill. I'm fine."

I turn around to find Carson undoing the cuff buttons on his crisp, white dress shirt before he starts rolling the sleeves. I'm once again mesmerized by the way his forearms work.

"Oh, that is definitely going in my book," I mumble to myself.

Carson turns to face me. His smile is smug like he knows how much he affects me. "I'm glad I could spark some inspiration."

"There's still so much that remains left to my imagination though." I wink at him.

He bites his lip and chuckles at that. "Be careful what you wish for."

After we learn how to make our own casoncelli pasta, the chef leaves the two of us to enjoy our meal.

Carson moans when he takes the first bite. "Mmm. Is it always better when you make it yourself, or is it just because we're eating a homemade meal in Italy?"

"I think even if we tried to replicate this exact recipe back home, it would never measure up because of the ingredients being locally sourced here," I reply.

"You're probably right," he says as he wipes his mouth with his napkin. "So, now that we're officially a couple, I feel like I've got to ask the hard-hitting questions," he tells me.

"Is that so? Such as?" I roll my fork in the air as if to say, *Go on.*

Taking a sip of his wine, he begins with, "Would you consider getting married again one day?"

Not anticipating that question right off the bat, I nearly choke. Taking a sip of wine and clearing my throat, I reply, "Woah, you really went for it, didn't you? Um, well, yeah I think I would if I was confident that the relationship was healthy, and I was truly in love."

And that's the honest truth. I really could see myself getting married again one day. But I know if I do, I won't go into the marriage lightly.

"What about you? Do you see yourself getting married one day?" I ask.

"Honestly, I never thought too much about it until recently. I knew I wanted what my parents have—a loving relationship and someone to share my life with—but I didn't put much thought into it beyond that. But now, yeah, I know I'd like to be married one day," he responds.

Butterflies take flight in my stomach once again from his words and how confident he is in his answer.

"What about kids?" The question slips from my lips before I've even processed what I've asked. But I need to know his answer. The topic was a major point of contention with Aaron. He only wanted kids to fulfill his parents' wishes.

Carson's face lights up with a genuine smile. "Yeah, without a doubt, I want kids. And you?"

I take a hesitant breath. "I do. I've wanted to be a mother for as long as I can remember. I think I'd like two so we're not outnumbered. But I guess I'd be willing to see after the first two whether or not our family is complete."

"We're talking about our future children on the first date. I can hear the church bells already, Austen," he teases.

My cheeks heat as the realization sinks in. I just said "so we're not outnumbered" and "our family" to him. He chuckles when I hide my face in my hands.

"I love it when you're bashful. And I love it when you include me in your future, Dream Girl. In case the nickname wasn't obvious enough, you're all I see when I think of my future. Marriage, children, pets, careers—I only see you by my side when I think of them."

He's looking at me with such hope and sincerity shining in his eyes, that I can't help but give him a piece of me in return.

"I see you too," I confess. "But I'm scared that my feelings for you are too strong too fast," I add.

Instead of the frown I expect to see on his face, his smug smile has returned. "You like me," he states, not asking.

Shaking my head at his antics, I chortle. "I do," I admit to him, and his expression heats. The way he's looking at me right now is downright sinful.

"Don't do that," I demand, pointing my finger at his face.

"What?"

"Don't give me that look."

"What look, Austen?" His face breaks out in a smile, and he can barely ask the question through his laughter.

"Don't try to distract me with those bedroom eyes. I can feel you undressing me with your gaze, Mr. Wilder. Not here."

"I can't help it. Look at you." Carson gets up from his chair, grabs his suit jacket, and then offers his hand out to me. "Come with me, the night isn't over yet."

I lace my fingers through his and follow him through the lobby to the hotel's dock on the Grand Canal, where a beautiful gondola is waiting for us.

"Would it be okay if we took dessert to go?" Carson asks, nodding his head at the gondola.

"I'd love nothing more," I tell him.

Once we're situated in the gondola, Carson offers his suit jacket to me. It's a little brisk this evening, and he knows the Texan in me isn't as acclimated to the cold as he is. When I've got it on, I inhale his masculine scent and bask in the way he wraps his arm around me.

We sit in comfortable silence as we take in the beautiful scenery, which is enhanced at night by the lanterns from the shops, restaurants, hotels, and homes along the Grand Canal reflecting off the water. Carson pours us champagne, and we eat Tiramisù.

After dessert, my mind is still racing from our discussion during dinner, and I decide to ask some questions of my own.

Turning in his arms, I look up at him. "Alright, Golden Boy, it's my turn. Where do you see yourself in ten years?"

That earns me a deep chuckle. "I didn't realize I needed to prep for an interview tonight. Well, I hope like hell I'm still playing the game I love. It's weird. This trip will be the longest I've ever gone without ice beneath my feet. After only a week, I've already found myself missing it, which I think is a good thing because it means I'm playing a game I still love. But I'm ready for a life beyond just hockey, so I'd hope that in ten years, I'd be continuing to build and prioritize my family—a wife, kids, maybe a few pets."

"That was a good answer," I hum as I burrow my head against his chest.

"Aside from becoming a best-selling author, what is your ten-year plan?"

"I just want to write stories that I'm passionate about—that bring me joy. I'm under no illusion that they'll become bestsellers, but I think it'd be pretty cool if one day a book I wrote was someone's favorite book," I admit before continuing, "I too would like to build a family. I've always wanted a pet, but with my mom raising us on her own after my dad died, she said adding an indoor animal to the mix was too much."

"What about geographically? Where do you see yourself?" he asks.

I pause to think about it. "In my heart, I'll always be a Texan. But I've recently given pieces of my heart to a few people who live in Minnesota, so if all goes well, I'd see myself in the Midwest."

Carson hums in response before adding, "And would you be opposed to moving around if you had to?"

"No. I mean, I'd be devastated if I couldn't nanny Cadence anymore, and I've grown quite attached to Kenna. But if I were to move somewhere else with Uncle Car Car, I'd at least get to visit them a lot."

"So often that Mack would get sick of us. Though, if I'm lucky enough to stay in Minnesota, what would your thoughts be on having a place in Texas to visit during the off-season?"

The question hangs between us for a moment before I reply, "I think my mama would be upset that you wasted your hard-earned dollars on a place when she's got more than enough space for us to stay on the ranch."

"Which brings me to my next question . . . when do I get to officially meet my future in-laws?"

I swat at his chest again, and he bends over in laughter.

"Right, right, right . . . too soon. Moving on to safer questions. What kind of pets are we talking?" Carson questions.

"That cat today was cute," I suggest. "I think I'd also like a dog someday. Seeing Cadence and Ranger together has converted me into a dog lover."

"I loved having a dog growing up and would like that for our kids one day. As for the cat, he was so fucking cute. One of the workers told me his name was Omen, which I said was badass. What would you name our future dog and cat?"

I don't even tease him over the fact that he just did what I did back at dinner—talking about the future as if it's *ours*. And I think it's because

I like making plans with him. Even though it scares the shit out of me, I also can't imagine Carson not being a part of my life now that he's in it.

"I mean, that depends on so many things. What kind of dog or cat is it? What color is their fur? It's impossible to say if a name would suit them."

"Okay, I could see that. But now you've got me curious, and this is kind of a dealbreaker for me, so just take that into account."

My stomach twists with nerves in anticipation of his question.

"When we have kids one day, are you going to want to find out the gender ahead of time or wait until the baby is born?"

I let out an unattractive snort that is also somewhat of a sigh. "Oh my gosh, Carson. You had my mind racing thinking about what you were going to ask, and then you asked *that*. Who says their dealbreaker is whether or not a gender is revealed?"

"Hey!" He feigns hurt. "I just think it's important to be on the same page about these things."

"What if the baby doesn't cooperate, and you can't determine the gender until he or she is born?" I counter.

"Well, then I'll have my answer—only a stubborn little girl who's just like her mama would make me wait longer than necessary for something I want."

Holy. Shit. I think future daddy Carson is going to melt hearts one day when he holds his baby in his arms. And now I've got images in my head of that baby being ours. Would they have his eyes? His blonde hair? God, I hope they'd get his patience and caring heart.

"So, what's your answer?" he presses, pulling me from my daydream.

"Um, I think I'd like to know ahead of time, if possible."

Carson pumps his fist in the air. "I knew you were my dream girl!"

When the gondola pulls back up to the hotel's dock, Carson guides me inside and up the staircase.

"Come here. I want to show you something," Carson says as he leads me down the hallway opposite of our room. He pushes open an intricately carved set of double doors that leads us to what appears to be a library. It's dark outside, so it's hard to make out the room from only the dim lighting of the wall sconces.

"I thought this would be a good spot to do some of your writing while you're here. There's a few books about the different places we're visiting while we're in Italy that I wanted to read too. You know, if having company while you write isn't too distracting."

Throwing my arms around his waist, I squeeze him with everything I have. "Thank you for being so thoughtful—for just being *you.*"

Lifting up onto my tiptoes, I press my lips to his. It's a whisper of a kiss—he ghosts his fingers over my collarbone, tracing a line up to my jaw before tangling his fingers in my hair and tugging softly.

When he breaks the kiss, he leans down. "I think it's about time we turn in for the night," he murmurs into my ear, brushing his lips along the slope of my neck.

My heart begins to race erratically in anticipation of what's to come. We somehow make it back to our room before he lifts me up and presses me against the wooden door.

Our kiss is heated, frantic, even. "Tell me you need me as much as I need you, Austen."

I pant, desperately trying to catch my breath. "I need you, Carson. I need to feel all of you."

He growls his approval at my compliance as he carries me into the bedroom and places me on my feet. With his hand resting over the zipper on the back of my dress, he asks, "May I?"

I nod in response before his request from last night that I give him my words rings in my head. "Yes," I breathe out.

He unzips my dress at a torturously slow rate until it finally falls to the floor. When I turn to face him in nothing but a black lace lingerie set, Carson's eyes darken with desire.

"You're ravishing, darling. Come here," he requests.

I go to him, watching his jaw tick as if he's barely able to keep it together right now. My core tightens with need when he picks me up, bringing me in for a searing kiss before setting me on the bed. I watch Carson undress with rapt attention, taking in the way his muscles flex as he tosses his shirt to the ground before he goes to undo his belt buckle. He stops when he looks up and finds me watching him.

Crawling toward him, I kneel on the edge of the bed and reach for his belt. The sound of his buckle clanging, followed by his zipper opening, only enhances my impatience to have his body against mine once more. I make haste as I strip him of his pants and briefs at the same time. When his cock springs free, I gasp as I take it in for the first time. He is so thick and long that I worry he'll split me in two.

"Carson," I stammer, gripping his cock in my hand and moaning when I realize I can't close my fist around it. "There's no way," I state. His abs clench in response to my touch.

"Fuuuuckk," he grinds out through clenched teeth. "I didn't take you for a quitter, Austen."

I scoff at that. "I'm not a quitter, but this will destroy me." I squeeze my fist so he knows what I'm talking about.

"Good. I was hoping to ruin you for anyone else." His gruff voice turns my nipples impossibly hard.

Oh, fuck. That was stupid hot.

Carson leans down to kiss me before lifting me into his arms. Wrapping my legs around his waist, I feel his length against my center. He walks us toward the fireplace as I get lost in the feel of his lips, pulling him closer as I tangle my fingers through his hair.

When he places me on the mantle of the marble fireplace and breaks our kiss, I let out a yelp. "Carson! What are you doing? It'll break!"

"Nothing is going to break. You're tiny, Dakota." He stands between my legs and begins trailing kisses down my chest as he unclasps my bra with one hand and tosses it over his shoulder. The moment he takes my nipple into his mouth, my hips lurch forward, searching for friction.

Before I can plead for more, Carson reads my mind, pushing the fabric of my thong aside as he circles his fingers through my drenched entrance.

"Mmm, Austen," he growls against my breast. He begins kissing down my stomach but looks up as he does, his eyes locking with mine are molten with desire when he says, "I need to taste you."

"Lord, have mercy on me," I plead but don't realize I've said it out loud until I feel the vibration of Carson's chuckle against my clit. I nearly shoot off the mantle from the sensation, but grip a hold through his hair instead.

He flattens his tongue and glides it from my opening through my slit where he begins lapping my overly sensitive clit. And in this moment, I realize I am at the mercy of no one other than Carson Wilder. When he works two fingers inside me and begins pumping them, my legs start to shake frantically as I feel the brink of my orgasm pull at my core.

"Oh, yes! Just like that," I chant through bated breaths.

When he plunges his long fingers deeper, hitting the most delicious spot, black dots begin to spot my vision and my legs convulse against his shoulders. The moment he sucks my clit while fervently flicking my clit with his tongue, I shoot off the mantle and barrel toward an earth-shattering orgasm. Carson doesn't miss a beat, without ever breaking his mouth from my pussy, he stands to full height while I'm on his shoulders, his fingers still thrust inside me, and holds me while I ride out my orgasm.

I've only just come back down to earth when he sets me on the bed and pulls my panties off. He leans over and begins kissing my inner thigh and I stop him with my foot against his shoulder. "Nuh uh," I tsk. "It's my turn to taste you," I tell him.

Sitting up, I go to kneel before him when he shakes his head at me, tapping his hand on the edge of the bed as he says, "Lay on your back and put your head right here, Austen."

I stare at him in confusion but do as he said.

"I'm big," he starts and I cut him off with a snort.

"Thank you for pointing out the obvious," I sass.

"Careful, Kota. I might just fuck the snark right out of that mouth of yours," he warns.

"Promises, promises," I say before I even realize what I'm pushing him to do.

He peers down at me and shakes his head. "Like I was saying . . . I'm big, so with your head angled like this, you should be able to take more of me."

"What little faith you have in me, Carsey. Have you ever been given head by someone who doesn't have a gag reflex?"

I think I hear him whimper at my question, and it makes me feel powerful, urging me on.

"Fuck my face already, Golden Boy," I taunt.

With my head resting on the edge of the bed, Carson nudges his cock against my lips, and I open for him, licking a line from his tip to the base. When I take him into my mouth, he lets out a low groan as he bends forward and sucks my clit into his mouth again.

He thrusts his hips forward, hitting the back of my throat, and I smile around his cock when I realize I've taken him all. A small chuckle gets caught in my throat when he pulls back and thrusts back in. Wanting to make him lose control, to be the first to come, I roll his balls in my hand and hum around his length.

"Holy shit!" he growls against my clit.

As if he can sense the unspoken challenge between us, he wraps my legs around his head and begins to feast on my pussy.

"Hold on tight," Carson commands before surprising the hell out of me when he lifts me off the bed, my mouth still around his cock. Again, he doesn't miss a beat with me upside down in his arms. The feral way he is devouring me has me gushing with arousal.

I realize he's only holding me up with one arm when he plunges his fingers back into me.

This is the hottest fucking thing that has ever happened to me.

I've barely a moment to think that when he begins pistoning his hips, fucking my face with fervor. I take him to the back of my throat and gently scrape my teeth along his length as he pulls back, sucking hard on his tip.

"Oh, fuck!" he grunts. "Dakota, fuck, I'm going to come." He tries to pull away.

Gripping his thighs, I urge him deeper, not giving him the option to pull out.

"You want me to come down your throat while you come on my tongue?" he questions before hooking his fingers so deep inside me I see stars again. Though, I'm not sure if it's the blood rushing to my head or the impending second orgasm.

Nodding my head in reply, I take him deep again, using my teeth a second time. His cock swells in my mouth just as a sensation I've never felt before pools at the base of my spine. Tension pulls taut at my core, and when Carson's tongue rapidly flicks at my clit again, the pressure in my core releases and I have the most intense orgasm of my life.

Did I just . . . ? Holy shit, I did. I just squirted. On his fucking face.

Carson lets out a feral growl as his cock pulses in my mouth and he comes down my throat and I moan as I swallow him down. His legs shudder beneath my palms, as he pulls out of my mouth.

In a move I'm not sure how he pulls off, he swings my other leg over his head, hikes me up over his shoulder, and makes his way into the bathroom. Setting me down, he starts the shower before pulling me into his chest.

"You. Are. My. Dream. Girl," he tells me, punctuating each word with a kiss. Carson holds my head in his hands as he gazes longingly into my eyes. "How fucking privileged am I to call you mine?" I don't get a chance to utter a single word before his lips crash against mine. Steam begins to fog the bathroom by the time we come up for air.

"Come on, let's get cleaned up so I can fall asleep with my girlfriend on my chest again."

My heart expands in my chest as he and I take turns washing each other with care. The feelings I have for this man eclipse all others I've ever felt before. It's at this moment, as I'm safely wrapped in his arms in Venice, that I realize I've fallen inescapably in love with Carson Wilder on only our first date.

25

Carson

When we traveled from Venice to Florence yesterday, we stopped for lunch in Bologna before we got to our cottage tucked away in the countryside. The immaculate home overlooks the rolling hills of a nearby vineyard, with greenery that frames the windows and doors, covering the stone exterior, giving it the cottage feel. We're not exactly roughing it, especially considering there is a butler and chef that stay on the property, but it has the most amazing vibes for my dream girl to write.

The entire reason I booked the place was because it has a private office that overlooks the vineyards, and the house is secluded, offering Dakota the opportunity to get in as much writing time as she can. Meanwhile, I plan to be in the pool that happens to be right outside one of her office windows, giving her all the inspiration she needs.

Waking up this morning, I feel on top of the fucking world. The other night, I made Dakota come twice on my tongue. And when she squirted on my face, I came so hard I thought I might spontaneously combust.

That was, hands down, the hottest night of my life. I'm wrecked in the best way. No one else could ever compare to Dakota. The way she feels nestled in my arms, the smell of her jasmine perfume, the sound of her sweet laughter filling the room—I'll never get enough of her.

I'm out of my mind obsessed with her. But it's okay. It's the healthy kind of obsession. The kind of obsession I would feel okay sharing with my therapist during a session . . . probably.

"Your heart is racing," Dakota informs me when she stretches in my arms.

"It does that from time to time. Well, really, just whenever you're next to me. Good morning, gorgeous," I murmur into her hair as I begin planting kisses all over her face.

"Stop! Oh my gosh!" she exclaims in between giggles.

Rolling her onto her back, I continue trailing kisses over every inch of her skin.

"Being with you like this has me feeling like I'm still dreaming," I admit.

She tugs on my hair, bringing my face to hers. "You're not dreaming, Carson. This is real," she places my palm over her heart, which also means I'm palming her naked boob. Giving it a squeeze, I realize I've already ruined the sweet moment, so I might as well make the most of it.

Peeking up at her, I take her in. The way the morning light shines off the caramel highlights in her hair, which are lighter from the Italian summer sun. Her bronzed skin is on display for me, a stark contrast to the crisp, white sheets. Her sleepy eyes are hooded with lust. When she tries to bite back a smile, I tenderly pull on her chin and watch as her plump bottom lip breaks free.

"You're sure I'm not dreaming?" I question before suggesting, "I think I've got the perfect test to let me know whether or not I'm still asleep."

"Go for it," she says with a yawn.

Leaning down, I pull her nipple into my mouth. When I do, her yawn turns to a gasp at the contact. I proceed to tweak, pinch, and bite her nipples, getting her worked up.

"I need more," she mewls after I torture her for few minutes.

"I've got you," I say as I shoulder my way between her thighs. "I'm going to start my day the best way I know how—with you splayed beneath me, begging and writhing for my cock, grinding on my face while I devour your sweet pussy. I am a man obsessed, Austen. I can't get enough of you—the way you taste on my tongue, the way you moan my name, the sexy whimpers you make when I suck your clit. I'm greedy for every part of you."

I don't wait for an answer; instead, I languidly stroke my tongue through her slit. She loves when I flick my tongue over her clit, but this morning, I'm going to bring her to the brink and edge her a bit.

Once I've got her thoroughly riled up, she curses me while her fists clench the sheets.

"Carson," she whimpers. "Why are you doing this to me?"

Chuckling at her frustration, I delve in to give her what she wants. When I latch onto her clit, she becomes a writhing, quivering mess until she falls apart in the most beautiful way.

Starting at her pussy, I leave a trail of kisses along her skin until I find her mouth. She urges me closer, and I'm not surprised that she fits perfectly beneath me. Propping myself up on my elbows, I roll my hips over hers, and she responds by grinding herself against my rock-hard length.

The feel of her pussy against my cock without a barrier is unlike anything I've ever felt as I continue to glide against her slick slit.

"You're fucking soaked," I murmur.

She sinks her nails into my lower back, pulling me closer to her as she moves her hips faster and trails her lips along the scruff that spots my jawline. When she kisses my Adam's apple, I swallow, and she moans.

I release a drawn-out groan of my own when she bites the chain dangling from my neck. "Fuuucckk."

Why is the sight of her with my medallion between her teeth the sexiest thing I've ever seen?

When she grabs my hips to halt them, I wonder if I've pushed her too far.

"I want to feel you. All of you," she requests as she fists my cock in her hand, stroking it a few times.

"Shit, I don't have a condom," I blurt, realizing how fucking stupid that sounds.

"That's okay. I mean . . . we don't need one."

I freeze and peer down at her. "I'm negative, I haven't been with anyone since long before my last test. Are you on the pill?"

She shakes her head. "No, I have an IUD, and I'm negative too. I trust you, Carson."

"Okay," I reply in disbelief that we're really about to do this.

Knowing I need to get her ready to take me, I slide two fingers inside her, slowly pumping in and out of her until she can take a third. When I can tell she's ready for me, I pull my fingers from her and line myself up at her entrance, slowly nudging the tip of my cock inside her pussy.

"Fuck, Austen. You're so fucking tight." Taking a deep breath, I urge her to breathe with me so I can slide in another inch.

Her pussy is suffocating my cock to the point where I'm worried she'll cut off blood flow.

"Oh, my *fuck*. I don't think I can take any more," she whimpers.

Resting my forehead against hers, I tell her, "You can take all of me because you were made for me, Dakota. Now take a deep breath so I can fill you."

She takes a deep breath, and after a few more thrusts, I bottom out.

"You're such a good fucking girl, taking all of me."

"I can take more," she moans.

"Tell me what you need."

"Harder, Carse."

Sitting back on my heels, I thumb her clit while I piston my hips harder against her. "Fuck. You're taking me so fucking well," I praise her, watching the way her pussy stretches to fit my thick cock. I stay just like that, but take one of her legs so it rests on my shoulder as I lean forward. The change of position has me sliding even deeper inside her.

"Is this okay?" I ask her.

"Yes, it's perfect. Now, fuck me," she demands.

Her wish is my fucking command.

I pull back and slam my hips against hers, thrusting in and out of her as the echoes of our skin slapping against each other surround us.

"Let go, Dream Girl. Unravel for me," I tell her, knowing that she's on the brink of a second orgasm.

My pace quickens, and after a few more thrusts, Dakota's pussy clenches my cock so violently that white spots dance in my vision. Flames of pleasure lick at my spine as my cock swells inside her. Leaning down, I groan into her mouth as I follow her with my own release.

I can't bring myself to pull out of her, wanting to stay frozen in this moment for as long as I can.

Resting my forehead against hers, I place a kiss on each corner of her mouth before stealing her lips in a sweet kiss. "You've enraptured my heart, Dakota," I whisper.

With our lips still touching, she replies, "Only because you revived mine first."

Her stomach grumbles, causing us both to laugh.

"Is my girl hungry?"

"Famished."

I pull out of her, sitting back on my heels again to admire my cum spilling out of her. "I've never done that before. Gone without a condom. But, fuck, Austen. You look fucking exquisite marked as mine."

"Only yours," she whispers, brushing her fingers over the scruff spotting my jaw. My heart feels like it expands in my chest as her words sink in.

Seeing her like this—looking satisfied and perfectly content—has me wanting to hold on to this moment forever, to these feelings cultivating between us. I fell for my dream girl long ago, and by the way she's looking at me right now, I think she might finally be catching up to me after all this time.

"I'll be right back," I tell her as I run into the bathroom to get a warm washcloth to clean her up. When I walk back into the bedroom, Dakota is just slipping on the dress shirt I wore to dinner last night. We stayed in just the two of us, but we thought it'd be fun to dress up. We ate our dinner on the back patio that overlooks the vineyards.

She looks so fucking good standing there in front of the full-length mirror in nothing but my shirt. As she rolls up the sleeves, I circle my hand around her waist from behind, lifting the hem up to expose her perfect pussy.

"Look how stunning you are with my cum dripping down your leg, Austen. I'm entranced." Pressing the warm washcloth against her pussy, I continue, "I'm a good guy, so I'm going to take care of you right now. But make no mistake, I'm only doing this to ease any pain taking me for the first time might've caused. As an unfortunate result, I am cleansing the mark I left. Just know I plan to dirty you up again every fucking chance I get," I rasp into her ear before she tosses her head back against my chest.

"You've made a mess of me, my lord."

We lock eyes as we stare at our reflection. Our chests rise and fall in rapid succession as I slowly drag the cloth up and across the apex of her thighs. My hands tremble with need and her heavy breaths only spur me on.

Unable to resist any longer, I move in front of her and kneel down.

"Carson, what are you doing?" She looks down at me, and my god, I want to worship at her altar.

"Seeing you like this, disheveled and completely satisfied, has me becoming unhinged. I want you to watch how feral you make me." Without breaking eye contact, I flatten my tongue and take a languid stroke through her slit.

"Holy fuck. S-sensitive," she whimpers.

I stop and look up at her. She has her bottom lip between her teeth, her chest heaving as she tries to catch her breath.

"Am I hurting you?"

"No. I just have never come that hard, and now I'm just really sensitive down there. I don't think I could come again. I–I've never had back to back to back. You're the only person to have made me come twice," she clarifies.

A smug smile eclipses my face as a soft chuckle escapes. "You just told an overly competitive professional hockey player that you've never had a hat trick of orgasms. Scoring is my specialty, Dream Girl. Now let me make my newest fantasy come true so I can go make you breakfast."

Within minutes, my girl is falling apart on my fingers and face. I've never been high in my life, but I imagine this feeling of euphoria that I feel in this moment is what an addict craves day in and day out. Dakota has turned my world upside down, but I'm ready to thrive in the chaos.

Pucking Legends:

daughter. Meaning our captain fucked the team owner's daughter at your wedding.

Benny:

J, what the actual fuck is wrong with you?!

G-Baby:

I was asking Carse if he's told Dakota he's in love with her . . . but tell me more about what went on at my wedding.

I have not told her yet. But it's so pathetically obvious, she has to know.

Jaxy, spill the details. Carlisle's DAUGHTER?!?! Benny, I thought you were just going to ask her to dance at the wedding, not do the naked tango . . .

Benny:

middle finger emoji I hate you all.

Benny left the group chat
Jaxy added Benny to the group chat

G-Baby:

omfg. You're cooked, Benny Boy.

You don't hate us. Looks like our boy is in a predicament. The only girl to interest him is off limits. I'm telling Super Nanny to write her next book about this.

Benny:

I'm definitely not interested in anything with her now that I know who she is. And there's no way she didn't know I was one of the players on her father's team.

Jaxy:

Yeah, you heard him. He's definitely not not interested in Little Red.

Benny:

Quit fucking calling her that. Her name is Scarlett. And we don't need to discuss her any further because she's a non-factor.

G-Baby:

Until daddy-dearest finds out . . .

"Dream Girl! Where are you?" I call down the hall of the cottage as I head in the direction of her office. "I've got tea," I say as I swing open the wooden door.

Dakota is sitting at the writing desk, her fingers flying over the keys of her laptop. She's wearing noise–canceling headphones similar to the ones I use for my video games.

Not wanting to interrupt her when she's in the flow, I go to shut the door when she slips off her headphones.

"Hey, sorry, I didn't hear you come in," she explains.

"No need to apologize. I was just going to spill some tea I learned. It would honestly make for a cool storyline in a book,"

"Oh, I love this. Let's hear it." She motions with her hand for me to continue.

"Do you remember at the bachelorette weekend and the wedding how Bennett met that redhead?" I ask.

"Yeah, the girl he sang karaoke for, right?"

"Yep. Well, that same redhead just happens to be the daughter of our team's owner."

I watch as Dakota's eyes widen, and her jaw falls open. "Oh my gosh. Shut up. No she isn't."

"She is. Her name is Scarlett Carlisle. But it gets worse, or maybe better for the storyline's sake . . . Bennett slept with her the night of Griff and Mack's wedding. And now that he knows who she is, he's dead set on believing that she knew who he was all along."

Dakota gasps. "Stop it. This is *so* going in a book one day."

"Will I ever make it in one of your books some day?" I question.

"You're already woven into this storyline, and likely will be for all of my books. You've shown me what it's like to feel intimacy and romance again."

I can't help the feeling of pride that swells in my chest. "Would that make me your muse?"

A shy smile lights up her face. "I suppose it would."

"Good. I'll let you get back to work. I don't want to be a distracting muse. Plus, watching you type away so passionately has me dying for you to get to the spicy scenes." I waggle my eyebrows exaggeratedly at her and she rolls her eyes in response.

I take a few strides toward her to close the distance between us and give her a kiss. It was my intention to give her a quick peck and leave her to work. But when she leaps into my arms and wraps her legs around my waist, my good intentions are put to the test.

I squeeze her ass before giving it a playful smack. Breaking the kiss, I groan as I rock my hips against hers to show her what she does to me.

"Back to work, Austen. There's plenty of time for more of this. You looked like you were on a roll. I'll go get you a snack and some water while you get back in the zone."

She sighs as I set her back on the ground, mumbling an incoherent response. "What was that?" I question.

"I said, you're too good to me. And then in my head I thought, I'm going to show him my appreciation later."

Her words along with the devious grin she's wearing has my cock springing to attention.

Down boy, I think to myself.

"Taking care of you is one of my love languages." My cheeks heat as soon as the words escape, but I'm not ashamed for her to know how I'm feeling. I've been dying to let her know I'm head over heels for her, but I still don't know if she's ready to hear my love declaration.

"Alright, well, snacks," I pivot, pointing over my shoulder as I back out of the office and shut the door behind me. Resting my forehead against the door, I sigh in relief that I didn't blurt my feelings just now. Dakota deserves a grand declaration, and as soon as she's ready, I'm going to shout it from the rooftops.

What she had before wasn't love. I'm ready to do everything in my power to show her what it should be—what my love for her will always be.

26

Dakota

Rome was beyond my wildest dreams. Watching Carson geek out and rattle off historical facts about the Colosseum and Sistine Chapel might've made me fall even harder for him.

It's been nearly two weeks since our first date in Venice, and with each day that passes, I'm finding myself not only getting lost in Carson but also rediscovering myself. I feel like a butterfly breaking free from my chrysalis.

Florence was what fantasies are made of. The house Carson rented for us was tucked away in the countryside and I got more writing done in the six days we spent there than I have since I decided to begin writing my book. I'd be lying if I said the landscapes of the rolling vineyards outside my window were the inspiration that put me in the right headspace to write so much.

We didn't see much of Florence outside of our little countryside haven, and that was fine by me. Each morning, Carson woke me up with his head between my thighs and I've never been so deliciously sore in my life. It's been nearly two days since he was last inside me, but I still feel self-conscious as we walk down via Lorenzo D'Amalfi.

Our last two days in Italy will be spent on the Amalfi Coast before we drive north to fly out of Naples.

Looking to my side, I take Carson in as we walk to the rental company, where we plan to rent a Vespa for the day. He's wearing olive green chinos and a white linen dress shirt. If I didn't fall asleep to the sound of his beating heart each night, I'd swear he was immortal. The way he looks so put together all the time, without a single hair out of place, free of imperfections, should intimidate me. But the validation and reassurance this man gives me each day is uncanny, making it impossible to feel any insecurities when it comes to how he feels for me.

Now, I know we've been on a month-long vacation, where I've fallen head over heels in love with him, but Carson showed me how much he cares about me long before we touched down in Italy.

We make it to the rental place, where they give us the key for a cream-colored Vespa with a cute wicker basket on the back that is all ours for the day. I want to squeal and do a happy dance at how adorable it is. And seeing Carson in the cute little bucket helmet has me even more smitten with this man.

Carson insists on driving a few side streets solo so he can get a hang of driving before I hop on the back. Once I'm on, I hold tight around his waist and press my front to his back, loving the feel of his muscular body against mine. Even though we've been on vacation for a month, he's made it a priority to work out each day and practice stickhandling drills in the hotel rooms or rental houses we've stayed in. It's fun to pursue my passion and write my book while he's refining his body and skills for hockey at the same time.

The midi dress I'm wearing keeps me modest while riding the Vespa. When we woke up at the hotel this morning, Carson said we were going to do "cute, coupley things." So I chose to wear a light blue mid-length dress and cream Esmeralda wedge sandals that tie at my ankles. The dress has a corset top that had Carson trying to lay me back on the bed for round two.

We've wound around the streets of the coast when Carson pulls to a rest stop on the road so we can take in the views. We park the Vespa and place our helmets on the back before walking to the guardrail to take in the view. The iconic, colorful coastal buildings provide a beautiful backdrop as I grab ahold of his hand and gasp when he gently squeezes mine three times.

"Carson," I whisper before squeezing his back four times.

His head snaps up to meet my eyes.

Tears fill my eyes as I say, "*Ti amo, ragazzo d'oro.*"

"Say it again," he pleads.

"*Ti amo.*"

"You love me?" he asks incredulously.

"I do. So very much," I admit, nodding my head.

"*Ti amo anch'io, ragazza dei sogni,*" he replies as he scoops me into his arms, and I giggle as he spins me around. My laugh is cut off when he claims my mouth in a searing kiss that steals the breath from my lungs.

When we finally break our kiss, I ask, "What does that mean, exactly? I only asked how to say, 'I love you, Golden Boy.'"

"It means I love you too, Dream Girl. And I do. So fucking much. I've been dying to tell you for a while now, but I didn't know if you were ready. You had a skewed perception of love because the marriage you were in was toxic and abusive. All I've wanted to do is show you what love should be, Austen."

It's my turn to shake my head incredulously. "You've shown me what love should be from the very beginning of our friendship. Our love may not have started with romantic intent, but that doesn't mean I didn't fall hard right away for your friendship—for your irresistible charm and witty humor. You quickly became someone I couldn't imagine going a day without talking to long before we made things official, and that is due to you consistently supporting me and showing up for us."

Carson pulls me into a tight embrace, and I feel the deep rumble of his chuckle against my chest. "I can't believe you love me back. It's about time you realized you have feelings for me."

"Oh, Golden Boy. I've known I loved you since at least our first date."

"Such a late bloomer," he teases me before declaring, "This calls for a celebratory selfie."

He wraps his arms around me from behind, holding my phone up in the air and flipping the camera so it's facing us. After he takes a few pictures, he swipes to video mode and starts filming the two of us.

"Hey, kids, it's your mom and dad here in Italy. Your mama just told me she loves me for the first time. Isn't that right, Mama?" Carson asks as he looks down at me and places a kiss on my temple.

"Carson, what are you doing?"

"Uh, you've got to call me Daddy. The kids are watching. They can't call me Carson."

Rolling my eyes into the camera, I say, "Daddy, what is this about?"

Leaning down, he whispers a muffled, "Holy fuck that was hot," before facing the camera again.

"Haven't you seen the TikTok trend where couples who are dating make videos for their future kids to watch? I saw it a few weeks ago and have been dying to do one together while we're here. I thought now was the perfect moment." He pans the camera to show the scenery in the background. "I mean, look at these views, kids," he tells the phone before continuing, "But the most *bellissima* view is of your mama. Isn't she stunning?"

I turn and burrow my face into his chest to hide from the camera.

"One thing you'll learn about your mama is she's bashful, and when she is, her cheeks turn the sweetest shade of pink. Alright, we've got to go celebrate our love. Goodnight kids! *Ciao!*"

He looks at me expectantly, and I sigh in defeat, rolling my eyes at his antics.

"Goodnight, babies. Mama and Daddy love you! *Ciao!*" I say as I blow a kiss to the camera.

When he stops videoing, he spins me in his arms and rocks me side to side in his embrace.

"Thanks for being a good sport, Austen. I think the kids will get a kick out of that one day." He's so confident in our future. It should probably scare me, but I can't help but feel self-assured too in what we have.

Just as he's handing me back my phone, I get a FaceTime request from Brody. I click the accept button and hold the phone up to get both of us on the screen.

"Hey, Golden Boy. Look who's calling before his preseason game."

Carson's smile is wider than I've ever seen it and I'm not sure if it's because we just confessed our love to each other or if it's because he's talking to his man crush.

"Brodes, how's it going, buddy?" he asks my brother.

"Hey, Carse. It's going. About to play in our second preseason game, and I needed to have my pregame chat with Kota Lynn. Are you taking good care of my sister?"

"Always. In fact, 'Kota Lynn' just told me she loves me for the very first time," Carson informs Brody, and I give him a gentle elbow to the side when he uses air quotes to mock my nickname.

"Ouch," he grumbles, which has Brody doubling over in laughter.

Once he finally composes himself enough to talk, Brody says, "I mean, what's not to love about you, Golden Boy?" Hearing my big brother call Carson by the nickname I've coined him doesn't sit right with me.

Huh, maybe this is how Carson felt when Jackson called me Super Nanny.

"Where has this bromance come from? Have y'all been talking behind my back?"

Carson shakes his head and gives my shoulders a reassuring squeeze. "It's not talking behind your back if it's not about you. We chat from time to time. Besides, you're the one who gave him my number."

I scoff. "Only because he threatened to miss his playoff game if I didn't tell him who I was moving in with unexpectedly."

"Semantics," he says, trying to play it cool when I know internally he's likely freaking out at casually chatting with Brody. I also didn't miss the way he called my brother "Brodes."

"Next thing I know y'all are going to tell me you asked for permission to date me from my brother." I chuckle to myself, only to have that laughter quickly die when I see the guilty look on Carson's face and watch as Brody fights back a snort that eventually escapes.

"God, this is good stuff," Brody says as he points to the two of us. "You two are hilarious. If I play well tonight, we're going to have to make this my new pregame ritual."

"Your superstitions are getting out of hand, Brodes," I say in exasperation.

"What I think your sister meant to say is, of course, man. Anything you need. I take my pregame rituals very seriously as well."

Rolling my eyes, I mumble, "Kiss ass," to which Carson begins tickling my sides so badly I think I'll drop my phone.

Unable to catch my breath, I let out an unbecoming snort-gasp, to which Brodes gives me shit for.

"I know you were raised on a ranch, but you weren't born in a barn, Kota Lynn. Get a hold of yourself," he gripes, not sounding one bit serious.

"Alright, you've had your pregame chat. Good luck, *Ciao!*"

"Y'all be safe, ya hear me? Carse, I'm counting on you to take good care of my baby sis," he says in warning.

"Her safety and happiness will always be my number one priority," Carson assures him.

On that note, I end the call and turn around to face Carson.

"So, y'all are on a nickname basis now?"

"I know, isn't it amazing? It's like the second best thing that's ever happened to me. Well, third, actually."

I lift a brow in question before he clarifies, "The first best thing is when you told me you love me just now. The second being the day Cadence was born."

My face softens at that. "I miss that little bugga-boo so much," I admit.

Carson smiles affectionately before wrapping me in his arms again and agreeing. "Me too. Which reminds me, we've got to get her something from the shops downtown when we return the Vespa."

"Okay," I say but it comes out as a lovesick sigh instead. I love the way this man so fiercely loves and cares for the people closest to him. And I'm completely baffled that I'm now on the list of people he loves and cares for.

Being loved by Carson Wilder wasn't something I anticipated happening this year, or ever for that matter. The man is too good, one of the absolute best. But sitting here overlooking one of the most beautiful sceneries I've ever witnessed, nuzzled in his embrace, I feel fulfilled for the first time in a long time. It may be one of the greatest gifts he's given to me—helping me realize my self-worth again. Carson validates my feelings and builds me up every chance he gets.

When he grabs my hand, leading me back to the Vespa and puts my helmet on with the greatest care, I send up a little prayer of gratitude that I get to love this man, and nothing and no one can take that away from me.

27

Carson

AUGUST

I woke up to a text from Brad, the contractor I hired to do the renovations at my house.

Contractor Brad:

> Not great news to report today. We ran into a delay with the wall sconces the designer ordered. They won't be here for another two days, which is later than anticipated. The rest of construction is nearly complete.

Me:

> I appreciate the update, Brad. I think we can manage a two-day detour. I'd like to wait until she can see the full thing come together.

> Sounds good, Boss. Safe travels.

> Thank you! Keep me posted on the progress.

I don't blame them for not having the library done. Honestly, I'm impressed they've been able to get what I asked them to do done this quickly. If I were Brad, I would've blocked my number and stopped taking my additional requests after a while.

Between the color changes, my request to hire a designer to furnish the space, and my last minute request to add a custom built-in high-low desk so Dakota can have the walking pad she's been eyeing, it feels like I've requested something new every other day. But I just want it to be perfect for her.

Feeling Dakota begin to stir from where she's sleeping on my chest, I set my phone back on the side table.

"Mmm. Good morning," she mumbles, her voice laced with sleep.

"Morning, gorgeous. How'd you sleep?"

"Like the dead, considering you fucked me in the ocean, only to go caveman with your need to mark me twice more when we got back to our room," she says in a haughty tone.

That makes me chuckle. "I can't help it. I'm in love and obsessed with showing you just how much I worship you."

Rolling to her side, she pitches herself up on her elbow. She yawns as she asks, "What time did you say we have to be at the airport?"

Catching her contagious yawn, I let out my own yawny reply, "Change of plans, Austen. We're not going home tonight. I've got a little surprise for you, if you're up for it?" I ask as she reaches over and begins running her fingers through my unruly mane.

"Where are we going?" she questions as I inch closer to her and sigh, relaxing into her touch that I've grown accustomed to these past few weeks.

"I can't tell you, that would ruin the fun of it. You'll find out which country when we get to the airport."

Mostly I can't tell her, because I've still got to figure it out and plan the logistics.

"Country?" she squeals.

"I had a dream last night, and I've decided we must cross it off my list of fantasies."

I'm not lying. I had a dream last night that I took her somewhere special. Did the dream conclude with a happy ending? Of course.

"Your fantasy includes taking me to a different country? Other than Italy and America?"

Kissing a line up her torso, I press a deep kiss to her lips. Sometime after Venice we ditched our clothes at night, and I have appreciated the easy access sleeping naked allows me each morning. It's a hard decision to make though, whether I'm going to start my day with her coming from my mouth or cock. So I quickly learned not to choose and have her come on both.

"It does," I answer between kisses.

Where? I'm not exactly sure yet. Maybe England?

Shifting her on top of me, I rock my hips against hers as she sits back so I can watch my cock glide against her.

"You feel so good," she mewls.

"I can think of a way to make you feel even better," I practically growl. "Turn around and sit the fuck down on my face while you suck my cock like a good girl."

Dakota doesn't immediately comply, instead she gives me a few more teasing strokes of my cock against her drenched core. Biting her lip, she finally replies, "I'll suffocate you."

"Eating your sweet pussy would be the absolute best way to go," I say truthfully.

When she finally turns and wraps her lips around my cock, situating herself above me, I yank her hips down impatiently and groan against her clit when I finally get a taste of her. She moans around my length, making my balls tighten with uncontained lust. I need this woman in every possible way I can have her.

Fighting back the urge to thrust up into her mouth, I focus on trying to make her come as quickly as possible. I refuse to come anywhere but her pussy this morning, and whatever she's doing with her mouth and teeth right now, feels good enough to alter my brain chemistry. Just as she clenches around my fingers and I feel her fall apart above me, I lift her off of me, spinning her around.

"Grab the headboard, Austen," I command.

As she does, I spread her cheeks and coat my length in her arousal. Lining myself up behind her, I work my way inside her inch by aching inch.

When my abs are flush to her delectable ass, I give it a light smack.

"Oh, fuck," she moans.

"You were made for me," I growl possessively into her ear as I drag my fingers down her side before finding her clit.

Desperate to give her a second release, I sit back and slam my hips forward. Once, twice, and on the third time she cries out, "Yes, Carson! Right there!"

"Play with your clit for me," I tell her.

"Only if you grab my hips and fuck me harder, my lord."

My cock swells inside her when she calls me that. Doing as she asked, I firmly grip her hips and piston my hips into her from behind. I push down on her back, and when she arches her lower back up, I nearly pass out with how much deeper the change of position gets me. With each thrust my balls slap against her at the same time as her hand frantically works her clit.

"I'm going to come," she whimpers, and thank fuck, because I'm right there too.

"Be my good girl and come, Austen. Soak my cock."

After a few weeks, you'd think I'd be used to the intensity at which I come when I'm inside of her, but I don't think my body will ever acclimate to the need I have for this woman.

"I love you. Oh, god, I love you so much," she chants and it's my undoing. My spine tingles at the same time my abs tighten, and I come inside of her with a ferocity I've never felt before. Dakota shatters around me, her pussy choking my cock has it spasming inside her and I swear to god I think I could come again.

"Goddammit, I love you more than anything," I croak against her spine. Completely spent, I rest my forehead between her shoulder blades, placing open mouth kisses along each of her vertebrae.

I reluctantly pull out of her, and she rolls onto her back, arms splayed across the bed, hair disheveled, and she's never looked so beautifully *mine*.

"No. Shut up!" Dakota exclaims as she realizes where we've just arrived. "Oh my god, you're joking. Stop it."

"Welcome to the Jane Austen House Museum, my lady," I say as I open the door and hold my hand out for her to take, bowing before her.

She takes my hand and gets out of the rental car. "You've spoiled me so, my lord."

Pretending to be a gentleman that I most certainly have not been around her lately, I offer her my arm and escort her through the gardens toward the front door of the museum.

When we get inside, I urge Dakota to take a seat at Jane's writing desk. I wouldn't be a good boyfriend if I didn't fill my camera roll with dozens of photos of her sitting at the desk.

"My favorite author sitting in her favorite author's writing spot," I say out loud as I finish sending off my favorite photo to Mack to print out for the home library reveal when Dakota wraps her arm around my waist and squeezes me tight. I hurriedly put my phone in my pocket and pray like hell she didn't see the text exchange.

Dakota gets lost in the details of the house for the next hour, and I watch her take it in with rapt attention. I could watch her do the most mundane things for the rest of my life and never get bored.

I'm so lost in her, I don't realize how much time has past. This isn't the first time this has happened—she easily captures my attention, especially when her smile reaches her eyes, making her nose scrunch up in the most adorable way.

"This is so amazing. But now that we're here, I'm dying to know how this was one of your fantasies," she whispers into my ear as she balances on her tiptoes, placing a peck on my cheek.

Slipping my hand into the back pocket of her jeans, I pull her closer and continue to walk the path that leads us to the Greyfriar, where we plan to grab lunch. I'm sickeningly in love with my girl, and I want everyone around us to know it.

"Anything I do with you is my fantasy. Truthfully, I just wanted to see your reaction to visiting this place. And the smile that lit up your face for the past half hour is everything I could've imagined and more."

That earns me a chuckle, and my chest puffs with pride.

I'm obsessed with Dakota's smile, but I crave the sound of her laugh each day. Even better, I love earning her laughter. How crazy would she think I am if I recorded her laughing so I could listen to it on the road when I'm missing her? She'd probably think I'm demented, but I'm oddly okay with it.

I've just got the front door open to the tavern when my phone rings in my pocket.

"Why don't you get that while I use the restroom?" Dakota suggests.

"Sounds good," I say in reply before seeing it's Griff who's calling. Swiping to accept, I answer, "G, what's good, buddy?"

"Hey, Carse. How's the detour going?"

"Really good, we just got done touring the Jane Austen House Museum. We're flying home tomorrow morning."

"Good to hear man. Look, that's kind of why I'm calling." He pauses on the line before continuing, "I was talking to Brad today because he's going to do some work at our place. Anyway, he said there was a guy hanging around the outside of your house last night when he was heading out for the night. He said he didn't get a good look at the guy, but that when he caught him scoping out the place, the guy took off. Do you want me to get in contact with my buddies from Boston and see if they can install an upgraded security system at your place? I think it wouldn't be a bad idea for us to get one installed here too."

My stomach churns as unease slithers its way up my spine. "These paparazzi have gotten out of hand. I'm so fucking sick of the media." That's been a huge bonus of this trip—no one knows me as the NHL's rookie golden boy. I take a deep breath trying to ease my frustration. "If you don't mind, I think it'd be a good idea to have someone do an upgrade."

"Consider it done. Do you think it's the same photographer that crashed into you and Cadence?" he questions.

"I don't know, but I'd like to have more cameras in place around the perimeter of the house so we can catch these scumbags."

"I'll give them a call now. Maybe the girls should stay together at our house once the season starts until they figure this out," Griffin suggests.

"Yeah, or even with my parents. I don't want to take any chances," I agree.

"Alright, well sorry to be the bearer of bad news. Safe travels, we'll see you guys once you get back."

"Thanks, G. Love ya."

He chuckles over the line. "Did you tell Dakota that yet?"

"I did. She actually told me first." A huge smile takes over my face, pressing my cheek against the phone.

"I can hear you smiling through the phone you simp."

"Takes one to know one, fucker."

"Touché. I'm really happy for you, Carse."

"Thanks, man. We'll see you."

I hang up and try to shake the feelings of unease so I don't ruin our last day together, but I can't help the sinking feeling taking hold of me. I'll never jeopardize Dakota's safety or happiness, and part of that is making sure she feels secure—in our relationship and in what I hope will soon become our home.

28

Dakota

"Oh, you were supposed to take that turn," I inform Carson as we make our way back home from the airport.

"I know." His gaze dances with mirth as he sneaks a glance at me.

"So, you missed the turn on purpose?"

"Yeah, this way is longer and has more stop signs," he says as he pulls the truck to a stop, leans over the center console and places a whisper of a kiss on my lips.

My cheeks heat from the quickening of my pulse. This man. This unabashedly wonderful man. He can't be real, can he?

"Mmm. I can't wait to get you home and suffocate you with snuggles. I'm feeling like I want to wrap around you like a koala tonight." My man loves to cuddle, which, let's be honest, Carson was never going to *not* be a boyfriend who cuddles. And it's not that I don't like to snuggle, but this man becomes extra clingy when he's feeling anxious. I can't for the life of me figure out why he'd be anxious or nervous right now.

When he pulls into the garage a few minutes later, I squeeze his hand three times and he gives me three in return paired with a dazzling smile that I can't help but mirror. Carson gets out of the truck and quickly rounds the hood to hold open my door for me. Gripping me around my waist, he lifts me out of the truck before wrapping me in his arms.

"Will you do me a favor, Austen? Would you close your eyes when we get upstairs? I've got a bit of a surprise for you."

I chuckle in response. "Your dick better not be the surprise, Golden Boy. While I'm thoroughly impressed by it, I don't consider it surprising at this point."

"Yeah right. What about last night when I fucked you so deep you said—" I cover his mouth with my hand.

"A cocky attitude will get you nowhere," I tell him as I pull my hand away.

"My confidence got me this far, Dream Girl. Don't act like you don't love me."

Wrapping my arms around his neck, I lace my fingers together, bringing my lips to his ear. "I'll never act like I don't love you, Carson. I'm yours and you are mine. Now quit your bickering and take me upstairs."

"You don't have to ask me twice."

Carson sets our suitcases in the laundry room before turning his back to me and squatting down. "Hop up," he says, shrugging his shoulders, but I'm far too busy admiring his bubble butt in the gray sweatpants he's wearing.

"Dakota, I've got a surprise for you, but if you keep eye fucking me like that, I'll have my way with you right here in the laundry room."

That snaps me out of it, because as much as I'd love for that to happen, I'm not someone who has received many surprises in life. Hopping on to his back, I can't help but let my hands rake over the rigid muscles on his back and shoulders. I nearly let out a whimper when he wraps my legs tighter around his waist, causing my core to rub against his solid lower back.

"Careful, Austen," he growls out in warning, his gruff voice causing heat to pool in my stomach. I can't seem to get enough of him; I've never been so attracted to another person in my life.

When we get to the top of the stairs, he heads to the left instead of the right where our rooms are. Which brings me to wonder whether we'll keep separate rooms now that we're back or if we'll share like we did on vacation. I'm honestly not sure I could sleep with him across the hall now.

As if he can read my mind he says, "We'll need to work on moving all of your things to our room before my preseason training camp starts. But your surprise is down this way."

He tells me to close my eyes when we're in front of what used to be Cadence's playroom. I do as he says and listen as he opens the door and takes a step forward.

"I'm going to set you down, but don't open your eyes just yet."

"Okay," I say as he places me on my feet and gives my shoulders a gentle squeeze.

"Alright, open your eyes," he tells me.

I do, but when the sight before me is too much to take in, I bring my hand to cover my mouth and squeeze my eyes shut again in disbelief.

"Carson," I whisper, but it echoes in the silence of the room. Opening my eyes again, I start to take in the details of the room that looks nothing like it did when we left for Italy. Tears prick at the corners of my eyes.

Instead of the bright white and beige playroom, the room is painted a dark hunter green with walls of floor-to-ceiling built-in bookshelves along three of the walls with beautiful crown molding and a ladder that runs the length of the room. Between the shelves are wall sconces that look like real gas-lit lanterns. In place of the closet that used to be against the one wall, there is now a wooden desk that looks like it's been custom built for the space. In the corner of the room sits an oversized brown leather chair and a matching ottoman big enough to fit the both of us. A large Persian-style rug covers the hardwood floors and ties in with the colors of the walls and shelves. The ceiling is the same deep green as the walls, but it has an ornate floral pattern to it.

"I had it remodeled while we were gone. It wasn't quite ready when we were supposed to leave the other day, that's why we took that little detour," Carson explains as I continue to take in the room in wonder.

"I don't know how you managed to pull this off, but thank you so much. This is the greatest surprise I've ever been given, Carson." The tears break free and start to cascade down my face when I see a piece of artwork hanging above the writing desk next to a wooden sign that says "This is where the magic happens."

As I get closer, I recognize it's a canvas full of my handwritten notes to Carson. He even wrote the ones I sent him via texts on post-its and had it made into a piece of art.

"One of my love languages is words of affirmation. So, in my mind, you've been telling me you love me everyday for the past four months," Carson explains as he follows me toward the desk. "Look how beautiful your words are, Austen. They're visual poetry. I want you to type them in your computer, write them on the walls, just like you've written them on my heart. You've claimed me, whether you meant to or not. There's no going back to just friends for me now that we're back home. Because that's just it, this place isn't home without you in it. Without you, it's just walls, plaster and roofing. So be mine forever, Dakota—move in with me and be my home."

Being with him these past few weeks has taken some getting used to—it's like I'm retraining my brain after years of experiencing such a polar opposite form of what I thought was love. Carson showers me with adoration and praise. He makes me feel needed, loved and cared for. I've never felt more safe and secure than I do in his arms. But I can't help this tiny voice in the back of my mind that blares that this is all too good to be true. Moving in together, in an official capacity, feels like it should be a decision made with careful consideration.

The moment the suggestion left his lips, I felt the urge to leap into his arms and shout yes. Instead, I find myself breaking eye contact and staring down at the floor, struggling to form a response.

"You don't have to make a decision right now. I'm sorry if I put pressure on you, that wasn't my intention. I'm just crazy about you, and I want you to know now that we're back, no longer on a dreamy vacation, that I'm still all in and completely in love with you."

I know in my heart I don't want to push him away or hurt him. But for a moment there, my insecurities had me worried I may be making another mistake blinded by lust. I know for certain that he would never treat me the way Aaron did. My heart knows Carson would never hurt me, never raise his voice at me in anger. But my heart isn't the one that needs reassurance, it's my head.

Carson Wilder is a walking green flag. He's kind, caring, endearing, selfless, the list goes on.

So why am I sitting here making him sweat over a question that I absolutely want to say yes to?

Bracketing my chin between his fingers, he lifts my face so his eyes can meet mine, and when they do, I realize I have nothing to fear. Before I can overthink this any further, I whisper, "Yes."

"Yes?" he questions. The hope in his eyes has emotion clogging my throat.

"Yes. Yes, I'll be your home. Always," I choke out.

He wraps his arms around me in a tight hug, lifting me off the ground. "Fuck yeah!" he exclaims as he spins us around.

"Quit it. You're making me dizzy!" I try to catch my breath through my laughter. "And I still need to check out the rest of the room," I tell him.

He stops spinning, but wraps my legs around his waist instead of placing me back down. Grasping my ass in his hands, he holds me against him and rests his forehead against mine.

"I don't think I've ever been happier than I am in this moment," he admits.

"Me either. Is this what you were nervous about earlier?" I question.

"Yeah, I mean, I've never surprised someone with something like this, and I wasn't sure how you'd take it. Do you like it?"

"I do, it's amazing." I don't hold back the smile that takes over.

"Good," he says as he places a kiss on each corner of my mouth. "I fucking love seeing you happy." With a pat on my butt, he sets me down and turns me back around to the room so he can point out different details I may have missed.

"I wasn't sure where you'd want all of your books, so I had the designer place some of them on the shelves," he explains before sweeping me over to one of the drawers that is below each shelf. "And in the drawers, I asked them to put some of our board games we've accumulated the past few months. Oh, and then because you said you knew how to play chess, I asked for this cool chess board I saw online." He walks me over to the square coffee table that is next to the oversized chair. There are floor cushions surrounding the coffee table, the perfect spot to sit and play our games together. The chess board is massive, taking up a good portion of the coffee table. Lifting one of the pieces to examine it, I feel the weight of it and ask, "Wait, are these glass?"

He stands beside me, bringing his hand over mine as he brushes his thumb over the ridges of the rook piece. "They are. Half are clear and the other frosted. I saw the board online and knew we had to get it."

Setting the piece down, I turn to face him. "This is unreal, Carson. I'm amazed they were able to get all of this done while we were gone."

He scratches at his head and lets out a sheepish sigh. "Me too, honestly, considering I was kind of a diva to work with. I kept making change orders and asking for updates, but it's only because I wanted it to turn out perfect."

Wrapping my arms around his neck again, I bring him in for a chaste kiss.

"Thank you, thank you, thank you," I tell him as I pepper kisses over his jawline. The moment is broken up when his stomach growls so loudly it can't be ignored.

"Why don't you look around and I'll go start a load of laundry and get us some snacks," he suggests and I can feel the heart eyes I'm staring at him with.

"Are you sure? I don't mind coming with you and starting the laundry."

"I'm sure that I want you to sit in here and finish the book you were reading on the plane. Or arrange your shelves. Really anything besides laundry. Does popcorn sound good to you?"

"Yes, extra salt please."

"Duh, is there any other way to eat it?" Carson gives me another peck before he leaves the room.

I don't care if it's cliché, but I do the fairytale spin in the middle of my new library, feeling like a damn queen in her castle.

Carson sets down the bowl of popcorn on the new coffee table in the library.

"Do you want to read some more?" he asks, and when I look up I realize he's now shirtless, leaving him in only a pair of low-slung gray sweats that match the ones I've got on.

Smirking down at me, he catches me ogling him.

"Let me just finish this chapter," I answer as he sits on the ground beside my chair. Finding myself feeling needier than usual, I slide off the chair and place my head in his lap. Carson tosses popcorn into his mouth, feeding me kernels while I continue reading.

A soft moan escapes my lips when he threads his fingers through my hair and begins massaging my scalp.

"What are you reading?" he asks.

Using my thumb as a bookmark, I close the book to show him the cover. "Do you remember me telling you about my indie author friend I met through Instagram?"

He nods before I continue, "Well, this is her debut and I'm completely obsessed. The MMC has been in love with the FMC for eleven years. Can you imagine waiting to be with the love of your life for eleven years? That man has perfected the art of patience."

"He sounds like a saint. I could hardly keep it together for a year," Carse says, making me laugh because his feelings for me became glaringly obvious right around the bachelorette weekend.

"Alright, I'm done with this chapter," I tell him.

"Do you want to watch a movie?" he asks, fingers still combing through my hair.

"Could we play a game instead? Maybe Scrabble or chess? Seems like a waste to have such a beautiful chess board and let it sit there as an unused decor piece," I suggest, placing my book down next to me.

"I didn't realize you were in the mood to lose. I'm low-key a chess master. Not on an official level, but I don't lose."

"Oh, Mr. Bigshot. Put your money where your mouth is. I think you may have met your match," I tell him as I sit up and take a seat on one of the floor cushions.

"Shall we make things interesting?" Carson asks with a quirked brow when he joins me on the cushion opposite of me.

"What do you have in mind?" I query.

"Strip chess."

"Strip chess?" I repeat.

"Yeah. One item of clothing for every piece taken. The more valuable the piece, the more significant the item of clothing. Checkmate would obviously be strip naked."

"Obviously," I deadpan. "You can't be serious. You're hardly wearing any clothing as is," I suggest waving my arm at his naked chest.

"We'll both go get more clothes on to make it fair. How about ten items each?" he asks.

"You're going down, Golden Boy."

Racing down the hall to my closet, I put on more items of clothing, along with some fuzzy socks and slippers. When I get back to the library, Carson is waiting for me, tossing popcorn in the air and catching it. Why is something so simple so much sexier when he's doing it? And why for the love of god does he catch me staring every time? He winks at me as I make my way over to the chess board. My panties are going to be a tortured mess once this game is over with.

"Do you want to be the clear glass or the frosted glass?" he asks.

"Is the frosted glass the black pieces?" I question, and when he nods in response, I turn the board around so the frosted glass is in front of him.

"Ladies first," he suggests.

"More like, the white pieces go first," I correct as I move my queen's pawn forward two spaces. Carson doesn't say anything as a cocksure smile spreads across his face.

"Your cocky attitude is unbecoming," I inform him.

That makes him chuckle. "You seem especially fond of my cock, Austen."

I snort in response. "Carson!"

He makes his first move, which is a mirrored move across the board. It doesn't take long for our articles of clothing to start coming off. And as each item comes off of him, I become increasingly distracted.

Carson's body is a work of art. He has spent countless hours in the gym and on the ice to earn every inch of muscle on him. I find myself itching to trace his veins and kiss every dip and swell on his body.

"Strip. All of it."

"What?" I question, still focused on the board, trying to strategize my next move.

That's when I notice my king piece is knocked over. "Checkmate."

I'm still staring in shock at the board when he says, "Did you really try to Queen's Gambit me?"

"Well, yeah, I did." I scoff as I begin to take off my remaining two items of clothing. When I go to unclasp my bra, Carson pauses my hands.

"Slower," he commands. "I want to milk this for all it's worth."

I do as he requests, slowly dragging the straps of my white lace bra, which happens to be my best matching set, down my arms until my breasts are exposed to him.

In past relationships, I'd felt self conscious about my body, but everything is different with Carson. He makes me feel so beautifully worshiped.

As I hook my fingers into the waistband of my thong, Carson stops me, before lifting me up, and laying me down on the ottoman of the chair. He takes his queen piece from the board and brings it to my lips. He then slowly drags it down the nape of my neck, trailing it over my collarbones, where goosebumps erupt in its wake. My body hums to life with every sliver of skin he touches as he continues down between my breasts until he reaches the delicate lace of my thong.

"I've never been so offended by a scrap of fabric in my life," he murmurs as he grabs a hold of my thong and tears it from my body.

"Carson! Those were my most expensive pair," I whine.

"I'll buy you a dozen more tomorrow, Austen. Actually, no. I think I like it better when you go without."

Without the fabric stopping his progress down my body, Carson sits back on his heels and brings my one ankle to rest on his shoulder, spreading my legs, leaving me completely exposed.

He drags the glass chess piece from my ankle to the back of my knee, causing chills to scatter from the sensitive spot. When he reaches my inner thigh, I fight the urge to clench them together at the sensation.

My body squirms as he teases the queen piece over my slit, before dragging it to my other thigh, I'm so soaked that only one swift pass has the piece drenched.

He circles my opening before dragging the piece up to my clit. My skin burns feverishly as he brings the tension to a precipice.

"Carson, please," I whimper.

"Is my dream girl feeling needy?" he questions.

"So fucking needy for you," I reply, desperate for his touch.

Perching myself on my elbows, I watch as Carson drags the piece down my slit before slowly pushing it inside me. The oversized piece feels cool and erotic as he pumps it inside me at a torturous rate.

Knowing I need more without me having to beg for it, he brings his mouth to my core and takes one delicious pass with his flattened tongue. When he sucks my clit and plunges the queen piece deeper, accompanied by his two fingers, I nearly scream from the overwhelming sensation. My core tightens as my orgasm threatens to pull me under. Legs shaking, pussy clenching, and my clit trembling from his mouth, I come completely undone only moments later.

"Carson!" I cry out as I hit the precipice of my orgasm.

Feeling emboldened as he pulls the queen from my pussy, I take it from his hand and drag it over his lips. "Suck it clean for me while I suck your cock, Mr. Wilder."

"I'd do anything you told me to right now," Carson croaks before he grabs it from my hands and stands up. I pull his pants and briefs down, the only remaining articles of clothes he had on, and toss them in the pile of clothes.

Pumping his cock a few times, I bring his leaking tip to my mouth and place a whisper of a kiss on it before lapping up his precum. I moan at the taste of him on my tongue.

I take him as deep in my throat as I can, his thickness stretching my lips at the same time as he hits the back of my throat. Trying to take a deep breath through my nose, I can't hold back the slight gag from his length.

So much for not having a gag reflex.

"Holy. Fuck. Mmm," he groans out. "Austen, you need to stop or I'm going to come like this and I refuse to come anywhere but your tight cunt."

Pulling out of my mouth, he lifts me up and presses me up against one of the book shelves.

"From the moment I decided to build this room, I've pictured what it'd be like to fuck you just like this. With you pressed against the shelves and desperate for my cock," he rasps into my ear.

"Then allow me to make another one of your fantasies come true, my lord," I whisper back as I fist his length in my hand and guide it to my opening.

His essence is laced with passion as he kisses me deeply. When he pushes inside of me, we gasp in unison. Holding me up with one hand below my ass, he grips a shelf with his other and begins to frantically piston his hips against me. With every punishing thrust, my back bumps against the wood. The sound of our flesh smacking against each other makes for one of the most erotic sounds.

"I will never get enough," Carson growls against the nape of my neck before he clamps down with his teeth then soothes my aching skin by sucking it into his mouth.

Knowing he's marking me as his, I give in to the need to claim him with marks of my own. Running my nails down the defined muscles of his back has me on the verge of a second orgasm.

"Carson. Don't. Stop," I plead, panting to try to catch my breath.

Letting go of the shelf, Carson grips my ass with both hands, and spreads my cheeks. The moment he does, he's able to penetrate even deeper inside of me, giving me just what I need to unravel for a second time. Whatever he's doing with his hips right now, it's mind-bending—life-altering. My pussy flutters around his cock as the heat of my orgasm heats my skin.

He continues to thrust through my release, only setting me down after he's milked it out of me. My legs wobble as I attempt to stand on my own.

"You good?" he questions.

When I nod in response, leaning against the wood of the shelf for support, he goes back to the chess board. Grabbing the round pawn piece, he asks, "Do you trust me?"

"Always," I reply.

"Good," he says as he walks me over to my desk, and bends me over it, pressing my chest against the smooth wood. He drags the pawn down my spine and drenches it in my arousal before pulling my hips back so my ass juts out.

His touch ignites an inferno in my body—every cell alight from just this single trace of his fingers down my spine. He licks down my spine, trailing his fingers and the heat of his tongue is like liquid flames, lapping against my skin and setting me ablaze.

Kneeling behind me, he soaks the pawn in my pussy one more time before dragging it back toward my ass and circling my virgin hole. "Is this okay?" he questions.

"Y-yes," I breathe out my stuttered response.

Applying a small amount of pressure, the tip of the rounded piece penetrates my ass, and I gasp at the unfamiliar intrusion.

Carson places a kiss on each of the dimples at the base of my spine before he rasps his question against my skin. "Tell me, has anyone ever claimed you here, Austen?"

"Never," I admit, but it comes out as more of a whimper.

Letting out a groan, Carson stands behind me and nudges the tip of his cock inside my pussy as he slowly works the pawn into my ass, using it as a makeshift plug. I've never felt so gloriously full in my life as I do when he bottoms out inside of me, pushing the pawn even deeper.

"Fuuuuckk, Dakota. You're so fucking tight," he groans, and that alone has my pussy clenching around him.

"You're so deep," I whine in response as he pulls almost completely out before slamming his hips back against mine.

"I need one more," he growls against my shoulder blades.

Gripping onto the edge of the desk, I tell him, "Fuck me harder and I'll come one more time for you."

Carson shifts me so my legs are pressed together, his bracketing mine. "Cross your ankles for me," he requests. I do as he says, and somehow this has me feeling even more full.

Grabbing my hips, Carson begins to thrust so deeply, I swear I can feel him in my chest. Each punishing slam of his hips against my backside drives the pawn further into me. The cool rigidity of it works me into a quivering mess.

"Ah, Carson!" I cry out as a lone tear of pleasure escapes, trailing down my cheek.

Lifting my hips and placing my knees on the desk, he spreads my knees and pushes down my lower back.

"Be my good girl and come for me," he chokes out between bated breaths. "I won't last much longer. You feel too fucking good."

Reaching between my legs, I cup his balls. As I do, I can feel his cock swell inside of me. Knowing he's on the edge, accompanied by how full I feel, has my pussy spasming around him as I come so hard I fear I'll black out at the same time as Carson lets out a guttural groan as he spills inside of me.

"Dakota," he murmurs against my lower back as we ride out our orgasms.

Carson carefully pulls the pawn out, while he remains inside of me.

"Stay right like this," he requests as he pulls out of me and I hear his feet pad across the rug.

When he comes back, I feel the cool glass of the queen against my thigh as he drags his release back up my thigh and pushes the piece inside of me.

"Did you just . . ." I trail off before continuing, "use a chess piece as a plug?"

"Twice actually. Before as a butt plug and now a cum plug—we can't be wasting a single drop, Dream Girl."

"Carson!" I guffaw.

"Call me a caveman, maybe it's the primal part of me taking over, either way I fucking love seeing you filled with my cum."

I stare over my shoulder at him in disbelief. Sitting in this position—with my ass still in the air, and a chest piece inside of me as a plug—I should feel embarrassed or ashamed; instead, I feel revered and empowered.

Carson gives my ass a light smack before scooping me into his arms. "Let's go take a bath before we christen the rest of the house."

Being with him these past few weeks has skewed my perception of time, and I'm only now realizing that this was the first time we had sex in his house. *Our* house. *Our home.*

It only took a matter of months for Carson to shift from a stranger to a best friend to now, where he has quickly become my whole world. I wouldn't change a thing about our story, and how lucky are we that it's only the beginning?

29

Carson

"Unwritten" by Natasha Bedingfield plays over the locker room speakers, and I can't help the smile that steals my face as I think about my author sitting at home working on the rest of her unwritten novel.

Today is Dakota's birthday, and I wanted nothing more than to skip our practice this morning so I could spend the whole day with her, but she refused to let me skip, which is probably for the best because I would've got my ass reamed by our captain and our newest alternate captain, Griff.

Speaking of the fucker, I turn to the locker stall beside me where he's using his elbow pad as a makeshift microphone as he scream-sings the lyrics.

"You're so off-key it's actually pathetic," I tease him.

"Oh fuck right off with that nonsense, Carsey. Let's have the expert weigh in. I'm pretty good, right Jax?" Griff asks.

"Yeah. I bet your wife tells you you're the next John Legend. Maybe you should sign up for *America's Got Talent*," Jax suggests sarcastically.

For some reason, a dopey smile lights up Griff's face. "I love hearing Kenna referred to as my wife. But the two of you both suck," he says as he points to me and Jax.

Always the first on the ice and the last one off, Bennett walks into the locker room and turns off the music, and a hush falls over the room. The respect he commands is impressive and admirable as hell.

"We had a good practice this morning, fellas. Everyone worked their asses off. Let's carry that momentum into our first preseason game tomorrow night." The locker room erupts with our teammates clapping and hollering in agreement.

"Don't forget the cookout at my place this evening. You're all welcome to bring your families and significant others. It's a good opportunity for everyone to get to know one another a bit more," Bennett tacks on.

"What about the rocket I brought home last night that probably hasn't left my bed yet?" our teammate, Pacer, asks.

Bennett shakes his head at one of our team's playboys. "Let's keep it to plus ones that you know the last names of, yeah?"

"You got it, Cap," Pacer replies.

Starting the music back up, Benny goes to take a seat at his locker stall to strip out of his equipment. He's been even more intense during this preseason training than he was last year, if that's even possible. I wonder if it's everything that went down with Carlisle's daughter that has him so worked up.

I'm brought out of my thought spiral when Jax asks, "So, are you bringing Super Nanny to the cookout?"

"If you're asking if I'm bringing my girlfriend, who now shares a home with me, to the team cookout on her birthday, the answer would be hell-fucking-yes."

"You're so fucking smug, slipping the fact that she's officially moved in with you into your answer like that," Jax quirks. "But I'm glad Dakota is coming tonight. She's not going to want to miss the little team competition I have planned."

"And what would that be?" Griff asks.

"A food-eating competition," Jax answers with a sly smirk.

"Fuck that. Why would we get ourselves sick the night before a preseason game?" Griff questions.

"Let's just say it won't be your conventional food-eating competition," Jax retorts.

Not willing to miss another minute more of Dakota's birthday than I need to, I hang up the rest of my gear and rush through my shower so I can get home to my birthday girl.

"Happy birthday, Austen!" I shout as I walk into our house with her birthday surprise clinging to my chest.

"Thank—Carson, what is that?" she questions, staring at me wide-eyed.

"It's our baby," I inform her.

"Carson, that is not a baby," she protests.

"You're right. He's our fur baby," I correct myself.

"He looks like a lynx—he's huge!" she exclaims.

"Takes after his dad that way," I coo down at the little guy. "Don't you, buddy? He's a Maine Coon cat. A total badass, isn't he?"

"Carson Warren Wilder, you cannot just bring home a cat and expect me not to have questions. Did you—" She cuts off, holding her hand to her forehead. "Did you steal him?"

I scoff at that. "Steal him? Dakota, do I look like I could steal anything? I *saved* him. He's a rescue. We're giving him a second chance. So what should we name him, Mama?"

Her face softens when I call her that, and I can see she's about to crack from the puppy dog eyes I'm giving her.

"You crazy man. You're not supposed to just bring home pets without discussing it with me first." Her weak attempt to scold me is cute.

"We did talk about it. In Italy, remember?" I remind her.

"I don't think I'd count that as agreeing to get a pet. We were talking about them in the future sense. You know, kind of like how we also talked about marriage, babies, and everything else."

I bite my lip seductively, waggling my eyebrows at her. "Don't tempt me, Austen. I'll knock your sweet ass up right this minute."

She nearly chokes on air at my suggestion. "Carson, oh my god!" she guffaws in exasperation.

"What?" I scoff as if she's the one talking crazy. Looking down at our nameless fur babe, I point at him before finding her gaze on us. "I think our little guy is already getting lonely. We should consider siblings for him in the near future."

"Not. Happening," she grumbles.

"Alright . . . putting a pin in that for now. Got it. But, we do need to choose a name for our first baby, and I'm already feeling the pressure. It's got to have a name that I can make nicknames out of that he'll understand. You *know* that's my love language. And this little guy needs all the love he can get. Can you believe someone left him in a dumpster?"

As if she is only now realizing I have a cat clinging to my chest, she approaches me and gives the big guy a kiss on his head.

"Hi there, handsome. Welcome home," she coos.

Fucking hell. Watching her take a liking to a pet should not be a turn on or something to get jealous over, but I find myself feeling both of those things at the moment.

"What about Sirius? I know you love *Harry Potter* so much," she suggests.

"Nah, Sirius was a black dog. What about Shadow?" I ask.

"That could work, but then what would his nickname be?"

"Good point. Hmm . . . what about Midnight and we can nickname him Night."

"Is this an homage to Taylor Swift or because he's a black cat?" she questions.

"Can't it be both? I'm still not over that 'Lavender Haze' you put me under in Italy."

"*Midnights* is a great album. What do you think, buddy?" she asks the cat and looks at him as if he can understand her question. When he purrs at her, she takes that as his approval. "Midnight it is!" she exclaims, and when she does, her Texas drawl comes out just a bit more than usual.

"I love when I get to hear that Southern twang make an appearance. Now that we're official, when are you going to take me home? I've got a bit of a break around Thanksgiving if you want to go back together."

Dakota's cheeks burn an adorable shade of pink at my suggestion. "I'd love that, Golden Boy," she says as she grabs Midnight out of my arms. "Do you want the grand tour of your new home, Midnight?" She takes off around the house, showing our little guy his new home.

When we get to our bedroom, I cut her off. "This room is off-limits to you, Midnight. Daddy gets Mama all to himself when we're in here."

My remark makes Dakota start laughing so hard she snorts. "Oh my goodness, I didn't realize I was living with someone so delusional."

"If by delusional you meant deliriously in love with you, then yeah," I say as I pull her in for a kiss on her forehead, which earns me a *meow* from Midnight.

"Carson, you can't expect him to sleep all on his lonesome. Besides, he's got to be my snuggle bud while his *daddy* is on the road," she points out while he nuzzles into the crook of her neck. My cock springs to attention hearing her call me that.

"I'm not so sure I like how much he's taken a liking to you already," I point out. Looking down at Midnight I say, "We talked about this on the way home. We've got rules. Number one, I'm your favorite. Number two, no cock blocking, which means no sleeping in the same room while Daddy is home." I waggle my brows at Dakota, giving her a wink when I catch her biting down on her bottom lip.

"You didn't stand a chance being his favorite and you knew it, so I suppose your rules were just for fun."

"If you want him to sleep in here, fine. I can never say no to you, Dream Girl."

A blinding smile takes over her face as she kisses Midnight's head before setting him down. She links her arms around my neck and I lift her up, wrapping her legs around my waist and kissing her deeply.

When she breaks the kiss, she says, "Thank you for the best birthday surprise. I love him already."

"Well I'm glad you loved your first birthday surprise, because I'm a bit nervous about the second one," I admit.

"Carson, our little guy is more than enough."

I scoff at that. "Getting him was as much of a present for me as it was for you. Now that I think about it, the second one is sort of a gift for me too," I tell her. And it totally is. She might kill me for it, but I wanted peace of mind that when I'm on the road, she's not only safe in our home, but safe on the road too.

So when I guide her out the front door into the driveway, I'm not surprised to find her speechless as she stares at the white SUV with black rims that matches my truck.

"Surprise," I singsong as I do jazz hands like an idiot. To add to my pathetic attempt to use humor to mask her fury, I continue in a Bob Barker voice. "For your twenty-ninth birthday, you get a brand new carrrr! This Acura MDX received the highest safety ranking two years in a row. While you're driving this vehicle, you won't find yourself spinning out on slick roads or getting stuck in a ditch in the dead of winter while your boyfriend is on the road."

"Carson, I love how caring and thoughtful you are, but I can't accept this gift," Dakota says exasperatedly.

"Well, it's a no-backsies gift from your brother and I. We both decided we'll play better while I'm on the road knowing you're driving a safe and reliable vehicle."

"How dare you say Carol isn't reliable. She's been with me for over a decade—if that isn't commitment, I don't know what is."

"And Carol can stay in the garage, where she belongs. She can be your summer car," I suggest.

With her hands on her hips, she huffs out a response I can't quite make out.

Desperate to have her not be mad at me, I pull out my phone and FaceTime Brody.

"Let me guess, she's madder than a wet hen," Brody says when he answers my call.

"I'm not even sure what that means, but yeah, she's furious with us."

Turning the phone toward Dakota, I approach her with caution.

"Hey, Dream Girl, look who called to wish his baby sister happy birthday."

"Brody Garreth Meyer, what in Sam Hill were you thinking? You knew I wouldn't accept a gift this extravagant."

"I did, that's why I told Carse that it should be from the both of us. See, it's not that extravagant when it's coming from two professional athletes, who just so happen to love you and want you to be safe."

"Oh, ho ho. Y'all are good," she says as she wags her pointer finger between me and the phone screen. "But what you perhaps forgot to remember is that Carol is a perfectly safe car."

"Come on, Kota Lynn. You aren't going to blow smoke up our asses with that statement. Accept the car, name it something ridiculous, and go have fun at Carse's team cookout," Brody tells her.

Dakota crosses her arms and lets out a huff as she rolls her eyes.

"Is that a 'thank you so much, big bro' eye roll?" he questions over the phone.

Sighing in defeat, she says, "It's a 'you're both on my shit list' eye roll and a reluctant thank you for the far too generous gift."

I fist pump in the air. "We'll take it!"

"Happy birthday, Kota. I hope you have the best day. Be sure to send me pics of my nephew later too, would ya?"

"Wait, how do you know about Midnight?" she presses.

Brody chuckles on the other end of the line. "Carse FaceTimed me when he was signing the adoption papers and introduced me to the nameless fella. So his name is Midnight, huh? Seems fitting."

"He's the cutest, isn't he?" I gush as I turn the phone toward me.

Shaking his head at me, Brody responds, "That he is. Alright you two love birds, I've gotta get ready for practice."

"Bye, Brodes," I call out as Dakota grabs the phone from me.

"Bye, Bubba. Love you so big," she tells him.

"Love you too, Kota Lynn. Bye now."

Dakota hands me back my phone and lets out a huge sigh of defeat.

"Please tell me this was the last birthday surprise. I don't think I can take any more."

Telling her a teeny white lie, I reassure her that it is.

"Well, I know I didn't initially say thank you because I was shocked and a bit upset," she starts and I cut her off.

"Just a bit," I deadpan.

"You know, I was going to suggest we take my birthday present for a spin while I give you road head to show my appreciation, but now I think I've changed my mind."

My cock twitches in response. "Austen, don't tease me. I've fantasized about getting road head from you hundreds of times since we first rode together in Italy. Why do you think I got the windows tinted?"

That earns me a laugh as she throws her arms around me and peppers kisses across my cheeks and along my jaw.

"We can take her for a spin when we go to Bennett's house later. For now, let's go christen the kitchen island. I just finished baking my mama's famous peach cobbler for the cookout."

I lift her up bridal style and run back into the house to properly wish her a happy birthday.

30

Dakota

OCTOBER

Carson has been needier ever since the season started. He's been apprehensive about leaving me alone at home, but he won't say why. It's not like I haven't noticed the upgraded security system, the way he's checking the locks every night that he's home, and how when we're on FaceTime, he asks me if I've checked them. But he hasn't said what's brought on the sudden fear and heightened his anxieties.

Staring back at my reflection in the full length mirror, I run my hands over the stitching of the black and lime green Wolverines jersey. I turn around, and with the claw clip holding my hair up, it's easy to spot "WILDER" across my back. This afternoon is Carson's first regular season home game, and it will also be the first game I wear his jersey to. I'm oddly nervous to have him see me in it.

Taking a deep breath, I make my way down the stairs to grab my purse and keys from the front entry table. I've just pulled the strap of my bag over my shoulder when I realize I left my phone on the nightstand upstairs.

"Shit," I murmur to myself. I'm already going to be late, and I don't want to worry Kenna.

Running up the steps, I grab my phone off the charger when it vibrates in my hand in rapid succession with incoming text notifications.

Unknown:

Hello, my beautiful Belle.

You thought you could just ruin my life and then trance off to a foreign country with another man, and there wouldn't be consequences? It's like you never knew me at all. But I know that can't be the case. You know perfectly well what I'm capable of.

Picture message attachments

My heart sinks as I click on a blurred photo of me and Carson naked in the pool in Florence. The second photo attached is of me and Carson in our home library. Even though it is a bad angle and the blinds are in the way, it's still very clear what's going on. Tears sting my eyes as a lump forms in my throat.

Fear like I've never known slithers its way down my spine as the hair on the back of my neck stands on end.

Unknown:

You have two days to pack your shit and leave him like you did me or this picture, and the accompanying videos, will be released to the media. Don't fucking test me, Dakota.

With shaky hands, I try to type out a reply, but have to start and retype it several times.

Me:

Aaron, you're not supposed to contact me.

What are you going to do? Call your lawyer? I wonder what Theo will think of his son's name being dragged through the mud because of a stupid whore.

> Tick, tock . . . the clock is running. If you're not out of his house in two days, the videos I have will be released to every website and news station.

> You're not willing to risk your golden boy's squeaky-clean reputation are you? Or have you really become that reckless?

I release the sob that was stuck in my throat.

Me:

> And if I leave? How do I know you won't release them anyway to seek revenge?

Unknown:

> If you leave him, that's enough for me. You don't deserve happiness after you took everything from me. Do as I say, and I'll send you the original files and all copies to your mom's house. And don't think I'll stop at the footage. Remember that little fender bender your beloved Wilders were in? Who do you think hired the photographer that crashed into them?

At this rate, nothing he says or does should surprise me, but I'm shocked that Aaron would go so far as hurting Carson and Cadence. They're innocent in all of this. I don't know what his end goal is or what this game he's playing is, but I know him well enough to know he'd never turn the photos and videos over so easily. But until I know more, I have to play along. My stomach churns, and I know I'm going to be sick as I type my reply.

Me:

> Consider it done.

Unknown:

> Oh, this should be fun. I'll be watching, Belle.

Shivers of fear race up my spine knowing he's been watching us all this time. I won't allow Aaron to ruin Carson's life or steal his shine. If upending my life can save him, I'd do it without question—I'd do anything for Carson. Even if that means obliterating my heart in the process.

Carson

Surprised I didn't find her by the fireplace, I jog up the stairs in search of Dakota. It's a cold October night, the perfect excuse to curl up by the fire together, which I plan to do once I check on her and make sure she's okay.

After Mack told me Dakota never showed up to our game tonight, I raced home right after our postgame press. I was surprised to hear she hadn't been there and have been anxious ever since, considering Dakota told me before I left that she couldn't wait to cheer me on wearing my jersey for the first time.

There's noise coming from the bedroom that I can't quite make out.

"Dream Girl, are you okay?" I ask before freezing in the doorway of our bedroom when I see a frazzled Dakota hectically tossing clothes into a suitcase.

"What are you doing, Austen?"

"Packing. I-I just need some time."

My heart sinks at her words and her frantic tone.

"Time? Time for what?" I question, panic lacing my words.

"T-to think." She can't even look at me as she continues to shove clothes and toiletries into her bag.

"I'm so confused. What do you need time to think about?" I bite out the question in a frustrated voice I don't recognize as my own.

She winces, and it just about kills me.

"I'm sorry for raising my voice. Where are you going?" I ask again after taking a deep breath.

"Home. Just home," she monosyllabically replies as I catch a glimpse of her tear-stricken face.

"Home? But this is your home."

"No, it's *your* home. I'm going back to Texas, Carson."

"Why are you doing this? What happened? Please talk to me," I plead.

"Don't you get it?" she questions. "This is all too much for me and far too soon. I shouldn't have agreed to move in. I shouldn't have jumped head-first into a relationship so soon after my life was shattered."

"B-but we love each other," I shudder. "We made promises, Austen. Promises to start a life together. To talk to one another. To be partners. Don't quit on us. Talk to me. Let me hear what's causing your hesitation or fears."

She turns her back to me and closes her suitcase, bracing her hands on it as she hangs her head and sighs. "Carson, I'm sorry if this is hurting you, that isn't my intention. I just think I made a mistake and I need time to think about my decisions. My mama said I could stay with her for a while, so that's what I'm going to do. I talked to Kenna already, and she said your mama would help her with Cadence."

I smooth my hand over my chest to ease the ache that's spreading. "So that's it? How come I don't get a say in any of this? What if I hadn't raced home tonight? Would you have just left without saying a word?"

"Yes! Don't you get it?"

"No, I don't. I don't understand any of this, Dakota," I choke out.

"I can't do this. I can't ruin you too—I'm broken," she cries.

"Austen, if you're broken, what the hell does that make me?" I counter. "Is this about the car? If it is, I'll take it back. Carol is still in the garage. If you want to drive her, let's just get snow tires for winter. And if it's really snowy, you can take my truck."

"It's not the car, Carson. It's everything else. I mean, just the fact that I'm seven years older than you should've been enough of a deterrent. We're not good for each other." She sinks down to sit on the bed with her head in her hands. Her shoulders shake as her muffled sobs echo throughout the room.

Closing the distance between us, I fall to my knees in front of her, begging her to tell me what happened to change her mind. "We're so good together, Austen. Please tell me why you're really doing this. What happened?"

Taking a shaky breath, she looks up at me through tear stricken eyes and says, "You've got to let me go, Carson. I have to do this. Please. If you love me, you have to let me go."

My chest cracks down the center as my heart spills out and falls to her feet. This isn't how it's meant to end—it was never meant to end at all. I'm not supposed to lose the girl of my dreams for a reason I don't even know.

But the thing is, I do love her. I love Dakota so fucking much, I have no choice but to let the love of my life walk away. My stomach churns as tears cascade down my cheeks.

Closing my eyes, I drop my head and attempt to plead with her one last time. "Tell me this isn't real, Austen. Tell me this is just another nightmare that I'll wake up from with you in my arms right where you belong," I croak.

With shaky fingers, Dakota cups my face in her hands. "Look at me," she whispers, and when I do, I can't help but wipe the tears streaming down her cheeks over the bow of her upper lip.

Bringing her forehead to rest against mine, she murmurs, "I am not being cliché or lying when I tell you, it's not you, it's me. This is my problem, and I just need time to figure this out, Carson. I promise you I will fix this."

She kisses my forehead and I can't stop the quivering of my chin or the whimper that escapes realizing this could be the last time I touch her like this intimately.

"I thought we were a team. I thought you loved me," I say as I stand on unsteady legs.

"I'll never stop loving you," she sobs as she stands as well. "I just need to go, Carson. Let me go."

So I do.

I stand by as she gathers her bags before heading downstairs. And when she closes the front door behind her, I sink to the floor of the entryway, wondering if I'll ever experience agony more crushing than this.

With what little strength I have left in my limbs, I pull my phone from my pocket and dial the only other person besides Dakota I'd allow to see me like this.

"Hello?" she answers.

"I need you," I choke out.

"I'll be right there," she reassures.

My chest squeezes with a debilitating ache, and my head has already brought me under by the time McKenna opens my front door and finds me lying on the floor.

"I'm here," she says, rubbing my back as I struggle to take air into my lungs.

When she sits me up and encourages me to lean my head between my knees, I can't help but wonder what the point of it all even is.

"She's gone," I gasp between panted breaths, my chest heaves and cracks open all over again.

McKenna doesn't say anything, she just holds me in her arms and remains the one constant I have in this life.

31

Carson

My favorite holiday has officially been ruined.

I should be ecstatic that Mack agreed to my costume idea for the third year in a row. Cadence, as usual, looks adorable dressed as Tinker Bell, while Griff and Mack hold her up dressed as Peter Pan and Wendy. I'm in a Captain Hook costume, but I feel more like one of the lost boys.

Dakota left for Texas three weeks ago, and I haven't heard from her other than a few texts letting me know she had arrived safely. She drove Carol down there, refusing to take the car Brody and I got her.

I've kept in touch with Brody these past few weeks, and from what he tells me, his mom says Dakota is just as devastated as I am. So I can't for the life of me understand why she would break what we had.

"Can I get a picture with all of you?" my mom asks.

I do as she requests because I'm a mama's boy, even though taking a picture is the last thing I want to do. Cadence doesn't particularly like my costume, so I don't blame her when she doesn't want to be held by me. Instead, Griff and Mack each hold one of her hands and I stand off to Griff's side. He went all out and is even wearing the green tights I got him mostly as a joke. That sappy motherfucker would do anything to put a smile on his girls' faces.

We're just getting ready to go trick-or-treating at my parents' house when I get an alert on my phone that my home security system has been tripped. Opening the app, I click the video to see a man dressed in black trying to break in through the back patio door.

My dad sees the look of concern on my face and comes over to me.

"What is it?" he questions.

"My security alarm went off. I opened the app, and some guy broke into the patio. The app says they alerted the police, and a dispatch is on the way," I explain.

Grabbing his keys off the counter, my dad says, "Let's go. I'll drive."

I only live about eight minutes from my parents, so when we pull up to my house five minutes later, it's no surprise that we've beat the cops. Shedding my costume jacket and wig, I swing open the passenger door.

"Stay in the car, Carson. We have no idea who this guy is. He could be armed and dangerous," my dad says, trying to pull me back in the car, but I'm already out the door. The moment I saw the camera feed, I saw red.

The culprit in my house isn't some thief out on Halloween night or even the photographer from the accident. That photographer was far too tall and had a wider build. The man on the camera tonight had the same scrawny build as Aaron Ackerman. What he's doing breaking into my house, I have no clue, but I'm about to find out.

Storming in through the front door, I look around the main floor open area and don't see him, so I pause and listen to see if I can hear him. The video footage didn't show him leaving, so I know he's still here somewhere.

My dad comes in the house behind me, shaking his head at my actions. "You've always marched to the beat of your own drum, but this is reckless, Carse," he hisses.

"It's Aaron. He's in my house and I've got to know what he did to scare her away. That's the only thing that makes sense," I explain in a hushed voice. There's a loud bang that comes from upstairs, and before I can think twice I'm taking the steps two at a time. He's in our bedroom, that sick fuck doesn't deserve to be in our space.

Turning the corner, I freeze just outside the doorway and peer my head into the room. Just as I thought, Aaron is the one standing in my room rifling through my dresser drawers. There is an unfamiliar black duffle bag on the chair in the corner of the room.

"Lying fucking whore," I hear him mutter to himself.

Squaring myself to him, I call out, "Can I help you with something?"

Aaron spins around, his eyes full of fury.

I pretend to look surprised that it's him, but I'm a shit actor. "If I'm not mistaken, you're not supposed to come within a hundred yards of my home."

"That no longer applies since Mrs. Ackerman no longer resides at this residence."

"It's Ms. Meyer, soon to be Mrs. Wilder, actually."

Aaron's face reddens in anger, and I'm starting to piece together the puzzle.

"What made you think Dakota no longer lived here?" I press.

"I watched the chaos unfold earlier this month when she left your ass, just like she did me. Don't take it personally, you see, she's a runner. Her daddy issues should've been the first of many red flags."

My barely restrained anger radiates off of me in waves. It takes everything in me not to charge and pound him into the crest of the earth.

"I'm pretty sure you were the abusive husband that caused all the issues. Now can you tell me what the fuck you're doing in our home?"

"It isn't supposed to be her home. She's supposed to be with me—she's *my* wife."

"*Ex*-wife," I growl. "You nearly killed her with your bare hands. You have no right to talk about her, let alone claim her as your anything."

Aaron lets out a demented laugh that has the hair on the back of my neck rising. "Well, if I can't have her, neither can you. That was our deal. But I see she hasn't kept up her side of the bargain. Now I'm going to look like the asshole for keeping my word. I'm sure you understand why I need to do this. I told her there would be consequences, but she never listened, that one."

Before I realize what he's doing, Aaron pulls out a knife from his pocket and charges toward me.

My dad comes out of nowhere and tackles Aaron to the ground, but not before the blade of his knife grazes the right side of my stomach. Dad has Aaron restrained in the corner of the room. The sound of their heaving breaths fills the room as my vision begins to blur.

Looking down, I watch as the lower part of my costume's white shirt slowly stains red. I've never done well with the sight of my own blood, so it doesn't take long for the black dots speckling my vision to overcome my consciousness.

The final thought that pulls me under is a mirage of Dakota's deep brown curls splayed on my chest as her emerald eyes dance with mischief.

32

Dakota

Opening my camera roll for the sixth time today, I click on the folder Carson labeled "Forever and Always" and begin swiping through the photos. My thumb hovers over one of my favorite photos of us. It's the two of us in Italy, moments after we admitted our love to one another. Carson has his arm wrapped around my waist from behind; his face is slightly hidden, peeking out from behind my head, but his smile is still blinding. Tearing my eyes away from his face, I drag my thumb over my face in the picture. The joy and unwavering happiness I felt are evident in the smile on my face. I don't think I've ever been as happy as I was at that moment. Don't think I'll ever be that happy again.

Tears prick my eyes as heat rushes my face. My throat works to hold back the sob threatening to escape. How could I be so reckless? I should've known better than to underestimate Aaron—to think he'd leave us alone.

It's been almost a month since I left Minnesota, and Aaron still hasn't sent the videos. I didn't expect him to keep his word, but I thought he'd show the rest of his cards by now.

My mama suggested I ride Buttercup to our west pasture to clear my mind. Mama knows that riding typically helps me feel better, but even the sun beginning to set isn't cutting it tonight.

Swiping my thumb across the screen, I feel tears roll down my face as I stare at one of our last photos. Carson surprised me with a JCPenny portrait session with me, him, and Midnight. He insisted we needed a family portrait of the three of us to hang in our home. I can't help the sad smile that takes over my face when I look at how dorky yet sexy Carson looks in a cream cashmere turtleneck that looks like it was painted on his body. His gold chain is out over the turtleneck, and his defined muscles bulge beneath the fabric. He's got Midnight cradled in his arm like a football, kissing his fury head just above his ear, while I'm snuggled against Carson's side, looking at the two of them like they are my whole world. Because they *are*.

"I had that one printed on the biggest canvas they sold for above our bed."

"Carson?" I gasp in disbelief, looking up to make sure my imagination isn't playing tricks on me. When my eyes land on him, I shoot to my feet, or at least attempt to. My knees wobble at the realization that he's here, standing right in front of me.

My fingers curl around his biceps as his hands steady my waist to keep me from falling over.

"Hey, Dream Girl," he rasps, tears stinging my eyes from the sound. I haven't heard his voice in weeks. When I look into his aqua eyes they're filled with tears of his own, making them look like seaglass.

"You're here? How?" I question.

"The team plays in Dallas tomorrow and there wasn't a chance in hell I wasn't going to come get my girl. Come back home with me, Austen. I promise we can work through anything together. Don't cut me out for a single minute longer."

Bringing my hand to my mouth to muffle the sob that wants to escape from his words, I shake my head. "I-I c-can't," I choke out.

"You can. It's all over now. Aaron is in jail. He's going to go to prison for a very long time."

"What? How? How did you know?"

"He came back to our house a few nights ago on Halloween—he was trying to break in. I caught him on the cameras around the perimeter of the house. At first, I thought the person sneaking around was a photographer, maybe even the one who caused the car accident with me and Cadence."

"Aaron hired that photographer," I interrupt.

"I know that now. The phone he contacted you on and threatened you with was confiscated when they arrested him for stalking, breaking and entering, attempted nonconsensual dissemination of private sexual photos and videos, and assault with a deadly weapon," he explains. "Why didn't you tell me about the threats he made to you?" he asks.

Ignoring his question, my stomach churns as his words sink in. "Assault? Carson, what happened?"

Carson braces his hands on my shoulders and bends down so he's looking me in the eyes. "It was nothing. I'm okay now; my dad's okay, and Aaron is locked away. There is nothing standing in our way. Come home, Dakota. Come back with me. Let me be your rainy day comfort. Let me be your cozy night by the fire. Let me be your everything, just like you are mine. I love you, and if you let me, I'd love to show you just how much for the rest of our lives."

Wrapping my arms around his waist, I pull him in for a hug but freeze when he winces.

"Carson, are you okay?"

He takes a deep breath as he steps back slightly before pulling up the hem of his denim button-up shirt. My confusion from his actions quickly transitions into concern as I take in the bandages on his lower right side.

"Oh my god, what happened?" I cry, reaching out to touch him but pausing when I realize I might hurt him.

"I really am fine, just a bit sore. Aaron had a knife, but my dad was able to restrain him before he did any major damage."

"Wait, I thought you said this happened on Halloween."

"It did."

"Carson, today is only the fourth of November. What in the hell were you thinking hiking out to this pasture in your condition?"

"I didn't hike out here; I rode Blizzard."

My eyes widen as I bend to look behind Carson only to find my brother's white Arabian grazing beside Buttercup.

"Didn't you say you were scared to death of horses?" I point out, still in disbelief that he rode one out here. "And I'm pretty sure your doctor would not clear you to ride a fricken horse four days after being stabbed."

"I wasn't stabbed . . . he grazed me with the knife. It was a surface wound at best. And hold the damn phone, I never said I was scared to death of horses." Carson leans forward and, in a hushed voice, says, "Will you keep it down? Horses can smell fear. If Blizzard hears I'm terrified of him, all bets are off."

Rolling my eyes at his antics, I rise to my tiptoes and tenderly kiss his lips, followed by the scruff on his chin and one on his Adam's apple, before placing a final one on the hot skin just above his bandages.

"Why didn't anyone call me?" I ask.

"I didn't want you to worry. By the time you would've heard, I was probably discharged anyway. Now, help me feel better and answer my dang question."

"I'm sorry, I didn't realize you were asking. It sounded more like a demand."

"You're right. I'm demanding you come home with me tomorrow night, Dream Girl."

"Oh, Mr. Wilder," I tut. "You're lucky you're so cute. Otherwise, you'd never get away with being so demanding."

"I'm just trying to be assertive like all those alphaholes in those books you love."

"What did I tell you? I love you just the way you are, Golden Boy. No fictional man could ever compare to how you make me feel. Take me home," I whisper against his lips.

"Ma'am, yes, ma'am," he drawls before sealing his lips with mine. I'd chuckle at how adorable his attempt at an accent was if I weren't lost in the way it feels to finally have his mouth open for mine.

Each night we were apart, I yearned for this man. For the way he looks at me like I'm the most precious thing in the world. For the feel of his hands against my waist as he traces lines down my back. For the way his breath fans against the nape of my neck as he worships every inch of my body.

Carson lowers me down to the blanket I was sitting on. The two of us laugh as we stumble to the ground and fumble with each other's clothes. Once I'm completely undressed, he hovers above me, and I moan with deep pleasure when I finally feel the weight of him against my skin once more. Roaming my eyes over every inch of his skin, my heart pounds in my chest when I spot something on his chest.

"What is this?" I ask, bringing my hand up as I trace the delicate black ink right above his heart that reads "Austen."

"I missed feeling you against me. If I could, I'd wear you on my skin. But I can't, because that'd be crazy, so I did the next best thing. I got a tattoo on my heart that makes me think of you every time I see it."

Tears blur my vision as I try to put into words how much I love it—how much I love *him*.

Stealing the breath from my lungs, Carson kisses me so deeply, so passionately, that I can't help the tears that escape the corners of my eyes. He laps them up from my cheeks before placing a scattering of kisses across my collarbones and chest.

"Please don't ever leave me like that again," he pleads with his forehead against my chest. "I was so scared I had lost you, Austen."

Bracketing his face in my hands, I lock eyes with the most beguiling blues I've ever seen. "Never. You'll never lose me," I promise him.

And he won't. Because his soul is stitched with mine—we're intertwined. My heart was akin to his the moment we met in a way that only star-crossed lovers can be.

I know I'll love and be loved by Carson with every breath I take for the rest of our lives. He has shown me what true love is, what it should always be: unconditional, selfless, intimate, empathetic, respectful, affectionate, secure, and unwavering.

Epilogue

CARSON – NOVEMBER

"**I** did a thing," Dakota calls out to me after I walk in the house and hang up my winter coat. I just finished shoveling the few inches of snow we got overnight so we can leave for the airport soon to pick up her mom. Jolene is staying with us over Thanksgiving, which happens to be the same weekend Brody's team plays in Minnesota. We're excited to have the two of them join us for the holiday.

"Oh, yeah? What's that?" I ask as I join her on the floor in front of the stone fireplace that she's decorated with golden and orange foliage garland and a smattering of wooden pumpkins.

The front walk and entire main level are decked out with fall decor, and I've never felt more at home. I wonder if after we take down the Christmas decorations, she'll let me convince her we should add more oranges and browns to our regular decor.

Dakota uncovers her legs and straddles my lap before I wrap us back up in her blanket. "I typed 'the end' on my first draft," she says, her face lighting up with a dazzling smile that I match with one of my own.

"Stop. Are you for real?"

Nodding her head, she replies, "I am."

I pump my fist before wrapping her up in a tight embrace. "I'm. So. Damn. Proud. Of. You," I tell her, punctuating each word with a peppering of kisses on her face.

317

Looking over her shoulder at my watch, I tell her, "We've got just enough time to celebrate this milestone before we need to leave for the airport."

"Is that so? We've somehow yet to christen this spot in front of the fireplace," she informs me.

"That feels like a travesty considering it's one of your favorite places. Come here, Austen," I murmur, bringing her in for a searing kiss that communicates everything I couldn't begin to express with words: my pride in her, my happiness for this life we're building, the amount of joy she brings me, and the fire of passion she ignites in me.

Dakota breaks the kiss and lifts her arms for me to take off her sweatshirt. I groan with pleasure when I find she wasn't wearing anything underneath it, leaving her in nothing but a pair of boyshorts.

My hands tremble slightly as I skim them down her arms until she wraps them around my neck. I continue trailing my fingertips over her ribcage, gripping her waist when I reach it.

Resting my forehead against her sternum, I breathe her in as she rakes her fingers through my hair still damp from the snow.

Unable to restrain myself any longer, I pepper kisses along her collarbones and sternum before bringing her nipple into my mouth as I squeeze the other, rolling the taut bud between my fingers.

Pulling off with a pop, I ask, "Have I ever told you how much I love your tits? They're fucking perfect. You're perfect."

She lets out a low chuckle. "I can't say you've admitted it aloud, but you've shown me how much you love them." Bringing her hands beneath my henley, she strips me of my shirt before slipping off my jeans and briefs.

Standing between my legs, I pull Dakota closer to me and slide her boyshorts down her legs at a torturous rate. I place a kiss on each of her thighs and marvel at the tiny goosebumps that trail my touch.

She straddles my legs and I grip her hips, guiding her back down. The moment her wet heat makes contact with my cock, it twitches against her clit and she mewls for more.

Lifting up on her knees, Dakota grips my cock, giving it a few firm strokes before lining me up at her entrance. She slowly sinks down and we moan in unison when I bottom out.

Wrapping our arms around each other, she wraps her legs around my waist, and it feels like we're as close as two humans can possibly get. She grinds against me, and when I tilt my hips forward, she keens in pleasure the new position offers.

"Don't move," she pants as she continues to rock her pelvis, rubbing her clit against me over and over again until I feel the telltale signs of her impending orgasm. Her pussy flutters around my cock just as she reaches the precipice of her climax.

I lock eyes with her just as she shatters apart. Her mouth hangs open as she throws her head back in ecstasy, letting out a melodious cry.

Only after she's rode out her orgasm, do I shift her onto her back and hover above her. Chest heaving, she works to catch her breath. I gape in wonder as I take her in—she looks ethereal as the flames of the firelight reflect off her sweat-slicked skin.

My chest tightens when Dakota looks up at me with glassy, lust-filled eyes.

"I am so privileged to be loved by you, Dakota."

Not giving her the opportunity to reply, I steal her mouth, sucking her bottom lip and raking it between my teeth.

"Show me," she pleads breathlessly.

I bracket her face with my arms, balancing my weight on my elbows as I deeply thrust back inside her tight pussy. Letting her adjust for only a moment before I pull almost all the way out and slam my hips back in. I repeat the motion over and over until she's chanting my name.

"Carson! Yes!"

Bringing my lips to her ear, I rasp, "Tell me you're mine forever, Austen."

"I'm yours, Carson! Only ever yours," she shrieks out, and fuck, the chorus of her cries combined with the way her pussy is squeezing my cock has me groaning into her ear.

"*Mine*," I let out just as I sink further, coming so deep inside of her that I'm not sure where I end and she begins.

I reluctantly draw out of her and roll onto my back, pulling her against my heaving chest with one arm wrapped snugly around her waist.

"So, when do I get to read this draft?" I pant out as I tuck my other arm beneath my head.

"Not until I get through edits, Golden Boy. I want you to read the polished version, if I let you read it at all," she responds through bated breaths.

"*If*? What do you mean if? Once you publish it, I can read it whenever I want."

"I don't even know if I'm going to publish it yet."

"You know I'll support you no matter what you do, but I'll say this, your story deserves to be told."

"Thank you, Carson. For everything. For giving me a safe haven when I had nowhere else to go, for being so supportive, for inspiring me just by being you, and for giving me a relationship that is more loving than I ever could've dreamed of."

I have the urge to take advantage of the serenity of this moment, to make a grand gesture, but we're interrupted by the alarm I set to remind us to leave on time for the airport.

"Let's get cleaned up quick and then go get your mama," I suggest as I roll onto my side to shut off my phone. "I bet Jolene can't wait to wrap me in another hug," I taunt, knowing Dakota gets fiery when I tease her about how much her mama has taken a liking to me.

"You think you're just the sweetest thing since sliced pie," she huffs under her breath as she marches up the steps to our bathroom.

Knowing I should just keep quiet, I do the exact opposite. "You're tempting me with those sassy lips and swaying hips," I tell her before racing after her up the steps. When we get to the top, I lift her over my shoulder and carry her into the bathroom, where we get lost in one another until our final alarm clock sounds, and we rush out the door to get on the road.

"How do you manage to stay so lean when you eat like that?" Brody questions, waving his fork at me across the table. We're eating an early Thanksgiving meal at my parents' house before we head out to do our traditional post-turkey skate. Tonight will be Dakota's first time on the ice, and I'm stoked to teach her how to skate.

I shrug. "What can I say? I'm a growing boy who likes to eat."

"He certainly does," I hear Dakota murmur under her breath before shoving a forkful of mashed potatoes in her mouth. Chuckling to myself, I give her thigh three playful squeezes under the table. I'm not sure if I'm telling her *I love you* with that one or *wait until later*.

"Hey, Carse, I didn't realize you played chess. I was in Kota's library you made her and saw the board. She said something smart about how you're a chess master, so you'd kick my ass. Care to place a wager?" Brody asks.

I nearly choke on my bite of food as his words register. Taking a long pull of water, I turn and watch Dakota try to hide her laughter behind her napkin.

Setting my glass down with a thud, I clear my throat. "Sorry, the turkey must be a little on the dry side," I sputter.

"Don't talk about my turkey like that. I practically killed myself over this masterpiece all day," Griff huffs out.

His reaction has Dakota and Mack bending over in hysterics—literal fucking tears stream down their cheeks.

"That chessboard is more for decoration. We've got another board I'm sure I could kick your ass on," I tell Brody, trying to reclaim my dignity. There's no chance in hell I'd play chess against anyone but Dakota with the chess board in her library, especially not her big brother.

"You're on, Golden Boy. I can't wait to make you eat your words after we get Kota Lynn out of urgent care. Texans are not meant for ice," Brody taunts across the table.

Dakota turns to where Mack is cutting up more turkey for Cadence and asks, "I'm going to do just fine, aren't I?"

Mack gives her a pitying smile, placing her hand on top of Dakota's. "I'm sure you'll do just fine. But I'd wear two pairs of leggings or sweats to add extra padding, just in case."

"Was that your Minnesota nice version of 'bless your heart'?" Dakota gasps.

My shoulders shake with barely restrained laughter. Brody howls obnoxiously, but it's me who gets a swat to the chest.

"Do you want me to tell them about our little ride in the pasture earlier this month?" Dakota queries, making my laughter die on the spot.

I never want a soul to discover what happened when Brody's horse, Blizzard, took off galloping after Buttercup.

"Play nice," I pout.

"Same goes for you," she retorts.

The rest of the meal is filled with our families getting to know each other. Griff's dad, Jack, and his girlfriend had a delayed flight, so Griff and Mack left to pick them up from the airport. They're going to all meet us at the outdoor rink.

After I finish my second slice of Dakota's homemade pumpkin pie, I'm considering going in for a third when she wraps her arms around my shoulders from behind.

"You better quit while you're ahead, or you won't be able to teach me how to skate," she murmurs in my ear.

I turn around and pull her into my lap, pressing a kiss against her temple before I ask, "How was that?"

Dakota said she was going to talk to Brody about everything that went down with Aaron while they ate dessert together on my parents' four-season porch.

She sighs against my chest, and I rub her back in encouragement. "Better than I anticipated. He was hurt, rightfully so, that I didn't tell him when things were happening. But he also told me he's never seen me happier than I am right now." Holding her against my chest, my heart swells with pride from her courage to have the tough conversation with her brother.

"I'm proud of you, Austen. I know it wasn't easy for you, but I'm sure it meant a lot to Brodes."

"You're right, it did." She nuzzles further into my chest, and I wish I could freeze time. Here I am with the woman of my dreams in my arms, a belly full of my favorite pie, and a house full of our families.

Dakota scootches back and asks, "Are you ready to work off all that pie, Golden Boy?"

"Sure am, let's go," I say as I lift her off my lap.

Thirty minutes later, Dakota's sitting on a bench while I kneel at her feet, lacing up her skates. Snow falls down around us in thick, cottony flakes.

"What is it about a man tying a girl's skates that is so damn sexy?" she asks.

I don't bother hiding my cocksure smirk. "You think I'm sexy?"

She scoffs and rolls her eyes. "As if that wasn't already glaringly obvious. But I'm having a hard time restraining myself watching your hands work like that."

"You love what these hands can do, don't you?" My grin turns lethal when I grip her thighs, and her breath hitches, causing her to squirm. "Don't worry, I plan to trace my hands over every inch of your gorgeous body later, Dream Girl."

Hopping to my feet, I offer her my hand and help her stand up, giving her a moment to get her bearings on the small blades.

We walk hand in hand down the padded path to the outdoor ice. I step onto the ice and turn to help Dakota, offering both my hands to help her balance. She takes a few timid steps onto the ice, and I have to bite back the chuckle that rumbles in my chest.

Seeing Dakota on the ice is like watching a baby fawn taking its first steps—she looks completely awkward like her legs might give out at any second.

I guide her to the boards and have her hold tight while I demonstrate how she should stride. After a few passes around the rink, she gets the hang of things, and we're able to hold hands side by side.

Once I spot Griff, Mack, and Cadence making their way onto the ice, I nod over to them, and Mack gives me a thumbs-up.

Knowing that's my signal, I place my hands on Dakota's waist to stop her since she still doesn't know how to stop. She whirls around, and confusion mars her face until I take her hands in mine. Her eyes soften when she sees mine are tear-filled.

"Sometimes it's hard for me to remember what life was like before I met you. I used to have a one-track mind that was solely focused on hockey as my entire future. But then you came in without warning and turned my whole world on its axis. I can't imagine my life without you, Austen." Clearing the emotion clogging my throat, I continue, "You have shown me what all-consuming, maddening love is like. There has been no greater privilege in my life than being called yours."

Pulling out a Tiffany blue box from my coat pocket, I drop down to one knee and open it. Dakota's eyes never leave mine, even as her mitten-covered hands cover her mouth with a gasp.

"I promise to show you what love should be like for the rest of my life. My love will never be contingent—it will be unwavering, and my heart will be wholly yours until my last breath. Will you make me the happiest man in the world by doing me the honor of becoming my wife?"

I don't have to wait more than the time it takes for Dakota to barrel into me as she squeals, "Yes!"

"Yes?" I press, not wanting to have heard her wrong.

"Yes! Yes, of course, I'll marry you," she murmurs against my cheek as I stand us up and spin her around.

With one arm wrapped snugly around her waist, I throw a fist in the air and shout, "She said yes!"

We make our way over to the entrance, where our families cheer their congratulations as they crowd around us.

"I'm so happy for you two," Mack says as she wraps us both in a hug.

Dakota gets picked up by Brody in a bear hug, and I take the moment to give Mack a big squeeze of my own.

"Believe it or not, but I knew she was the one from the moment I saw you lock eyes with her. Call it twin intuition, I'm not sure, but I could feel that she felt like home," McKenna tells me as tears well in her eyes. "I've never been happier for you, Carse."

"Thanks, Mack," I choke out, taking a deep breath as I attempt to keep my shit together.

"I'm just surprised she said yes," Griff teases as he punches my shoulder, giving me just the distraction I needed.

"Yeah, yeah. Well, if you could convince my sister to marry your ass, I figured I might as well shoot my shot with my dream girl."

"Did I hear my name?" Dakota calls out, walking back over to us after giving our parents hugs.

"I was just saying I can't believe I get to call the woman of my dreams my fiancée," I remark, wrapping her in my arms.

Dakota's face lights up with an endearing smile, her eyes full of warmth. "How lucky am I to have stumbled upon the love of a lifetime at a job interview?"

"I'll forever be the lucky one," I admit.

And I am one hell of a lucky man to love and be loved by this woman.

"Repeat after me," Dakota whispers against my lips.

"Okay," I hum in reply.

"I have the best fiancée in the world," she chuckles.

"I've never heard a truer affirmation. I have the best fiancée in the world," I mimic. "Now you repeat after me," I tell her before giving her ass a firm squeeze. "I'm ready to go home and make sweet, sweet love to my fiancée."

She lowers her voice to a hushed whisper and repeats my words back to me.

"Carson!" she squeals as I dip down and throw her over my shoulder, being careful not to get cut by one of her skates.

I give her a playful smack on her butt as I walk us over to the bench where our boots are. Setting her down, I untie her skates and slip her boots on.

"So, am I taking your last name, or are you taking mine?" I ask.

That earns me a soft chuckle. "Your last name says everything about you, Golden Boy. I can't wait to become a Wilder. Though, I do think my pen name will be Kota Lynn. Is that okay with you?"

I look up at her from where I'm kneeling before her. "You never have to check to see if I'm okay with a decision like that. But, yeah, I love that idea, Austen."

She nods her head at me. "Good. Now take your fiancée home and make sweet, sweet love to her."

I'm not sure I'll ever get used to referring to her as my fiancée, but I'm sure right when I do, she'll become my wife. Hope blooms in my chest as I think about the future we're about to embark on. We've got a lifetime of wild adventures in store for us, and I can't wait to experience them with my dream girl by my side.

Extended Epilogue

Dakota – July

Someone please pinch me because this can't be my life right now.

Carson and I are back in Texas for our wedding with only our families and close friends here to witness us exchange vows.

It's the morning of our wedding, and I just got a call from my publicist Trisha that my publishing deal for my football series was announced. A couple months ago, a major publishing house asked if they could meet with me. Never in my wildest dreams did I think they'd end the meeting with an offer to publish the series. I submitted my manuscript to my editor two weeks ago, but the announcement hadn't been made public yet.

Too excited to wait, I swing open the door to the room we're getting ready in and march down the stairs in only my robe and head to the den where the guys are hanging out until they need to get ready.

Peeking my head around the door, I ask, "Hey, Carson, can I steal you for a minute?"

Carson stands with his back to me, and a laugh slips from my lips when I see his shoulders stiffen before he squeaks out, "Austen, what are you doing? I'm not supposed to see you—it's bad luck!"

"Oh, I don't believe in that. Come on, Golden Boy. Take a quick walk with me," I implore.

He slowly turns toward me, and when his eyes land on me, his face lights up with an enigmatic smile. "You look beautiful," he tells me.

Pointing at my head full of rollers and the gel under eye patches I have on, I roll my eyes at him before he pulls me in for a tease of a kiss.

"I'll meet you on the front porch," he says as he disappears into the kitchen. When he joins me on the porch swing, he hands me a cup of black coffee and I smile at him.

"Thanks."

"You're welcome, Dream Girl." Carson pulls my feet into his lap and begins kneading my arches. "So what did you want to talk about? If it's a case of cold feet, I can keep them warm."

I sit up and playfully push at his shoulder. "Never. My feet are nice and toasty over here."

"Good," he says as he gives my foot three squeezes.

"I love you more," I singsong.

"Hmm, I don't think so," he murmurs.

"Well, I brought you out here because I couldn't wait any longer to tell you something—" I trail off as Carson grabs my mug and sets it down on the side table.

"Is it official? Did they announce? Where do I go to look?" he presses.

"They did. I just got off the phone with Trisha," I tell him as I pull my feet from his lap and stand.

"Did they tell you when they think it'll release?"

Turning to face him, I place my hands in the pockets of my robe. "Not yet, but I just told Trisha it's very important to me to have it published before April, because I don't want to be worrying about my book release while I'm trying to soak in snuggles on maternity leave."

"Right, that makes sense—" he stops mid-sentence, shooting his eyes up to look up at me. "Wait, did you just say . . ."

When he sees me nod with tears in my eyes holding a positive pregnancy test in my hands, he leaps to his feet, throws his arms around me, lifts me up, and twirls me in circles.

"Golden Boy, stop! I'm going to be sick!" I tell him as tears stream down my cheeks.

"Are you serious? When did you find out?" he asks.

"I'm serious. Just this morning, but I took five tests to be sure it wasn't a false positive. And don't worry, I didn't tell Trisha why I wanted the book published before April. You're the first to know."

Carson doesn't say a word as he just drops to his knees, places his hands on my waist, and rests his forehead against my stomach. I see his shoulders quake before he looks up at me with tear-filled eyes and says, "This is the best gift I've ever been given. I'm so overwhelmingly happy. A-are you happy?"

Biting my lip to stop the quivering, I nod my head in response. "So very happy," I assure him.

He peppers my abdomen with kisses before shooting to his feet and wrapping me in his arms again. Feeling around his thighs, I pull his phone from the pocket of his athletic shorts.

"Easy there, Austen. Watch out or we might end up with twins," he teases, and I'm shocked to find I don't mind the idea of twins. At least if we had twins with our first pregnancy, we wouldn't know any different.

"I can practically hear your thoughts, and I'm right there with you. If it's twins—hell, if it's triplets—they'll be the most loved babies in the world."

I spin in his arms, my back snug to his chest, as I hold up the phone and press record.

"Hey, baby or babies. It's your mama and daddy here on our wedding day and we just found out we're not only going to be husband and wife, but we're going to be your parents!"

Carson wraps his arms around my waist and gives my stomach three gentle squeezes. Resting his chin on top of my head, he smiles down at the phone. "Hi, sweet babies. I'm saying plural because even if this first one is a singlet, there's not a chance in heck I won't be knocking your mama up again first chance she gives me."

I nudge his side with my elbow, and he just chuckles.

"I'm so excited to watch you grow inside your beautiful mama's belly. Get used to my voice because you're going to be hearing a lot of it when I talk to you each night. Be kind to your mama, keep the kicks to her bladder to a minimum. And if you could refrain from making her eat heinous things like your auntie did, that'd be cool too. You've got the sweetest big cousin waiting to hang out with you and the craziest uncles and auntie who I'm sure can't wait to hear all about you. *Ti amo, piccolo miracolo.*"

"I love you too," I say and blow a kiss at the phone before turning off the video and tossing it on the porch swing cushions.

"What does that mean?" I question.

"Little miracle," he whispers in my ear before placing a lingering kiss on my temple. "Today is already the best day of my life because you're about to become my wife, but finding out that we're going to be parents too has made this day the greatest of all time."

I place my hands on top of where his are still resting on my stomach and lace our fingers together. We stand like that, tears streaming down our cheeks as we share our hopes and dreams for the new adventure we're about to embark on as parents. My heart has never been more full, and I've never felt more fulfilled than I do at this moment.

Also by Grayce Rian

The Off Ice Series

What It Was
(Griffin & McKenna's story)

What It Should Be
(Carson & Dakota's story)

What It Must Be
(Bennett & Scarlett's story)
Coming Summer 2025

Acknowledgments

First and foremost—thank you, my dear readers. As an indie author, my dreams wouldn't be a reality without your support!

To my forever book husband: thank you for loving me each and every day. Your unyielding support means the world to me.

To our three children: you have changed me in inexplicable ways, all for the better. I will never be able to express how much and how fiercely I love the three of you.

To my parents and two big sisters: I love you all immensely. Thank you for allowing me space to grow, for your unwavering support, and fostering my creativity growing up!

I have to thank my amazing in-laws. One of the biggest bonuses to marrying my husband was gaining the large, loud, and loving family I married into. Thank you so much for your support and love!

I want to give the biggest thanks to my incredible editor Ciara. You have helped me grow as a writer so much already and I cannot wait to continue to work together on the next project!

To my book designer, Kateryna: wow, your creativity amazes me! You were such a joy to work with and your enthusiasm for this project had me so much more excited. I cannot wait to work on the rest of the covers in this series together!

Samantha: Becoming friends with you has been one of the best surprises on this indie journey. Thank you for being a critique partner and for all of our plot brainstorming sessions!

Hannah: You're the best friend I never saw coming! Thank you for being an alpha reader, for sharing your creativity, for your spreadsheet skills, and all your words of wisdom. I cannot wait to hug you IRL.

To my betas: I couldn't have shaped this book into what it was without your input and feedback! Brittany, Brit, Chelsea, Ginsa, Jen, Morgan, Rose, Sariah, and Sam.

To Sam, Ginsa, and Jess: Thank you for being my safe place and the best author support system. You're each so talented and I love that I get to cheer you on as we share in this journey!

To the Goddesses group chat: Y'all are my favorite humans. Ever.

Lastly, I'd also like to thank Alli, Anna, Roxi, Megan, and Mindy, friends I didn't make until later in life but couldn't imagine raising my kiddos without.

About the Author

Grayce Rian is a contemporary romance author living in Wisconsin. *What It Should Be* is the second standalone novel in the Off Ice series.

Grayce's stories perfectly combine spice, angst, and sweetness to make readers swoon. When she's not writing about your new, favorite book boyfriend, you can find her with her high school sweetheart, chauffeuring their three kids to every activity imaginable, or with her nose buried in a book.

Grayce fell in love with reading and writing at a young age and pursued the creative outlet as a minor in college. She contributes a lot of her creativity and passion for reading to her mother, and Grayce now shares the same love for fictional escapes with her oldest son.